THE ARTERIAN SERIES: BOOK TWO

OF BLOOD & BANES

COURTNEY WHIMS

Developmental, Copy, and Line edits done by Noah Sky
Proofreading by Brittany Uller at The Author Experience.
Cover art, design, interior map, formatting, and interior design by
Courtney Whims.
Map base by Inkarnate.

LCCN 2025914229
Paperback 979-8-9908379-4-2
Hardcover 979-8-9908379-5-9

To Adam,

"Together is my favorite place to be."

♥

PRONUNCIATION GUIDE

ARTERIAS: *Ar-tier-ee-us*
ARTERIAN: *Ar-tier-ee-uhn*
VITALIS: *Vit-alice*
VITALANS: *Vit-allens*
SERAHAVEN: *Sarah-hay-ven*

KATERINA: *Kat-er-eena*
DAEJA: *Day-shuh*
COLE: *Coal*
DARIAN: *Dare-ian*
ARCHIE: *Arch-ee*
MARGE: *Mar-juh*
MELAINA: *Mel-ain-uhh*
SETHAN: *Seth-uhn*
CORVIN: *Core-vin*
GAVIN: *Gav-in*
NOLAN: *No-lan*
CELESTE: *Suh-lest*
TAWNY: *Taw-knee*
LELAND: *Lee-land*
AARIC: *Are-ick*
AVICE: *Ay-vis*
ELARA: *El-are-uh*
A'NALA: *Uhh-nala*
BRISTOL: *Bris-toll*
NADJA: *Naw-juhh*

Readers who may be sensitive to certain elements,
please take note.

Your mental health matters. ♥

Of Blood and Banes is a fast-paced fantasy romance
that takes place in a kingdom where dragons are forbidden.
This is an adult series which contains elements that might
not be suitable for some readers.

For the most updated list of elements,
please refer to the URL below:
courtneywhims.com/book

NORTHERN FOREST
THE OUTPOST
SKYLARK
MISTWOOD
STONE SHIRE
WINDMERE
KAT'S HOME
BLACKFELL
WYNNBAN
HORNWOOD
PADMOOR
SPILLBURG
ARTERIAS
GROVEDEN
SILVERPEAK
HELMBROOK
BROOKVALE
SHADSTEAD

SERAHAVEN MOUNTAINS
VITALIS
THE ACADEMY
MOSSMEAD
MILLTON
EVERDEN
PINEPOINT
FORBIDDEN FOREST
NIGHTFORT
SILKWOOD
ELDIRE
BAYROCK
ASHFALL
DRIFTMOND
KILAMBER
MIDKEEP
VATHSTONE
SOUTHLIGHT
DRAGON'S BACK RIDGE

OF FLAMES AND FALLACIES RECAP

"It all started when—"

"Daeja, I thought we both agreed I'd be the one doing the recap? They might not even understand what you're saying."

"...but...they're looking at me like they do know what I'm saying? Oh! See! They do!"

Katerina sighs. *"Fine...go on, then."*

"So, anyway. It all started when Kat found my egg buried in her father's grave. She was so beyond excited to find me that she took me into her hometown, Padmoor, to a guy named Pillar to figure out how to hatch me—"

"Willard," Kat corrects softly.

"Right. Willard told her to take me back to wherever she found me because King Aaric of Arterias banned dragons long ago and executed all the dragon riders. Being associated with my kind would mean her or her ill mother could be killed. But Kat was so elated to have me, she rebelled against Willard's advice and—"

"Now, now. I definitely didn't rebel. I just...didn't know what you were."

"Okay. Well then, her house caught on fire in the middle of the night, and she definitely knew what I was then. I hatched! Her mother warned her to find Cole and take me to the Dragon Lands. We began our trek to Blackfell to find where Cole was stationed as a newly appointed captain of a military outpost. On the walk there, we discovered Kat's father was a rebel before he died. He had an entire journal based on his studies of elemental dragons and his time spying on King Aaric at the castle in Arterias! During our travels, we sadly couldn't save a little girl and her family from rebels setting the town of Hornwood on fire. But we did pick up a sword from a rebel we killed. And then we made it to the military outpost where Cole was. Kat had to fake being a healer's apprentice and Cole's sister! All while hiding me! How am I doing?"

"You seemed to have left out the part that I was engaged to Cole at one point…"

"Oh…right…so that happened, too. But long before I was hatched. They had split on bad terms and hadn't seen or spoken to each other since then. So, we weren't sure if Cole was going to help us. But he did. One night, I woke up to an intense urge and followed it to the forest where we found a blue flame! I sniffed it, and the next thing you know, I tripled in size! Then Kat and I were able to start communicating. Kat stayed at the military outpost while she worked with Cole in locating a map so we could get to the Dragon Lands safely. And undetected. But during her stay, the smelly, grumpy lady Marge—"

"She's not smelly."

"I disagree."

"Probably has something to do with her being Spoiled. I'd imagine consuming dragonblood might alter someone's pheromones.

"What are pheromones?"

"Okay, we're getting off topic here."

"Right. Anyway, Marge found Kat's father's journal and demanded we take her to the Dragon Lands with us, rather than her turning us in. One man, Archie, told Kat the sword she had was a King's Close Circle sword. When the neighboring town of Blackfell was attacked by rebels, we swooped in to save the day! Kat rescued some hostages. I ripped a guy's head off—"

"But we aren't doing that again. Right?"

"Riiiight…and then Kat found out Cole was engaged the whole time and kept it a secret! So, she decided we'd go to the Dragon Lands ourselves without the map. But as I waited in the forest for her, she got caught by some asshole named Darian. And rather than ripping his head off—"

"Yes, yes. I think they remember that part. Let's skip it."

"Whew, thanks! Then Cole's fiancé arrived at the outpost and took Kat out dress shopping. But the whole time Kat thought

Celeste was Darian's ex-lover, considering she wrote him letters and was arguing with him late at night telling her she loves him. Fast forward, and Kat found out Celeste is actually Darian's half-sister, and they share the same father—Jurrock. A few nights later, back at the military outpost, Kat was on her way to leave with me to the Dragon Lands, but Cole stopped her. He told her how sorry he was and sent her with a map, his mother's ring, and Kat's father's journal. We thought he burned it, but he ended up keeping the journal because he knew how much it meant to her. But then Kat went back to the military outpost to save a rebel woman who was held hostage. And a full-on battle started between rebels and Arterians. I saved Kat and still have a badass scar to prove it!"

"Careful wiggling your wing. It still hasn't properly healed!"

"Funny you're telling me to be careful…anyway! Kat promised me a whole carriage full of chicken. Which…she has yet to pay. The end."

"I thought you don't like chicken anymore?"

"What? When did I say that?"

"You said you've had it so often now you're sick of it?"

"Beside the point. Anything I missed?"

"Well, we ended up in the Dragon Lands. And found out their leader is Sethan, who is Melaina's father we all thought was dead."

"Okay…now you're the one missing information."

"Oh?"

"Yeah. Is there a reason why you conveniently forgot to mention that guy Darian is the prince of Arterias?"

"…no?"

"…I'm not sure I believe you. Maybe I'll ask you again at the end."

ONE

A LOSS OF BLOOD AND TITLES

Little did I know living was scarier than dying. After my first brush with death in Arterias, I realized living was hard—full of pain, heartache, and uncertainty. But death? Death is final. Quiet. Dark.

And in an odd way…peaceful.

"You were out for several days after the battle in Arterias. You lost so much blood, I'm surprised you've managed to survive," Marge chides and smacks the top of my hand with the head of her staff. Though it's gentle enough to bar a warning, the top of my hand still stings from the contact.

She hisses, "Woman, are you not listening? You need to take it easy. Give your body the rest it needs to recover."

Glaring at her, I hesitantly retract my hand from the door handle. The memory of the sword hidden within the wooden staff is a ringing reminder of all the things I don't know about Marge. While some innate part of me trusts her, I'm hesitant to listen. I need to see Daeja. I need answers as to how long we'll be held as so-called prisoners. Or…hostages? Are they one and the same?

I grumble, "And smacking me with your staff is supposed to help my body recover?"

"If you weren't such a stubborn thing, I wouldn't have to resort to such violence." She presses the length of her staff against my chest and forces me away from the door.

I laugh. "Are you really herding me right now?"

"If that's what it'll take for you to listen to me."

She sweeps me back away from the door and to one of the beds lining the room in neat rows. The same bed I'd woken up in, with several blood-flecked rags layering the mattress. I'd angered the wound in my ribs yesterday when I found out Darian's true heritage and passed out shortly after. Even now, my side aches with every move and breath. As if a shard of glass is wedged between my ribs, and with every unmeasured breath, it burrows deeper.

"Now sit down," Marge commands.

When I finally sit on the bed, she removes her staff from my chest. Her nimble hands pull the loose, cream-colored shirt tucked into my pants free, and her fingertips graze the thick bandages wound around my torso. Probably wasn't the best idea, putting me in a light-colored shirt. Small flecks of blood bloom like roses on the material.

She clicks her tongue and shakes her head. "See? You've ruptured it. It's bleeding again."

She turns away from me and hobbles over to a wooden set of cabinets tucked up against a stone wall. Her staff clicks on the wide stone tiles as she returns with a handful of materials.

She slowly peels off the bandages, sticky with my blood, then presses a fresh cloth to my wound. Crimson immediately bleeds onto the material. I level my breathing, straining to focus on anything but the pain throbbing in my ribs.

Five things I see: sunlight leaks through several sets of windows barred in iron grates, washing the stone walls around us in warmth. Almost twenty beds fill the room from wall to wall, with the wooden cabinets Marge retrieved materials from earlier spanning one side of the room. Wooden beams arch overhead, accentuating the soft curve of the ceiling.

Four things I feel: I grip the bed sheets in my fist and bite down into my cheek. A throbbing pain pulses harder in between my ribs—

"This is going to hurt," Marge murmurs with a twinge of sympathy.

A sharp object tugs at my skin, the sensation mixing with my pain. I avert my gaze, looking everywhere but where she stitches my wound closed. But I can't ignore the pain. Nor the sensation of her needle piercing me, then threading the stitch through my skin as if I'm nothing more than a torn blanket.

Near desperate for a distraction and through gritted teeth, I ask, "Marge, what happened that night back in Arterias? After I passed out?"

"Well, after you fainted word got out the rebels captured Darian. They started to close in on us, but your dragon kept them back. That rebel woman you set free is apparently the lead of this southern town, and she called a halt on their advances. They took whoever was still alive after the battle as prisoners."

"You said I was out for…several days?"

"Yes. Many of us thought you were dead. Or were going to be. But the Gods have greater plans for you. The rebels let Cole carry you the whole way here, and your dragon followed like his shadow."

My heart flutters at Cole's name. Gods, the fear he must have felt while holding me in his arms, bleeding and unconscious. I look down at my hands, and his mother's ring still wraps around my finger. Like a distant promise.

Marge pours a warm liquid onto my wound, and the splintering pain melts like frost in the morning sun.

"It's a miracle you survived…" Marge whispers as she winds a fresh wrap around my torso. Once she finishes, she places her hand softly over mine. "You need to take care of yourself, first. We cannot lose you."

I glance from her gloved hand up to meet her eyes. "Who is we?"

Her expression softens. "Everyone. We all need you."

I scoff at the idea. "Does that apply to Darian, too? Or… pardon me for being so informal. *Prince* Darian? How could you not tell me?"

"Because titles can be dangerous things. And I didn't need you to focus on it."

"And what did you need me to focus on instead? Learning medicine?"

She grabs my right hand and traces the dark stain ringing my middle finger—the mark I got when I met Daeja.

"This. Your dragon. You are the first dragon rider of your generation, Katerina. And of all things, you have a *black* dragon. It is no coincidence."

I slip my hand out of hers and fight the temptation to look down at the dark ring on my finger. "You knew all along?"

"I did. The day I saw you cutting those mushrooms, it had never been about how you cut them. I saw your fingers and that ring. When I gave you those gloves, it was to protect you."

"Protect me from what?"

"Not what. *Who*."

I flinch. "And who is that?"

"All of the people who want you dead."

I swallow under the severity of her stare. "People want me dead?"

"Many." She pats my leg. "Both you and your dragon. Which is why we need you to get started on your training again. But you cannot until you've properly healed. Otherwise, you risk being worse off than you are now. Rest for a few days, and then we can reassess you."

"But I—"

"I mean it, Katerina. And if you only listen to one thing I ask of you," she removes the black leather gloves from her hands and flops them onto my thigh, "keep these on at all times. Nobody else needs to know you wear the ring."

"Does everyone know what the ring means?" I ask as I tug the gloves onto my fingers.

"I'm not sure. Commoners in Arterias likely wouldn't, since the King is quite prone to erasing all the history and any information pertaining to dragons and dragon riders. The King's Close Circle is a different story. And as for the rebels…just…keep the gloves on."

The stir-crazy drive to leave this bed forces me into a frenzy. Had it not been for the waxing and waning exhaustion washing over me, Marge might have needed to shackle me to the bed to keep me down.

"Blood loss," she tells me when I groan through the struggle of keeping my eyes open.

The rest of the day is a blur. Every time I open my eyes again, the light in the room has shifted to a different part of the day. When a soft hand wraps over my shoulder and squeezes, I open my eyes to find a set of warm amber ones looking back at me.

"Hungry?" Cole whispers and takes a seat on the edge of the bed near my knees. A platter of food rests in his palms.

Shadows stretch across the floors in the telltale sign of sunset, with orange and yellow bathing Cole in a glowing light. I edge onto my forearms and wince at the pain throbbing in my ribs. Cole sets the tray down and wraps one hand around the nape of my neck and lower back to help me sit up. He then adjusts the pillows behind me to support my spine.

My stomach growls when I notice the wide array of fruits,

cheeses, and breads on the plate he's brought me. As soon as he hears it, he grins and places the tray over my lap. I pluck piece after piece. Each bite triggers a deeper sense of the ravenous hunger within me.

I glance up from the tray as Marge shuffles out the door with Archie, leaving Cole and me alone in the room of empty beds and warm light. I swallow. Cole's watching me with the intensity of a thousand burning suns. Calculating every angle of my movements, as if he's expecting death to claim me at any given moment.

"Thank you," I whisper.

"For what?" His soft expression is lost in concern.

"For this," I motion down toward the food, "and for getting me to the Dragon Lands. Marge said you carried me the whole way."

"I told you one way or another I'd be getting you and Daeja to the Dragon Lands, didn't I? Though, I wanted to be here when you woke up…" His smile weakens, the warmth in his eyes fading. He clears his throat, breaking our eye contact. "I'm sorry I couldn't."

I stop mid-chew, analyzing his expression as if it'll tell me what he's actually thinking. "And where were you instead?"

"Negotiating."

"Sethan mentioned his proposal was to leave Darian here and we could all go home, right?"

He sighs, shaking his head and still not looking me in the eyes. "His proposal has changed."

"To what?"

He pats my shin, then stands. "Don't worry, I'll figure out a way to get us home. The only thing I want you focusing on is recovering."

I lean forward to weakly grip the hem of his shirt, garnering a side-glance and pause.

"Don't do this again," I mutter under my breath. "What is it you're discussing with Sethan?"

"I don't want you to worry about it. You can hardly keep your eyes open as is." He gently plucks my fingers from his shirt until the fabric falls loose. He lifts my hand to his lips and dusts a soft kiss to my knuckles. "Get some rest, and let me take care of it."

Before I can argue, he lays my hand back down on the bed and tucks a strand of hair behind my ear. His touch is lightning in my nerves as he swipes a nostalgic slow line around the corner of my jaw. Those calloused fingertips graze the column of my neck, before he tosses me a small smile that cracks the ice in my heart.

Then he leaves.

As the door closes behind him, it jolts me out of my distant longing. I snort, popping a piece of cheese into my mouth as I stare at the door. I know he'll figure out a way to get us home, but…

Where is home now?

When I turn onto my side in my sleep, my injured ribs scream at the contact with the bed. Wincing, I flip over onto my back and stare up at the dark ceiling. Sucking in a slow breath, I fight against the pain until it dissipates. A collection of deep exhalations echo around me, and I flick my gaze to the left.

Rows of beds stretch out into the room, all occupied by Arterians: Cole, Archie, Melaina, Marge, Gavin, Nolan, and several others I hadn't quite gotten to know back at the military outpost. Archie is tucked under the sheets with his hand stretched out, holding Melaina's in the bed next to his. Cole looks pained even in the depths of his dreams. And, unfortunately for those of us sharing this room with her, Marge's snoring seesaws in and out of the otherwise quiet room.

I peer over at the door. My skin prickles, and an uneasiness settles into my stomach as I stare at the wood. When the light seeping through the crack of space between the bottom of the door and floor flickers with the passing of shadows, I slowly shift out of bed and slip my boots on. With no one awake to scold me, it's the most opportune time to slip out and see Daeja. Tip-toeing around the room and between the beds of other sleeping Arterians, I slink closer to the door. When the shadows stretching into the room from the outside disappear, I press an ear to the wood and wait.

A heartbeat.

Two.

Three.

Lowering to the floor and ignoring the ache in my side, I scan underneath the door to find the cobblestone street stretching out into the town empty. Instinctively, I pat my sides for a dagger to use as a reflective surface to better my range of visibility. Or to use it in the event I need to defend myself. It's too damn bad they've confiscated all our weapons. Though, not sure I blame them.

Slowly creeping back to my feet, I glance over my shoulder to ensure everyone is still fast asleep. I push the door handle down in what might as well be slow motion. Swallowing against my building apprehension, I part the door open and peer out. The streets are still empty. When I slip out of the rebels' so-called "healer's quadrant," the cold winter air immediately kisses my skin numb.

A glimmer of movement off to the left catches my attention, about fifty feet away, and I make out only enough in the darkness to see two separate groups of guards exchanging hushed whispers.

They must be changing watches.

Before they notice me, I sneak off through the quiet streets toward the forest, following that magnetic thread. I'll be damned if they think they can keep me from seeing Daeja. And they can kiss my ass if they think they'll dictate when and where I can see her. I won't allow the distance forced between us back in Arterias to resurface. Because one thing's for certain—we belong together.

And no king, man, nor law will ever separate us again.

My heart rate slows with each step I take closer to her. The pine trees' sticky sap is the smell of home, and their towering skinny silhouettes frame me in a dark nostalgia. It must feel familiar to Daeja, too, because she spends her nights out here.

Her dark figure is curled in on itself, and the steady rise and fall of her silhouette makes me pause mid-step. But as her muscles shift beneath her, she lifts her head out from where it was tucked beneath her wing. Those breathtaking white eyes flash open, her pupils adjusting to the moonlight.

She exhales, her breath visibly billowing out in a soft cloud. **"You're awake. What are you doing out here?"**

I close the gap between us and stretch out a hand toward her snout. *"I wanted to come see you."*

Her nostrils flare, likely sensing Marge's scent on my leather gloves, but she doesn't move away from me as I stroke the ridge of her nose. Instead, she closes her eyes and tilts her muzzle into my hand like an affectionate, needy house cat. I slide my hand underneath her chin and caress that favorite spot of hers.

A thick purr drums within her broad chest, and she turns her head sideways to lead the rest of her body to flop onto her back. With her size, the ground rumbles underneath her lazy fall. **"Shouldn't you be...I don't know...sleeping?"**

I crouch with a small smile and rub her long column of a throat. *"I'll sleep when I'm dead."*

"I don't find that statement funny in the slightest. And as much as I'm enjoying this..." Her purr still rumbles like an accordion of thunder in her chest with every stroke of my hand on her black scales, her eyes still closed. **"You shouldn't be out of bed until you've healed enough to not ache."**

"If you thought a little soreness would be enough to keep me from you, then I've sadly misled your perception of what you mean to me."

Her eyes flash open, and she rolls away from me to lie on her belly. Stretching her wings out to the side with a gentle wobble, she pulls them back in and folds them into her sides. Her gaze is soft and serious. ***"I've never doubted your affections for me. I only want you to recover. And not just because there is no me without you."***

A slow smile spreads across my lips. I drop down to my knees and sit back on my feet as I gaze upon the truest companion I've come to know. This magnificent, fearsome creature who's so much more than others assumed she'd be.

My gaze settles on her wing where a spear punctured her during the battle in Arterias. The wound has quickly healed over, leaving a gaping hole in the webbing. If it weren't for her, I would have likely been six feet under by now. She'd saved me. More than once. And now, she has the scar to prove it.

"You risked your life…for me."

She stretches her neck forward so her nose touches mine, lightly. ***"Because I can't bear the thought of being in a world longer than one second without you."***

A surge of warmth and light swells within my chest, and I bite down on my bottom lip to contain it. As I'm locked into her colorless eyes, a current of memories flash across my vision, all from her perspective. Me teaching her how to fly. Me holding her as a hatchling to my chest at night to keep her warm. Me slipping her pieces of chicken as she hid in the cover of my hooded cloak.

When she breaks our contact, the memories stop. She nuzzles my shoulder with an insistent prod. ***"Now, go. You can come tomorrow if you'd like, but get your sleep. I'm not going anywhere."***

Too touched to argue, I nod and rise to my feet. After kissing the tip of her nose, I turn back toward the town the rebel woman I saved back in Arterias—Tawny—calls Midkeep.

Tawny became the leader of Midkeep several years ago. The proximity to the border with Arterias classified this town as a sort of military one. Each of the buildings are fortified in stone and brick, and the roofs are constructed with thick wooden beams. Cobblestone streets wind through the town, and all the soldiers I've seen so far have been adorned in metal suits.

As I near Midkeep, the thrum of approaching footsteps catches my attention, and I whip toward the sound. Long, stretching shadows approach from around a building down a street.

Shit. Guards.

We aren't supposed to be out without supervision, especially this late at night. I can only imagine how suspicious I look. I quickly scan my surroundings. To my left is a stone building on the southern outskirts of the town. The footsteps close in, and the louder the sound of boots on the cobblestones, the harder my pulse works. Holding my breath, I dash toward the building and reach for the door handle. My breath slips from my lips when the handle turns, allowing me entrance. Pulling the door closed once I'm inside, I wait in darkness. The footsteps come…and then they fade. I push the door open slightly and peer out as four guards round the corner of a building out of sight.

Smack! The sound reverberates from behind and below me, and I flinch forward, nearly tumbling out the door.

I turn to find a stone staircase winding down into the ground behind me. The steps are illuminated by a dim flicker of flame from somewhere at the bottom of the stairs, away from my view. A miserable groan rises from its depths, and a chill races down my spine. Part of me whispers to not venture past the top step as I stare down the staircase.

But the other part is louder.

After ensuring the door is closed, I inch down the stairs and quiet my breath by breathing through my nose. As I descend, the light glows brighter, washing the stone walls arching above me in orange.

Another slap echoes in the walls. I turn a corner, pause when I realize the staircase ends, and quickly backstep. Dropping back behind the cover of the curved wall, I press myself against the cold, wet stone. Panic floods my skin with heat. *Did someone see me?*

I wait. Holding out for a calling or footsteps to approach. But when another smack sounds, I finally peer around the wall's edge.

The staircase opens out into a room encased in stone walls and floors. Torches fastened to the wall bookend the room, casting long shadows across the ground. Two men clad in black face away from me, one of which I recognize is the rebel's leader—Sethan. His ash-gray hair is stark against his dark brown skin.

The other man flicks his wrist. Liquid flies from his drenched fingers and splatters onto the ground. As he takes a few steps back closer to Sethan, he reveals a man crumpled on his knees before them. The man kneeling on the ground has a string of crimson drool dripping from his mouth, blood matting his brown hair.

My stomach drops.

Darian.

TWO

They've Made a Mistake

Sinister pools of blood splatter the stone floors all around Darian. His chest flutters with ragged breaths, and as he hunches forward to cough, the thick metal bands shackling his wrists clink as he catches himself on the ground. More blood spews from his lips. His arms tremble with the miserable effort to keep himself upright.

"Tell us," Sethan thunders, his attention set on Darian.

As slow as if he were lifting the weight of the world, Darian's sullen gaze sweeps off the floor and up to Sethan. Dark shadows trace his eye sockets, with bruises and cuts littering his skin. His bottom lip is swollen on one side to the extent it makes me flinch.

I wait for the snicker. The sneer. Those venomous insults he never hesitates to spit. But rather than antagonizing his captor, his eyes flutter closed as his head sags, accepting his fate.

Sethan nods at the armored man next to him. The soldier turns to the farthest wall and retrieves a whip hung up on a hook. My breath catches in my chest as the man walks back toward Darian and circles around to stand behind him.

"Then I suppose we'll bleed you dry," Sethan threatens with an icy calm.

The man behind Darian plants his feet, pulls his arm back behind his head, and rips the whip down across Darian's back. Not even Darian's clenched teeth can hold back his cry as he jolts forward. My stomach bottoms out, and I shudder.

The man raises the whip again, and I race out from behind the cover of the staircase wall.

"Stop it!" I grab at Sethan's shoulder to turn him to face me.

He swivels, anger sparking in his brown eyes as he instinctively snatches my wrist. Instantly, I recognize the shade of brown in his irises, realizing exactly where Melaina got it from.

"What are you doing here? Get back to your room," he snarls.

"Fuck you, you don't command me," I hiss, attempting to slide my forearm out from his strong grip.

"Need I remind you, girl, that you are no longer in Arterias? Which means you fall under my authority." Sethan nearly throws my gloved hand out of his grasp and turns back toward the man with the whip. "Again, Corvin."

Corvin hesitates, staring directly at me with wide eyes. His short brown hair is cut close to his skull. Swallowing, he flicks his gaze from Sethan to me and back again, as if he's contemplating the lesser of two evils.

Sethan narrows his eyes as he demands, louder, "Again!"

Corvin raises the whip behind his head, his arm now shaking. Shoving past Sethan I spring forward, throwing my hand out to stop the whip before it cracks down on Darian's back. Corvin swings down, and the wicked leather snaps into the back of my hand. I bite down a scream, buckling to my knees before Darian. I can only imagine how it would feel on someone's bare skin. Pain rises to the surface, throbbing in the back of my hand and bubbling beneath my wounded ribs.

Corvin drops the whip to the floor as he shuffles backward until he bumps into the wall. "I-I'm so sorry…"

Darian lifts his head enough to look at me. Those desolate green eyes, hazy with pain and a distant delusion, watch me through slow blinking lids. His face. Oh, Gods, his *face.*

I break eye contact with him, unable to bear the heaviness of his stare as I glare up at Corvin, then back over my shoulder at Sethan. "What the fuck is wrong with you?"

"How else do you expect us to glean any information to help save Arterias?" Sethan asks, his arms tucked behind his back, ever so nonchalant.

I rise to my feet. "There are other ways!"

"No. No, there aren't. And if you want to win this war, you'll do what is necessary."

"This is not necessary!" I spit. "And who said I want any part in your war?"

The slight lift to his lips lowers as he tilts his chin down at me. "If you want to save your dragon, then surely you will come to your senses."

"She's safe, we're in the Dragon Lands."

"Not for long," he counters.

I narrow my eyes at the open-to-interpretation statement for both Daeja's safety and our residency here in the Dragon Lands. I haven't had long to consider what our plans will be, but Daeja can't go back to Arterias. She belongs here. And if she belongs here…well, I suppose I do, too.

My voice dips low. "If that's your attempt at threatening me, you'll be sorely mistaken."

A step sounds behind me, and I turn back to Corvin edging the side of the wall as if he might not be noticed.

"Get. Out," I growl. And I swear to Gods the man *flinches.*

"You stay, Corvin," Sethan calls behind me.

The poor soldier flicks his attention from me to behind me, his forehead glistening with nervous sweat. The longer the seconds tick by, the harder the realization washes over me. He's weighing mine and Sethan's commands. He's hesitating because of *me.*

I turn back to Sethan and point down at Darian, betting on my intuition. "Leader of the Dragon Lands or not, you will not touch him again."

Sethan snorts, seemingly amused at the conviction in my tone. "Then I suppose you'll be the one responsible for questioning him? Please. Go ahead. Find out why the King wants all the dragons dead."

He holds my gaze. Waiting for me to back down. I clench my jaw, forcing myself not to break under his narrowed stare. To not flinch at the thought of uncovering a truth I'm unaware of. But part of me is just as eager for the answer.

Finally, he waves his hand as if pestered by a horse fly. "Let's go, Corvin. We'll try this again tomorrow."

Corvin hangs the whip back up on its hook with a speed that reeks of desperation to get out of this room and throws me an apologetic look over his shoulder as he meets Sethan at the staircase.

Sethan levels me with a look. "I'll show you this one act of respect—and mercy. Do not be quick to forget it."

He and Corvin ascend the staircase out of view, their footsteps fading into silence.

A wheezy breath tugs my attention away from the stairs, and I turn to face Darian. The wounds patterning every inch of his face, neck, and chest makes me hurt as if I sustained the injuries myself. They've stripped off his shirt, revealing more lacerations than I can count. Ungodly amounts of blood stain his matted hair, his pale face, the stone floors, and his filthy pants.

My stomach churns at the realization of how long he must have been down here to have so many brutal injuries. I've been out for several days.

*Days…*my stomach does an uncomfortable flip at the thought. He's miserable looking. Painful to behold. He doesn't even look up, eyes still squeezed closed as he uses every bit of his strength just to fucking *breathe*.

"Are you okay?" I whisper, crouching to his level. A distant pain spiders in my ribs at the maneuver. *Gods, he needs Marge. Desperately.* I pat my sides, searching for anything I have on me to help him but find nothing.

"Leave…me." His voice is ragged. As if those two words took every ounce of his strength, and he forfeited a few precious breaths to mutter it.

"I'm not leaving you. Darian, they'll kill you—"

"Fuck 'em. If they do…they'll be doing me a godsdamned favor—" He's ambushed by a violent cough and attempts to cover his mouth with the inside of his wrist while sputtering bits of blood and drool.

I reach out to him with a shaky hand, gently place my fingers under his sharp, stubble-dusted chin, and tilt his attention off the floor to me. Anything to beg him to listen. "You need a healer. You need Marge."

He snatches me by the wrist and throws my hand away from him, the metal chains on his shackles jingling from the motion. "Get your fucking paws off me."

His bloody handprint is wrapped around my wrist, and I stare at the splash of red against the black leather of Marge's glove. He retreats, sitting back to lean his head against the wall.

How he's managed to lose so much blood without passing out is beyond me. But if anyone can do it, it's Darian. This man would stare death down in the face and have it running for the fucking hills. But there's no denying the hint of defeat in the way his shoulders sag, and the dullness in those green irises. His rich, olive skin now borders ghastly.

"Darian…" I try again, gently.

Lifting his head off the wall, he glares at me with a fierceness reminiscent of a wild animal before it bites.

I inch toward him. "Let me help you up. We need to get you out of here so we can find someone to help."

"There's no helping me. It's far too late."

"Humor me."

He doesn't move or argue. His gaze is still locked on mine, though his eyelids flutter like he's fighting a losing battle.

Don't make me regret this. I slink forward and slide my arms underneath his, then lock my hands over my opposite wrists. He wraps his arms around me, and with a grunt, I help pull him up to his feet. Pain throbs in my ribs with warning, though I ignore it.

Darian finds his footing and releases me, his legs trembling as he leans back slightly against the wall to gather his balance. I pull back away from him, and my hands brush over his manacles. I pause—stuck on the metal slick with grime and blood constricting his movements.

He's the prince of Arterias. His grandfather murdered countless dragons, riders, and rebels. Daeja and I are a target. Any doubt he isn't led by his grandfather's beliefs is whisked away by the memory of him executing two men who were reported to be sympathizers. He nearly killed Archie in a sparring match the first time I saw him. And who knows what other things Darian was responsible for?

He's a prisoner of war. Perhaps he deserves this. Perhaps this is fate or karma.

And yet, Gods…looking at him crosses that line of morality in me—

Darian lunges at me, taking full advantage of my hesitation. He raises his fists to wrap the chain connecting his shackles around my neck and shoves me backward in one swift motion.

I stumble, nearly tripping over my own feet as he glides us to the stone wall and pins me against it. The chain from his shackles squeezes the breath out of my throat.

I search his eyes, digging for a hint of mercy, but he's back to his signature glare. I'm not sure what happened between now and those soft moments with him at Windmere: sweeping me off to his room, wrapping me in his jacket, and tucking me into his bed. Even teasing he was going to bring me breakfast in bed. Perhaps it was all a game. Or a fever dream.

Darian presses himself into my chest as he lowers his face closer to mine. His laboring breath stirs my hair. "Let. Me. Free."

"Darian…s-stop…" I wheeze out as I arch my back against the wall and push up onto my toes, searching for a meager inch of space so I might catch a breath. I sink my fingers into the chain and attempt to pull it away from my throat. But my grip is slippery, and my strength is waning by the second. He doesn't shift his grasp. If anything, he pushes harder. My vision sparkles in black, and when my eyes roll back into my head from the lack of oxygen, he pauses.

Slightly.

Lifting the chain off my throat, he then loops it behind my head to pull at the nape of my neck. I suck in a strangled breath through my burning throat as the haze of asphyxiation lifts.

"You so much as make a move to escape, or try to fight me, and I'll fucking kill you. Do you understand?" he growls, and tugs me hard enough my face bumps into his bare chest.

"Yes…" I rasp out, still struggling to steady my breath. A dizzying sensation wracks my head, and I rest my forehead on his pecs before I black out. I run through all the possible scenarios of how to get out of this. Even in his disadvantageous state, I'm no match for him. Especially considering my wounded side—any hard twist will easily split the stitches open again. Besides, he'll catch me long before I can slip out of his grasp and run.

"Put your hands on my chest," he barks.

I hesitate.

"Don't fucking make me ask again."

I skip a breath and shakily rest my palms on his bare chest, sticky with blood. His muscles flex underneath his skin as he pats down my sleeves, shoulders, back, and sides. I wince when he brushes my injured ribs. His assessment moves on to my waist, my hips, my…rear.

I flick a glare up at him. "The fuck you think I'm hiding in my *ass?*"

He uses the tip of his boot to tap against the insides of my ankles, ignoring my question completely. Repositioning the chain back behind my head, he growls in my ear, "Turn around. Away from me."

I obey, slipping my hands off his chest and slowly turning in his arms until I'm facing away from him. He collars my throat with the chain once more, pulling me back with him a half-step until my shoulder blades press into his chest.

"Move," he grunts in my ear, and then shoves his groin into my ass so I step toward the staircase.

If I wasn't still dazed from the air he squeezed out of my lungs or the aching pain in my ribs, I might have even blushed.

"You…f-fucking…idiot…" I gasp as we edge up the stairs.

He tightens the chain on my throat, silencing me. My boots slip off the steps, the edges of my vision bleed into black. I lean back harder into him for support.

We ascend the rest of the stairs, step by painful step, as I hold on to the chain around my throat for dear life. At the top of the staircase, he commands me to open the door. I push it open slowly, and after he scans the quiet cobblestone streets, he slips us out into the cold. His pace doesn't quicken until we leave the outskirts of Midkeep and head south into the forest.

In the back of my mind, I know he won't hurt me. I *think.*

He would have easily killed me in the dungeon if he really wanted to. He had me right there—all he had to do was strangle me a second or two longer. And yet, he didn't.

I still have no idea what he's playing at, or why he wants me alive. He can't possibly think he'll walk to Arterias from here. He'd be caught before he got halfway. And given his hands are shackled, he wouldn't be much of a fight. But a terror looms over me like a shadow as I consider all the wild possibilities that might run through someone like Darian's head. There's no telling what he's planning.

"Let…me…go…" I wriggle against him as we tread deeper into the forest.

The chain against my throat is far too tight, and my face grows unbearably hot.

Tight.

Tighter.

My lungs scream in withered protests. All the pine trees around us blur into a single mass. My thoughts dull to a whisper as I begin to wink out of consciousness. I overestimated his mercy.

"Daeja…"

As if in slow-motion, I fold to my knees. This fucker *is* going to kill me.

"Shit," Darian mutters under his breath. He catches me in his arms before I can fall face first. The strain on my throat disappears, gifting me a shaky breath.

A branch snaps off behind us and a menacing growl splits the silence, quaking the air around us.

"Fuck," Darian hisses. He yanks me off the ground to my feet, pulling me back into his chest, his heart hammering against my back like it might jump through both of us.

Behind us, Daeja's head-splitting roar blasts strands of my hair out in front of me. Birds stir in the trees, shooting into the starry night sky with startled cries.

Darian spins us to face Daeja. She flares her wings out to the sides, her lips curling and exposing her rows of vicious fangs. Every horn crowning her head and neck gleams in the moonlight, with her slitted white eyes hooked into Darian.

"Now's…your chance…to run," I rasp.

Darian removes the chain from around my throat and shoves me to the side. I stumble and fall to my knees, catching myself on my hands before I completely collapse. Another shot of pain explodes in my ribs, and I instinctively cup a hand to my side. When I pull my hand away, blood stains my palm.

I glance up as Daeja snarls and lunges toward Darian, who's bolted in the opposite direction and leading her farther away. Daeja's heavy footfalls shake the earth beneath me as she chases after him. I force myself up to my feet and turn to follow, but Darian doesn't get far. Daeja races past him and whips around to face him head on, blocking his escape. She lowers her head with a growl, her black talons digging into the soil.

Darian goes rigid before he backpedals at a measured pace. Daeja takes a taunting slow step toward him, her mouth parting open and tongue flicking out between her rows of teeth.

She strikes like a snake, snatching his shackles' chain and ripping him up off the ground. He kicks out at her neck with a grunt. But it's no use—he hangs helplessly from her mouth, flailing in her grasp like a caught fish.

"Don't hurt him," I warn Daeja as I stumble forward, fighting against the pain rolling wave after wave over me, begging me to slow down.

Her head swivels to me, swinging him in her mouth, and her icy white eyes glare at me. ***"I ought to kill him just for threatening you. And eat him for putting his hands on you."***

I stop ten feet away from her. *"I've got this, trust me. Just put him down."*

She snorts and tosses him to the side. He flies off several yards and hits the ground before sliding into the base of a tree with a thud. Pushing up to his forearms, he struggles to get to his feet. The moonlight etches all the angled edges of his shoulders and ribs, still blooming with bruises and cuts.

"Maybe a little gentler next time."

"He doesn't deserve gentle," she growls, slinking in behind me.

I shrug lightly, partly agreeing with her, but not wanting to encourage any bad behavior. As I stop a few feet in front of Darian, Daeja lowers her chin just over my shoulder, and I pat the side of her muzzle.

Darian drags his gaze up to me, his eyes widening in shock. The color drains from his face as he realizes Daeja isn't going to just *not* hurt me. Recognition dawns on his expression, and his fear of Daeja transforms into something greater.

A fear of *me.*

Daeja roars from beside me, the sound sending my hair into a flurry, and ringing in my ears. As I hold Darian's gaze, I don't even flinch.

He jerks away, pressing his back into the tree trunk as he flicks his attention between Daeja and me. "You…you! I should've known you were a *dragon rider.*" He spits out the last word.

I smile. He must not have been paying attention when Sethan mentioned *my* dragon.

"You're not the only one with secrets, your *highness.*" I give him an exaggerated bow before I swoop the chain to his shackles and yank him up to his feet.

"Unarm me, you peasant." He rips his chains out of my grasp, the metal clinking together at the motion as he snarls.

On second thought…maybe I should *let Daeja eat him.*

"Gladly…" Daeja snakes forward.

I hold out a hand to her. *"Didn't realize I shared that one. It was a hasty thought."*

She licks her maw and takes a half-step forward to lean into my hand. **"Or a tasty thought."**

As I toss her a glance, a group of shadows stretch across the forest floor from behind us.

Daeja twists her head to survey the area. **"We have company."**

When I turn to face the approaching group, Sethan catches my gaze at the front of the throng. His eyes narrow, hinting at what he's already thinking—*see, I told you.*

Daeja snorts, clearly attuned to my own irritation as she positions herself between Darian and me but keeps her focus set on the rebels walking our way. Sethan is accompanied by ten others, all with their weapons drawn. With a few of Sethan's gestures, several of his guards break off from the group, pass Daeja and I, and seize Darian before escorting him back toward Midkeep.

The few who remain are frozen at Sethan's side, poised and ready for the next command. Sethan makes eye contact with each of them and dips his head, dismissing them one by one. Silently, they turn and walk back to Midkeep. Leaving only me, Daeja, and Sethan.

"I can take him. Though, quite confident of him to send off the rest of his men."

"I don't think he's here to fight…"

But Sethan stares at me as if he's taking off every brick, piece by piece, of my self-confidence. Waiting for me to crack. Waiting for me to give in. It might have only been seconds, but it ticks by like hours. A drop of sweat rolls down the back of my neck.

"What?" I bark, attempting to mask my nervousness with irritation. Anything to break through the awkward silence and readying myself to hear the *"I told you so."*

His expression doesn't change. "They've made a mistake."

"They?"

"Whoever decided you're the one to save us."

THREE

WHOM I'M SPEAKING TO

Sethan and I argue over what should be done about Darian with Daeja lingering behind me. Her rigid posture silently challenges Sethan to say the wrong thing or take the wrong step. Eventually, we settle on a shaky agreement that Darian will stay in the dungeon untouched for the night. We can discuss more tomorrow.

After I persuade Daeja I'll be fine returning to the town, we part ways. Sethan escorts me back to the healer's quadrant in a painful silence. After he leaves, Marge tends to my once-again-ruptured sutures with whispered scoldings. In the middle of clenching down on a rag and digging my fingernails into my palms to stay silent while the other Arterians sleep, I finally agree to take it easy. After the liquid burning in my ribs subsides, I stretch out the tension in my jaw and sleep.

The next morning, a group of soldiers usher all of us Arterians out of the rebels' healer's quadrant. I'm not the only one disgruntled by the guards surrounding us, herding us like sheep down the cobblestone streets of Midkeep as passersby watch us with stunned intrigue.

We wind down several busy roads, bumping shoulders with one

another as the guards keep us in close formation. We're led to a massive stone building near the center of the town, its tile roof spanning higher above the rest of the multi-story homes and shops surrounding it. Four other soldiers stand guard at the building's…*entrance?*

It's in the style of a drawbridge. Except, there's no moat or anything to cross. The thick, heavy wooden panel lies flat on the busy cobblestone street. I lean forward to peek across the other two Arterian squad members on my right to exchange a confused look with Archie, who shrugs with splayed hands.

Just as I turn to scan the rows of Arterians behind me for Melaina, a rebel soldier barks, "Keep it moving!"

Our tightly formed squad—with no option *not* to—follow the rebel soldiers surrounding us over the drawbridge door, past the four guards, and into the large building.

The cavernous stone ceiling spans at least sixty feet up into crisscrossing beams with dragons of all shapes and sizes carved into the rock faces. Long, rectangular tables stretch out in front of us, with at least thirty seats on each side of them.

As I scan the room, not a single thing is made of wood. All of it is made of stone. Even the windows lack drapery. Instead, thick iron bars cage the outside of the windowpane with the glass itself being a hazy shade of gray.

Despite the ample amount of sunlight washing in through the two-story tall windows aligning the entire western and eastern wall, several sets of iron chandeliers are strung across the length of the room, their flames flickering with a quiet serenity.

On the farthest wall from us, beyond the tables, is a colossal fireplace that nearly steals my breath. Positioned at the head of the table, directly in front of the fireplace, is Sethan. Already he has his soldiers filling the seats closest to him as he stares down the long table.

Directly at me.

A drop of sweat rolls down the back of my neck.

"You just say the word and I'll quit pretending like I can't take them all out in one breath," Daeja chimes in my head.

I bite my tongue to keep myself from snickering as I hold Sethan's gaze and push away my nervousness. *"This building we're in is made of stone and iron. I have a feeling it was built specifically so it couldn't be burned down."*

"Oh, and you think that'll stop me?"

The soldiers surrounding us part, and the screeching sound of metal grinding against each other has us all whip back to the entrance. The drawbridge closes with a thunderous *slam.*

"Take your seats," Sethan commands, the room naturally amplifying his voice.

Underneath the watchful, heavy stares from Sethan and his soldiers, we all shuffle into the available seats at the table by Sethan's. As I settle into a seat next to Melaina, Archie leans over from the other side of her and flashes a toothy smile.

"Good morning, sunshine!" He's completely oblivious to the tense hostility hanging in the air between our group and the rebels.

Nolan looks like he's about to burst out of his damn skin while Gavin pulls him down into a seat. Meanwhile, the soldiers posted near the walls have their hands already bracing their weapons. The few rebels who sit at the same table as us scan our expressions like we may explode at any second. As if one wrong look or movement may splinter whatever morsel of peace we are currently holding on to.

Tawny sits across from me, her eyes meeting mine, and a part of me relaxes. Something tells me I can count on her to keep her people in check—even if it's so obvious they detest us. Servants appear out of a hallway in the far corner of the room and begin to distribute plates of steaming food to all of us.

"Welcome to the Midkeep community hall! How are you feeling?" Tawny's gaze darts down to my side as someone sets plates in front of us.

I follow her gaze down to my ribs and gingerly touch the area where bandages wrap around my torso, hidden by thick black layers of winter clothes she gifted me yesterday.

"You're going to need these for later," she'd said.

As if I didn't need them currently. Now that we're in the dead of winter, and this far north? It's cold enough to freeze the hells over. The clothes I had back in Arterias wouldn't have been enough for the chill here.

I smile, peering up at Tawny. "Good, I think. And…thank you for the clothes."

"If you want to thank me, convince the rest of your group to accept our help. The least they can do," she glances over to Gavin and Nolan, her nose wrinkling as she beholds the stains mottling their clothes, "is change into something clean. We have more than enough clothing and food to share with everyone."

Nolan shifts his attention from the untouched food on his plate to Tawny, his brown eyes narrowing. "We don't need to smell and look like you. I'd rather parade around naked than be associated with you barbaric, traitorous excuses for people."

Tawny arches an eyebrow, her expression teetering between anger and amusement. "Oh, really? Then by all means," she waves her hand in the air, "parade. You have a lot of nerve speaking to me like that, you—"

"Tawny," Corvin warns farther down the table.

I can't help my own sense of disgust and anger piquing when I recall last night's events and how merciless Corvin had beat Darian. How easily he pulled the whip back and struck him. How Darian's blood dripped from his fingers.

Maybe I'm not so hungry anymore.

I scan the room for Darian, my mouth growing dry as I begin to accept he isn't here. It'll be a conversation I need to have with Sethan.

Tawny growls at Nolan, "We are trying to show you kindness—"

Nolan leans over to spit across the table in her direction, and it lands directly on the back of her hand.

Oh…fuck.

When she flicks her gaze up from her hand to Nolan, her eyes burn with an unkempt fury.

Everyone explodes into action.

Rebel against Arterian.

Tawny shoves up from her seat as she draws her sword from her side. Nolan snatches his plate off the table, dumps the food onto the floor, then wields it like it might be a serviceable weapon. The servants muffle shrieks as they scurry away from us, and the guards at the walls rush in. I hold out a hand to Tawny to keep her from attacking, and the rest of the people at the tables draw their weapons, sliding metal ringing in the air as sword after sword is unsheathed.

Nolan lunges across the table at Tawny as Gavin dives after him, barely catching a fistful of his shirt. Nolan climbs over the stone table and drags a muttering Gavin with him. Melaina snatches the front of Nolan's shirt and rips him down off the table with a vigor that would make any father proud. His back hits the stone tile floor with a shudder.

"What are you doing, Nolan?" she spits as she pins him down.

Archie scrambles out of his seat and draws one of the forks from the table. It's too bad they hadn't decided to trust us with knives yet. I scan the other Arterians around us, finding Cole several seats down near the entrance. He breaks up a fist fight between an Arterian and a rebel as other guards crowd in.

Tawny, thank the Gods, has the self-control to still be watching from the other side of the table as Melaina wrestles to keep Nolan still. My discipline is wearing thin as I keep reminding myself I promised Marge I'd take things easy. I'm lucky enough the first two splits in my stitches haven't led to a serious infection or immediate death. And I'm not trying to test the 'third time's a charm' theory. Considering Marge throws me a pointed stare from across the room, she's thinking the same.

"Oh, so now that daddy is their leader, you're on their side?" Nolan snarls at Melaina. "You're just as much of a traitorous bitch—"

Melaina slams the side of her forearm into his throat, cutting off the rest of his sentence. "Watch your mouth!"

Nolan swings a left hook, connecting with the side of Melaina's jaw and spinning her off him. Archie drops onto Nolan, straddling him with ease before pressing a fork to his throat. Got to give the man some credit—at least he's resourceful.

"*Stop!*" a deep voice rolls over across the room as loud as thunder.

All of us freeze, turning to the front of the room where Sethan stands. Even Nolan has the sense to discontinue his fighting.

Sethan clears his throat, scowling as he rakes his gaze across the room. "Need I remind you all of what's at stake here? I will not tolerate this childish bullshit. One more outburst, from *any*one, and you'll be thrown into the dungeons. Is that clear?"

He looks at Tawny, waiting for a response. She dips her head and sheathes her sword. The rest of the rebels follow suit, sheathing swords and daggers before settling back into their seats.

Leaving us Arterians still standing.

Sethan then settles his attention on me. "You," he jerks his head over his shoulder, "come."

I can't help but look over my shoulder to make sure he isn't referring to someone else. My gaze skips past the other Arterians to Cole, waiting for him to step forward. My skin heats as everyone turns their stares onto me.

Oh Gods…not Cole. *Me.*

"Now!" Sethan barks.

I flinch before hesitantly turning and following Sethan and his guards out of the room through the hallway the servants came and out a side door to the streets.

We wind through the town wordlessly, and I glimpse Daeja's black figure following us from a distance where the streets spill out into the forest blocks away. Every townsperson watches her pass street after street, their stances all rigid with wonder. Despite her keeping a comfortable distance between us, I know if things turned south, she could reach me within the blink of an eye. The awareness of which settles my nerves.

Even Sethan's guards positioned around us toss her wary glances.

"Tell her you're not in danger," Sethan calls without looking my way.

I snort. "I will not tell her of which I do not know."

"Tell him he's the one in danger," Daeja growls.

"I'm not sure he'd be keen on threats…when did you wake? How long have you been following?"

"Long enough to keep an eye on you."

We arrive at another large structure at the northern end of Midkeep—the same one I'd first met Sethan at and found out Darian was a prince. Sethan leads me into the building, with two of the guards staying outside and the other two following us in. As one of the guards closes the door, Sethan stalks around to the other side of a large mahogany desk and swivels to face me. His hands are tucked behind his back and out of sight. Something about it makes my fingers dance anxiously at my hip, where my sword should be.

Sethan stares at me. So completely still he could convince anyone he's a figment of imagination. I'm starting to think this is his technique of intimidating others into his will.

"What?" I ask finally. "I don't play silent games. What do you want?"

"You need to get your people—"

"*My* people?" I laugh. "I'm not the captain here, Cole is—"

"Don't you interrupt me, child. They are just as much—"

"First of all, I am *not* a child."

He growls and slams a fist into the desk. "You need to practice some self-discipline."

I take a half-step back before I snap, "And *you* need to learn to speak to me with respect. I will not be spoken to like this—I'm not a child. I'm a grown-ass woman."

"Then act like it," he snarls.

"Excuse me? I was just trying to stop you while you were ahead—you're talking to the wrong person. I am not their captain."

"I know to whom I am speaking."

"Then you should know, one, I'm not a child. So, stop referring to me as one—it's not going to make me listen to you. Nor will it make me respect you. And two, Cole is the one who commands this squad. Not me."

"Yes, you are," he says with a tight tone that conveys a deep frustration, despite his mask of cool apathy.

"No. I'm not. What do you not understand about that simple statement?"

"What I don't understand," he clenches the wooden lip of his desk until his knuckles turn almost white, "is why in the Gods' names you've been chosen."

I raise an eyebrow. "You mentioned that last night, too. What makes you think I'm this so-called 'chosen one'?"

"The prophecy."

"Well, you must have things wrong. I don't know what prophecy you're talking about, but I can assure you, it's not me." I turn away from him and take a few steps to the door.

The soldiers cross their swords in front of me.

Sethan says behind me, "Do you think this is what I want? What any of us want? We're all relying on you, Katerina. It could have been anyone else, but for some unknown reason, it's you. You are the chosen one, whether or not you like it. And if you sit idly by, more innocent people will die. The King will slaughter all the dragons. And all their blood will be on *your* hands."

I swivel at the threat of people dying on my behalf. "You just said it yourself. It could have been *anyone* else. Maybe it is someone else—maybe you're confused. I've come to the Dragon Lands to live in peace with my dragon. I'm not here to fight in your war."

He clenches his jaw, working and failing by the second to disguise his frustration. "I am not confused. There is no one else but you. The elders translated the prophecy, and it stated Arterias would be restored by *air* and *night*—who else could that *possibly*," he spits that last word out, "be? Your dragon is a moon dragon. Air. And. Night."

FOUR

MOON DRAGON

A shadow falls over one of the windows in the office behind Sethan, and I jump. A white eye with a slitted pupil appears, scanning the room from the outside. When I make eye contact with her, her pupil dilates.

"*Very subtle of you,*" I snort.

"***I wasn't going for subtlety.***"

"*What in the Gods' names is a moon dragon? Have you heard of one?*"

"***No. I know about as much as you do.***" Her attention shifts over to Sethan, and she pulls her head back to face the window head-on. As her lips curl up to reveal her jagged, dripping teeth, the window clouds with her hot breath.

I turn my gaze back to Sethan, finding him anything but intimidated. "A…moon dragon? I only know of fire, water, earth, and air dragons."

He sighs, rolling his eyes as he walks from his desk to a matching mahogany bookshelf crammed tight with rows of dusty, muted tomes. "Of course you don't."

I narrow my eyes. How can he possibly be irritated with me

for my lack of knowledge when I've lived my entire life in a kingdom that forbids even the mere mention of dragons? The only knowledge I have is because of my father's journal. And I shouldn't even have that, considering it could have cost me my life had I been caught with it. Or cost Cole his—since he hid it within his possession for so long to keep me safe. And because he knew how much it had meant to me.

I lift my chin. "So, you expect me to just know these things? I don't. I didn't grow up here in the Dragon Lands."

"Neither did I. Many of us sacrificed our families, friends, and livelihoods to be here."

"You mean like Melaina and your wife?" Probably should have toned down the disdain. I can't help it. I stare at him as I consider the depth of pain he caused Melaina and her mother by faking his death and living his life out in the Dragon Lands. And never returning. I can't imagine how difficult it is for Melaina to process. She must have felt a surging mix of relief, longing, and anger when she first saw him several days ago. I wouldn't blame her for being upset with him, if she is. It's a lot to process.

Sethan ignores me, but there's a small tic to his jaw. He pulls a thin brown book from the shelf, strides over to me, and shoves it into my hands. "Educate yourself and make a decision. You need to be the one to choose and to command your people. They'll listen to you."

Taking the book from his grasp, I scoff. "What sort of command do you think I'm capable of instilling? I'll save you some disappointment—they won't listen to me."

"You and all the Arterians must swear to stay and never leave the Dragon Lands, and must give up your weapons permanently. And if your people won't listen to you out of respect, they will listen to you out of fear."

"I will not threaten them to listen to me."

He grabs my forearm, his eyes boring into mine. A warning growl rumbles outside the office, quaking the window panes.

"He's got three seconds until I break this window…" Daeja warns.

Sethan still won't pay any mind to her, his grip firm on me. "We don't *get* a choice of if we lead through fear or respect. We don't have time. You do whatever is necessary to get them to listen to you. You do what needs to be done for the good of the people. You have two days to decide, and if you don't, we'll kill all of you Arterians."

My mouth drops open as I flinch. "You…will not. You wouldn't kill your own daughter?"

Intended as a statement, it comes out more as a question. The truth is, I don't know him. And based on the fact he deceived his own daughter about his death, maybe none of us do.

He pushes past me without a response. I turn to face him, my mouth still open as he slips out of the door, leaving me with the two guards.

"Do you think he's bluffing?"

"If he isn't…I need to somehow convince the entire squad to stay here. Permanently. And without their weapons."

"It's a good thing you're lousy with a sword. Missing it won't hurt as much."

I slide my attention to the window where she's watching me. *"Very funny."*

Her shoulder shifts like she's shrugging. *"Count on me to keep you optimistic. Or realistic…one of the two."*

The thought of so many people relying on me is terrifying. Clenching my hands tighter around the brown book Sethan gave me to still the shakes, I ignore the stares of the two guards at my back. I failed to save my mother, my brother, and the little girl in Hornwood. How can I scale that responsibility up to an entire squad or more? An entire *realm?*

Sethan's voice echoes in my head, sending a chill down my spine. *"And all of their blood will be on your hands."*

This isn't something I wanted. Gods, I long for the easy days

I spent by the river, where I was only responsible for one other person. My mother.

I leave Sethan's office, Daeja still following along the town's outskirts until I arrive back at the healer's quadrant. When I slip inside, the room is empty and quiet. Everyone must still be in the community hall. Sitting on my bed, I take out the weathered book Sethan gave me. I flip open the cover and past the first stained and tattered page.

A curving, floral script fills the pages. My interest wanes as I read—I've seen it all before. The same information was written into my father's journal: fire, earth, water, and air dragons. Hatchlings. The history of dragon riders and bonding. Everything is the same except the handwriting. I became so accustomed to my father's handwriting that I can't help but mentally note the differences.

As I flip to the back of the book, my heart stops. Loose pages are tucked between the last page and the back cover. The inner edges of the paper are ragged, as if they were torn from a different book. My eyes widen as I realize *this* handwriting is familiar.

I scramble for my satchel tucked underneath the bed and retrieve my father's journal. I compare my father's entries with the loose pages from the book. Side by side. Letter by letter. I flip to the back of my father's journal, where miniscule scraps of parchment had still been attached to the spine. As if…

As if pages were ripped out.

My hands shake as I take one of the loose pages from the book Sethan gave me and line it up with the ragged edges of my father's journal.

It's a perfect match.

I stare in shock. I never gave much thought as to what pages might have been pulled from my father's journal. I just assumed he made a mistake on previous entries and scrapped it. Or perhaps, deep down, I accepted I'd never find out why, anyway.

I begin to read the missing pages.

Before any creatures and elements sprawled the realm, there was the sun, and there was the moon.

The sun had come first, but it was lonely and desperate for companionship. The sun searched all the worlds, far and wide, and found the moon in a separate realm. Rather than compete for the power of the sun—the moon reflected it. The moon couldn't shine without the sun. And yet, without the moon, the tides were unmanageable—destroying the lands. At once, the two became the very first dyad. Bonded and inseparable. Endless as a ring, with no beginning and no end.

The ancient carvings in the hatching grounds of Vitalis depict two dragons: one of the sun and one of the moon. The last documentation of a sun dragon in the era of dragon riders was Queen Elara's. Her sun dragon, Vue, was said to be of otherworldly beauty. His scales gleamed like porcelain and reflected the sunlight into dazzling shimmers when he stepped outside. The only thing dark about him were his black eyes, deeper than any shadow. He could control the position of the sun, channel solar power into beams of blinding light, and manipulate dragonfire. It was even rumored by some that he could resurrect the dead.

Unfortunately, Queen Elara and her dragon died before a moon dragon hatched. Many theorized it was the sign of the Gods cursing mankind, and this is the last cycle of life in this realm. As far as what has been documented, the sun and moon dragons are reborn every one hundred and fifty years in honor of the Gods' battle for blood. It's said that the Gods bring dragons as gifts to this realm, in memory of their war for the heavens. The sun and moon dragon eggs appear in the deepest part of the hatching grounds, coinciding with that sesquicentennial's celestial event.

Though, now that the sun dragon of this cycle has died, it's a question of whether the moon dragon is still out there. And if it is, how its hatching may alter the balance of magic and life.

I remove the loose entries from the book Sethan gave me and

tuck them into my father's journal. Where they belong. After I've put the journal in my satchel and slid it back under the bed, I exit the healer's quadrant. *Daeja is a reincarnation, reborn every one hundred and fifty years?*

"Daeja, does the name Vue sound familiar?"

"No. Why? Should it?"

"I don't know yet." But the truth is sitting there in front of me. Not wanting to be ignored and needing to be confirmed. I follow the path from earlier to the massive community dining hall, partly shocked none of Sethan's soldiers have been assigned to follow me. The drawbridge entrance is still closed, and after explaining to the guards my need to speak with Sethan, they lower it for me. Every set of eyes in the hall turn toward me as I stride into the building from such a grand entrance. The enormity of it already makes me feel smaller than I am. Ignoring eye contact with anyone along the several crowded tables, I approach the one where Sethan sits.

He pauses mid-conversation, pops a piece of potato into his mouth, and turns toward me expectantly.

"Can I…" I toss awkward glances toward Sethan's soldiers. "Can we speak in private?"

The room falls eerily silent, my skin prickling under the intense quiet.

Sethan stares at me, his jaw working in circular motions as he chews and considers. After he swallows, he says, "Whatever you need to discuss with me, you can say here. I don't hide information from my people."

I narrow my eyes. Is this his way of leading with respect? A willingness to converse with Arterians out in public?

Though, what's the difference between Cole and me? *Or is he scared of me the way the others are?* It's obvious the rest of the rebels shy away, giving me extra space whenever I walk by. Watching my every move. Even last night's stint where Corvin questioned Sethan's commands because of me. I swear Daeja would purr if she witnessed how much of a threat she is to them. Even when she isn't in the room.

But with Sethan, it's tricky to decipher where he stands and what he thinks. He hides it all behind his stone-cold mask and well-composed responses. If Daeja truly is a moon dragon, she might hold more power than I ever could have possibly imagined. And I'm willing to bet he knows it, too. I imagine it may work in my favor.

I clear my throat. It feels silly to ask, but I do it anyway, "Why do you think my dragon is a moon dragon?"

He tilts his head to the side. "Let me ask you a question first. Have you ever seen a black dragon?"

"Well…no. But I haven't seen many dragons, either."

He nods, as if it answers my question. A muscle tics in my jaw—he didn't need to be so damn condescending. Especially not in front of an entire audience. Gods, even if he is Melaina's father, I can't bring myself to like him.

I try again, forcing myself to level my tone. "Earlier, you spoke of a prophecy…and that the prophecy is tied to Daeja because it mentioned air and night. Why do you think it's me, though? What else did the prophecy say?"

He leans back. "The one son—"

All together, as if they'd recited it for years, the room joins in a collective whisper, *"The one son, chosen to lead them all. Wasn't a son but a maid. Until binds of death did that grave deed bade. In death blood is shed. But from blood there is life. Restored by air and night to end all strife."*

My blood runs cold. I've heard those lines before. My mother often recited it. And despite having heard it so many times throughout my childhood, it's the first time I've ever given any of the words space. Or a second thought. It's the first time I've ever considered they were more than a string of ramblings from an unwell woman.

All along, it meant something.

All along, it was meant for *me.*

FIVE

FEAR OR RESPECT

Sethan doesn't question why I need to take a seat in the closest chair. He even signals for the entire room to clear out. Quickly, quietly, soldiers clear the crowd of Arterians and rebels out from the community hall, leaving Sethan and me alone.

"You've heard it before, haven't you?" he whispers from across the table.

I nod, still staring blankly at a random spot on the stone beneath my boots. It can't be about me. I'm no one. Nobody. It must be a mistake. If it were true, how come I couldn't save my family? How come I couldn't save Hornwood?

"That prophecy has been around for hundreds of years, Katerina. And it is the single most important translation the elders brought back from the old libraries."

I break my staring contest with the ground and meet his brown eyes. I'd heard it before. Back in Arterias, Marge mentioned elders translating old tomes after King Aaric took the throne. "Why don't you want us to leave? What's the actual reason you haven't killed us yet and want us to stay in the Dragon Lands?"

"You know the answer to that already. Why even bother asking it?"

"Because I need to hear you say it." *Darian must be a red herring.* Sethan doesn't want us to stay in the Dragon Lands because he needs Darian. Or…maybe he still wants possession of Darian, but there's something greater. Something far more valuable.

Me.

Sethan looks me up and down, assessing me. "Because you are the one the prophecy speaks of. And if we lose you, we lose the war."

His threat of killing us if I didn't decide in two days was all a bluff. I snort. "And if I want no part in your war? If I refuse to side with you?"

"You will not refuse." His voice borders on condescension.

"You know nothing of what I will or will not do," I snap.

"As I said before—you rule out of necessity. And whether that means fear or respect, it must be done all the same." He stands up from his seat, looking down his nose at me. "My patience wears thin. We do not have time for your juvenile antics. The King is plotting to invade the Dragon Lands, and he will stop at no end to gain power. So, if you will not agree to help us out of mutual respect, then…"

I push up out of my own seat, resting my fingertips on the table as I lift my chin to look him in the eye. I will not be a fucking pawn. "You'll what?"

He blinks at me. Letting the threat simmer.

I lean forward in a silent challenge. "What will you do?" He's already proven he can't hurt me or Daeja. We are far too irreplaceable, if he truly believes in the prophecy. He won't hurt his daughter or Archie—if he knows it'll crush Melaina. He's having secret conversations with Cole. Marge would likely whoop his ass if he even looked at her the wrong way.

But…he has Darian.

The prince of Arterias. And as far as I know, if King Aaric's son Jurrock is dead and Darian only has sisters, it means Darian is the only male left to inherit the throne. Sethan can potentially use Darian as a bargaining chip, depending on King Aaric's feelings toward his grandson and the plan for succession. Unless…he knows King Aaric won't give up anything to get him back. Then Sethan can use Darian's pain against me.

Witnessing last night's brutality was more than enough proof to Sethan that some part of me cares. Or at least I have some moral compass. And it proves to *me* Sethan won't hesitate to force his desired outcome. And if I show a lick of hesitancy on the behalf of Darian, it may only fuel the fire.

My eyes narrow. I will not be manipulated into something I don't want. Especially because the trust I have in Sethan is equivalent to the width of a grain of rice.

He holds my glare. "If you leave me no room for respect… then…"

"You're mistaken if you assume I will respect *or* fear you, Sethan. So, if you think you can strong-arm me into getting what you want," I growl, pushing off the table, "think again."

I stalk out of the room.

On my way out of the community hall, I grab a full chicken from the servants. I leave the bustling town of Midkeep for the tranquility of the forest. Still, no guards follow me. I search near the river where Daeja has resided the last few days and find a massive dent in the grass where she's been laying.

Odd.

Considering how quiet she's been since we parted ways, I

figured she was dozing. Midday is her usual napping time. I've always assumed she's a nocturnal creature as she became accustomed to traveling through Arterias by night. Another hint toward her being a moon dragon.

Checking my surroundings, I remove a glove and crouch. I press my hand to test how warm the flattened grass still is. Closing my eyes, I reach out for her presence and begin following our magnetic thread south.

My eyes flash open, and I stare out into the forest, waiting for her shadowy figure to flicker through the trees. When I find nothing but stillness, I stride south through the forest, keeping the river to my right. Perhaps she moved spots to nap in the sun instead?

A chuckle bursts through the chirping birds and gurgling water, and I pause. Swinging my attention to the left, I spot Daeja farther in the trees nudging Archie's torso with her snout, her heavy breath audible even from this distance. Archie laughs again—this time a belly laugh—and pats her nose.

I walk to them and stop a few yards away. "What…is going on here?"

Both of them swivel into my direction. Eyes round as if they've been caught doing something they shouldn't, before they exchange a look. Daeja bumps his lower back with her nose, sending him forward a few steps.

Archie ducks his head with a half-smile. "Hey, Kat! We were just uhh…"

Daeja reaches forward to grab the edge of his jacket near his hip between her teeth as delicately as she can and tugs. Though, she is anything but gentle. The motion jerks Archie off his feet, lifting him overhead as he tosses out a surprised shriek.

I drop the feathered chicken to the ground and dash forward, ready to catch Archie. "Daeja! Put him down—"

"It's alright, it's alright. Here!" Archie fishes into his pocket while suspended in the air, his feet kicking out in a half-hearted attempt to balance himself, before he pulls something out.

Daeja sets him back down and slurps the item clear out of Archie's fingers.

Archie laughs again as he scratches her neck. "I've been bringing her snacks ever since you passed out from the battle in Arterias. Figured she'd be hungry. You know…she's actually really friendly."

Daeja freezes, her pupils dilating to the size of round dinner plates before she leans into Archie's touch and kicks one of her hind legs into a frenzy.

"You're…you're not afraid of her?" I tilt my head, perplexed. *"I suppose I didn't need to bring this…"* I whisper to Daeja, then toss the limp bird into her direction. She snaps it out of the air gracefully. Ever the bottomless pit.

Archie's eyes are still settled on Daeja, a warm smile on his lips as he answers, "I mean, of course I am. But that's the thing—you can still fear and respect something at the same time."

I swallow as I recount Sethan's words.

Lead through fear or respect…

Later, Sethan isn't in attendance at dinner. Tawny takes the lead table for herself and her closest guards. When I ask her if they eat all their meals in this extravagant building, she mentions this is the community hall, and each town in the Dragon Lands has something similar.

Cole is absent, which makes me suspicious he's with Sethan.

For believing I'm the chosen one, Sethan sure has yet to include me in their hours-long conversation. I'm adding it to the list of questions.

After our meal, I slip out to the forest to see Daeja. Her large silhouette sits at the base of a tree, staring up at the branches as she tilts her head back and forth.

"What…are you doing?" I ask her.

She jumps before glancing over at me. ***"It was looking at me."***

I stop next to her and follow her gaze up into the dark pine tree. On a branch thirty feet above us is a snowy-white owl, watching us with black beady eyes. It tilts its head unnaturally to the side, almost upside down, then flips it into the opposite direction moments later.

Daeja attempts to copy its movements, also twisting her head at undoubtedly uncomfortable angles. ***"Do you think I could catch it?"***

I chuckle. *"You probably wouldn't want to eat that one. Plus, didn't Archie and I give you enough?"*

"I always have room for more." She flicks her gaze over to me with a playful blow of steam.

I pat her thick neck, welcoming her hot breath in the cold winter night. *"Archie believes owls are bad omens, so I'd leave this one alone. Which…I wanted to ask you. You normally don't like humans—so why Archie?"*

"I suppose I can be easily persuaded," she purrs, still fixated on the owl.

I smile to hide my laugh—*definitely a bottomless pit. "Or food motivated? Noting that for future reference—"*

"I thought I might find you here," a feminine voice calls from behind me.

Following the voice, I turn and find Melaina. She stands with her arms crossed over her chest.

"If your father sent you here to escort me back…" I whisper, taking a half-step closer to Daeja, even though I'm not sure how to finish that sentence.

"You're not in trouble," Melaina covers quickly. She uncrosses her arms and walks closer, her gaze floating up at Daeja. "I still can't believe you had a dragon all this time, though…"

The owl startles and shoots into the air with a muffled 'hoo,' and Daeja tears her attention off the tree branch to Melaina. ***"Well, she better believe it,"*** she grumbles, clearly disappointed Melaina managed to scare off the owl.

Melaina takes a few cautious steps toward us, and Daeja snorts, causing Melaina to flinch and freeze, her gaze locked on Daeja in awe and wonder.

I throw out a half-hearted laugh, following her gaze to Daeja. "Yeah…it was no easy feat."

"A friend," I warn, patting Daeja's neck with a bit more force to prompt her to lower the bristling horns around her head. *"She's no threat."*

"I don't need to worry if she's a threat. I only need to remind her I ***am a threat."***

I shake my head with a laugh that spills out of my nose, and Daeja bumps her muzzle into my gloved hand. I pet her scaly snout, and the tension melts away from her, drip by drip.

"I imagine…" Melaina calls behind me. "My father says she hatched with you. Is that true?"

I nod before turning to face Melaina. "Though, that wasn't information I shared with him."

Daeja settles down into the ground, tucking her front legs underneath her chest and her back legs hidden underneath her belly. Like a clunky, giant loaf of bread. Her white eyes still watch Melaina with unmistakable caution.

Melaina mumbles, "My father also told me there's a prophecy. And…"

I finish for her as a silence settles between us, "And it's about me. And you believe it?"

Melaina shrugs. "I'm not sure. I don't know what to believe anymore. All my life, I was taught rebels and dragons were bad. I've spent years thinking my father was dead, and I trained to protect my family and the kingdom from those who killed him. From rebels *like him*. And now…now, I don't know. He's leading the people I swore to kill."

"I imagine that's hard to process."

"Ha, yeah…I was so overcome when I saw him. I couldn't believe it at first. And then the shock faded to relief, and now I'm a mix of emotions. I'm grateful, confused, and…honestly?" She laughs shakily. "Pissed. Off. My mother and I spent so long thinking he was dead. So many nights crying and feeling like we were broken…and for what? He played us for fools. He never came back."

"For what it's worth, I'm sorry," I whisper. "I can't imagine what these last few days have been like for you."

Melaina nods, offering me a small, appreciative smile. "I'm sorry, too. My father has been so hard on you, and he shouldn't be. I think…and don't ever tell him I said this…but I think he shows that hardened demeanor when he's scared. And whatever is going on—it has him *terrified*. Desperate, even. But it doesn't all rest on you."

I sigh, hoping it releases all the emotions clouding my heart. "It feels like it does. He said I must be the one to convince everyone to stay. He said I'm the chosen one…but for what? I can hardly defend myself. How am I supposed to save the entire realm?"

Her smile widens as she glances down. She spins a bracelet around her wrist, her eyes trained on the shining metal as she murmurs, "When I thought my father died, it felt like it was me against the world, too. I felt so alone. Like no one else could possibly understand what I was going through or what I felt. Every day was dark, every day empty. And then…Celeste showed up at my door. I hadn't answered her knock the first few days, but that stubborn-ass woman was persistent. She came, day after day, until I finally relented and opened the door. She gave me this bracelet and some flowers. She told me how sorry she was, and that whenever I felt sad and alone, even if she wasn't there, and even if I wasn't ready to have anyone there, I could look at it and think

58

of her." She takes the bracelet off her wrist and grabs my hand before placing it in my palm. The moonlight shimmers off its brilliant gleam, highlighting a hidden quote etched into the metal.

You can go through it or grow through it.

"I—I can't take this," I mutter and try to hand it back to her.

She shakes her head, patting my shoulder. "You need it more than I do right now. You're not alone, Kat."

Before I can respond, she brushes past me, taking a few steps away and then pausing. She turns to me slightly, her voice low. "I know…he can be difficult. He can get so lost in the greater good he sometimes loses sight of how it affects other people. But he is good. Even if I'm pissed at him, I know he's made the decisions he has for something bigger than me. It hurts knowing the good of the realm is his first priority. But I still trust in him. Just as I trust in you."

SIX

AN OLDER BROTHER

Melaina's silhouette disappears into the distant treeline toward Midkeep. I sit next to Daeja, shuffling in between her neck and shoulder, welcoming her warmth. I rest my head on her black, rugged scales as she lifts a wing and tucks it over me. Her easy breathing lulls me into drowsiness, and we sit in the quiet of the night. The only thing to break the silence is the rushing currents of the river in front of us. As I fight against my heavy eyelids threatening to drag closed, I watch the water glide by, glittering in the moonlight, before I drift off into sleep.

The blackness of sleep transforms into a room washed in golden light. Sunlight spills through the windows, dust motes dancing in the beams that drag across the room. The singsong chirping of birds rings in the distance. I scan the room, instantly recognizing the wooden table with several rickety chairs. The front door. The makeshift fireplace hearth.

It's my home back in Padmoor.

Immediately, I swing my attention to the wall with my mother's carving all those months ago: *secrets never die, they're just buried in a grave*. But it's free from any imperfections.

Someone touches the back of my head, and I spin to try and face them, but my hair is stuck.

"Stop, Kat! You're going to make me pull out more hair!" a boy's voice scolds me from behind.

A boy's voice I haven't heard in *years*. My heart shrinks into a piece of crumpled paper, and I fight to take a breath. *Am I dreaming?* I turn again to look at his face, but I'm only afforded an inch to my right. My hair screams at my scalp, preventing me from fully pivoting.

The boy snaps, "Will you hold still? I'm almost done with your braid!"

"You're pulling too hard!" It's my voice but…much younger. Echoing around me as if a ripple in a distant lake.

"I am not!" the boy snaps.

"Yes, you are! Oww! Mother!" the younger me calls out.

Footsteps approach us from the right, where the hallway leading to my mother's room is. My mother's chime of a voice rings out, clearer than I've heard in years, "You two, quit bickering! Kat, sit still for your brother. He's just trying to help you."

As I grit my teeth to block out the pain and turn to glance at her, the room blurs and swirls out of perception. The memory melts as if liquid, until it stills into an entirely different scene.

A small, trembling hand clutches an old, quill pen, hovering over a paper with wrinkles. The page has the same two unreadable words repeated a quarter of the way down. The sensation of the trembling quivers in my body—it's my hand as a little girl.

"Try again," my brother chirps from behind my shoulder.

I lower the pen and drag the inked tip across the page, but it jumps sporadically over the wrinkled paper.

"I can't!" I whine.

"Well, you shouldn't have given up so easily! If you hadn't crumpled the paper on the first try when you got frustrated, it would've still been smooth. You have to keep practicing if you want to be any good."

"I don't want to keep practicing! I'm not good enough!" I shoot back.

"Here!" my brother barks and wraps his hand around mine. His hand is only slightly bigger, but he holds mine with a steady confidence while directing the pen across the page. When he finishes the signature, he releases my hand and I drop the pen to the table. With his guidance, the two words I'd continuously attempted to write are clear.

Katerina Blackwind.

"See?" He huffs. "Stop giving up so easily, and you might actually be good at something."

I cross my childish arms over my chest and sink back into the chair. *"You're just better than me."*

"No—I'm older than you. I've been writing for four years longer than you have, so don't compare yourself to me."

I force myself to turn toward him. Fighting against some invisible barrier keeping me locked in place. I'm growing angrily desperate just to see his damn face—

The memory shifts and fades, as if sand gusted away by invisible wind. Everything turns black again. But two pairs of panic-stricken breaths echo around me, along with the rising drum of my heartbeat.

"Don't look, Kat," my brother commands with a tight voice.

My hands are cold against my sweat drenched face. I open my eyes, and light leaks through the cracks of my fingers. A hand is gripping my shoulder, both comforting and alarming. I can't help it—I'm terrified yet still morbidly curious. I split my fingers apart slightly to peek.

"I said don't look!" my brother snarls.

I flinch, terror creeping down my spine as I whimper, *"What's happening?"*

"Nothing! It'll be okay, don't be scared. Just keep your eyes closed and stay here. Okay? Do you understand me? Just keep your eyes closed—"

A glass-shattering scream rips through the unsettling silence, and I cry. A hand slaps over my mouth.

"Shh, keep it down, or she'll hear you!" he whispers near my ear.

The scream tears through the room again. With my face buried in my hands, I curl inward and squeeze my eyes shut so hard an ache flares behind my eyelids.

"Stay here," my brother whispers, and his warm hand over my mouth disappears before his footsteps hurry away from me.

Terrified of being left alone, I lift my face out of my hands and scan the room for him. Candlelight bathes my bedroom in dim, flickering light. I'm sitting on the floor, tucked back as far as I can be into the corner between my bed and dresser. I catch a glimpse of my brother's back and his sandy blond hair as he slips out of my door into the hallway. I stare at the door as he shuts it behind him—the same one behind which I last saw my mother, when our house was burning down.

"Wait," I whisper. *"Please don't leave me!"* Crawling forward, I inch across my room toward the door. I pry it open a few inches and peek out into the hallway across to my mother's room.

My mother sits on the floor against her bed, her arms crossed and fingers digging into her shoulders before scraping her nails down her bare arms, leaving angry red marks. Her eyes are round with a wildness and disheveled insanity I'd grown to know. But now, looking through my younger eyes, I don't realize what it is. I see my mother, but I don't *recognize* her. It fills me with dread so heavy I'm struggling to pull in a decent breath into my lungs. A cold terror drips down my back as if it were water from melted ice.

My brother crouches a few steps away from our mother and rolls something into her direction, the item *clink*ing as it bumps over the floor. She snatches it, fumbling with it frantically before pressing it to her lips and swallowing.

My brother leans forward into her direction. "Mother…? Are…are you…are you alright?"

She snaps her attention up to him, her face contorting, and eyes almost bug-like. "I told you…I told you!"

My brother falls back off his heels and catches himself on his hands, crawling backward to reveal pools of blood around my mother.

Oh, Gods.

Now that I recognize it—it's *everywhere*. Crimson stains splash her pale throat and blonde hair, coating her nightgown in an unsettling burst of color. The red scrapes on her arms aren't scratches—*they're blood*. Strange twists and jerks animate her movements as she drags herself toward my brother, her head twitching and eyes rolling.

He holds out a hand, panic lacing his voice. "We'll get you more, okay? We just need—"

Willard, I want to whisper, but it won't go past my lips. She needs medicine. And quick.

Black bleeds into the corners of my vision, threatening to overtake and drown out the memory. Everything dulls to a painful silence.

No, wait! No!

I sink my fingers into the floor, desperate to not leave them, my fingernails cracking under the pressure. But the wooden boards beneath my nails wave like liquid, and despite how many times I frantically try to claw at them, they meld into a sea of brown. And then…green.

As if someone snapped their fingers, sounds explode around me. Birds tweet and chirp, and a river gurgles nearby. The flat green beneath my hands pop into vibrant sprigs of grass, bursting between my fingers. A crisp moisture hangs in the warm air, and I scan my surroundings. Dew drops glisten against the pine needles, the grass, the rocks. The gushing river splitting the Northern Forest shines almost white with snow runoff from Dragon's Back Ridge. The water spills out past the shallow riverbanks my brother and I played in last summer, swallowing much of the land and growing dangerously close to the roots of the pine trees. I push up to my feet, and a pain flares in my right kneecap.

"*Ow!*" I whine, my voice still childlike, then grab my doll resting on the ground near me.

"I told you to stop running around! It rained last night so everything is going to be slippery."

I toss a glance over my shoulder at my brother. He's bent over near my father's gravesite, laying wildflowers we picked in the hills near our home at the cross's base.

I still can't see his face.

"I'll only stop if you can catch me!" My childish amusement kicks my voice into something high-pitched. I sprint past him with my doll in one hand.

"No! Stop!" My brother rises to his feet out of the corner of my eye.

Wind whips my hair behind me, the river roaring next to me as I race the currents downstream. His heavy footsteps sound behind me, closing in. I swear I can almost sense his fingers reaching out to grab at my collar. My feet nearly glide off the ground. The bend of the river approaches quickly, and I skirt right to run alongside it, stumbling as my feet lose traction on the slippery grass from such a tight curve.

"Kat—" his voice is interrupted by a loud thump and splashing sound.

I turn. My brother slides across the ground, and the river pulls hungrily at his legs, sucking him into its abyss inch by inch as he claws at the ground.

Hold on.

"Aiden!" I scream, my throat burning from how hard I shout his name. I dash forward, sliding to my knees and diving for his hand.

Hold on.

Before I can wrap my fingers around him, the river's current drags his legs sideways, pulling him deeper into the water. He scrambles, digging desperately at the ground glistening with dew, but it's no use. The river swallows him up to his chest, and the shock of the icy water drags a strangled gasp from his lips.

Hold on.

I snatch his wrist, my hand too small to wrap around his completely. As soon as I touch him, his head snaps up to me.

His *face.*

I know it all too well.

I've memorized every etched wrinkle creasing his pinched brows. The expanse of white around his brown irises. The unmistakable horror coating every inch of his expression before it settles into a Gods-fearing acceptance.

I know what comes next. I've tried so hard to push this memory out of my mind. This is the very last time I see him. And yet… and yet I can't look away. I can't close my eyes. Everything moves in slow-motion, trapping me in the moment and forcing me to look at him. The river behind him rushes by with a speed that's eerie, and the hammering pulse in my ears slows.

His skin, normally flushed with rosiness by our days playing in the sun, is zapped ghostly white. Gritting his teeth, his forearms tremble with all the strength he can muster into anchoring himself to the riverbank. His brown doe eyes hook into every corner of my soul.

"Hold on!" I cry, wrapping another hand around his other wrist. Summoning every bit of strength a five-year-old has, I pull him as hard as I can. But my heels slip on the grass, and I fall back, breaking my grasp on him. I fling forward, scrambling to him and snatching his wrists once more.

"No, Kat! Let go! Or you'll get swept off, too!" he barks.

But I can't. I can't let him go. A fierce determination flares within me, and I wrap my fingers even tighter around his wrists. My fingers ache at how hard I grip him. My arms tremble.

"Let…" he grunts, heaving himself up on one forearm to pry my fingers off his wrist. The motion allows the river to tear him farther back away from me.

His eyes meet mine.

One.

Last.

Time.

"Go," he breathes as my grip on him loosens, and the river sucks him in.

"No!" I scream, jolting forward but missing his fingertips by an inch.

He disappears under the roaring white waves and is swept into oblivion.

"Aiden!" I scream as I race downstream, scanning the surface of the river. *"Aiden!"*

I spot something dark clinging to a fallen tree, its gnarled branches reaching out into the water like angry claws. Running as fast and hard as my little feet can go, I slip and slide on the wet grass, slowing every stride. Hope rises in my chest the closer I get. Aiden's cloak is caught on a branch.

It's him. It has to be.

Ignoring the roaring water swinging the tree back and forth, I crawl over the trunk to get closer. I grab a handful of the fabric caught on the branch and sink my other hand into the river, its icy water biting into my skin. I seize another fistful of fabric beneath the surface and pull up with all my might.

It comes free. Easily. I stare at the freezing, soaked heap of fabric in my hands. But no Aiden. My heart shatters into pieces as fine as dust, and my own voice—new and old—echoes in my head.

Hold on.

SEVEN

NIGHTMARES ARE DREAMS

I snap awake, jolting forward off Daeja with a speed that makes me almost dizzy. The river in front of us is the first thing I see when I open my eyes, the moonlight glittering off the surface in scattered waves. Its soft, lazy lull is far from comforting.

Instead, it's a quiet reminder.

I lean forward and rest my forehead against my bent knees, wrapping my arms around my legs. My shoulders quake as I'm consumed by heartache all over again, the memories racing inside my mind at a blinding speed.

Hold on…

Daeja stirs and bumps her nose into my side, her exhalations warming me. ***"I'm here."***

I unfurl slowly and lean my head against her, my breath a rapid drum. Staring at the water blankly, my tears slow as numbness spreads throughout my chest. No matter how much time passes, and no matter how hard I try, the last memory of my brother still crushes me. Every time the memory resurfaces, I'm caught on the *what ifs*. What if I'd stopped running like he asked? What if the grass wasn't slick and the river's currents were peaceful? What if I had been strong enough to pull him out? The fruitless possibilities swarm me, as they always do, even when I bat them away.

Daeja nuzzles into me. ***"It wasn't your fault."***

"But it felt *like my fault then. And it* still *feels like my fault—"*

"Stop. If you keep beating yourself up about it, you'll never be able to move on."

"How can I move on? I don't know how. And what if…what if I don't want to move on?"

"Just because you move on, doesn't mean you don't love him. It doesn't mean it didn't happen."

I glance up at her and scratch under her chin, murmuring aloud, "How did you become so insightful?"

She blows a breath of hot steam in my face, the air brushing all the strands back from my face. ***"Become? You wound me so. Haven't I always been?"***

The laugh in my chest breaks up the vice grip around my heart, shaking away the pain as a landslide sheds stone from a cliffside. *"Thank you."*

Her pleased rumble reverberates in her black scales underneath my palm. My gaze lowers from my fingers to the bracelet Melaina gave me. The one she received from Celeste. I lock in on the words carved into the thin metal band and, though they are too small to see without holding it a few inches from my face, the words shine in my mind.

You can go through it or grow through it.

Daeja interrupts my distant staring by nudging between my head and neck. ***"Go back with the others. I imagine sleeping on a nice, plush bed is much more comfortable than the ground."***

"Is this your subtle way of asking for a mattress?"

"No…" Her pupils narrow to slits, and she glances at me sideways. ***"…maybe."***

I can't help but snort as I pat her head. *"I'll see what I can do."*

She nudges me up off the ground and to my feet, then bumps her nose into my lower back. ***"And don't come back until you do."***

I recognize her hidden intention as easily as noticing what color the grass is. Her discomfort is fake. She knows it'll be the prompt I need to leave her out here. Snorting, I playfully pull down one of the small horns on the side of her head in mock scolding. Her pupils dilate to circles, and she shoots her tongue out at me, the tip flicking my cheek before I squeal and backstep out of reach.

No matter what kind of emotional turmoil I'm in, she always manages to pull me out. Gods, even if the prophecy is right and having bonded her means it falls on the two of us to save this realm, I'm so grateful to be hers. My gratitude and attachment to her far outweighs any heavy responsibility for the rest of the world. I find a certain level of peace in the fact that our bond means our lives are intertwined, eliminating the fear of living a life without her.

As I walk back to Midkeep, I think of everyone I've met along the way. Their faces flashing through my mind with each step. Everyone who is still alive, at least.

Cole. Archie. Marge. Melaina. Gavin. Nolan. Darian. And now…Sethan, Tawny, and all the people I haven't yet met in the Dragon Lands. The townspeople who passed me by as I walked the streets of Midkeep.

How, if I deny or refuse to stop the King—they all might die. All their blood will be on my hands. No matter if I love them or hate them, it's blood all the same. I can hardly stomach and process my brother's death all those years ago. If the death toll ticks up to hundreds, *thousands* of people? I might be the one who can make a difference—can I really live with myself if I refuse?

The buildings of Midkeep come into view through the treeline, and I slink through the shadows, pausing as I wait for one patrol to disappear into the town. I get halfway through Midkeep before I'm caught. Once the guards recognize who I am and confirm I'm alone, they lower their weapons and escort me back to the healer's quadrant. I must have a lot more pull than I'm aware of if me sneaking about this late at night only garners me chaperones. Though, I don't doubt Sethan will hear of it. *Not looking forward to that conversation.*

"Where have you been?" a voice hisses as I close the healer's quadrant's door.

I about jump out of my skin and whirl to the voice. I realize who it is and slowly close my gaped mouth. "Sorry? Did I need to check in with you on where I go?"

"You look dreadful," Marge states. She's in a nightgown, standing near the edge of her bed while the rest of the squad slumber peacefully in the background.

I laugh quietly, dripping with sarcasm. "Thanks."

But the laugh is a hair too loud. Archie stirs in his bed, lifting his head off the pillow with his eyes still closed and hair strewn about like a hawk's nest. "You're welcome," he mumbles in a daze, then flops back over to his other side, slipping back into sleep.

Marge drags her gaze back to me the same time I do her, then whispers, "I don't mean to be curt…I'm just…I'm worried about you, Katerina."

I unlace one boot, remove it, and slide it near the bedpost. "Nothing to worry about. I just haven't slept much. That's all."

She scans me head to toe. "Have you been dreaming?"

What an odd-ass question. I balance on my bare foot, swaying around as I try to remove my second boot. "Yes…well, more like nightmares."

She tilts her head and watches me with a mix of mild curiosity and disappointment in my balancing skills. "My mother used to tell me sometimes dreams are your reality spilling over into your subconsciousness. Pay attention to them—they may know you better than you do."

Well, then my reality is fucked. And it's been fucked for a long time. All I've dreamt about has been previous traumatic events. Hornwood burning. The little girl and her family perishing. My mother's manic episodes and my brother drowning.

I place my second boot near the bedpost with the first one. "What did she say about nightmares?"

"Nightmares *are* dreams."

Silence falls between us, until Marge rests a hand on my shoulder. "If you need someone to talk to…I'm here for you. Or you don't have to tell me. Dreams are personal things. Hold on to them."

Hold on. I shake my head vigorously to dislodge the two words stuck inside my head. Sucking in a breath, I dip my head. "Thank you, Marge."

But what can *hold on* possibly mean?

EIGHT

HOLD ON

"Kat!" a whisper splits through my sleep. "Kat!"

I drag my eyelids open and stare up at the shadows stretching across the expansive ceiling. A hand is wrapped around my shoulder and shaking me gently. I turn to the voice, and my vision swims from grogginess.

"What?" I murmur, partly confused and dazed.

Cole is kneeling at my bedside, his eyes round with worry. He stops shaking me, but his hand is still tight around my shoulder. "Are you alright?"

I blink and rub my eyelid with the heel of my hand. "What? Yes. Why?"

He watches me cautiously. "You…you kept crying *hold on.*"

I fling up off my back and whip my head toward Marge's bed, the one next to mine. She still snores peacefully, and the rest of the beds are occupied with snoozing squad members.

"I…I did?" I whisper, dragging my gaze back to him.

It has to mean something. After dreaming of flames for so long, now all I can think or dream of is my brother? Perhaps Marge is right. Perhaps there's an underlying meaning.

Cole nods. "Do you…want to talk about it?"

I swallow, looking down at my hands. Anyone else I might be hesitant to share, but before all else, Cole was my friend first. My confidant. Admitting such a personal thing to him almost feels like second nature. "I umm…I keep dreaming about my brother. All our memories and the day he died."

"I get it. I still dream about—" He glances around the room to check and make sure no one else is awake. A heavy breath sags his shoulders before he continues, "My mother. Sometimes it's nice to see them again. But still painful, all the same."

Nodding, I look back down at my hands again, to his ring around my finger. I've been removing the gloves at night, since Marge suggested I only need to wear them outside in public. I pinch the metal ring and spin it around my finger, working up the nerve to remove it and hand it back to him. It just feels so…natural on my finger. Like it belongs there. *You're just heartbroken that you can't live in the reality of marrying him. Clinging to the familiar. Give it back—*

He rests a gentle hand atop mine, stilling my fidgeting. My heart skips a beat, and I twist my neck to look down at him, where he still kneels.

His eyes are a perfect, soft amber, his whisper like a summer breeze, "And I used to dream of you a lot, too. I…I still do."

Before I can respond, he removes his hand from mine and pats the bed thoughtfully. Avoiding my eyes as if he's embarrassed by the admission, he pushes up to his feet. Before I can stop it, the memory of the months I spent haunted by dreams of fire, my mother, and the family back in Hornwood I failed to save, flood me. The only time I can recall not dreaming was when Cole was next to me. As if his mere presence chased away all the fear and nightmares. A lifeline. I'm desperate for sleep and unwillingly longing for his steadfast comfort.

"Wait," I blurt, before I can stop myself. "Can you…can you stay with me?"

He scans the room, squinting through the dim starlight spilling in from the sets of windows, his jaw tense. As far as anyone knows, we're siblings. And though we're no longer in Arterias, no longer in the military outpost, it still feels necessary to keep up the front. He was…or *is* engaged?

Part of me wonders if pretending we're so platonic will protect the both of us from getting involved further. It's a clear line in the sand we should *not* be crossing. And besides, I'm not quite ready to admit the truth to the others. We've spent months lying to them about my true identity…and we already have enough tension between our groups. A new confession may break what thin ice we're currently standing on.

My fear outweighs everything else. And there's still a part of me drawn to Cole that I can't deny. "Until I fall asleep. Please…" I whisper. "It doesn't have to be anything other than what we make it."

Flinching when he recognizes the pain in my voice, he turns his hazel eyes to me. "You're sure?"

I nod and open the sheets with eyes that tip toward a silent plea. *Please…don't make me ask again.*

His body is rigid, holding onto his breath as he slides into bed next to me. The mattress sinks under his brawny frame. But rather than curling his muscled body around me and holding me in his arms as he always did, he keeps a courteous distance between us. We both lie on our sides, facing each other. He slides one hand beneath the pillow to brace his head, and the other lies in front of his chest on the mattress. The moonlight washes his features in a softness, his expression a touch heavier than peace. As his eyes lock with mine, I swallow down the thickness collecting in the back of my throat. The tip of his nose is only six inches from mine. It's the closest we've been in a while. With nowhere to look but each other, my gaze flicks down to the soft set of his lips.

Inches. Just inches away. I feel myself being pulled into him like a tide, reeling me in.

Marge's snore hits its loud, ragged peak, and both of us flinch before melting into silent chuckles.

"Why is it always the ones who snore the loudest fall asleep first?" he whispers.

Biting my bottom lip to keep myself from laughing, I flick his hand. The urge swimming in my chest to kiss him recedes. For a moment. And I'm wearing his godsdamned fiancée's bracelet Melaina gave me. What kind of woman does that make me? Foolish? Heartless…? Definitely jealous, even if I don't want to admit it.

The humor in his face falls into something serious. "What? What is it?"

I shake my head. Not wanting to give my emotions words. Not right now.

He slides his hand across the mattress until the outside of his pinky finger touches mine. The most innocent way to touch me. But the way his eyes dig into my soul, they flay my heart like the butcher he is. "You can talk to me. You know that. We're friends, aren't we?"

But friends don't steal glances across a crowded room. And they don't share a bed after midnight, staring into each other's eyes with smiles that hint at how much they want to lean in and touch like they're starved. Every time he looks at me this way, it crushes me. Because I know he shouldn't. Just like I shouldn't want him to.

"Friends?" I chuff out.

"It hurts me, too, you know," his whisper cracks. "What else do I call you? What do you want me to call you?"

"I don't know."

"Kat…" He threads his fingers into the backs of mine.

"Don't…" I mutter and slide my hand out of his. "It's not fair. Because if you keep touching me, I won't want you to stop."

A broken sigh. "I'm sorry I put us here…"

"I don't want to talk about this right now."

"Okay…okay. Get some rest. I won't leave until you're asleep."

"Thank you," I murmur, lost in the honey pools of his irises until I drift off to sleep.

The rest of the night is dreamless. I wake the next morning to a tingling beneath my ribs, like fire ants have been set free underneath my skin. Flinching forward, I yank my shirt up, catching only a glimpse of rippling skin as my wound heals completely. The only remnant is a faint four-inch-long scar on my ribs.

I touch the skin, as if I'll blink and it'll have been a hallucination. But even the pain has faded to only a dull ache. Scanning the rest of the room, I find Cole gone and Archie's concerned gaze.

"Are you alright?" Archie asks from a few beds down.

I nod. "I…I think so?"

"What was that?" Daeja grumbles, her voice rough with sleep.

"My wound is gone. It wasn't your doing?"

"No. Or…at least, I don't think so?"

I lean into my side, testing the muscles. Even though I'm partly relieved it doesn't sting like it has been, the lack of it strikes a hot flash of alarm through me. Because if it wasn't Daeja…who was it? Or *what* was it?

"You could feel it, too?"

"Yes, it woke me up."

After I dress and grab the book under my bed, I slip out of the room to head for Sethan's office. After requesting a private audience, the guards at the entrance let me through. Sethan sits at his massive wooden desk, its legs carved into clawed feet. The rich mahogany gleams in the sunlight sparkling through the sets of diamond-patterned windows lining the walls. A large rug, colorful and worn, spans the space around his desk, covering most of the gray stone tiles. I glance toward the several bookshelves lining the wall, searching for the spot where Sethan pulled the dragon journal from originally.

"Yes?" Sethan asks, not bothering to pause or look up from the letter he's writing.

I take the book and lift it for him to see. "I wanted to return this to you."

"And?"

I stride across the room, stopping at the edge of his desk, and drop the book onto his desk a few inches from the letter he's writing. The move isn't enough to gather his attention, so I place my fingertips on the cover of the journal and stare at him.

I clear my throat. "So, Daeja is a moon dragon."

Finally, he looks up. "Great. That's all you've come to tell me? We've already had this conversation. As you can see, I'm quite busy right now."

He's still pissed about our last encounter. But so am I. Except, I'm willing to push away my feelings to do what is right. As I lean forward, readying myself for a bite of a response, a glimmer of light catches my attention in my peripheral vision. Turning to the shine, a streak of sunlight glitters on a gold frame hanging on the wall. The canvas its framing is shredded, with bits of colored scraps still hanging limply like ribbons.

I wince, unable to imagine what or *who* could have caused it.

Sethan follows my stare, then turns to grin at me. "Cyrus was known to lose his temper quite easily, and frequently. Though, I suppose it could have been attributed to his heritage."

I stare at the brutally tattered canvas. It's as if a bear waltzed in here and tore its thick, gnarly claws down the painting. The rest of the room fades away, aside from its golden frame. I feel beckoned forward, as if it holds the key to all the answers I need.

I shake myself from the indescribable pull and turn my attention back to Sethan. "Why would you keep something like that?"

He shrugs nonchalantly. "It's a good reminder of all the things he was capable of, I suppose."

"Who was he? What happened to him?"

"He ruled the Dragon Lands before I did and died in combat."

I slide the journal across the desk closer to him. "I want to know everything."

He snorts, leaning back into his chair. "You don't get to know everything."

"Then why should I trust you? When rebels have been burning down innocent towns and murdering men, women, and children?"

His eyes darken. "*Hold on…*"

I flinch at his choice of words.

Sethan breaks into a sarcastic laugh, sharp with a hidden anger. "You think *we* are doing that?"

"I witnessed it myself," I snap.

Sethan glares, the weight of his stare on me heavy. With strong, scarred fingers, he quickly undoes the top few buttons on his shirt and rips the top open, exposing a few inches of his brown chest. "Do you see this?" Scars scream across his skin in jagged, angry angles—deeper than the ones that mar his neck and hands. "This wasn't the rebels. This was *King Aaric*. I was on your side as an Arterian, Katerina. Make no mistake. I was second in command to Jurrock, and when I discovered his letters from the King—"

His eyes blaze, and he swallows hard. "I couldn't believe it. Jurrock had been my best friend for ages. And when I confronted him, he brushed me off. He told me it was *necessary*. That the towns hosted rebel families and were sending provisions to the north. He convinced me the rebels were evil, and we had to put an end to any sympathizers before it got out of hand. We had to cleanse our kingdom of any traitors, before there was a full-blown rebellion in Arterias. I wanted to believe him. And for a while, I did. Jurrock had been my best friend, so I didn't want to believe he was wrong, that we were wrong. But…we were."

I watch him cautiously and back off his desk as he pushes out of his chair and stalks around it toward me. He passes a wall stretching high into the ceiling, each panel creating a massive picture depicting the Dragon Lands. Dark clusters of towns, villages, and a variety of landscapes decorate the wall.

A map.

I not-so-subtly scan it, eyes wandering over the unfamiliar snow-dusted mountains clustered at the most northern part of the map. Down to rich green forests spreading out over the entire continent. The lakes, rivers, canyons, and volcanoes. At the furthest southern piece of the map is Dragon's Back Ridge, where more towns are noted, and I spot Midkeep. Black splotches jump out at me, bleeding over the outline of multiple neighboring towns. I focus on the stark explosions of ink and am unable to look away. Sethan comes to stand next to me, facing the map and waiting for the unspoken question between us.

"I…I've never seen anything like it," I murmur.

"That's because King Aaric doesn't want Arterians knowing just how much else is out there outside of his kingdom. He wants you to fear us. Which…I suppose you should. But not enough to want us exterminated. Only enough to respect us and honor our requests for peace."

My father's journal entries trickle into my mind. He wrote the rebels had been requesting peace treaties with the King—but were met with silence.

I glance sideways at Sethan, finally asking, "What are the black spots for?"

He folds his hands behind his back. For the first time since I've been here, a solemnity relaxes his angry expression. "It might be better if I show you. Will you come with me?"

I hesitate.

Can I actually trust him? If he wanted me dead at this point, it would have been done long ago. We're far outmatched here. The prophecy must provide some sort of security for me and Daeja. Though…he could have me tortured alongside Darian if he wanted to.

But Melaina trusts him. Trusts that he honors the good of

the realm above all else. I suppose I should at least honor her faith by giving him a chance.

We leave his office and walk through the cobblestone streets toward the eastern part of town. Each townsperson we pass dips their head in acknowledgment, and Sethan mirrors the gesture. Despite Sethan's every effort to mask it, a hint of a limp stalls his gait. The chatter from the town fades as we slip away from the buildings and into the cover of pine trees.

"Where are you taking me?" I ask finally, sweeping my gaze left and right through the forest. I've only been on the western side of Midkeep, and the trees around me are entirely unfamiliar.

"Call your dragon," he commands, ignoring my question.

I narrow my eyes at his authoritative tone and stop in my tracks.

He turns to me, completely unamused. "Do you want answers or not?"

Working my jaw and crumbling under his intense stare, I finally tear my attention away and stare off into the forest. *"Daeja? Can you meet me at the eastern part of the town in the forest?"*

She yawns. ***"On my way."***

Sethan and I stroll farther into the forest. The sun creeps above the treetops and stretches shadows into long stripes across the ground. Something loud snaps a few yards off into the forest at my right, and I whirl toward it.

My breath catches in my throat as a large dragon stalks through the trees toward us. Its scales shimmer like ruby-red armor in the sunlight, each magnificent muscle gliding with its stride. It stops a few feet away, towering over me as its lip curls up to reveal yellow-stained teeth. A growl rumbles in its throat as its golden cat-like eyes meet mine.

I pat at my sides, cursing for not having anything to defend myself with. As I backpedal to put space between me and the fire dragon, Sethan walks up to the dragon and rubs its neck. "Katerina, meet A'nala. A'nala, Katerina."

A'nala keeps their eyes on me as they lower their head and stretch toward me with flaring nostrils. My hair stirs as the creature pulls in two long, hard sniffs.

Mouth agape, I flick my gaze back and forth between Sethan and the dragon. "You…you're—"

"A dragon rider," he finishes for me.

NINE

DRAGON RIDER

"Now, where is your dragon?" Sethan asks impatiently, scanning the forest.

"She…umm…" I struggle to wrap my head around this reality as I stare into A'nala's golden eyes. I have to physically twist my shoulders to drag my gaze back to Sethan. "I-I thought all the riders were executed?"

"They were."

"So then…how?" My gaze floats back up to the magnificent crimson dragon, thick, gnarled horns blending from ruby red to black at the tips.

He huffs. "We can speak of this later—"

The trees stir around us, followed by the beating of wings. I turn as Daeja lands with a thud on the ground, a few feet behind me. She keeps her wings outstretched as she growls, the horns on her head and neck bristling. Taking a step forward, she stretches her head over me protectively, the bottom of her chin brushing my scalp.

Sethan strides over to A'nala's side, and the dragon lowers itself as if it's done it a million times. Those yellow eyes are still trained on Daeja.

"Have you ever ridden your dragon before?" Sethan calls.

"Well…yes. Sort of?"

"Wonderful." He snags something behind A'nala's neck and pulls himself up and onto her back. He pats her thick muscled neck. "Let's fly low and slow, girl."

A'nala rises from the forest floor, revealing black leather straps and buckles encircling her chest and back. I must not have noticed it. As A'nala turns away from us, I glimpse Sethan seated in a black saddle, positioned perfectly between A'nala's neck and shoulder blades.

Patting Daeja's shoulder, she finally turns her attention to me and lowers for me to scramble up toward her back. She noses her muzzle under my foot and nearly throws me over to the other side of her spine. Schooling my heavy breath, I settle into the crook of Daeja's neck. I lower myself, squeezing my legs around the back of her neck and grabbing on to two of her long, skinny horns.

Without another second to spare, A'nala and Sethan slingshot into the sky.

"Are we following them? Do we trust them?" Daeja mutters.

"No, we don't trust them. But…we are following them." I clench my fists tighter around her horns.

"Sometimes I question your judgment…" She lowers her head and breaks into a run, her wings flapping before we lift off the ground.

"You and me both," I whisper back.

The pine trees flash by us at an alarming speed. I fight against my racing heart to calm myself and glance up at A'nala gliding off in the distance. At least Sethan has a fucking saddle. My thighs are sure to be sore tomorrow after how hard I'm trying to balance myself on Daeja. And thank the Gods my ribs have miraculously healed, even though the scar aches dully as my body rolls with each flap of Daeja's wings. We skim over the treetops, staying low. The ground taunts me from beneath us, reminding me if I fall there is no water to catch me. Just unyielding, solid earth.

It's a mistake looking down. So, I glance back up to A'nala. They still have a good two-hundred-feet lead on us. *This is slow for them?*

"I could go faster," Daeja murmurs, reading my thoughts. **"I'm still a little sore from when that rebel punctured me with the spear."**

But I know she's holding back. For *me*. She can sense my anxiety and fear. And something tells me she's only using her wing as an excuse to calm my emotions. Because she could absolutely, definitely fly faster.

A'nala's red shape cuts south toward Dragon's Back Ridge. The mountains reach staggering heights, lurching above us into the sky, with some of the peaks blanketed in snow. We fly for another twenty minutes, deeper into the mountain range and closer to Arterias. The views alone at this height are heart-stopping. I've now added another reason to regret blacking out after the battle in Arterias. It's gorgeous out here. Something about it feels like a home I've never been to.

A valley opens up in between towering mountain peaks, and A'nala descends. Daeja follows suit and flares her wings, slowing her speed until we land on the ground. Sethan hops off A'nala, and I fumble down from Daeja, lacking any grace or experience. When my feet strike the ground, I feel the vibration ring through my body. My thighs are on fire, hands are already aching from clinging so hard to Daeja.

Sethan wordlessly prompts me forward with a hand. His features are unreadable. Daeja and I follow him and A'nala up a steep incline, the wind picking up as we near the top. A'nala and Sethan pause at the peak, their stares fixed on something in the distance. Daeja and I climb the rest of the way, and as we crest the hill, the wind wipes away all of my breath.

In the valley below, a black ash settles over the land like an ominous veil, reaching up to the edges of the hills and mountains. Stone buildings are either crumbling or toppled over completely. Piles of stone and brick lay buried by dust. Scattered throughout the ruins are black, withered tree trunks with mangled branches curling in on themselves. Violent, ragged lines shred the streets, as if claws tore across the town.

"What…what happened?" I murmur. "Dragonfire?"

"No. Not dragonfire," Sethan whispers.

"Then what? Why are you showing me this?" I drag my gaze away from the decimated town and to him, terror settling in my chest like a heavy stone.

Sethan's brown eyes are set on something in the distance. An aching sadness pulls at his brows. "Because this is all that's left of them, and we need your help. This is what happens every time and will continue to happen if we don't stop King Aaric."

"What do you mean every time? What is this?"

"When I was still in the King's Close Circle, we were dispatched to Wynnban one night. It was the closest the rebels were rumored to have ever gotten to the castle, and when we got there, it was night. There wasn't a single person stirring—no one to fight back. We were instructed to bar the doors and set fires to the homes. Every. Single. One." He looks down and clenches his fist. "They commanded us to leave no one alive. One home, I recognized the family's sigil. And that's when I knew I couldn't do it. There were so many innocent lives—so many people who didn't deserve such a cruel death. Children, elderly, the sick…I had to get them out. Even if I couldn't save them all. But the fire grew so fast…*too* fast. It wasn't like anything I'd ever seen. It was almost as if it had a life of its own. As I broke through someone's window and climbed into the house to save them, I felt something. The air turned cold, heavy, and sharp. As if it crackled with the electricity of a storm, despite the raging fires. I turned back to the window and watched the fire bleed through the streets at a rapid pace. The King appeared in the flames and walked through the fire without even flinching. I watched him pull a canister out and pour the liquid on his hand. He coated every inch up to his wrist. And as I watched it drip—I could be wrong—but I *swear* it looked like blood. He reached into the fire and it flared brighter. Stronger. And as he moved his hand, the fire followed him as if it were…"

"Alive?" I murmur. Remembering the night I passed out in Arterias, and how the flames almost responded to each sweep of my hands.

He nods. "That night I managed to rescue the family whose house I'd broken into. We ran as fast and as far north as we could. When we got to the hills on the outskirts of town, the ground shuddered underneath our feet. We turned and saw the flames engulfing Wynbann morph from red, to blue, and then white. And as quick as it had transformed, something sucked all the flames into the center of town like the receding of a tide…"

He drifts off, staring at the demolished town before us as if he's reliving the memory. After a few moments of silence, he blinks and shakes his head, finally looking at me. "You might not trust me. And that's fine, because I don't necessarily trust you, either. But we must work together if we're going to save Arterias, the Dragon Lands, and all the dragons. We *have* to start somewhere. And maybe you don't believe you're the key to all of this…maybe you think we're wrong. But that's all we have left—our hope. And if that means betting on you, then I suppose I'll bet on it."

My mouth parts as I register the information. What if all along the fire that happened in Hornwood hadn't been the rebels, and it had actually been the King's men? That the ones who killed the little girl, her family, and her entire town wasn't who I thought it was? Nausea at the thought of something so cruel churns in my stomach. The realization rushes over me and drowns out all of my senses, pulling my attention toward it.

The sword I took from the 'rebel' who tried to kill me and Daeja back in Hornwood had the symbol of the King's Close Circle. I think some part of me wanted to believe a rebel had taken it from a battle they won against the Arterians. I favored that idea more than this one, a reality that sickens me to my core. Denial is a powerful negotiator—but now there's no rejecting it. No matter how hard I try to ignore it or refuse to swallow the reality.

A low, rumbling cry splits across the vast expanse, shuddering the blood in my veins. Daeja at my side winces, tucking her head low as she squeezes her eyes shut. A'nala mirrors her discomfort, and Sethan cringes.

The menacing sound alone unnerves me. A tingle flickers in my hands, and I nearly squirm out of my skin. "What is that?"

Sethan tics his head to the side at the next ringing wail. "A ripple."

"A ripple?"

"Yes. When a dragon is slaughtered by a magical weapon and its magic isn't returned to the earth, it's stuck here, somewhere…else. Trapped reliving its final moments."

A'nala's top lip curls up, her pupils narrowing and widening repeatedly.

Daeja shakes her head as if trying to rid the sound. ***"Make it stop."***

"Let's go." Sethan motions for me to mount Daeja, and he climbs into his saddle on A'nala's back.

The four of us take back to the skies, and the ripple's wails fade into the distance, replaced by the sound of the whipping wind. We land back in the forest outside of the Midkeep.

"Why have I never heard a ripple before?" I ask Sethan and slide off Daeja. "Back in Padmoor, I watched the King's military kill a dragon. I never heard anything then?"

He works on tying up some of the loose straps from the saddle. "Had you bonded your dragon at the time?"

"I'm not sure what you mean by that question. At the time, she hadn't even hatched. I wasn't even aware of her existence."

"Then the reason you didn't hear it before is because only those with magic can hear it. You can now since you and your dragon are bonded. That, and I imagine King Aaric is careful to not create ripples in his kingdom—it serves as a better reminder for us in the Dragon Lands and our people."

"So…that creature is stuck there? For eternity?"

Sethan tosses me a side-glance. "Unless *you* release it."

"Me? How?"

He strides forward and holds out an open palm. "Remove your gloves, and give me your hands."

I snort, taking a step back. Marge had mentioned the ring on my finger was tied to being a dragon rider and I should keep it hidden. But now knowing Sethan is also a dragon rider…does that make him trustworthy? I'm still unsure how I feel about him.

He flicks his fingers impatiently. "Come on. You have nothing to hide from me."

Daeja growls in warning. ***"If you don't want to take them off, don't."***

I pat her side to quiet her as A'nala locks in on Daeja. *"Easy. Let's not aggravate either of them."*

"Why should we care? They aren't our friends or allies. I might be a little more than half the size of the she-dragon, but I bet I could outrun her."

"She's double your size, and considering the scars littering her scales, she has far more experience in combat."

"Some people just call it old age."

I toss her a glance. *"Daeja!"*

When I look back at Sethan, he has an eyebrow quirked up. "Or…*do* you have something to hide?"

Chewing on my tongue, I race through the possibilities. If I don't remove the gloves, it'll only make me seem suspicious. And besides, what do I have to lose other than the fact he'll know for certain I'm a dragon rider? Sliding my gaze to Daeja, she's already watching me. *And it's already obvious I am a dragon rider.*

Removing my glove, I reluctantly offer him my right hand with the dark circle that represents my bond with Daeja. In our proximity, I recognize a band of dark skin wrapping around his wrist, with its shape mirroring something of the ring around my finger.

He shakes his hand and motions to my other hand. While I lock onto his steady gaze, I pull the glove off my left hand finger by finger and hold it out to him. His brown eyes fix to my hand, sucking in a gasp as soon as I rest mine in his. He hovers a fingertip above my fingers, right over the ring Cole gifted me. Not daring to touch it.

"This ring…" He clears his throat and drops my hand before taking a step back. His brown eyes are still glued to my hand. "…this ring has much power. More power than you could ever imagine. Enough power that you could release a ripple."

"I could?"

"With some training…" He nods, before shaking off his mesmerization. "Look. If you really don't think you can trust me or those here in the Dragon Lands, then we can make a blood pact. But we need you. The dragons need you. And the entire realm needs you."

"A *blood* pact?"

"A blood pact is a binding agreement. Should either party venture outside of the agreed to terms, they'd die. So, you won't have to trust me, and I won't have to trust you. Because we'll be magically bound to it."

I flinch at the severity of such an agreement. If I don't hold up my end of the bargain, Daeja will also die. But it also means him and A'nala dying if *he* doesn't hold up his end. If I can't trust his words directly, I can at least trust the magic of such a pact. *Right?*

He jerks his head into the direction of Midkeep. "But there's one last thing that belongs to you, that you need to see before you make a decision."

Back in Sethan's office, he pulls open a hidden drawer in his desk and hands me a letter. I take it from him, and when I note the front is blank, I flip it to the back. A broken wax seal with the symbol of the rebels—a capital 'A' with a dragon perched on top—is stamped across the two folds. Unfolding the paper, Sethan stalks around the room out of sight.

Sire,

I pray this letter finds you well, and I apologize for such a lengthy silence. I write to you to inform you of my official resignation as a spy. During my return to the Dragon Lands I was caught by an Arterian in Padmoor. She held me prisoner and, somewhere along the way, we fell into an undeniable companionship.

And now I have a child on the way. As you can imagine, I can't leave the babe in this kingdom or at the very least, not alone.

I can only hope someday I see you again. May the Gods grant you a lifetime of peace and prosperity. May we win this war. And may we set our people and dragons free from tyranny.

Forever,

Leland Blackwind

I fold the letter closed and scan the room to find Sethan leaning up against a wall and watching me already.

I shake the letter. "What does this mean? Why did you want to show me this? I already knew my father was spying on the King."

"Because of how he addressed him," Sethan whispers.

I blink, opening the letter back up and scanning the first word. *Sire.* "How is that relevant?"

"Because no one called Cyrus sire. Many of us have reason to believe that your father, Leland Blackwind, was *sired* by Cyrus. Making you the granddaughter of—"

"Cyrus," I breathe.

TEN

IN LINEAGE AND PACTS

I'm the granddaughter of the rebels' previous leader? The realization steals my breath.

Sethan lifts his chin, looking at me through lowered lashes. "Yes. Your father and grandfather fought on our side. Do you really think so little of them, that they'd be on the wrong half of this war?"

"No," I admit, setting the letter down on his desk and staring at the wax seal. Despite never having met them…it still feels like an insult to not trust them. Where my allegiances *should* lie has been a continuous, flickering thought at the back of my mind. Especially after I began reading my father's journal back in Arterias. And *especially* as I became more and more intertwined with Daeja.

"We need your help, Katerina," Sethan says softly. "We need you."

I tear my gaze away from him to glance at Daeja, who watches me with a twitching tail. *"What do you think?"*

"I'll follow you wherever you go. And I'll stand behind you in whichever decision you make."

I turn to Sethan as thoughts race through my head, increasing in speed and weight. When I lock gazes with him, the thoughts quiet as I murmur, "Alright."

He takes a few steps in my direction, his boots clicking on the stone-tile floor. "Will you swear secrecy for anything you find out about the Dragon Lands, kingdom, and magic?"

I lift my chin with a sigh. "Yes. I suppose."

"Great. And you and your squad will not leave the Dragon Lands unless I grant you permission."

I scoff. "How do you expect me to keep an entire squad under command? I'm not even their captain—"

"You'll find a way. You just need to try."

I grumble, "Can you guarantee your people won't hurt mine?"

He crosses his arms over his chest. "Not entirely."

"Seriously? How am I supposed to agree if you can't even guarantee our safety?"

"There are always those who don't believe in and won't follow the commands of their leaders. I'm in an elected position, and it wasn't necessarily a unanimous vote. Everyone is aware I was born and raised as Arterian, so not everyone trusts me. In fact, there was a bit of an upheaval at my appointment. But…I can agree my immediate comrades would be bound by our deal, as they're already sealed to me by their own blood pacts."

I cross my arms over my chest, mirroring his stance. "Fine. But you also agree to allow us our own separate quarters outside of what is currently provided."

"Granted, but you all have a curfew."

"Excuse me?" I scoff. "What are we, children?"

"That's my requirement."

I glare at him. "What for?"

"I don't need to express the reasons for my request, do you accept it or not?"

Tapping a finger against my arm in thought, I grumble, "Okay. But you also stop torturing Darian."

He blows out a breath. "Not likely—"

"Or the deal is *off.*"

His jaw flexes, and he runs a hand over his nose and mouth, down his short gray beard. "If…you agree you'll do what is necessary to save this kingdom."

It's vague enough of a request that it doesn't scare me. "Great. You'll also release Darian to me."

"No. Absolutely not. He is just as much a danger to you as he is to everyone else."

"We can keep the manacles on him, then, but he stays with me. That's final, and I will not negotiate on it." After having witnessed the brutal whipping nights ago, the idea of Darian alone with them doesn't sit well with me. Even if Sethan and I agree on a blood pact, and his soldiers follow his orders of not harming anyone in our squad, I know if someone else in the Dragon Lands gets Darian it'll likely mean he's killed. That, and deep down I have a fierce determination I can be the one to get information out of him. Information that might save the entire realm. Sethan's just been going about it the wrong way.

Sethan spins away from me, pacing about the room, his eyes glued to the floor as he considers. After a few sets of strides, he finally whips to me. "Very well, then. But I take no responsibility for whatever happens to him. Many may know him here in the Dragon Lands, and people will do anything they can to spill his blood. That's not even considering his heritage."

I level him a look—I'm already steps ahead of him. "You and those you can commit for don't kill him."

Sethan rolls his eyes, clearly understanding the more time we take discussing terms, the more he must agree to. As soon as I'm about to jokingly request a dragon-sized mattress, he intercepts my thoughts by unsheathing a dagger tucked into his belt.

Slicing the blade across his palm until the blood wells, he holds his open hand out to me. "Deal?"

I stare at his hand for a long moment. There's no going back from this. But I'm not willing to risk him killing us Arterians if he wasn't bluffing about the two-day deal.

"Katerina, deal or not?"

With a sigh, I nod and remove one of my gloves. He offers me the dagger, and I slice my own palm open and place my hand in his. A tremble sparks to life in our grip before shaking up both of our arms. The initial sting in my palm after I split open the skin transforms. As his blood mixes with mine, every nerve in my body spasms. I curl up onto my toes, my spine arching and head falling back as I fail to let it take control of me. My lips part in a strangled gasp, my hand still holding onto his as if it's my only lifeline.

The sensation fades as quickly as it came, and I lower back onto my feet, my breath chasing after my rapid pulse. "What was that?"

"That, my dear, was your first blood pact."

After I've put my glove back on, Sethan hands me the key to Darian's manacles. I slide it in my brassiere, regretting not having enough pockets on my pants. He then walks me back over to the community hall, lined with the tables occupied by Arterians and rebels. Our squad is tucked off in a corner, with a generous amount of space between them and the other rebels at the same table. Sethan announces to the room he'll be gone for a couple of days to speak to their council and then exchanges a few whispered words with Tawny.

Tawny nods, gathering some of her soldiers and leaves the room with Sethan following her. I stride after them and out of the hall, meaning to ask if and when we'll get our weapons back. *Should have negotiated that.* A few steps into the street and a hand rests on my shoulder before tugging me back. I turn, finding myself face-to-face with Cole. His expression is soft with that signature worry and discreet longing.

"What's going on?" he asks. "Why is Sethan leaving to speak to their council?"

"I made a pact," I answer simply as I spin back toward the direction where Tawny and Sethan's group slip behind a set of buildings a few blocks away.

Cole strides after me, keeping pace alongside me. "What do you mean you made a pact?"

"A blood pact to ensure our safety."

Cole throws out an arm to stop me from walking and spins himself in front of me, blocking my path. "*What?* Are you joking?"

"If I am, you're not laughing."

"Because it's no laughing matter," he growls. "What the hells, Kat? You just agreed to a blood pact with Sethan? Do you understand what a blood pact might mean?"

I tilt my chin up at him to look him in the eyes. "Oh, and I assume you do?"

"I can make some guesses."

I move to shift around him. "Great, then I'll leave you to it."

He snatches my forearm to keep me from advancing, his jaw clenched in frustration. "I know you're still mad at me but—"

"More like pissed, yeah!" I glare. Not that I need to justify my decisions, based on whatever emotion I was feeling at the time. I don't dare think about our tender moment the other night when he stayed with me until I fell asleep. Because perhaps the anger is resurfacing that the one thing we had—which used to be so pure and simple—is disastrously convoluted.

The fact is, I did this for the realm.

I drop my voice to a quick whisper. "Let's remember you had many secretive discussions with Sethan you have yet to fill me in on.

So don't pretend like I've gone behind your back to make a decision without you when you've shown me no such consideration."

Cole shakes his head. "But this goes beyond our relationship. He singled you out—what did he ask of you?"

"If this goes beyond our relationship, then I suppose it's none of your business, right?"

"Wrong—I care about you."

"And you're scared I made the wrong decision?"

"No. But your choices affect more than just you, you know," he murmurs, the tension in his expression softening.

That spark of anger inside of me glows. "Don't you think I know that? Don't you think I made the decisions I have for people *other* than myself?"

"That's beside my point. What did you agree to?"

I glare at him, swallowing down the tension collecting in my throat.

"Please…" he whispers. "I only want to help you."

His gentle tone breaks down part of my wall. I am no match for those warm amber eyes. "I…swore secrecy of any sensitive information he discloses. And that the squad doesn't leave the Dragon Lands. And…to a curfew."

Cole screws his nose up. "Of all things, he asked for a curfew?"

"Yes. In turn we get our own quarters, safety from the rebels, and—"

I pause, uncertain if I should share the agreement Darian is to be released. To me. That I'm the one with the key to his manacles. But at the end of the day…I'm done having to defend my decisions. "And Darian is to stay under my supervision."

A flicker of tension resurfaces in his jaw at the mention of Darian's name. "I'm thankful for our own beds and safety, but…Darian? Why?"

"I think he may know Aaric's secrets. Secrets no one else would be keen to, and that may turn the tides in our favor."

"Our favor? And now you're fully siding with the rebels?"

I nod. "I am. I've seen and heard things you can't even imagine. I always questioned King Aaric, and part of me pushed it to the back of my mind because I didn't want to accept the cruel reality of it. But I don't think the King is who he says he is, and I don't think the rebels are the ones who've been setting the towns on fire."

He flinches. "You don't actually believe that…do you?"

"And what do you believe?"

"I…" He scans the streets around us with townspeople meandering by. Finally, he drags his gaze back to me, his voice low and serious, "If there's anything in this world I believe in, it's you."

"Then believe I've made the right choice."

He sighs, running a hand through his hair. "Do you have a plan on how to get critical information out of someone like Darian?"

The question makes me flinch. I haven't given it much thought, other than I'll find a way. From a logical standpoint, I don't know Darian, and he doesn't know me. We aren't friends. We aren't…anything, really. What makes me think he'd be privy to sharing anything with me?

Cole waves the question away. "That doesn't even matter right now. What's most important is how are you planning to keep our squad here in the Dragon Lands? Why wouldn't they just try to leave?"

"Because staying is the safest option for them. I made the pact with Sethan to ensure everyone's safety. And if they do try to leave, they'll kill them."

ELEVEN

HAUNTING OF A PAST

Tawny leads me later in the night to the most northwestern part of Midkeep where there are rows of uninhabited stone buildings. She tells me that here in the Dragon Lands each town has a designated sector of buildings mostly fitted for dragon riders traveling through the realm. And at the heart of each sector is one singular building that's always reserved for Cyrus.

She leads me to the most lavish stone building on the street. The face of which has two stone dragons sitting on the marbled steps leading up to it. The scaled creatures curl into pillars holding up the roof. Tawny swings open the door for me and ushers me inside, apologizing under her breath for any dust the attendants might have missed.

I step inside, my gaze sweeping across the room. A man neatly folds a plush red blanket on a massive bed near the farthest wall. The bed's frame twists up into a convergence of multiple golden dragons, their brilliant sheen the focus of the room. Other splashes of red decorate the grand space: an ornate rug underneath the bed, curtains lining the windows on the wall opposite the bed, and glittering rubies set in the sconces lining the walls. The man preparing the bed bows before us and exits.

Tawny turns to me, murmuring, "This was Cyrus's last residence before he died."

"So…you know?" I ask as a shiver runs down my spine.

She nods, unsheathes a dagger from her belt, and hands it to me. "Sethan told me you were related to him, yes."

I slowly take the dagger from her, lifting an eyebrow. "What is this for?"

"Hide it. In case you need it," she whispers. "You'll get the rest of your weapons tomorrow."

My shoulders sag in relief. Just as I'm about to ask her if it was Sethan's will to return our swords and daggers, the door opens again. Four soldiers spill into the room, two of which hold someone between them. I slide the dagger behind my back out of view, then tuck it into my waistband. Their prisoner—Darian—lifts his head and glares at me through strands of his chestnut brown hair. I fight against the surge of nervousness that I might have made the wrong decision.

The four soldiers half-drag, half-fight Darian to the far wall parallel to the bed. Two of them take the end of the long 'leash' of a chain from his shackles and secure it to a metal loop in the stone wall.

I squint. *Why the hells did Cyrus have shackles in his room?*

"Don't worry," Tawny whispers. "Those chains have been tested and won't break. The only way out of them will be if you release them. And the chain connecting him to the wall is about nine feet long. There's another six-foot gap between the bounds of what the chains will allow him to move, and the edge of your bed. So long as you stay out of his reach, you'll be safe. If you need us to remove him, just send word."

The soldiers test the chain's strength by tugging on it repeatedly, before stepping back and turning their attention to Tawny, who nods her dismissal. The men slip out of the room, and as Tawny shifts to follow them, her gaze snags on me.

I can see it in her eyes—*are you sure this is a good idea?*

I nod, and she leaves. She watches me as she closes the door, leaving me alone with Darian.

"Can you tell me why the fuck I'm in here with you?" Darian growls.

Clenching my hand around the dagger's hilt, I turn toward his direction. His breath falls in and out heavily, and he jerks against the manacles like a wild animal. Every time he stills, his body trembles like a leaf. My attention is focused on the metal entrapping him and waiting for it to bend or break. But it doesn't. Though, it does little to relax my tensed muscles.

Shoving my anxiety out of my own limelight, I stride over to the bed between us and slide the dagger underneath a pillow.

"I'm talking to you!" Darian snarls.

And here I thought I was the one at mercy from his bad temper and egotistical, self-entitlement. I turn to face him, thankful they at least decided to clothe him. Wounds still pattern his face in bruises and cuts, though they look mostly scabbed over. His face, hair, and clothing look fairly clean considering the last time I saw him. At least they've afforded him a bath.

"Answer me!" he barks again.

Makes sense he's the prince of an asshole. Forcing the fear and intimidation out of my body and face, I snap back, "Because I requested it. You're fucking welcome!"

Gods, the way he watches me, seething with his pupils blown to spheres nearly drowning out his green irises. It sends a chill racing down my spine. Perhaps this *is* a mistake. But it's too late now—if I go back to Sethan and request Darian be returned to the dungeons, it will only look bad. It'll make me look weak. And I can't afford for Sethan, or anyone else for that matter, to think that of me. Besides, I have to start believing I have this under control.

I turn my back to him and hesitate for a moment before undressing. I shouldn't care. He's already seen me naked. Lifting my chin, I undress down to my undergarments with my back to him, ignoring the metal chains clinking and screeching against each other as he tests the shackles again and again. I find sets of clothes in an ornate wooden dresser near the bed and pull out a nightgown before sliding it over my body.

"You might as well quit trying. You're not getting out unless I see to it," I call, shifting into the sheets and wrapping my hand around the hilt of the dagger tucked beneath my pillow.

"Listen, bitch," he hisses from the far wall. "If you don't let me go—"

I flip toward him and pin him with a glare as he strains against his confines. "Watch how you speak to me."

"Bi-tch," he pronounces slowly.

Throwing the sheets off me, I whip out the dagger from beneath the pillow and tear out of bed, anger fueling each step as I storm toward him. I have to set these boundaries. And I have to set them now. If I'm to share such an intimate setting with him for an unknown amount of time, I must establish the rules.

I will not take his bullshit.

I will not be scared of him.

If anything…he will be scared of *me*.

He's fucking lucky I don't throw him outside and let the dragons have him. This is his last option, unless he wants to stay in the dungeons again. At which point, I'd have no control over what happens to him.

I close the distance between us, watching him with a lifted chin as I press the tip of my blade to his throat and growl, "Don't. Fucking. Test. Me."

He tips his head back in defiance, a grin tilting his lips as he swallows against the blade. Testing me. Narrowing my eyes at the challenge, I inch my hand forward, letting the edge of the dagger prick his skin. A thin river of blood trickles down his neck.

"Look at that…the kitten has claws," he purrs. "Come a little closer, won't you? I want to see how far you're willing to go."

Funneling all my anger into my narrowed eyes as if he'll back down from the intensity, I clench my teeth. He thinks I'm bluffing. And here I used to think he's a cunning man. I drag the blade up his throat, leaving a slow trail of blood under his chin, and apply pressure until his head tilts back as far as it'll go.

I slink closer to tower over him, my hair sweeping down into my face. "You will obey me. And you will respect me. And when I tell you to shut the fuck up, you will close your godsdamned mouth. Do you understand me?"

He snickers as if I only told him the most humorous joke. Taking the blade off his throat, I wipe both sides of the dagger on his cheek, smearing blood onto his skin. Jerking forward, he grabs behind my knees and rips my legs out from under me. I lose my grip on the dagger as I fight to catch myself in the backward fall, landing straight on my ass. The dagger clatters to the ground a few feet away from me.

We both lunge for it.

He snatches one of my naked legs with one hand and tries to grapple for the dagger with the other. I kick at him, my heel connecting with something hard before I swipe the dagger off the ground and escape his grasp. I crawl over to the bed like my life depends on it. After I've cleared his chained perimeter and scramble up into the bed, I glance over at him. A wicked look of amusement and disdain burns in his eyes, with a small trickle of blood seeping out the corner of his mouth. He swipes the blood away with the back of his fist. I must have kicked him in the mouth.

Good. Fucking asshole.

"Don't try that shit again," I warn as I burrow into bed. With my hand still tight around my dagger, I watch him, unable to turn my attention away for more than a second.

He shifts down to the floor and mirrors my body language. His fingers dance along the stone tile, a faint trembling still in his hands. "Sweet dreams, kitten."

It feels more like a threat than a well wish. And at this rate, those sweet dreams will be filled with gutting his pompous ass.

Thump.

My eyes flash open, waiting for another sound. But nothing comes, and I chalk it up to a groggy delusion. Closing my eyes, I begin to slip back into sleep.

Thump.

I jerk up out of bed, whipping my gaze around the room before stilling. Darian's eyes are closed, an easy rhythm to the rise and fall of his chest.

Thump.

I slide the dagger out from underneath my pillow and edge toward the sound at my door, constantly checking Darian's slumped figure over my shoulder.

Thump.

Turning the knob slowly, I open the door a few inches to peer out. Nothing stirs out on the cobblestone streets. The other buildings are dark and quiet. Opening the door a bit more, I poke my head out. A few feet to the right of my door, Cole stands on one leg with the other bent, his sole resting on the exterior wall of my room. His thick arms are crossed over his chest, his head slowly sagging forward as his eyes flutter closed. As soon as his head reaches the lowest point, it dips and he jerks back, slamming his head against the wall behind him.

Thump.

He struggles to keep his eyes open, each dragging blink threatening to keep his eyes closed.

"Psst!" I whisper.

Jerking awake as if thrown into a frozen river, he spins toward me, his expression wide and still dazed.

"The hells are you doing out here, Cole?" I grab him by the jacket and pull him closer to my door, scanning the streets around us as I whisper, "Did you forget we have a curfew!"

He takes a breath, blinking the haze of sleep out of his eyes as he runs a hand through the crown of his head. "Oh…shit. Sorry. I… umm…" He glances around, clearly embarrassed.

"Are you seriously guarding my room? It's well past midnight. Darian is chained to the wall. I'm *fine*. Go back to your room, and get some sleep."

He blows out a breath. "It's not Darian I'm worried about… or at least, he's not my main concern."

I pull him inside and shut the door silently before I lead him out of the main room where Darian sleeps, down a side hallway and into a lavish bathroom. Gods, even the bathtub gleams in the moonlight with an expensive porcelain sheen.

I release my grip on his jacket. "What's your main concern that you'd risk breaking curfew, then?"

He takes a few steps forward so I can catch his mumbled whisper. "The rebels. There's something they aren't telling us."

"You're being paranoid."

"No," he growls. "I'm not. I don't trust them. Something is going on, and they aren't telling us. Something that involves you."

"They don't necessarily trust us either, but we all have to start somewhere. We have to work together."

"Fine, you can trust them all you want. You made a blood pact—but I didn't. These people might want to save you because you'll save the world, but I want to save you because I *love* you."

"Cole…" I sigh, taking a step back away from him. *Now isn't the time for late night confessions.* As much as I don't want to hear those three little words from him, I'm hungry for it all the same.

He splays his hands out to the side in a silent apology. "I'm not trying to scare you. I'm just trying to protect you."

I snort. "By guarding my room?"

"By making sure anyone who tries to hurt you has to go through me first." His warm, honey eyes search mine. "If I tell you something, will you promise not to make any rash decisions?"

I cross my arms over my chest, leaning back into the wall. Tossing a glance over my shoulder down the hallway, I scan the shadows like I won't have to agree. "Maybe."

"I need a yes, Kat," he nearly pleads.

I meet his eyes. "Fine. Yes. What is it?"

He grabs my wrist gently, twisting my hand so his mother's ring catches the moonlight and glimmers brilliantly. "Marge told me this ring needs to stay with you. On you. You cannot take it off."

Sethan's words ring in my head. *This ring has much power, more power than you could ever imagine.* As far as I know, it has enough power to release a ripple. But what else can it do?

"Why does Marge say I can't take it off?" I murmur.

"Because…" He blows out a quick breath. "…because it links you to the King."

"What do you mean 'links?' And since when do you have private discussions with Marge?"

"This ring links your life to King Aaric's. Which means, if you die, he dies. Arterians won't kill you, even if you're a dragon rider."

I recoil, the news striking me with a sudden rush of panic. "How…how is that even possible?"

"I don't know. Some ancient magic, Marge said. She didn't want me to tell you, and I was hesitant because we didn't want you thinking ahead of yourself. But…I don't want to keep things from you anymore."

Must be why I woke up with healed ribs. Not because of any-thing Daeja or I had done…but because the King must have done something to mend them. I thumb my ribs, testing to make sure they're still healed over, and am met with a faint soreness. "Then what's this rash decision she's wary I'll make—"

As it dawns on me, my eyes round, and my face falls. If I die, King Aaric dies. I could shove a sword through my heart, sacrificing myself to single-handedly take down the King.

TWELVE

Touching and terms

"I wouldn't risk Daeja's life," I whisper, crossing my arms tight over my chest.

Cole's voice dips even lower. "Even if you decided not to, the ring puts a massive target on your back. If any of the rebels recognize it, they could decide to kill you because it'll kill their greatest adversary."

"That's…why you were standing guard outside? Not because of Darian, but because you think the rebels might kill me in the middle of the night?"

He nods.

I clear my throat and push off the wall. "I signed a blood pact—a binding contract with one of the terms being our safety. Do you really think they would go through the trouble of such a thing if they intended to kill me?"

"*Sethan* signed the blood pact. It doesn't mean everyone in this entire town will agree to it. And this is just one town—there's the entire northern continent who might question Sethan's decision and decide they don't need to follow it."

I swallow. He has a point, and it's one I had already considered. But hearing it resurface from someone else only strengthens the fear.

Now, not only does the King and all his subjects want me dead…but I'm in the Dragon Lands where I can be an easy victory for the rebels.

Fuck. I might be in more danger here than I was back in Arterias—not that my own safety concerns me as much as Daeja's. I can't risk her. The thought alone tears a rip in my heart.

"Don't let that scare you. I'll never let anything happen to you…" Cole trails off and mindlessly brushes a strand of hair out of my face. Instinctively, he twirls the piece of hair before tucking it behind my ear.

Because he loves me. Staring, I tilt my chin up toward him, my lips parting of their own accord, knowing what usually comes next. It feels as natural as anything. Wanting to kiss him. To touch him. Blushing at the overwhelming longing, I lick my lips and pull my head away before I give into temptation. Getting lost in his eyes swept away all the memories of why we aren't kissing. Why I feel so distant from him. Why my heart screams inside of my chest like a caged animal, broken and bruised. He can always say the right things. And yet…it doesn't matter. Not right now.

"I'm not scared," I murmur finally.

Hurt isn't scared. And the only thing I can possibly think of right now is how hurt I am. After all this time, he still cares. But it doesn't change the fact he was engaged and refrained from telling me for several months. It also doesn't change the fact I slept with Darian—something he still isn't aware of. But as I look into his eyes, glassy with exhaustion, longing, and pain, I know I can't tell him. Not right now, at least.

He drops his hand on the side of my face before clearing his throat. "I'm sorry, I…I shouldn't have touched you. Habit, I suppose."

I bite my lip and nod. "Listen, I want you to go back to your room, and get some sleep. We'll discuss this tomorrow."

When he hesitates, I sigh. "I'm serious. Trust that I can take care of myself. I'll be fine. I'll barricade the door with a dresser if it'll make you feel any better."

He snorts a laugh and looks down at his boots. "Okay…" He drags his eyes back up to mine and whispers once more, "Okay."

I escort him out and watch him disappear down the road and behind a line of buildings as sadness tugs at my heart. In another reality, if he felt so worried about me, I would have invited him in and had him stay with me. Months ago, it was all I would have ever dreamed of. I still find myself fighting the knee-jerk reaction to be close to him.

A complex mix of emotions stirs in my heart, and before I linger too long on it, I slip back into my room. Locking the door, I then eye Darian's sleeping figure off against the wall. After a few quiet moments, I stride over to the dresser and hook my fingers under its top lid. Pulling a solid breath into my lungs, I shove it forward, the feet screeching against the tiled floor.

Darian's head whips up, his chains rustling as he pulls himself up to sit and scan the room wildly. "What the fuck are you doing?"

I push again, ignoring him, and the feet scrape against the ground.

Darian rubs a sleepy eye with the heel of his hand. "Are you seriously rearranging furniture in the middle of the night? Have you lost your fucking mind?"

My response comes out in huffs as I scoot the dresser closer to the door, "Just…go back…to…sleep."

He snorts. "How am I supposed to sleep with all your panting?"

I ignore him, sliding the dresser only another inch closer to the door. *What kind of wood is this shit made out of?*

He snickers, "Looks like you need a big, strong man—"

"I need no one," I grit out, not bothering to look his way.

"I know just the guy—come over here, set me free, and I'll help you." His voice is edged with mischief.

"Unlikely," I grunt.

"Wait…" He laughs, realizing my intention. "You're scared, aren't you?"

I finally shove one last time, sliding the dresser right in front of the door. Wiping my sore hands against each other, I turn to face Darian. "No, I'm not."

He snickers. "Don't worry, darling. I'll be sure to protect you from all the scaries out there."

I slide back under my sheets, back to him and not bothering to look his way as I grumble, "Can't imagine you'd be able to do much without your hands."

"Oh, kitten. If you could only see the things I could do without my hands."

I don't respond. Shuffling deeper into my warm sheets, I close my eyes. Thankfully, he has the decency to not carry our conversation further. Silence settles around the room, and the more the seconds tick by, the more my fear of recurring nightmares creeps in. Not to mention, the ridicule from Darian if I wake up in a cold sweat, hyperventilating. But as I edge closer to sleep, nearly falling into the void, a noise rips me out of my doze.

Clink.

I grab the pillow's edges and pull it over my ears to block out the sound before relaxing back into the mattress.

Clink.

My eyes flash open.

Clink, clink, clink.

Oh, for fuck's sake, am I not going to get any sleep tonight? I turn over my shoulder and glare at Darian who is arching his back into the wall, shifting his hips uncomfortably and attempting to adjust his pants.

"What are you doing?" I hiss, a cold chill racing over my naked legs. I must have kicked off all the blankets. My gaze fixes on him as he rolls his body, and I follow the motion from his chest down toward his groin. I stiffen—nearly as stiff as his cock bulging beneath his pants. Unable to tear my eyes off him, I can't help to stifle a laugh.

"Maybe if you pulled your nightgown over your *ass*," he grounds out, "I wouldn't be in this predicament."

I laugh again. *Simple-minded man.*

"You won't be laughing when I get out of these," he growls, the perfect balance between a threat and sensual promise.

Retrieving the dagger from beneath my pillow, I hop off the bed and strut toward him. I can't help but smile at his unmistakable frustration. "Is that a threat I hear? Need I remind you of how to speak to me?"

His eyes follow every curve of my body, from my bare feet up my legs to my hips, then he locks onto my eyes. In this situation, he's so easy to manipulate. His green eyes flare with an explosion of anger, frustration, and…*craving*. I suppose I wouldn't be too surprised if he still fantasizes about our one night we had back in Arterias.

Stopping a few steps outside the reach of his chains, I lower to the balls of my feet. Perhaps physical torture wouldn't work on Darian—but there are other ways. I only have to find out what those ways are. And seeing the raging mix of desire and hatred in his eyes is prompting me in one specific direction.

Edging my knees open slowly, I whisper, "I'd be…*happy*…to negotiate a deal with you."

The cold air rushes between my legs, and my skin pebbles. He flicks a narrowed glare from my face down to my legs for a split second, before he jerks his head away, straining against his manacles once more. Desperate to put space between us.

It could be the lack of sleep prompting me. Maybe even the fact I'm hungry for answers that could lead to eliminating King Aaric and restoring peace in the kingdoms. Or…or perhaps it's that, no matter how much I try to mask my ulterior motives, something in me wants him as much as he does me. I've been trying to lie to myself that I'm not drawn to him like a moth to a flame—hungry to touch him even if it means my own demise. Some undeniable and indestructible burn that catches me by surprise every time. And out of him and Cole, I can't feel guilty about this. Only a touch of self-hatred.

"If you tell me why the King is burning down the towns, I'll touch you," I whisper as softly as I can.

Pressing himself back against the wall to get as far away from me as possible, he growls, "Don't you dare."

But caught within his burning stare, I see it. How his breath hitches, how his eyes keep wandering lower. He's as tempted as I am. Resting my hands on my knees, I slowly drag them up my thighs, the hem of my nightgown sliding with my hands and revealing more and more of my undergarments. The flat side of my dagger glides across my skin in my right hand, sending a shiver up my back.

"Would you rather…touch me, then?" I ask innocently, before sliding my free hand between my legs and over the warming fabric separating my fingers from my flesh.

He jerks his head away again as if I slapped him, a muscle in his jaw flickering as he clenches his teeth. *Good. I have him right where I want him.* He's much more bothered than I thought he'd be. And Gods, I can't lie. It's intoxicating seeing the effect I have on him. Of being in control.

Pushing up to my feet, I strut toward him as I hold the dagger at my side so he can see it. Fueled with a fire I can't quite control, I seize the hair on the top of his head and pull his face back to look up at me.

"One way or another, Darian Raventhorn," I rumble, tapping the tip of my dagger right where his artery pulses in his throat. "You'll tell me. So which way is it going to be? The easy way? Or the hard way?"

His eyes dilate, his lips parted as he struggles to level his breathing. "I'd love to know what your definition of hard is."

Slowly, I drag the dagger across his skin to nick the thin flesh, and a trickle of blood races down his throat. "Does this give you a hint?"

"You won't know the true definition of hard until I bend you over that bed and fuck you like you need to be," he rasps.

"Watch your tongue," I warn, but my skin heats with desire swirling inside of me, like a thundering whirlpool just waiting to be unleashed.

"As you wish," he purrs and leans forward, ignoring the fact I have his hair tight in my grip. He parts his lips, sticks out his tongue while watching it, and drags it up the inside of my thigh to my undergarments.

Oh. My. Gods.

The wickedly hot sensation shatters every bit of my artificial self-restraint. I freeze, my thoughts completely wiped out of my brain. His tongue is too hot, too close. And yet…not close enough.

I pull his head back before he gets too carried away, and before I'm lost to the burning need for more of the sensation, I say, rather breathlessly, "A negotiation."

He smirks. Gods, the most sinister and tempting expression I'm hungry to keep *and* wipe off his face. "The terms?" he asks rather plainly.

"You tell me why the King is burning down towns."

He tilts his head to the side. "And I get what?"

"To touch me," I breathe.

"Deal," he growls and jolts forward. Wasting no time, he slips two fingers into the edge of my panties and pulls them to the side enough to swipe that dastardly tongue against me. He groans, clearly tasting my arousal, and buries his face deeper between my legs. Lapping up every drop.

A shock wave of pleasure pierces through every nerve ending in my body as I nearly stumble, moaning. He holds the back of my knees, digging his nose and tongue deeper into me. Working me. I roll my hips into his face, greedy for more, and a soft breathy whimper whispers off my lips.

"This is…technically…tasting—oohh," I squeak as he swirls his tongue round and round my clit, my legs shaking and threatening to crumble. Gods, his stubble-dusted lips scratch and pull at me in all the ways that shouldn't feel good. But I can't stop—I can't stop him.

"Stop talking," he growls into my wet cunt, his deep throaty voice rumbling a sinfully hot vibration into my core.

But I don't want *him* to stop talking. I want more. I grind into his face as my head falls back and eyes flutter closed. He burrows his tongue deeper inside me, pleasing every silent request I have. As soon as I'm about to come on his tongue, he stops, somehow sensing how dangerously close I am. He pulls back to look up at me, and I whimper as his saliva cools against my skin.

"Release my hands, and I'll release you," he pants. He looks so damn hot with my arousal glistening on the tip of his nose, his glossy full set of lips, and his strong chin. He's made an absolute mess of me, and I'm fighting to keep myself balanced on these wobbling legs.

"I can't," I rasp.

"Yes…you can." He takes his thumb and rubs too slow against my swollen clit. His index finger teases my slick entrance.

"No," I breathe, trying my best not to buck against his skilled hand.

"Release me, kitten," he commands, dipping his finger inside of me and stroking me slowly as he flicks his thumb against my clit.

"What happened to not needing your hands?" I whine. "You seem to be managing just fine."

"No one can know what I'm about to do to you. So, I want to take you to that bed, shove your face into the pillows to mask your screams, and fuck you into the mattress until you forget your name, okay? And I can't quite do that if I'm chained to this godsdamned wall, can I?"

Gods, he's really tempting me. I'm on fire for him—to have his hands all over me, unrestrained and willing. To have him fuck me with every long, hard inch of himself that I forget all my other problems. Temptation and craving lures me into testing the limits of what he promises. To have him ruin me until I can't breathe.

But a small voice in the back of my head whispers this isn't right. I came into this situation to take hold of it—not to be so easily overcome by the temptation of a good fucking. The more time passes, the more I *want* to let him free. Even if that small voice keeps screaming he's only manipulating me. Just as I tried to manipulate him.

He presses a light kiss to the inside of my thigh. "Be a good girl…" He plunges his finger inside of me deeper before adding a second digit. "…and let me free."

My hand trembles around the dagger I still point at his throat. It's only a matter of time before I drop it completely. My heart pounds in my ears, my blood heating to something almost unbearable as he drags me closer and closer to a climax. "Say it again."

"Good," he growls, slipping a third finger inside me and fucking me roughly with his hand. His eyes burn into mine, his lips pulled back into a devious smile. *"Girl."*

I moan, "Darian, I'm about to come—"

My eyes flash open, and I jolt forward off the bed. My breath is wild in my chest as my gaze darts around the darkened room. The dresser is still in front of the door where I pushed it. And Darian lies quietly on the floor with his eyes closed. The buzzing in my head and between my legs mellows out, and I swipe at the sweat on my forehead before I slowly lower myself to lie back down. Pulling the sheets up to my chin, I try to quiet my heavy breathing.

Gods, perhaps this is dangerous having him so close. Especially if he's getting to me in my sleep.

As Marge's words about dreams trickle into my mind, I slam the thought out before it gets too far and flip onto my side away from Darian. A rumbling laugh sounds off in his direction, and I peek over my shoulder at him.

"Were you having a nice dream?" Darian's voice is husky with sleep.

"No," I grumble and turn back over.

"Why did you say my name then?"

"I didn't say your name."

"You're right. You didn't say it…you *moaned* it." He chuckles.

A scorching heat blooms in my face, and I cringe, squeezing my eyes shut. "You're delirious."

"Not nearly enough to miss when you're calling out for me."

"You sure love to talk."

"I know," he rumbles.

Silence falls for a few moments, concluding our conversation. Pulling a breath in through my nose, I clear my mind to slip off into sleep once more.

"I could make your dreams come true, you know," he purrs.

I snag my pillow from underneath my head, spin, and chuck it straight at his head. Lucky for him, he catches it.

Rumbling an arrogant laugh, he tucks the pillow underneath his head and pats it. "Thank you. About time you showed me some hospitality."

THIRTEEN

I DON'T REPEAT MYSELF TWICE

"Candidly speaking, why in the Gods' names would we do that?" Nolan challenges me, his fist wrapped tight around a fork. His thick brown brows are furrowed by the mounting frustration bubbling around us in the other squad members seated in the community hall.

Good grief, here we go again. How can Sethan possibly think these men and women will listen to me? I don't necessarily blame them for wanting to return home, but it's imperative they stay. Even if they don't agree with it.

I can't quite place why Nolan has gotten so irrationally angry since our time here in the Dragon Lands. Melaina mentioned back in Arterias he was hired to protect her after they believed Sethan died.

The rest of our squad and the rebels occupying the long tables in the massive hall turn their attention toward us. Piece by piece, a silence falls like snow in the room. Until the only thing audible is when Archie drops his fork to his plate.

"Because if you leave, they'll kill you anyway," I say, holding Nolan's gaze, unwilling to show a lick of anxiety.

"You're just saying that to save your own tail. We all have

friends and family we want to go back to. We don't belong here!" Nolan flicks his hand out to the room.

Other Arterians chime in with their mumbled agreements, and I glance around at the angry faces. Shit. It might have been a mistake telling them I made a blood pact. Sethan made it sound so simple that they would listen to me. And now look at us—half the men and women can't even look at me without wanting to drag my face through the mud for such a decision.

Not to mention the tension spiking between those individuals who support my decision and those who don't. We don't even need to worry about the rebels fighting us—we do a perfectly fine job fighting *ourselves.*

"Do you even have a family, Nolan?" Gavin bites back.

It's the first time I've ever heard such a tone from him. He normally melts back into the shadows, far from anyone's attention. His onyx eyes narrow as he jerks his head toward Melaina, his long raven hair swinging with him. "Last I remember, you and I swore an oath to Sethan and Melaina to protect them."

"Just because you apprenticed Sethan and feel so obligated to follow him around like some eager puppy doesn't mean I will. Our vow was voided as soon as he became part of the rebels," Nolan barks.

Gavin slams his fist onto the table, silencing the rest of the squad's arguments bubbling to the surface. Melaina darts her hand out and grabs Gavin's shoulder to keep him from launching across the table at Nolan.

"A vow is a vow. Have you no honor?" Gavin challenges.

Before Nolan can respond, Archie jolts up to his feet, his hands splayed out to both men. "Guys, guys. Let's slow down for a second. I have family back in Helmbrook, too. But we should hear her out—"

Nolan interrupts, glaring at me. "She's an incompetent woman who made the hasty decision to—"

"Enough!" Cole roars as he shoots to his feet, the sound deafening in my ears.

Everyone stops and turns to him, and even Nolan has the sense to be quiet.

"You speak about her like that once more, Nolan," Cole points a finger at him, that's just as threatening as a weapon, "and I'll kill you my fucking self."

Nolan holds his stare but swallows uncomfortably.

Cole scans the rest of the group as he leans forward onto the table, his eyes challenging each individual, picking them apart one by one. "You may not agree with staying here, but there is no choice. Even if Kat didn't agree to this blood pact, they would have killed us if we tried to leave. Or they could have killed us to get rid of this mess. We're outnumbered. Either way, you wouldn't have made it back home alive. Don't you understand? She made a decision that potentially saved all of your lives. She pledged her own blood and life for your safety—how could you *possibly* be angry with that?"

Silence. Even the conversations at the other tables are at a standstill. I swallow, heat spanning from my chest to my cheeks. Thankfully, everyone's gazes are glued to Cole. He always has a natural tendency to draw people to him. An air about him that commands people to listen. That, and he has everyone beat in height and muscle. Challenging him would be asking for a death sentence.

"Well?" Cole threatens, spinning his attention back to Nolan. "Anyone care to answer?"

"You fucking imbecile," Darian spits from down the table. "You'll all die if you stay here."

I instantly regret allowing him out of the room, even if he's managed by someone I trust. Curse my own sympathy. Next time, I'll leave him to stare at a brick wall for a few days. Melaina holds the chain to his manacles and tugs it to silence him.

Cole stills his fidgeting fingers into fists. "What did you call me?"

A coy grin tugs at Darian's mouth. "Do I need to speak slower for you?"

Cole shoves off the table and prowls toward him. Darian stands and kicks his chair back, Melaina mumbling something under her breath as she tightens her grip on the chains and rises from her seat as well. Cole stops in front of Darian, towering over him by inches. Both lock into a tense glare—neither of them faltering.

Cole lifts his bearded chin at him. "Say it again."

Darian snorts, his lips pulling up in a half smile. "I don't repeat myself."

Cole leans forward and whispers, "And I don't ask twice."

I jolt out of my seat and stride across to the two of them before someone throws the first punch. Melaina tugs at the chain confining Darian half-heartedly, her wide eyes bouncing back and forth between the two heated males as she slides her free hand to her waist where her sword should be. I'm cursing myself, we still haven't had our weapons returned yet.

Cole's knuckles whiten. "Need I remind you, I'm your captain."

"You ain't shit. Look around you, we aren't in Arterias. Which means I owe you no loyalty. And if you remember correctly, I'm your prince, you lowly fucking bastard."

I fling myself straight at Cole, shoving my hands directly into his chest to back him up as he lunges toward Darian. "Stop!"

Melaina rips Darian's chain back. Other squad members and rebels rush in to help me push Cole back, while others crowd around Darian and Melaina. An earth-cracking roar bursts out from behind me, so loud I almost see waves. Everyone turns to the sound, eyes wide and faces drawn pale as they recognize where the roar is coming from.

"Listen!" Daeja's voice melds with the roaring. Though only I can hear the words, I imagine everyone else understands.

No wonder this building is enormous, and the entrance is a drawbridge. Despite her size, she fits comfortably inside the dining hall. Along with A'nala at her side, who slinks with pounding steps toward the table where Sethan is. *Sethan's back? So much for leaving for a couple of days.*

The squad and rebels still, and Daeja ceases her roar. Her lips are still pulled up into a silent snarl and twitching to reveal more of her fangs longer and thicker than any man's forearm.

"Thank you," I whisper.

She blows a short breath into the crowd, several people flinching. I swear that's going straight to her head.

"A'nala says when the two leggers don't listen, we make them."

I'll have to ask her what she's been doing with A'nala lately. With a grateful smile at her, I take a few steps away from Cole to address the squad. "I know some of you may be upset with me. You might feel like I've made a wrong decision. But the truth of the matter is, if you don't stay, you die. And that would have been the case whether I made the pact or not. Look around you. We're all sorely outnumbered here. You wouldn't be able to make it to the border of Arterias. I've made a blood pact with Sethan—one that binds the *both* of us. I negotiated our safety with this pact, so none of our squad will be hurt or killed. Sethan's own soldiers have already sworn allegiance to him through their own blood pacts, therefore binding them to my agreement with Sethan. So, if you don't wish to stay, then be my guest. Leave. Now."

I scan the group, but no one moves, all frozen to their spots as they stare at me and Daeja. "Anyone?"

Daeja growls from behind me, and several people shake their heads. I catch Tawny's gaze from across the room, and I swear I see her smile.

Ignoring the racing beat of my heart, I tear my attention away from her and the rebels. "Good. I understand many of you have family and friends you want to return to. But the best thing we can do for them right now is to stay put until we figure out what the King is up to."

"What do you mean, 'what the King is up to?'" Archie asks.

Darian looks up at me, his brown, messy hair dipping into his eyes.

With a steady breath, I announce, "The rebels haven't been burning down the towns. The King has."

A collective gasp rolls through the group of Arterians.

"This is an outrageous claim! She's making it up because she bound herself to Sethan and the rebels!" Nolan fumes. "Propaganda!"

"I could just end him right now," Daeja purrs casually.

"That won't be necessary. And not exactly the way I want to convince them."

"If you don't believe her, then perhaps you should all go see for yourselves," Melaina grumbles, watching the squad with Darian's chain wrapped tightly around her fist.

"I believe her," Archie chirps. "Kat wouldn't lie—and she wouldn't put herself above the rest of you. Don't you remember our battle in Blackfell? She was supposed to be a healer's apprentice, and she risked her life to sneak into Blackfell. She saved all those civilians who were being held hostage and set them free."

I can't help the grin lifting my cheeks as I watch Archie. He looks back at me, his brown eyes shining as he mirrors my smile.

He continues, "If she were selfish, she wouldn't have risked her life for those civilians. Just as she wouldn't have risked her life returning to Blackfell to try and rescue me."

"Or me," someone says.

Everyone turns to the voice.

Marge slinks through the group, her staff tapping rhythmically until she stops in the center of the crowd. "When we were attacked in the middle of the night at the outpost before Blackfell, Katerina came to the healer's quadrant to defend me. She didn't even have the proper training the lot of you do. The fact that she risked herself for me when she barely knew who I was spoke volumes. You don't have to trust the rebels—you only have to trust Katerina."

More silence.

Cole pushes through the crowd, his heavy footsteps splitting the silence. He stands next to me, facing the squad in a wordless declaration. Marge hobbles toward me next, dipping her head as she stops at my other side, then turns to face the rest of the group. Archie follows, then Melaina who tugs Darian along with her. Gavin. And one by one, Arterians join the line of people beside and behind me.

Nolan is the last one standing before us, his gaze flicking from person to person. Finally, after he's undoubtedly weighed his options, he dips his head before tightly mumbling, "I suppose I have no choice."

I can't help but smile. Sethan's wrong. Leading out of fear is poisonous. And leading out of respect will have to be earned. We have to start smaller.

Instead, I lead out of a hesitant unity.

FOURTEEN

LATE NIGHT RENDEZVOUS

Lost to dreams of blood and fire, my sleep is interrupted by a force smacked over my mouth. Flashing my eyes open, I instinctively arch up off the bed and grapple for the hand covering my mouth, then slow my fight as a pair of hazy amber eyes fill my vision.

Cole.

He shakes his head, throwing strands of his auburn hair around his face as he holds a single finger up to his soft lips.

Quiet…got it. I flash a glance off to the right where Darian's back is to us, his slow breath the only movement in his dark figure. I sweep my gaze over the windows, the door. How in the hells did he get in through the locks without making a peep? And why is he out past curfew *again*?

Cole removes his calloused hand from my mouth finger by finger, his eyes still burrowing into me, reiterating the need for silence. I nod, and he leans away from where he stands at the edge of my bed before holding out an open palm for me to take. Slowly, I pull the sheets off my body and slide my legs over the edge of the bed. Placing my hand in his, he helps me up and motions to my boots on the floor. I glance up at him, arching an eyebrow.

After all the years we've known each other, we don't need words to communicate. He dips his head to the boots again. I slide them onto my feet, lace them up, and as I straighten my spine, he wraps my cloak over my shoulders and attaches the clasp at my throat. Once I've slid on Marge's gloves, he grabs me by the hand and leads me to the door. He opens it and scans the streets in every direction before pulling me out of my room with him and closing the door. I squeeze his hand, silently questioning what's going on.

He squeezes back—*it's okay.*

We edge along the front of the building, my heart thundering in my chest. *Where is he taking me?* He whips to me, pressing a finger to his lips. His eyes fall to the floor, finger still pressed to his mouth and stance rigid as he strains to listen. After a few still seconds, he leads me wordlessly down street after street to the northern part of Midkeep. Once we cut down a corner into an alley bathed in shadows, he turns toward me, but I beat him to the punch before he can say anything.

"Why the hells are you pulling me out of bed after curfew? Don't you realize it's a breach of—"

"Not for me," he interjects before I can get far. "I didn't agree to the blood pact."

"Yes, but I—"

He grabs the space between my neck and shoulder, leaning his face down closer to mine so I might listen to him. "Look, I don't know how much time we have, but I saw something earlier in Sethan's office when he and I were discussing getting our weapons back."

"Tawny said we were supposed to get them back earlier today. Did you piss Sethan off?" I ask.

"No. I've been told maybe tomorrow. It makes some of his soldiers nervous knowing we'll be allowed to have them back. But that's beside the point. I need you to see something, and I don't think you'll believe me until you see it for yourself."

"What is it?" I whisper.

He suddenly whips his attention back to the main street, then pulls the both of us down into a crouch and shuffles me back into the wall. Our direct sight line of the main street is blocked by two stacks of wooden crates. His hands still grip me between my shoulders, his laser-focused attention caught on the street beyond the crates. That godsdamned fidget sparks in his fingertips, dancing in my muscles and spiking my own anxiety.

What happens if we're caught? They can't kill me…or at least I don't think they will. But what about Cole?

A steady fall of footsteps approaches, growing louder and louder until they reach their peak and begin to fade away. Cole finally turns his face toward me, and we are close enough I notice sweat beading on his forehead. Though I'll admit, out of the two of us, he's much more functional than I am under pressure.

His quirked eyebrows ask the question his lips don't have to. *Do you want to do this?*

I nod.

He lifts the hood on my cloak over my head, then tucks the long strands of my silver-blonde hair into the back and out of sight.

"C'mon," he mouths and then tugs me back toward the main street. He peers around the corner of the alley wall, still managing to find and lace his fingers through mine.

Is this for my own peace of mind or his?

I don't have long to determine which, as he tugs me after him into the street. A mob of shadowed figures shifts far down the road, and Cole follows them at a slow, cautious pace. We stop a block away from Sethan's office and slink down a shadowed alley with multiple barrels up against the brick wall of an old tavern. As we peek around the corner, down the street are two guards posted at the front of the building. Their spines are straight and gazes fixed on the distance.

Cole draws me back from the corner and unlaces his fingers from mine. He flips my palm up. With a series of points and drawing words with his fingertip across my gloved palm, he sketches out a plan.

My eyebrows raise as the pieces click together. He wants to be the distraction. To lure them away as I slip into the office by myself, and he'll meet me inside. I shake my head. I don't even know what I'm looking for, and I'm not trying to chance that even if I get in there, he can't join me. It'd all be pointless. I glance down at my boots, mentally searching for another way. A grin splits my lips as I stare down at what's beneath our feet. I grab a small loose cobblestone in the street and pluck it free, my gaze anything but innocent as I smile up at Cole.

I chuck the stone down past us in the opposite direction of the guards, and as planned, they both flinch, exchanging a glance before one of them heads our way. Cole leans his head to the side. Eyes wide in a *are-you-trying-to-get-us-killed* look.

But we don't have long to discuss it because the guard unsheathes his sword from his side as he walks toward us. As he passes the entrance to our alley, Cole strikes like a serpent. He snatches the unsuspecting soldier and rips him into the shadows with us, clapping a heavy hand over the man's mouth to muffle any sounds as I pry the sword from him. Quick as the night, Cole wraps his second hand around the thrashing man's throat and squeezes. I keep watch on the second guard still posted at the office down the street and flinch when Cole's victim kicks a stone and it skitters across the road.

The second guard's attention whips from the stone that stills in the middle of the street to our direction.

Now or never.

A heavy, sliding thump hits the ground behind me, followed by Cole stepping in front of me as the second guard approaches. He does the same as he did with the previous guard, quick to silence and knock the second man unconscious. After checking to make sure they're still breathing, we take their swords and slice off strips of their tunics and wrap the fabric around their wrists and ankles into makeshift restraints. Cole takes another piece of fabric and bunches it into a ball, his eyebrows pinched in shame as he opens the guard's mouth and stuffs it in. I follow suit, and then we slide them into the empty barrels stained with a stench of old ale. Once we close the lids, I pull out the stoppers on both barrels to ensure they can breathe.

I tell myself at least this way, it'll afford us extra time if they awaken. Without another moment to spare, we head to the office, checking over our shoulders and down every direction the street splits into with each step.

I reach the door and turn the handle. Locked. *Damn…well, it was worth a try.*

Cole and I turn to each other at the same time, and he nods toward the eastern side of the structure. We slip away from the front and edge around the side of the building until we get to a set of tall, skinny windows. The inside is nearly pitch black, with only vague silhouettes of furniture scattered inside.

Cole tries each window then stops at the third one, finding with a little resistance and a creak, it opens. We freeze, waiting for any neighboring buildings or guards on patrol to hear it, but slip inside after a few still moments. My heart pounds in my chest.

Something about seeing this room in pure darkness is eerie, and my gaze is immediately drawn to the painting Cyrus shredded. The shadows accentuate how violently the art had been torn through. And I'm supposed to be related to him? It's still a truth I can't yet swallow.

Cole takes a few steps across the room, his profile blocking out half the painting against the far wall until he turns his attention to me. "What? What is it?"

When I don't answer, he turns, following my gaze over his shoulder toward the painting, before he blows out a soft breath through his nose. "Yeah, Sethan has quite an eclectic taste in furnishings…"

I shake my head, ridding myself of the distant intrigue tingling at the base of my skull. "He said Cyrus did that. But I still can't understand why he'd hold on to something so damaged."

Cole blinks, as if the statement drives a dagger into his heart. Like I meant it in some other, roundabout way. Before I can try and say anything more, he stalks across the room to Sethan's desk and waves a hand over the pieces left in plain sight, squinting in the dim light. "Shit…I don't see it here."

I sigh, then join him. "Can you at least tell me what we're looking for?"

"It was…" he turns to the bookcase, scanning each tome. "It was a book. Or a journal, I suppose."

"He already showed me the old dragon journal."

"No. It wasn't a study on dragons. This spoke of breaking magical bindings."

I suck in a breath, blinking away the shock. "Like…"

Cole stops his searching of the bookcase and turns toward me. "Yes. Like breaking a blood pact."

"He wouldn't—"

"And how do you know he wouldn't?"

I open my mouth to respond, then slowly close it as realization dawns on me. I don't. The only, single thing I can trust is Melaina trusts him. And maybe that's even a blind mistake.

Cole turns his attention back to surveying the shelves. "Exactly…and I know I broke your trust in me. So, I wanted you to see it yourself. If he's going to break the pact, perhaps you can read in the journal how to stop him from doing so."

"What does it look like, so I can help?"

He crouches down to the bottom shelves of the ornate book-case. "It was a small, thin book. Smaller than anything here…"

I walk over to the other side of the desk and open the drawers.

He continues, "But it was hard to see. In my meeting, we met by candlelight. And he had stacks of maps and other things on top of it. All I could see were the words 'Breaking Magical Binds' on the cover."

I begin to sift through the stacks of papers, folded letters, scrolls, magnifying glass, and items to complete a wax seal. "Did he say why he returned so early? He was supposed to be gone for several days."

"No, he didn't. I don't think he ever left, to be honest."

"It's not in here." I sigh and slide the drawer closed, almost pinching my fingers between the top of it and the lip of the desk. I pause, tilting my head to the side as I stare at the engraved intricacies in the thick wooden edge.

Squinting through the darkness, I kneel on the floor and run my fingers across the length of the ridges until I come across a bump. I pinch it between my forefinger and thumb and tug it toward me gently. What should have only been a two-inch-thick edge of the desk, turns out to be a secret drawer no bigger than the width of one book and deeper than the lengths of two. Sitting there, in the darkness, is a small, black book.

"Is this it?" I whisper and pull the book out gently as if it'll disappear in the wind should I remove it too quickly. But he doesn't have to answer because as I draw it near me, there on the cover in red it says 'Breaking Magical Binds.'

Cole looks up from where he's been sifting through books on the shelf. A hopeful smile cracks his lips.

"Great." I toss a look toward the windows. "Now let's get out of here before those guards wake up and alert someone."

As we both rise from the floor, a key rattles at the front door, and we turn toward each other, color draining from our faces. There's no way we can make it to the window and out without being noticed.

Cole motions toward a massive, ornate wardrobe tucked into the corner of the office, and we both dash toward it. He swings one of the doors open and I climb inside, pressing my back up against it as Cole slides in with me. He stands toe-to-toe with me, a few inches separating us. But as he goes to close the door behind him, it won't budge.

I slam the book to his chest, grip his sides, and rip him into me. My breath rushes out of me as his full weight crushes my chest, and the door closes behind him. Leaving us in almost complete darkness.

My breath rises and falls in quick succession with his, the side of my face flush with his chest. I don't dare move my hands from his ribs. Don't dare move at all. The only movement I allow myself is breathing, and even that I force myself to steady.

Sethan's characteristic growl is muffled by the wardrobe we're hiding in. But based on the cadence, he's shifting around the room. "Have you swept the patrols across the outskirts?"

"I already have a group of soldiers on it now, sir. A second group is posted at the southern part of town in case any intruders try to head south," Corvin responds.

"Have you checked all of the Arterians?"

"Not quite, sir. We're planning on checking all of their quarters next after we ensure the borders are secure. That way no one gets out."

Fuck.

Cole manages to slip his hand to my shoulder, squeezing me to calm my nerves—*it's going to be okay.* Though, it's hard to ignore the slamming of his heart against his broad chest as the side of my face is pressed against it.

"We thought you might want to confirm nothing is missing, in the event we need to question anyone we catch tonight," Corvin continues.

Shuffling sounds about the room outside, drawers sliding open and closed. My heart hammers in my ears, picturing him getting closer and closer to finding out that the little black book is missing from his secret drawer. And him getting closer to the wardrobe we're hiding in. Cole leans his head down to rest his head on top of mine. As if he's trying to help contain my buzzing panic.

"If you catch them with something of mine, no need to question them. Just kill them," Sethan responds plainly and slams a drawer.

Hard.

I squeeze my eyes shut, even though it's only a touch darker than it is in the wardrobe. He definitely found that the book is missing. Just in the way he slammed it—I know.

"Sir, the two missing guards have been located," an unfamiliar voice calls.

"Bring me to them. Corvin, take a group and check in with those at the southern point."

"Right away, sir," Corvin responds.

Heavy footsteps fade into the distance, followed by a door clicking closed. After a few frozen moments of listening to the leapfrog of mine and Cole's pulses, he finally inhales slowly and lifts his head off mine. A crack of light leaks into the wardrobe as Cole leans back and bumps the door open with his shoulders. He grabs the black book between us before it falls.

The light affords me more detail. Like the way his lips are parted in longing, his eyes soft and focused solely on mine. His warm breath stirs my hair, and a flush of heat creeps down my spine. Sweat glistens at his forehead, the scent of him surrounding me with a deep familiarity in this tight, dark space.

As he inches slowly away from me, his heat fading from where his body pressed against mine, I realize how hopelessly longing I am for him to stay.

Oh…shit. My hands are still fisted tightly into the shirt at his sides. I let go, my fingers rigid from how hard I clung to him. He sucks in a breath, the motion clearing his dazed expression. He clears his throat, tucks the book under his arm, and steps out of the wardrobe. Then, he offers his hand to help me out.

We don't dare speak. It's already known how dire it is for us to get back before we're noticed. We slip out of the room through the window, past the alley where we knocked the guards unconscious, and through the winding dark streets of Midkeep. We're close. So close my heartbeat starts to slow as I recognize the street my room is on. As we turn a corner, Cole whips toward me, his eyes wild.

"I'm sorry," he whispers.

"What—"

He shoves the small book to my chest and seizes the back of my thighs, lifting me clear off the ground with an ease as simple as taking a breath, then pushes me back against the stone wall in the alleyway. The air in my lungs rushes out of me in a single breath as my shoulder blades collide with the hard wall. And suddenly.

Instantly.

Cole's lips are on mine. Stealing every breath from my mouth as he crushes himself against me. Demanding. Pleading. And desperate in all the ways I don't want to admit I miss. He doesn't allow a single inch of space between us, leaning into me as if his life depends on it. As if his entire existence hangs between us, and if we separate, it'll fall to the ground and shatter in a million, incomprehensible pieces.

Footsteps approach the alleyway.

And then I understand.

Instinctively, I wrap my arms around his neck and circle my legs around his waist, tight, and drawing him into me further. Arching my back against the wall, I force as much of my chest into his to hide the journal between us. Cole groans an approval into my mouth. An understanding. But Gods, does that deep, throaty sound send a chill down my spine. One of his hands slips from the back of my leg, and he shoves himself harder between my thighs. I accidentally whimper.

Oh, *fuck*. This is not the pressure I need. And definitely not the mouth I need. Not when I'm so godsdamned pissed at him. Not when each brush of his lips and beat of his pulse against my chest threatens to wipe my memory of it all clean. Goosebumps erupt on my skin, a gentle tingling falling across my nerves like a blanket of fresh snow with each press of his lips on mine.

Don't. Fucking don't, Kat.

But Gods…it's uncontrollable. A mix of desire and familiarity floods my veins, a heat collecting between my thighs where he is. The rest of the alleyway fades away, my own pounding heart drowning out the sounds of the approaching footsteps.

Stop it. But I can't. *We* can't. *You shouldn't be touching him like this, not when he's supposed to be engaged.*

Cole slides a hand up the wall behind my head, and I grab the back of his neck, pulling him into me as I swipe my tongue across the bottom of his lip. *Shit, that was a mistake.* And he knows it, too. He breaks off our kiss with panting breaths, his eyes peeking at me through heavy lids, partially in warning, partially in gut-wrenching desire.

A group of shadows stretch across the main street, and I rip him back against me. No time for thinking. Our lips meet again in a clash of warmth and unfettered, undeniable want. Claiming the other with each angle, each push and pull. Like it's a competition. Oh, how I've missed this. How I've wanted this. How I've hungered for what we once were.

"What in the realms—" someone mutters.

Well, at least we're convincing. Maybe too convincing. I pull off Cole's mouth, my breath loud and shaky as my hazy vision settles on our finder.

Sethan stands with several guards, all of them rigid with shock. Though, much to Sethan's credit, he wipes it clean off his expression and returns to his normal state of contempt. "I suppose your familial ties were just a ruse?"

Cole doesn't even bother to drag his attention off me. His heated gaze lingers on my mouth. Instead of pulling away from me, he leans his forehead into the crook of my neck with a broken sigh that doesn't need words. He wanted that kiss. Needed it as much as his next breath. And Gods, is it so terrible of me to admit I needed it, too?

"Yes," I answer Sethan and sigh to relieve the tension gripping my chest and throat. "Just a ruse."

The long inhale Cole sucks in at my neck prickles my skin. Like he's steadying himself before diving into a lake. He picks his head up off the crook of my neck and drags his attention to Sethan.

Sethan narrows his gaze. "You do realize you both agreed to a curfew?"

"I…" I clear my throat to get rid of the sandy texture rasping the single vowel. "Yes. Sorry…we just…"

I look at Cole, keeping a close watch in my peripheral vision of the journal still pressed between us. His auburn hair is mussed, lips parted as he fights to regain his own breath.

"Any extracurricular intimate relations does not negate that curfew, Katerina," Sethan scolds, then turns his attention to the guards at his side. "Escort them back to their rooms."

Cole clears his throat, his grip still tight on my waist, his torso pressed against mine. "Might we…have a moment to tidy our appearances before we return?"

Sethan waves a hand, then turns his face away to give us a small semblance of privacy, and his guards follow suit. Cole sets me back on my feet and grabs the journal between us before quickly pulling his shirt out of his pants. He tugs his waistband down, revealing his deeply chiseled lower abs and the curves down toward his…

I stop and avert my gaze toward Sethan, brushing my hair down the back of my head as Cole slides the journal into the front of his waistband and tucks his shirt over it. The pulsing of my desire slows, and my cheeks heat at how Cole can't take his eyes off me. Like I'm the only person in the realm. The two of us join Sethan and the other guards. He and his soldiers scan us, but to my relief, don't pat us down.

Sethan's glare is an almost deathly promise. "Don't let us catch you out after curfew again, understood?"

FIFTEEN

Your Side

"How's your side?" Tawny asks the next morning as I open my door. She presents me my sword and scabbard, then glances at my ribs.

I suppose Sethan's irritation after finding me and Cole out last night wasn't enough to keep from returning our weapons. I'm not going to question it further. Looping the sheath around myself, I pat my side. I'm still perplexed at the sheer absurdity of it healing overnight. "Thank you. Surprisingly, it doesn't even hurt anymore."

"I'm glad to hear it. Sethan will likely want you training with the riders when they return."

I blink. *Riders? There are more of them?*

She grimaces. "I'm not sure if that was sensitive information or not. Though, I imagine you'd find out sooner or later, since you entered the blood pact."

With Darian having been taken by Gavin and Nolan to bathe and eat, I invite her inside with a gesture. She dips her head before sliding into the room with me. I scan her face and the cut on her forehead I stitched up weeks ago, now a scar.

As soon as I close the door, I ask, "Do you have a blood pact with him?"

"I do. But I didn't need one."

At least I know if she has a blood pact with Sethan, she can ultimately be trusted. But I'm still not privy to asking her what she knows of Cole's ring I wear. Marge's warning to keep the ring hidden at all costs echoes in my head. I ask, "Then why enter one?"

"Because it shows my people I trust him. I was born and raised here, and he was not. It was quite the commotion when he was sworn in—and so I felt it was my duty to seal myself to him. As did many others in the Dragon Lands."

"But not everyone," I mumble.

"Correct. Those of us north of the border may share similar ideals when it comes to dragons, but we don't all agree with what needs to be done in terms of Arterias and King Aaric. We've always struggled with unity—even before Sethan came along."

"So why do you trust him?"

She shrugs. "What other choice do I have? I know our current reality is like a frozen lake, thawing as the seconds tick by. We're all standing on the surface, so consumed about being right, we push the others to the ground, not realizing if one of us falls and cracks the ice—we all go down. The more we push and shove, the closer we get to drowning."

I nod, sucking my teeth in thought. "Even the rebels have rebels."

She narrows her eyes. "You Arterians call us rebels. But we are so much more than that. We go by Vitalans."

A knock sounds at the door.

"You may come in," I call.

The door swings open and Corvin enters. Directing his attention at me, he dips his head. "Katerina, my apologies for the intrusion. Sethan requests your immediate presence."

I take a breath. Great. I can only imagine what this conversation is going to be like after having already broken the curfew rule. I follow Corvin to Sethan's office, and he ushers me inside.

Sethan lowers his head upon our arrival, then gestures to one of the tufted chairs on the other side of his desk. "Thank you for coming so promptly. Take a seat."

I lower myself into the chair, watching him all the while and readying myself to answer questions about my relations with Cole and why I was out so late at night. Sethan's hands are tucked neatly behind his back as he dismisses Corvin with a dip of his head, leaving us alone.

Sethan lifts his chin in the few seconds of silence. "I'm glad to see you survived sharing a room with Darian."

I shrug, thankful we aren't speaking of Cole. Yet. "Or he survived me."

Sethan's rough beard splits into a hesitant smile before it's whisked away. "I spoke with the elders, and they've all agreed to the journey to Vitalis."

That single word wipes away my question of why his trip was so short. "Journey?"

Glancing up at the large map stretching out across the wall, I trace a trail up to the drawing of the large, stone castle tucked into the mountain range. Even from this distance the intricate details etched into each building are immaculate, with depictions of waterfalls framing the lush castle grounds. But Midkeep is far. So far south, I imagine it'll take triple the time from Padmoor to the far eastern shores of Arterias.

I drag my gaze back to Sethan. "They want us to go all the way up there? Why?"

"Because that's where Queen Elara died. What do you know of the history of Arterias and Vitalis?"

"Honestly? Not much."

He nods. "Before King Aaric came into rule, Arterias and Vitalis were just the northern and southern capital of Osseus."

"Oss-*ee*-us?"

"Yes. Osseus was the name of our entire continent. After Queen

Elara died, many detested Aaric's claim to the throne, even though he was next in line—"

"Didn't King Aaric kill his sister, though?" I ask, recalling my father's journal entries.

"That's what many of the older generations say. It could be a rumor, or it could be true. There's no way to know for certain. Many of the dragon riders rose up and rebelled against Aaric's claim to the throne. They argued he wasn't fit to rule after the death of his wife and daughter and felt he was too mentally and emotionally unstable. King Aaric executed them, claiming the dragon riders were causing anarchy. But when he executed them—it divided the kingdom. There had always been people who were wary and jealous of dragon riders, and those people flocked to Aaric, believing in a new order of power—one without dragons. But the rest of the kingdom rose up behind those who lost their loved ones from such a gruesome, cruel execution. King Aaric and his followers, nearly outnumbered at the time, fled south to Arterias. Over the years, he's taken down our towns one by one. And as the older generations have passed on, the memories and histories have faded into oblivion."

"Then how do you know all of this?" I ask, still suspicious of his motives. I need to get that journal from Cole, see what it says about breaking pacts, and why Sethan would have information on it.

He motions toward his bookshelf with the many dusty and worn tomes. "Aaric crafted a detailed plan of erasing the history, but we were able to save some things from Vitalis before he destroyed it. The rest has been shared by our elders and council members. Aaric wants us and the rest of the realm to forget. That's why every one of our requests for peace has been ignored—because he *wants* to exterminate us. He wants complete and utter control."

I swallow. "So…what do the elders think we'll find in Vitalis that can help us?"

He shakes his head with a frown. "I'm not sure, and I don't think even they know. But they say you may be the key to answers we've tried to find for over a century. No one else has been able to enter Vitalis except Cyrus, since it's guarded by magic. Cyrus had been looking for that ring you have, claiming it could change everything. But he died before we could take down the King. Since you're his granddaughter, and the prophecy is about you and Daeja, we think you might be able to pass through the magical gates at Vitalis."

Of *course* it's me. I blow out a breath. "When are we expected to leave? And how long will it take us to get to Vitalis?"

"Well, by dragon back, it's maybe a few days. But seeing as we need to keep your squad together so no stragglers try to escape back to Arterias, it's maybe a few weeks or a month on foot."

A bit slower than I anticipated, considering the distance on the map from Midkeep to Vitalis.

Sethan grabs a long, skinny wooden rod off his desk, paces over to the map, and drags a trail up it. "From here to Driftmond is a full day's travel after we cut over the river. Then another day's worth of travel from Driftmond to Kilamber—"

"Why would we do that when we need to go north to reach Vitalis? Why would we go west?"

He points to a cluster of mountains with a massive volcano northeast of here. "Because Eldire is where fire dragons live. And we can't risk running into any wild ones."

I nod, taking mental notes.

He continues, flicking the wooden stick from spot to spot on the map to direct my attention, "Anyway, after Kilamber, we get to Vathstone and restock our supplies. We should zig-zag over the river toward Bayrock, and then it's several days to Silkwood—"

"Wouldn't that slow our pace? And we'd run the risk of losing supplies to the currents if we're having to pass through the water multiple times?" My pulse skitters at the thought of having to cross a river several times over, the memory of my brother getting swept away replaying in my mind.

"Or running into water dragons." Sethan shrugs, as if I

shouldn't be worried about it either. "Though, with it being winter, I imagine most of them are dormant in the depths of the ocean by now."

"Do we have another option?"

"Well, we could cut north from Vathstone near Ashfall, trim the outskirts of the Forbidden Forest near Silkwood, restock in Pinepoint, and stay in Mossmead before the final stretch to Vitalis." He takes a step back from the map, staring up at it in deep contemplation.

He glances at me from over his shoulder. "So, what's it going to be?"

I flinch. "What?"

"What do you think we should do? Up to Bayrock or by Ashfall?"

"Ummm…" I glance back up at the map, caught off guard that he's expecting me to weigh in on the plan. "I guess through Ashfall, if it's faster?"

He nods. "Very well. In that case, prepare your squad. We leave in two nights."

SIXTEEN

THE SECOND RING

After I leave Sethan's office and head toward my room, I spot Marge hobbling across the cobblestone street a few blocks to my north and struggle to keep myself from breaking into an overeager pace toward her. She slips down an alley out of my view.

As soon as I'm close enough, I rest a hand on her shoulder to stop her from walking. "I need to talk to you."

I whisk her further away from Midkeep and into the forest, away from any potential listening ears.

As soon as we are outside of town, I turn to her. "Why the hells didn't you tell me about this ring linking me to the King?"

Irritation flickers in her narrowed gaze as soon as I use profanity, remaining when I finish my sentence. "He told you?"

"He did."

She mutters something inaudible under her breath.

I lower my hand to my side. "When were you planning on sharing that information with me?"

She grumbles, "You weren't quite ready to know that bit yet."

"But you felt like you could trust Cole over me?"

"That wasn't my intention, and you know it. But I knew out of everyone here, he can be trusted the most to protect you."

"And so you told my brother—"

"He's not your brother. So, let's stop pretending he is."

"W-what?"

"Everyone is so busy looking at you, they don't see how *he* looks at you. How he speaks about you, whether or not you're in the room. Let's cut the facade."

I take a step back. "But…you never said anything?"

Even after she knew Cole was engaged to Celeste. To King Aaric's granddaughter. It's enough to convince me of her loyalty to me. After all this time, she could have easily ratted me out.

She shrugs, turning her attention back to Midkeep. "I've learned not to stick my nose in affairs that don't involve me. It's none of my business. Besides, I see the way you watch him, too. The way you speak of him. You love him."

Or…maybe loved. I'm not so sure anymore, and if I let myself think about it for too long, it'll only open a world of pain. I shove it aside.

She must notice the turmoil in my expression, because she quickly averts her eyes and scans the forest. "I didn't want it to scare you. And I didn't want you to make any rash decisions. Cole understood that. Why he suddenly had a change of heart and mind is beyond me."

"Stop dallying, Marge. What else aren't you telling me because you don't feel like I'm ready for it? This ring links me to the King. You want me to hide it, and I know it's powerful. But what else?"

"Nothing."

"You're lying! For someone who loves to tell everyone else how much she trusts me, you have yet to share everything."

Finally, she turns to me with a sigh. "Do you remember what I told you back in Arterias? How there used to be an old, ancient language, forgotten after Aaric came to power?"

"Yes?"

"Do you know what the first word was in the common tongue?"

"No."

She slowly draws something in the dirt with the tip of her staff, leaving a single word a shade darker than the rest of the ground.

I tilt my head in confusion after she finishes. "Not a 'hello.' Or 'how are you?' *Blood?*"

She nods and traces the two Os again, linking the letters together. "Blood was the first word, because our ancestors believed there was power in blood, and we were all born with some bit of magic—all of which ranged in potency. The Gods created us through magic. So, naturally, some bit of magic courses through our veins. Our elders believed the Gods also created two rings. They forged them through the rawest form of magic and their own blood and bone. Those two rings could be used for powerful things—things you and I couldn't even think or dream of, if harnessed in the proper way."

I glance down at my gloved left hand, where I've memorized the cold ring against my skin. "Like healing a wound?"

"Your ribs…yes. That was likely magic. When you were wounded back in Arterias while wearing the ring, King Aaric suffered the same injury. And since it links you to him, you too were healed if he used magic to repair his ribs."

"So, he knows someone else is wearing it. Why wouldn't he just remove it?"

"Because the longer you wear it and the more you wield magic with it, the more ingrained it becomes with you. The King has worn it for over a hundred years—so it's sealed to him. He couldn't take it off even if he tried."

"And no one can take it off of him?" I squeeze my hand into a fist.

"Correct. Only the wearer can remove it. Unless the wearer is dead…that's why he's so desperate to find it. The Kings and Queens before us wore them. Since the two rings together were far too powerful for one singular person, the rings were split. One for the Queen, and one for the King. Thus, how the tradition of wedding rings came about. The rings were around far longer than the first dragon riders. And generations before Aaric and Elara were born, the rings were separated to balance the power of the two halves of the continent—Vitalis and Arterias."

She sighs. "And then when Queen Elara died and King Aaric took the throne, all of it changed. Aaric took the first ring from Vitalis where they resided, but the second one from Arterias disappeared." She motions to my hand.

I flick up a look at her. "This…this is the second ring? This was Cole's mother's ring—"

"Exactly. Cole's mother likely either got that ring by stealing it from the rebels, or she was a rebel herself," Marge whispers. "But I don't know if we'll ever truly have an answer."

She hobbles over to me, grabs my hand, and removes my glove. She lifts my fingers closer to her face to inspect the metal ring. "Based on what I've seen, the King has the Bone Ring. And I have a sneaking suspicion this is the Blood Ring."

"You…you've met the King? You've seen him?"

She chuffs. "Did you forget I know Darian, Edith, and Celeste?"

Truthfully, I had never asked. As far as I'd been concerned, I didn't need to know more about Darian. At the time, I didn't even know Celeste.

Marge continues, "Yes, I've met the King. Worked for him, even. I lived in the castle for years as a healer, and that's how I came to know Darian and his sisters. I often helped mend broken bones and stitch gashes. Darian in particular was a frequent visitor—the boy was rambunctious and often injured himself. Not to mention his rigorous training with his father."

"How did you come to the northern outpost in Arterias, then?"

Her voice dips. "Well…I suppose I was assigned to it."

Her answer is short enough for me not to ask anything further on the matter. I tilt my head to the side. "So, what could King Aaric possibly need both rings for?"

"I'm not sure. But one thing is for certain: there's never been anyone within our knowledge that's worn both. If he gets his hands on the second ring, it's sure to be catastrophic for the rest of the realm." She hands me her staff to hold, then fishes at her chest for something hidden beneath several layers of clothes. Attentively scanning our surroundings, she unclasps and removes a necklace. The chain carries a glass vial filled with a swirling gray mist, as if encapsulating a small storm.

"Here, I want you to have this." She urges me to open my hand before dropping the necklace into my palm. Quickly, she closes my fingers over it and pushes my fist close to my chest. "For an emergency. You don't let anyone know you have it. Understand?"

I nod, and ask her in a small voice, "What is it?"

She glances around the forest once more to double-check we're alone. "Remember when I told you about all the properties of dragon's blood? An earth dragon's breath has similar effects. But it's a less concentrated dose. It's mainly used for strength. Should you find yourself gravely injured, I want you to take it."

"I can't. Didn't you say dragons hate Spoileds—"

"It's not the same. First, your dragon is so attached to you, I doubt she'd be phased by anything you consumed. Second, dragon's breath is much milder. Dragons cannot sense it as much because breath fades much quicker than something that fuses with your blood as you drink it. Besides…it doesn't come with the nasty aftereffects that dragonblood does."

I finally open my hand to peek at the vial. "How did you get this?"

She dismisses me with a wave of her hand. "It shouldn't matter how. You only use it for yourself. Do you understand?"

"I…"

"*Katerina Blackwind.*"

I flinch. She knows—she knows my *actual* name. Hearing it for the first time in so long sounds nearly foreign.

She hisses, "Answer me."

I dip my head in response, securing the necklace to my neck and tucking it into my shirt. "I understand."

SEVENTEEN

BREAKING BINDS

"Cole...I need to tell you something," I whisper. Shaking my head furiously, I run a hand through my hair. It doesn't sound right. "Cole—"

I sigh, sagging to sit on my bed as I stare at my boots. Every practiced attempt at telling Cole of my night with Darian freezes me, my tongue refusing to move. Gods, this must be how it felt for him trying to tell me about Celeste. Even if I shouldn't feel as guilty as I do, the emotion still gnaws inside my chest. Especially after last night... whatever it was. I've been running it over in my mind, remembering his touch. His kiss...I brush my fingers longingly across my lips.

A knock sounds at my door, and my blood rushes from my face into my chest. Each step across Cyrus's old room to the door feels slow. I pull it open, and Cole is glancing over his shoulder down the street.

He turns to me. "Melaina took Darian from me and told me you sent her so I could speak to you in private."

I motion him into the room and shut the door behind him. I take a shaky breath, my hand resting on the wooden door as I linger in the still moment. As I turn to face him, he's unbuckling his belt and pulling the journal out from the space between his right hip and bottom of his ribs. He holds the little black book out to me, and I take it as he fastens his belt. Averting my attention down to the book, I rub a thumb over the title 'Breaking Magical Binds,' before I flip it open to the first page.

By Leland Blackwind.

I flick up a look at Cole. "My father wrote this."

He walks until he's a step away from me and cranes his neck. "All the more reason to believe it, then?"

I flip through the next few pages, detailing the history of dragons and dragon riders. Once I get past the information of the first dragon riders, I pause.

What has been gathered from the Book of Magic is that most magical binds and pacts can be broken through various ways. The first is the most simple—through the Blood and Bone rings. These rings source the purest form of magic, and so they can break the strongest of bonds.

The second way is through a series of rituals, mostly performed by using dragonblood and the ancient language. Though, much of the ancient language—the language of the Gods—has been long forgotten. What translations we still know are limited and not nearly enough to break a bond that has surpassed the six-month mark. The only way to potentially break a longer pact would be if both parties are in mutual agreement of it, and the ritual is held during a celestial event. Celestial events cause surges in the ley lines, which can enhance the magical potency of dragonblood.

"Why else would Sethan have this? Does it not give you a reason to believe he might be trying to find a way out of your blood pact in the event it doesn't serve him?" Cole murmurs.

I flip to the next page, only to find foreign characters scrawled onto it. "I don't know…but look at this. Do you think this is the Gods' language?"

Cole tilts his head and leans closer to me, his forehead nearly brushing mine. "I'm not sure. It doesn't look familiar to me."

After flipping through the rest of the book to ensure we haven't missed anything else, I return to the last decipherable page about breaking binds.

I underline the first paragraph with my finger. "The easiest, simplest way is through using the Blood and Bone Ring. Which means, if anyone's breaking anything, I have the upper hand." As a reminder, I wiggle my gloved fingers.

"Who's to say he hasn't broken anything already? Do you think you would have felt something? Especially since he caught us…"

He trails off, and I look up from the book at him. Kissing. Caught us kissing, after curfew. My heart leaps in my chest, heat rising to my cheeks. I close the journal as he locks me into his warm honey eyes.

My voice is light. "No…I…I suppose I haven't felt anything different…"

The rest of the room darkens around us, and I swear the lightest thing in the room is him. His heavy eyes fall to my lips, and he hesitantly brushes my hair off my shoulder to my back. He shouldn't be touching me like this. And I shouldn't be letting him. We're creeping back to the deadly edge we aren't supposed to be leaping off.

"You felt…nothing?" he breathes.

We aren't speaking of the pacts anymore. I swallow against the tension collecting in my chest as his fingers skate too lightly against my skin. His touch ghosts against my lower back, his eyes searching mine for an answer to a secret prayer.

"Tell me it doesn't haunt you, too. Tell me you felt nothing," he pleads. "Tell me anything, just…let me in."

"I…" *Won't…or can't?* A thin line separates the two words, and I'm not sure where I lie. But the truth is, I can't deny how much I've dreamed of his lips on mine again…how right it feels. Even if all the circumstances point to it being wrong.

His jaw clenches, tension drawing into his eyebrows like a bow strung tight. He knows I can't deny it. I don't even have to *say* it.

Something inexplicable draws us together with a magnetic force that's close to impossible to deny or fight.

He closes his eyes as he leans his forehead to mine. "Please, Katerina Blackwind. Please tell me to stop."

"I can't…" I breathe finally. I skate a hand from the top of his shoulder down to his elbow, my breath catching in my throat at how badly I want to kiss him again. Now we're just playing a game of who'll be the first to break this physical barrier we've tried so hard to build between us. Each of us lean in a little bit further, succumbing to the longing. Our noses brush, sharing a heated gasp of breath.

"I love you," he reminds me in a whisper as he cups my cheek with one hand, his forehead rests against mine.

As my eyes drag almost completely closed, I rip myself back before I can be enveloped in him.

Shock, disappointment, and longing pain flashes across his features. "What's wrong?"

Uncertain I'll be able to look him in the eyes, I tear my gaze away and stare at his muddied boots, toe-to-toe with mine. His hand slides from cupping my cheek to my chin, tilting my head up gently to look at him again. Warm, golden eyes stare at me, picking at every weak strand of my self-composure.

"Hey," he says softly. "If…if you don't love me anymore…if you don't want me…just say it."

I bite into my lip as I shake my head. "That's not it. But there's something you should know…and I need you to sit down."

Worry flashes in his eyes, his breathing picking up speed. Stiffly, he backs away and takes a seat on the edge of my bed. "Okay…?"

I'm still rooted to the spot I stand. "I don't know how else to say this…but I'm going to try anyway. Remember the night I found out about your engagement to Celeste?"

Darkness sweeps over his features, his eyes lowering as he recalls. He swallows thickly. "Yes. I remember."

"There was something else that happened that night."

His eyes snap up to me.

The words spill from my mouth like a hot liquid I can no longer contain. "It's been eating at me ever since. And I don't know what we are anymore, but I still feel obligated to tell you out of respect for what we once were. I almost left for the Dragon Lands myself that night, but as I was leaving, Darian caught me. And the only way I could think of to keep him from seeing Daeja was to kiss him."

Sucking in a shaky inhale, he clenches his jaw like he just got punched in the gut. He nods, his voice tight. "Alright. I can't say it feels good to know you kissed him but—"

"That's not all," I murmur in defeat.

His mouth parts. His realization doesn't have to be spoken with how stricken he looks. As if I reared back and knocked my fist straight into his strong jaw. And when I don't speak further—when I don't even try to fight the lingering silence between us—understanding floods in, drowning out every bit of his expression into something agonizing.

He jolts to his feet, turning his back to me and facing the wall. "You didn't," he breathes.

"Cole, I—"

"I thought he looked at you the way he did because he's a…" He shakes his head, hiding his face from my view. He runs his hands through his hair, gripping at the back of his skull as he breathes through his lips.

I pace toward him, gingerly touching his shoulder. "I hadn't meant—"

He spins out of my touch, his auburn hair sweeping down in front of his eyes as he keeps his head down, his gaze trained on his boots. His voice comes out weak. "Stop."

We both stand frozen in place, my hand still outstretched before I lower it. My heart shatters as I witness first-hand the tidal wave of pain crashing over him.

I whisper, "It was *just* sex, you can't be jealous—"

"I'm not jealous," he rasps, clenching his hands into fists. "I'm…I'm broken."

He turns to leave.

My breath tightens in my chest, and tears collect at the corners of my eyes. Fuck, this is so much more painful than I'd ever realized it would be. To know I held his heart in my hands—that he had given *so* willingly, time and time again, and crushing it like glass. Broken beyond repair.

It cuts me, too.

I grab his forearm as he passes me, and he glances at my hand, still avoiding any eye contact. He watches the way my fingers wrap around him, desperate and pleading.

I shake my head. "Wait, please…it meant nothing to me."

His lips part before tightening into a line. Squeezing his eyes shut, he shakes his head. "But it meant something to me." He slips out of my grasp and leaves.

EIGHTEEN

Reckless honesty

After I've spent some time in my room lying in bed and tearing up thinking about how broken Cole and I are, I force myself up. No time to let it keep me down. There's too much at stake.

Daeja escorts me through the cobblestone streets to Sethan's office. She's quiet. Sensing my heartache. Every townsperson gawks and shifts out of the way, giving us a healthy amount of space as we make our way through the town side-by-side.

"Don't let that go to your head," I tease.

Her head is lifted, eyes locked on the path, and her lips twitch into something like a grin. *Too late.*

Once we get to Sethan's office, I pound on the door a second before it swings open and I enter. Daeja's breath heats my back as she edges her muzzle through the door and opens her mouth in a hissing growl. The two guards who were standing at the door shift away, their hands sliding to their weapons.

"Thank you, but I think they get the point."

"Just in case they need a reminder…" Daeja snaps at the air with a sound that rings in my ears before she retreats.

I walk past the guards and straight for Sethan sitting at his desk. His eyes flick up from his letter, then he waves the guards out to leave us. They hesitate but exit anyway, their eyes trained on Daeja in one of the side windows before the door closes. The same side window Cole and I snuck in the other night to retrieve the black book, which is now tucked into my satchel.

"Yes? To what do I owe the pleasure?" Sethan prompts.

I flex my sweating hands in my black leather gloves to try and redirect the tension in my chest. But the longer I think of it, the more I know with certainty it's the best path forward. "I went against our agreement about the curfew."

"You did. And you've lied about your relations with Cole."

"Yes. We lied because back in Arterias I had to pretend to be his sister in order to stay at the military outpost. And…" I pause, not wanting to disclose the fact Cole was—or *is*—engaged. And to the King's granddaughter, of all people. "…and we've kept that front, because the rest of the squad doesn't know. Considering we're already walking on eggshells within our own group by a temporary agreement to stay, I don't want to disrupt it by revealing such a long-winded lie."

"I see…and you're trusting me to keep it a secret?"

"For now. I think sharing that secret with the squad would be disastrous, especially if we want to make it to Vitalis as a group. You told me you could lead through fear or respect. But…I think there's another way. I think you can lead through honesty. And while I can't disclose that secret right now…there is one thing I can do."

He leans back in his chair, crossing his arms over his chest and waiting.

Praying I'm not making a colossal mistake, I pluck the little black book from my satchel and rest it on his desk in an utter leap of faith. "The reason we were out last night is because we stole this."

Daeja's dark figure glides past the set of windows behind Sethan's back and pauses, her eyes fixed on him and waiting for any of my commands.

"My…" His gaze flicks down to the book. "I must admit—I'm impressed by the reckless honesty."

Despite my fear, I don't drop my chin, nor take my eyes off him. Waiting for him to also come clean. "I noticed after you caught us out after curfew, nothing happened. If I violated the blood pact we made, doesn't that void our agreement? Would I have felt something?"

Catching on to my train of thought, he glances up. "I haven't broken our blood pact, if that's what you're asking."

"What is this book for, then?"

"It's a study on how to break binds and pacts between *dragons* and their *riders.*"

"And why would anyone do that?"

"I'm not sure. But the elders thought the celestial event was an important piece of information. It was noted the currents of magic are strongest then. And we have reason to believe the King is waiting for one to test out the theory, since he doesn't have that ring." He motions to my hand. "Now comes our conversation about what your punishment should be."

"Punishment?"

"Is this the part where I break through the window?" Daeja grumbles down our bond.

He answers, "Yes. It's only fair, considering you could have just asked me about it rather than *stealing* from me."

I clench my teeth. "Do you truly blame me for not trusting you when you're not entirely forthcoming with your information? That, and you're also not the most approachable person to ask questions."

"You know, in thirty years from now when you're my age, you might not be the most approachable, either."

Daeja growls, and he turns to look at her through the window over his shoulder, before he turns back to me. "If you read the book, then you know you hold the upper hand here. With your ring, you can easily break our pact at any point. I have nothing to gain to break it and everything to lose."

"Like A'nala…" Daeja murmurs.

Though, I think A'nala is just the beginning of what he's referring to. *"Are you really able to hear all of this through the window?"*

She snorts, her breath fogging the glass in a cloud before it dissipates.

Sethan continues, "I'll do the best I can to gain your trust, but you need to give me the chance. Can you at least do that?"

As if delivering the book wasn't enough of an example? I watch him, debating the best answer, before I finally mutter, "I can try."

"Then that's the most I can ask for."

"I have one request."

"Name it," he mumbles warily.

"The curfew doesn't apply to me."

Cole doesn't show up to dinner at the community hall later that evening. After everyone finishes their meals, we all return to our rooms and settle in for the night. Melaina and Archie assist me in securing Darian's chains to the hooks in the far wall of the room. Darian looks ready to snap at Archie's hand as he sheepishly tugs to double-check the strength of the hooks. Archie squeezes my shoulder as he and Melaina leave the room.

I change out of my day clothes into a nightgown, blow out the wall sconce candles, and shuffle into bed. I drift off into sleep for a short amount of time before I wake to a soft knock. My eyes flutter open, and I scan the wall where Darian's chained up. His eyes flash open, meeting mine in the darkness. Another set of knocks.

"Well, I'm not going to get it," he grumbles.

I nervously slip out of bed, bringing a dagger with me to the door. A knock this late at night can't be anything good.

When I part the door open, I release a breath and open it more. *Does anybody know what a godsdamn curfew is?* "What are you doing here?"

Marge presses a finger to her lips. She beckons me out with an urgent flick of her hand. I gesture down to my nightgown, and she spins her hand in circles to spur me into action. When I open the door wider to allow her in, she shakes her head. Closing the door slightly, I return to the dresser, pull out day clothes, and turn my back to Darian as I remove my nightgown.

"Mmm," he purrs thickly, clearly enjoying the sight.

I ignore him, shuffling quickly into my pants and pulling a long sleeve on before grabbing a cloak.

"Wher*ever* could you be going so late in the night?" Darian's tilted voice mocks in innocent curiosity.

I seize my boots, pulling them onto my legs.

"Late night rendezvous? Scandalous thing, you," he taunts again.

"Careful. I might actually think you're jealous," I whisper as I shut the door behind me.

"Wait—" he calls but is cut off once I secure the door closed.

Marge leads me through the town, slinking through the shadows and sliding against the walls through alleyways. The silhouette of the forest appears off in the distance as we get near the outskirts of Midkeep.

I whisper, "Where are you taking me—"

"What are you doing out? It's past curfew. Get back to your beds," someone commands from behind us.

We turn, facing the direction of the voice. Two men with metal tipped spears scan us. One of them lowers their spears, pointing it directly at us. Marge's eyebrows quirk up, before settling down above her eyes in intimidation. I pity the man who dares to challenge Marge—her expression alone would scare the boots off someone.

The other guard recognizes me, his eyes widening as he elbows the one who spoke, and motions toward me silently.

The first guard lowers his spear, clearing his throat before he speaks, "My apologies. Please continue on your way. But hurry back, the forest is no safe place for two ladies on their own."

"We'll manage," Marge grumbles as she grabs the back of my arm above my elbow and steers me away.

We venture into the forest, the pine trees stretching into the sky like an army of still soldiers watching us coldly. The moonlight seeps through the pine needles, washing the forest floor in grays and shadows. Marge holds up a hand to stop me as we near the edge of a clearing.

"What? Why did you bring me out here in the middle of the night, Marge?" I whisper.

"Shh!" Her gaze is glued to something in the distance. A breeze picks up, lifting her hair and shuffling her cloak. She slowly looks at me over her shoulder. "Do you hear it?"

I blink hard, straining to listen between the whispering of wind in the leaves and bubbles of the river farther south from us. "No, there's nothing out there. This is ridiculous—"

"Shhh!" she warns again and hobbles toward me. "Close your eyes."

I eye the forest around us, my skin prickling at the thought of closing my eyes if she actually heard something in the distance. She hits the side of my leg with her staff, and a dull ache springs in my muscles at the contact. I squeeze my eyes shut and am swallowed by darkness. The breeze dies off, leaving an eerie stillness settling around us. I listen hard, looking for whatever Marge was trying to hint at, but still, I find nothing. I peek an eye open and Marge is still standing in front of me, staring.

"Focus!" she barks.

I squeeze my eye back shut, forcing myself not to shiver in the cold night air now that I'm motionless.

Marge murmurs, soft as if she might scare something off, "Listen…you've grown accustomed to its sound, because it's become a second nature to you. You've tuned it out because it's something you've heard your whole life, and it's been right under your nose, all along."

With my eyes still closed, I shiver in the bitter cold. Still straining to listen for whatever delusion Marge has convinced herself is out here, in the middle of the night. Perhaps I should be concerned for her mental stability if she's pulling me from bed after midnight for…a sound emerges from the trees. Sliding through the canopies, gliding along the wind, and whispering through the undergrowth. A soft, subtle, hum. My jaw drops. The longer I focus on it—the louder it becomes. The buzz surrounds us, echoing off the tree trunks.

"Yes…" Marge whispers, closer than she'd been moments before. Her body heat radiates near in proximity. "You hear it."

Perplexed and curious, I nod, considering opening my eyes. But something stops me, as if I know better. As if once I open my eyes, my focus will slip, and the sound will disappear. The deep humming relaxes every nerve ending in my body, singing in my bones, and slowing every rush of blood in my veins.

Marge's hand softly rests on my shoulder. "Good…I want you to kneel down."

My normal hesitation is swept away by an indescribable wave of enchantment. I lower myself to the ground, slowly and obediently, until my knee hits the cold dirt.

"Now…" she says, as soft as a breath. "Remove your gloves… put your hand to the ground. And feel it."

I remove my gloves and toss them to the side. Slowly, I bend forward, the humming growing louder as I reach my hand out to where I sense the ground is. I hesitate before I touch it, hovering above the surface. My skin grows rigid with goosebumps breaking out along my forearm, every microscopic hair on the back of my neck stands. A magnetic gravity pulls my hand closer, and I fight against it momentarily, before I push through my hesitation and press my palm flat to the dirt.

A living, surging essence breathes beneath the surface. It's buzzing energy whispers out around and beneath me. The black behind my eyelids glows with an incandescent burst of blue and white. I'm fully drawn to it as if it could tear me through the layers of dirt to get to the core of this world. It whispers to me—calling me. Tempting me. Nearly *pleading*. I put my other hand on the dirt and draw closer to the ground—

A pain flares in my shoulder, and I rip open my eyes. My sight takes a moment to adjust, the blurry shapes and lines around me forming a picture of Marge and the dark forest.

She's pale. Her eyes are wide and voice shakes. "That's enough for tonight."

The rest of my senses wash back over me, despite the fact I hadn't noticed they were missing before. The river bubbles in the distance, the whisper of a breeze snakes through the leaves, and the tapping of Marge's staff on the ground grabs my attention.

"Katerina, are you alright?" she asks.

I nod slowly. An unknown heaviness swarms my head, and I grab my gloves before I push up to my feet, stumbling as I regain my balance. Smoke taints my nostrils. "What was that?"

She scans me head to toe in suspicion. "Magic."

"Magic?" I nearly laugh.

"Had your mother never told you of the great magic?"

"No." I don't want to tell her my mother had been terribly ill and couldn't get a coherent word out. I don't need her pity, and part of me doesn't want to simmer in such painful memories.

"The magic of our realm flows like a river. But those rivers are underneath the ground in what are called ley lines." She drags her staff through the dirt to draw intersecting lines. "The essence of dragons come from the ley lines, and it's where their power to create elemental magic stems from. Though, dragons are second in power next to the rings. The rings are the one thing that can manipulate the magic however the bearer deems fit."

"Where do the ley lines come from?"

"We don't know too much about the nature of them. Other than sometimes they shift, sway, and surge depending on the seasons or celestial events. Or sometimes it's completely random. Only few have seen it surface, and those that have say it looks like a blue fire—"

"I've seen it," I mutter, recalling the night in Arterias where Daeja touched it, nearly tripled in size, and we were then able to speak telepathically.

She tilts her head, eyes studying me carefully. "You've…seen it?"

"Back at the outpost…near the lake. Daeja and I saw it. She touched it by accident."

"How old is your dragon?"

"Umm…" I pause, attempting to piece together the timeframe when she had first hatched. "At least four months. Probably five?"

"Interesting…she's quite young. You shouldn't be able to communicate with her so soon. Dragons don't bond with humans until well into their adulthood when they've matured. But if she touched it…" Marge trails off, staring off into the dark forest. "That could explain how she's so big for her age. And how you can communicate with her already. Did you touch it, too?"

"No."

She turns her attention back to me, not masking a relieved sigh. "Good. If you see it again, you avoid it at all costs, do you understand? You touch *nothing* until you've mastered pulling."

"Pulling?"

"Yes. Think of how you'd draw water out of a well. The Blood Ring is the bucket that collects the water—the magic. But you must know how deep to lower that bucket into the water, and how long to let it fill, before pulling it back up. If you fill it too much, you won't be able to draw it out. And if you pull too quickly, you risk the chance of spilling it. On the other hand, you pull too slowly and you will drain your strength. It's all about balance."

She glances around the clearing. "It's getting late, and we don't want those guards getting suspicious we've been gone too long. But every night, when everyone is asleep, you'll meet me outside your door, and we'll train you on how to pull."

NINETEEN

TRUTH AND GAGS

Marge and I make it back to Midkeep with only a lingering stare from the guards. Marge over exaggerates her limp around them, then returns to her normal gait as soon as we turn a corner out of eyesight. Clever thing. I slip back into my room and close the door silently.

Darian is sitting and leans back against the wall, an elbow resting on his bent knee as he watches me through his brown locks. "Well, you don't smell like sex."

I hang my cloak up, then turn my attention to unlacing my boots.

"Did you want to?" he jabs.

"You know, on second thought, I may just revoke the agreement I made with Sethan, and have you stay in that wet, freezing basement," I say without looking in his direction and toss one boot over near my bed.

He's back to that all-infuriating mocking tone. "Your sweet, tender heart wouldn't do that to me."

"Oh, really?" I finally glare over at him as I unlace the next boot. "Funny you think you know me so well. You know absolutely nothing about what I'm capable of."

He blows out a bored breath, examining the dirt underneath his nails. "Fine. I know you didn't strike that deal out of the kindness of your heart. You want something from me. And while that something might be a myriad of things…" He drags a heavy stare up and down my body with a grin. "I can't help but be curious as to what you *think* you want from me and why you wanted it so bad you decided I should be your roommate."

I pull my boot off and toss it with the other one. After undressing myself, I stand staring at him in nothing but my undergarments, my nightgown hanging from my hand. "You won't be my roommate for long. You'll be traveling with us to Vitalis, in which case, if you don't play your cards right, you may be reassigned to other sleeping arrangements. Like sleeping outside with the dragons."

He cocks his head to the side. "Really? The good ol' capital. What a joy."

I begin to pull my nightgown over my head and take a few steps toward the bed.

"Since our time together is fleeting, perhaps you keep that off," he rumbles.

"Do you ever stop talking?"

"Only if you'll shut me up."

I turn, pinning him with a glare as I pull the nightgown over my frame. The way he watches me…with that lazy, catlike half-interest, half-boredom.

On second thought… I strip the nightgown off, his eyes flashing in anticipation. I stalk over to him, drop onto a knee into the space between his legs, and lower myself face to face with him. Gripping his chin in one hand, I yank down and stuff as much of my nightgown into his mouth before closing it.

I pat his scratchy, stubbled cheek, meeting his narrowed eyes. "Much better."

I slide into bed, reveling in the silence as I close my eyes and drift off to sleep.

A strangled gasp cuts through my watered down dreams. Flipping up off the mattress, I glance at Darian who is arching his back against the floor, his eyes wide and mouth gaping. My nightgown is crumpled on the floor near him. And the long, nine-foot chain connecting his wristlets to the wall clinks as he thrashes. He claws at his chest, the tendons in his throat bulging as he struggles to breathe.

Racing out of bed and nearly tripping over my own feet, I slide onto my knees beside him and assess his throat and chest. No puncture wounds, nothing constricting his airways. I brush my hand over his forehead, and his skin is clammy. *Fuck…poison? Did someone poison his dinner?*

"Don't you die on me, you idiot—"

In a smooth, quick motion, he lunges for me, snagging fistfuls of my hair before ripping my head down. A searing pain explodes in my scalp.

"Fuck!" I writhe. "Let go, you fucking asshole!"

Slapping and grabbing his hands, I attempt prying his fingers from my hair but can't get him to let go. Gritting my teeth, I slam my forehead into his, ramming his head back into the ground. He grunts in pain and twists both of us to the left, throwing me over with his weight and smacking me straight down into the cold, hard floor. A new explosion of pain wrecks my back, shoulders, and skull. He's over me in a flash, straddling me with his strong legs. With this new vantage point, he takes the chain between his manacles and pins my throat down.

If I wasn't fucked before, I surely am now. *I should have just let him die.*

"You are far too easy," he laughs. "Do you not remember what I told you back in Arterias? In the sparring circle? Control your emotions, or they'll control you."

His voice echoes in my head from all those months ago. *"We have no room for deadly mistakes."*

I slowly slip my fingers under the chain trapping my throat, gasping for air. Attempting to knee him in the ass. "Get…off!"

He lowers his face to mine, staring at me eye to eye. "You have the key. Let me out."

"No!" I gasp.

"Then I'll just kill you," he says rather plainly.

"You won't," I croak. "Your *sweet*, tender *heart* wouldn't do that to me."

Something dark flashes in his eyes, and his jaw twitches.

"You know I'm your best chance at being free," I spit. "You help me, I help you. You kill me, you lose any chance of seeing your sister again."

Not to mention, I imagine he knows what the ring might mean. If he kills me, he kills King Aaric. And while I'm not privy to his relationship with his grandfather, I imagine that domino effect isn't something he's hoping for.

He growls, and with his fist tangled in my hair, he wrenches my head to the left, pinning the side of my face against the floor. I stare at the blanket spilling over the bed onto the floorboards stretching out to meet me.

A small smile stretches across my lips after a few breaths—*I'm right*. "You won't kill me, because you can't…can you?"

I fight against the pain screaming in my scalp as I pull against his grip to look him in the eye with defiance, my lips trembling as I clench my teeth under the searing pain. My entire vision is filled with his raging, forest-green eyes excavating every fear from my body. A seething, breathing nightmare.

He pushes off me, recognizing the truth of my statement and deciding better of it. All at once, the pressure in my scalp and on my throat from his chain, disappears.

He snags the nightgown off the ground and chucks it at me. "Put your godsdamned clothes back on and get your fucking ass back in bed before I change my mind."

"Pull a stunt like that one more time…" I rise to my feet, clearing my throat from the soreness wrapping around it. "…and I'll stab you in the fucking chest."

But at least now I know with absolute certainty Darian doesn't want to kill me. Or, at least, he has reasons not to. Reasons that far outweigh whatever he feels toward me. I only need to figure out what those reasons specifically are, and how I can use them to my advantage.

I'll break him.

I'll find out the secrets of King Aaric and take him down.

Even if it's the last thing I do.

TWENTY

I wake to the sound of raindrops pattering against the ceiling, rushing in a calm atmosphere despite Darian clinking in his chains. Yawning, I rise to sit in bed, stretching my arms above my head.

"Lovely. Is this how you always look in the mornings?" Darian taunts.

I haven't even gotten out of bed yet, and he's already at it. Sheepishly, I brush a hand down to flatten my hair and then braid it back. I dress, sheathing my sword and daggers before turning my attention to him. "I'll be back later."

"You're not seriously leaving me here, are you?"

"Thought you might want to stay out of the rain."

"So thoughtful, however I don't mind getting *wet,*" he slows on the last word.

I pause. If I leave him here unattended, I'm not worried he'll escape. But it leaves open the possibility of someone else slipping into my room and taking him. Or killing him. The fact of the matter is I need to have an eye on him or someone I trust to keep an eye on him.

"Fine." I unhook the long chain attaching his restraints to the metal loop in the wall, then lead him out of the room with it like it's a leash.

All of Midkeep is washed in gray and blue hues with raindrops ricocheting off the ground. The rain immediately soaks our clothes and hair. Squinting through the rain, we break out into a fast walk and wind down the streets to get to the community hall. We rush inside, the room warm with candlelight and a roaring fire in the grand hearth. Long tables lined with food and drink stretch out before us, and a dull buzz of conversation fills the room. The chatter dies out as everyone turns to face us. I recognize Archie sitting with Melaina, Gavin, Nolan, and Marge. But no Cole.

Water drips from my forehead down my cheeks and throat, and I swipe away the drops trickling into my eyes.

"Good morning," Sethan rumbles, standing from his place near the fire. "Come. Sit. We have things to discuss." He tosses a look at the guards standing near the wall.

They swoop in and take Darian's chains from me, leading him away to the table with the other Arterians. I shrug my cloak off and afford one last glance at Darian, who's being passed off to Melaina.

"He'll be fine. Sit," Sethan commands.

I take a seat next to Sethan, and someone pushes a plate of food in front of me. The fire at my back already warms my clothes.

Sethan watches me curiously. "We meant to start our travels today, but seeing as it's raining, it might be best to wait until the storm clears. In the meantime, we've been preparing the horses for those without dragons."

I cough, nearly spitting my water out. "Horses? Wouldn't the dragons be…I don't know, tempted to eat them?"

"Wild dragons, perhaps. Are you concerned about the mental restraint of your own dragon? That might need to be something you work on."

"She's perfectly capable of restraining herself, thank you."

He shrugs. "She's quite young—technically still a hatchling.

Besides, our dragons don't have to worry about their next meals. Here in the Dragon Lands, we have built dragon feed farmers into our society."

"Sounds like a lucrative business," I say as I pop a piece of cheese into my mouth.

"The older your dragon gets, the less they must eat. So not really, no. A'nala eats maybe once every few months."

Now that I think about it, when was the last time Daeja ate?

"A few minutes ago."

I really need to practice when to share my thoughts with her. *"And what exactly did you eat?"*

"Nothing that concerns you," she rumbles.

"You also need to work on that," Sethan interrupts.

"What's that?"

"You're quite obvious when you're speaking to her. You need to practice masking your features, otherwise others will know when you're talking. Especially if we are to ever run into trouble with rebels or Arterians."

Suppose I'll add it to the list of things I need to practice.

"There was one other thing I wanted to show you…" Sethan stands, offering a hand to help me to my feet. "Follow me."

I ignore his offer, standing on my own, and he leads me out of the community hall back into the rain and to another building a few blocks over. Swinging open the door for me, he ushers me inside. After a few blinks, my eyesight adjusts to the dim, cloudy light creeping through the windows. Boxes and heaps of items occupy the room in tidy, well-maintained lines.

"Storage," Sethan answers before I ask, and strides over to the back corner.

I follow him, glancing at the items around us as I pass them: black leathers, swords, daggers, maces, and axes. Crates of what looks like fruit. Stacks of folded blankets and pillows.

"Here," Sethan calls, tracing a hand over a black-as-midnight item resting on a table tucked back against the farthest wall. As I approach, I make out the curves, lines, and pair of horns at the top of it. Two straps hang down from the item, the bottoms ending in loops. *A saddle?* I brush one of the horns, the leather cracked and worn, yet smooth.

Sethan mumbles, "Cole requested a saddle for you, but don't tell him I told you. He asked me not to mention his name."

I flick my gaze to him. *Cole?*

Sethan turns his attention back to the saddle. "Funny enough, we kept this one for years. I wasn't sure why the elders demanded we keep it. But by the stars—this saddle was meant for you. Because it was Cyrus's."

I'm speechless. Unsure what to say. "He…was a dragon rider, as well?"

"No. While he seemed naturally drawn to the dragons, he never bonded one. This was a horse saddle, but we reconfigured it to fit your dragon. Though, I imagine we may need to adjust it as she grows. There's no telling how big she'll get, considering how large she already is for her age." He pats the saddle as if it's an old-time friend. "It'll make the journey much more comfortable. You're one of us, now."

Sethan and I return to the community hall, and I scan the crowd for Cole but fail to find him. I head straight to Archie, who uses a knife to expertly carve into an apple. When I stop a few feet behind him, I smile. He's carving a rose into the apple of all things.

"Hey, do you have a moment?" I ask, resting a hand on his shoulder.

He turns, his brown eyes bright with joy and teeth flashing. "Absolutely."

He flicks his attention over to Melaina a few seats down deep in conversation, whistles at her, and tosses her the apple. She catches it, and glances down at it in confusion as Archie pushes up from his chair and walks away from the table with me. A wide smile warms her cheeks.

As soon as we are out of earshot, I turn to Archie. "Have you seen Cole?"

Archie tilts his head, recognizing the worry in my voice, before answering easily, "He's probably off in the forest somewhere near the river."

"Doing…?"

Archie blinks and shrugs. "I don't know what he usually does out there. In Arterias, he would always slip off when it was raining and be gone for a few hours. I followed him one time, and he just sat at the river. Staring…" He frowns. "You know, I don't know what his fascination with the rain is. Did you not get much rain in Padmoor?"

"Umm…yes? During the winter and spring seasons but…"

I can't put my finger on it—Cole hates the rain. He detests the way his hair clings to his skin when it's wet. Loathes how his clothes would rub him raw, and despises how a drizzle can fog over an otherwise perfectly sunny day. He *hates* rain.

"I'm going to go check on him," I excuse myself.

Archie shakes his head. "No need. He always asks to not be bothered."

"Well, I'm his sister. So, I'll be bothering him."

Before Archie can argue, I slip out of the hall into the rain-slicked town and head into the forest toward the river. The deeper I go, the more the hazy drizzle washes out the environment, to the point I can't see more than fifteen feet in front of me. I follow the sound of the river until it grows louder, and I spot Cole. He sits with his back facing me, his head low. As I draw closer, his legs are bent up, head resting in his arms crossed over his knees. His face hidden from view.

"Careful," Daeja warns, and I glance around the forest, expecting to see her but not finding her. ***"I checked on him earlier. He asked to not be bothered."***

"You didn't tell me he was out here alone?"

She grumbles, trying to form a response, before finally saying, ***"I was keeping a close eye on him from afar. I didn't want to be in the middle."***

I pause, frozen a few footsteps away from Cole. *How is he not freezing his ass off out here?* Something about this feels personal and vulnerable. Something I'm not supposed to see. But the thought of leaving him out here, alone in the freezing rain…

I rest my fingertips on his shoulder. "Cole?"

He flinches, whipping toward me. "Kat? What are you doing here?"

I settle myself next to him, the rain splattering against us. He shrugs out of his jacket and holds it over my head.

I duck underneath it, glancing his way. "Thanks. I…"

My voice drops off when I observe his face. Strips of his muddied red hair hug his angled features. The rain slicks off his strong nose, off his bearded chin and down his corded throat. His lashes drip, his hazel eyes the only warmth in the blue-hued environment. Like the sun on a rainy day. And yet…a sadness lingers within them. A depth of longing and swirling agony. And just like that, I already know I'm the reason why.

"What?" he mutters, blinking rapidly and turning his face away from me, still holding his jacket over me to shield me from the rain.

I tilt my head to the side, trying to get a better look at his face. It looks like it wasn't the rain wetting his cheeks and reddening his nose and eyes.

"Look at me," I whisper.

The rain picks up in speed, hissing on the ground. He hesitates and slowly draws his face back to mine.

"What are you doing out here? You…" I sigh. "You hate the rain?"

His throat bobs as he swallows. "I do."

"Then why are you out here?"

"Because I hate the rain."

"I…I'm not following."

He takes a deep inhale through his nose, allowing the jacket to rest on my head as he folds his hands into his lap. His angled brows lower over his lashes as he stares at his scarred fingers.

"I…" he laughs, though it doesn't lessen the anguish in his face. "It sounds stupid. I could tear myself apart for you. But no matter how hard I might try, I can't seem to tear myself away from you."

I knit my eyebrows, still confused.

He tosses a glance my way, recognizes my confusion, and continues, "Every time it rained after I thought you died back in Padmoor, I was haunted by the memories of you. Of our first—"

"Dance," I breathe, realization flooding me.

We got caught in the Northern Forest in a torrential downpour years ago. Stuck with nothing but each other. He pulled me into his arms to warm me, and one thing after the next, we transformed into slow dancing as the rain sang a beat against the forest floor. Gods, it was…it was the most romantic moment I'd ever had in my life. Despite it being so fleeting anyone else would have thought that we were gods-damned crazy.

He nods, a small smile splitting his sad features. But the smile fades as quick as it appears. "And after you died, I'd return to the forest every time it rained. I'd sit at the river and think of you. I'd reflect on every last breath I shared with you. Every smile, every laugh, every kiss, and every touch. When I returned to the outpost, they never asked questions."

Because when they looked at him—wet cheeks, runny nose, and reddened eyes—they might have thought it was from the rain. Not from tears.

He continues, "I had to hide my agony from losing you because I had to lead this squad. They couldn't possibly know how much I was struggling. I hated the rain before I met you. But as I got to know you…as I fell in love with you…I began to love it. No matter how much it hurt me when you were gone. Because this is what I could have of you." He motions out to the hazy forest. "The color of your eyes when you wore gray. I could sit and remember our times together for hours and not be disturbed. It was the closest I could feel to you… even if you were gone."

Pulling a silent breath between my lips, I watch the rain streaming down his brow, his sharp cheekbones, his jaw. I reach out, rest a hand on his, and pull his attention lost on the river back to me.

"You're engaged," I remind him softly, nodding my head like it'll also convince me our story is over. "Celeste is a lovely woman, and you're promised to her."

His jaw flexes, holding me in his gaze with a sincerity that stabs me in the chest. "I made that promise before I knew you were alive."

"It doesn't void it. Your word is your word—"

"My word means *nothing* if it's not for you." He huffs, searching my eyes. "I tried. I drafted hundreds of letters to her, trying to find the right words to express I could no longer marry her. And all I could write was I was meant for someone else. I was meant for *you*. Marrying her would only hurt her. She deserves someone who will love her with everything they have. And I have nothing to give her. All I have left is blood and banes. Because every breath, beat, and part of what makes me, me, has already been given to you."

"Cole…"

He shakes his head, his voice growing taut. "No. Don't…please don't say anything more. Not in that tone. Not unless you're saying you're still in love with me."

I rub a thumb against the back of his hand; my throat constricts, overwhelmed by emotion. I have to break eye contact, looking down at our hands so I can force out the next words. "Maybe you need to let me go. Maybe you shouldn't love me."

He looks up at the sky before squeezing his eyes shut. The downpour splatters against his face, rivers of water streaming down his cheeks. "I'll be able to stop the rain…" he turns to look at me, tears slipping from his eyes, "…before I can stop loving you."

My heart crumples with the tormented gentleness of his gaze. Gods, how much easier it would be if he stopped looking at me like that. If he stopped these confessions. It's only making things harder. Painful.

He clears his throat. "I'm sorry…I don't know how to fix this thing between us…" He sweeps the strands out of his face as he rakes his fingers through the crown of his head.

He glances over to me, hesitant. "I really am sorry, Katerina Blackwind. For everything." He presses a quick kiss to my forehead, then leaves.

"Again," Marge barks.

Groaning, I lift my head up to look her in the eyes and squint through the soft rain. "It's not working."

Every inch of my clothes clings to my frame, hanging on me like a cold, wet blanket. I can't fight against the shivering or chattering of my teeth, and seeing how unbothered Marge is grows my frustration. We've been out here for hours in the middle of the night. When I mentioned practicing in something a little more sheltered like her room, she shut me down, claiming I wasn't quite experienced enough to pull that far away from the ley lines. And right here, near the river, is where the magic is strongest.

"You're not trying hard enough," Marge retorts.

"Are you trying to piss me off?"

She splays an open hand to her side and sweeps it around the forest surrounding us. "If that's what it's going to take."

I hang my head, far too exhausted to argue or fight with her. Every time I've pressed my palms to the earth, I've tried again and again to pull magic toward me. But it's like trying to pluck a single, specific strand of hair from a horse's tail. As it's fucking running away from me.

My breath saws in and out of my parted mouth, clouding with the cold, wet winter air. "I'm done."

"No, you're not."

That gains her another glare.

She has the unwavering confidence to stare back and taps the end of her staff underneath my chin until I've stretched my head back as far as it'll go. "Close your eyes. Focus on shutting out your vision first."

Rain smatters against my face, and I squeeze my eyes shut.

"Next, center your breathing. Count to ten if you have to, but slow your heart rate."

I shake my head with my eyes still closed. "This is stupid."

She smacks the side of my arm with her staff.

"Ouch!" I hiss but take her warning and still myself. With my eyes closed, I follow the ins and outs of my breath until it slows down my racing frustration.

"Now…" she whispers, her voice lowering closer to me. "Close off what you're feeling. Let the rain fall away, and the coldness seeping into your bones disappear."

Bit by bit, I let go of the sensations crowding in for my attention. Gone is the frigid damp hugging every angle of my body. The sporadic pattern of rain on my face becomes nonexistent.

"Good…" Marge's voice is only loud enough for me to discern from the hiss of rain on the forest floor. "Now focus everything onto that energy and pull it like you're stitching. Take it slow, deliberate, and steady. You are the needle, and you make the path. The magic is your thread to make do with what you wish. Find the confidence in yourself."

Nodding slowly, her voice and the sounds of the rain fade away and are replaced by a calm, harmonious humming. I sag my head and shift my weight back into my hips until I'm sitting on my folded knees. Spreading my fingers wider to call it to me, I gradually drag my hands across the wet earth to me, inch by slow inch.

Something heavy and magnetic underneath the surface moves with me, slipping a little more to my command the more intentional I am. As I pull my grip closer to my knees, I lift my stretched hands starting with my palms, waiting for the magic beneath to follow my lead. When it reluctantly does, I open my eyes and pull my fingers up off the ground by an inch. A soft, wisp of blue dances underneath my hand, completely independent of the rain and pools of water surrounding the tiny flame.

My chest heaves with each breath that passes as I hold the pulled magic, and as I glance up at Marge, the flame slips and disappears back into the earth. I let my head fall back with a frustrated sigh.

"Why were you looking at me?" Marge jabs. "I'm not going to flatter you. Especially not after it took you hours to do that."

"Of course not," I mumble.

"Because I know you can do better."

I straighten and sweep my heavy, wet hair off my shoulder onto my back. "That was my better. That was in fact, my best."

"I don't believe you."

"Then don't." I push up to my feet. "But I'm exhausted."

She lifts her staff and rests the end of it on my chest. "One more time. That's all I'm asking. One more of your best."

I flick my attention from her staff on my sternum to her, then back again.

She pushes the staff a touch harder into my chest. "King Aaric will stop at nothing to slaughter the dragons and everyone who opposes him here in the Dragon Lands. You are the only person who can take him down. Which means you will be his biggest target. If you don't master this magic, everyone will die. You and Daeja included."

Swatting her staff off me with a grunt, I lower back down to my knees to the temptation of mastering that pure magic. Of touching it again. "Fine. One more time."

TWENTY-ONE

DON'T FORGET TO BREATHE

Tawny smiles at me the next morning. "I will never forget the Arterian who risked her life to set me free. Thank you, Katerina."

She's to stay behind, considering she's the leader of Midkeep. She's needed here, and even though I haven't known her long, I prefer her much more over Sethan. As a going away present, she gifts me a black corset, shaped with water dragon bones that washed up on one of the eastern shores. She assures me the corset will provide enough protection for my ribs, should any blade strike me. That, and she was quite delighted to inform me there are hidden sheaths for daggers. Should I need them.

The rest of the squad and Vitalans gather for our trip.

I nod awkwardly at Tawny. "It was only the right thing to do."

She pulls me into a hug, whispering into my ear, "Remember that."

I blink at her, unsure of the implications, but I don't have much time to consider it as Sethan begins to round up his people and the squad. There are several horse-drawn wagons to store our supplies, along with any others who can't travel as fast on foot. Daeja lowers herself to the ground as I approach her, the tip of her tail twitching in anticipation.

"Nervous?" I ask as I tuck in a stray strand of silvery-blonde hair back into my braids. My body still carries a heavy ache throughout my muscles from spending almost half of last night in the rain practicing pulling magic with Marge.

Daeja snorts at me, the hot steam blowing my hair out of my face as I stop at her side. ***"Never."***

"I know." I smile, patting her neck. She's grown big enough now that I can walk underneath her, with the top of my head brushing the underside of her scaled belly. But despite her size, her exuberant confidence still mirrors her youth. I grab the saddle's foothold and claw myself up her side. Though, she eventually has to nudge me up into my seat with her nose.

Cole strolls over to us, still avoiding eye contact. I tighten a thick, leather belt around my waist, adorned with metal loops sewn into the material. Taking the long leather straps attached to the saddle with hooks on the ends, I secure each one to the loops on my belt.

"Are you all hooked in?" Cole mumbles softly as he stops a few steps away from us.

"I think so?" I shift my hips, settling into a comfortable position and double-checking I've secured all the hooks.

He reaches out a hand, and Daeja shifts subtly away from his touch as he tightens and double-checks each strap. Despite the fact he can't even look me in the eye, he assures himself with each tug on every belt and loop.

"I never said thank you for the saddle," I murmur.

He glances up for a split second before lowering his eyes again with a small nod. Tightening one more strap wrapped behind Daeja's shoulders, he pats her neck.

Her head spins into his direction, her eyes dilating and narrowing as she stares at Cole. ***"Watch yourself,"*** she growls.

"Be safe," he whispers at both of us, before walking off to join the rest of the group traveling by wagon.

"You too…" I mutter, though he's too far away now to have heard me.

Archie helps Marge up into the wagon, and the two of them take a seat next to Melaina. Several other men and women join them, crowding into the back. My attention snags on Darian, still manacled and held between two of Sethan's soldiers. Archie catches my gaze and waves enthusiastically with a toothy smile. With a small chuckle, I wave back at him. Melaina and Marge follow his gaze, dipping their heads at me a little more subtle than the level of Archie's blind enthusiasm.

A heavy thrum of gigantic footsteps approaches behind us, and Daeja's anxiety quivers the bond between us. Though, on the outside, she's completely still with her head held high and staring off at the group. A'nala slides in next to us, her movements heavy but serpentine.

Sethan sits in his saddle, his back straight and eyes set somewhere in the distance before he turns to me. "Ready?"

I have to look up at him to make eye contact. A'nala is close to double the size of Daeja. Rather than airing my anxiety about the thought of flying, I nod. My chest burning as a reminder that I've managed to hold onto a breath, until I release it.

He turns his attention back to that nonexistent spot in the distance. "Let's fly. To the skies and the stars."

A'nala's fiery red jaws part as she bellows, the sound tearing through the forest as she clambers forward, her wings beating hard and carrying her and Sethan up into the sky.

Tilting my chin down in determination, I wrap my hands tighter around the two horns protruding from the top of the saddle. The only thing combating my nervousness about falling are the small metal hooks secured to my belt and tied down to the saddle.

"Don't you trust me?"

"It's not you I don't trust." I blow out a breath and narrow my eyes. *"Let's fly."*

"To the skies and the stars," Daeja mocks Sethan, before she bursts into a run, flapping her wings a bit harder than A'nala had to, until she lifts into the air.

The Arterians crowded in the wagons watch with wide eyes as Daeja and I rise. Their faces and figures fade from view as we lift higher. The ground and trees shrink beneath us, and a cold wind zaps all the warmth from my face. Thank goodness for the extra thick layers of black leather and fabric Tawny gifted me. We rise until the horizon fades off into an unknown distance. We're higher than Daeja and I have ever flown before, and my stomach tightens as I get dizzy. The sky stretches out around us, a limitless blue canvas. Mountains and trees pepper the land as far as the eye can see.

"Don't forget to breathe," Daeja warns.

Sucking in a big inhale, the dizzying sensation lessens. I had indeed forgotten to breathe on the ascension. Glancing down at my aching, sweaty hands clenching the horns, I'm silently thanking Marge for the gloves. Finger by finger, I pull one off at a time, relief springing to my joints and muscles at the release of pressure.

"That's it, good, relax. Let go, I've got you."

Shakily, I release the horns completely but hover my hands an inch out from them, ready to grab them in a split second if I need to. My brain and heart won't listen to the fact that I'm strapped and hooked into the saddle—the only way I can possibly fall is if I unhook myself. But I can't ignore the nervous shake of my hands, the war drum of a beat in my chest, and the sweat dripping down my neck.

Daeja takes a sudden dive, my ass lifting off the seat a few inches, suspended by the hooks latching me in. My stomach drops into my godsdamned toes, and I shriek as I fling myself forward and cling to the saddle horns again for dear life, squeezing my legs and shutting my eyes.

Daeja's body quakes underneath me with unabashed humor.

"Not funny!"

"I thought it was funny."

"If I wasn't hooked into the saddle I would have splattered on the ground by now!"

"Maybe you need to learn to let go and actually trust me," she growls.

"I do trust you. It's just that…"

"What?"

"What if the saddle comes loose? The straps rip? A buckle breaks?"

"You tend to overthink things. The Red One made it pretty clear he triple-checked all those things before we left. I think he might have even done it just to reassure you, because he already checked it on me before you got there. Besides, even if all those things did happen, I would still get you. I would never let you fall."

I hesitate to respond, my mind buzzing from all the uncertainty.

"Don't believe me? Let's test it. Unhook yourself—"

I laugh, the motion trembling in my chest. *"Absolutely not."*

"Prove you can trust me."

"Or prove you can trust me when I say I trust you!"

She grumbles, about ready to bite back with something else when she quiets. She turns her head to the side, eyes fixed blankly in the distance. **"Wait, hold that thought…"**

I follow her gaze. A'nala's red figure glides in and out of the clouds. Six other dragon riders follow close behind her, forming a large V.

"A'nala wants us to join the dragon riders."

"Can you talk to all of them? Even at this distance?"

"Yes. Though, some of the others are harder to understand."

"Why do you say that?"

"Some of them have accents and different tones I'm trying to get used to. The second one on the right behind A'nala slurs his s's a lot. And the third one in the left line doesn't like to speak to me. Actually…I don't think he speaks much at all. A'nala says for me to not bother him."

She veers left, the wind slicing beneath her wings and ripping at my braided hair. I crouch down, pressing myself tighter into her to avoid the wind. Or, at least, that's what I tell myself.

"Tawny mentioned a few days ago about there being other dragon riders, and I've never seen them until today. But…it sounds like you've met them before?"

"Once or twice."

"And you didn't tell me, why?"

"Just as you feel you can handle yourself, I can also handle myself."

"I have decades of life experience over you, though."

"And I can speak with other dragons. You cannot."

"Touché."

"Plus, it's not like you tell me every time you meet someone new."

Daeja flies over to them, eventually joining in the back of the right line. While I've seen birds migrate over the Northern Forest back in Padmoor every winter, seeing dragons fly in such an organized formation was something else. Even one dragon gliding through the sky was majestic. Their heads dipping as the rest of their bodies rolled in rhythm. Their strong muscled shoulders flexing with each flap of their massive wings.

The other dragons within the formation are fairly similar: shades of reds, oranges, and yellows. Horns of different sizes crowd their skulls, spines, and tails. But what really draws my attention are the scars marring each of them. Holes tatter all of their wings, causing a soft whistle as the wind tunnels through them. Sections of scales are shredded with deep scars, the sheen of their bodies dulled by the ragged marks. One of the dragon's horns is broken in half, its wicked edges standing proud from its head. Another dragon has a chunk missing out of the top of its tail.

"You're staring. Even I can feel it."

"Sorry." I duck my head, focusing instead on the expanse of sky ahead. I can't look down. Because if I look down, my queasiness will

resurface as fast as the blink of an eye. At least admiring and watching the other dragons distracted me for a split second.

"A'nala wants us at the front with her and Sethan," Daeja explains before she cuts around the line of dragons we were following. She pumps her wings harder to pass the other dragons, each flap draining more of her energy. The dragons likely have years of experience over her—she's still only a baby. Their wings are almost double in size.

The group must notice or words are exchanged, because one by one the dragons slow to a glide, allowing Daeja to advance forward. I glance sideways at the other dragons and riders we pass, dipping my head awkwardly as they glance our way. We make it to the front of the formation, and A'nala's yellow eyes shift over to us lazily before refocusing on the path ahead. Sethan turns his head to me as we level out beside them.

He points at me, then holds up one finger, and taps his head. *My first lesson.*

He takes his hands off the saddle horns, unhooks the metal attached to his waist belt, and pushes up off the saddle through his feet in the stirrups. He stands with his hands held out open and to the side, tilting his head back and allowing the wind to whistle over his face, his eyes closed and face relaxed.

He makes it look so damn easy.

I scan A'nala, the positioning of Sethan's feet in the stirrups, his lonely saddle horns, and the hooked straps fluttering freely in the wind.

He turns to me with a challenge in his eyes, dipping his head in encouragement. Oh, *hells* no.

"You'll be fine. You've ridden me plenty of times before without a saddle and hooks."

"Yes, but we weren't even above the treeline! We had a lake beneath us whenever I did fall. And not to mention, we've never flown at this speed—"

Sethan shouts something inaudible and flips me a middle finger.

Ex-*fucking*-cuse me?

He must see the shock and annoyance wash over my features because he shakes his head vigorously and points at the base of his middle finger.

Ohhh. I flick my attention down to my gloved hands. Despite the dark tattoo of a ring around my finger being covered, I understand it all the same. Daeja won't let me die. And it isn't because our lives are interconnected. But because she genuinely wants me to live—I'm her family, just as much as she is mine.

"Take it at your pace. You don't have to do it all at once," Daeja murmurs. **"You don't even have to do it at all, if you don't want to."**

Pulling a breath into my lungs, I root myself in determination. Shifting my weight into my heels as I unlatch one finger at a time from the horns, the tension collected in my joints nearly snaps as I let go. I toss a sideways glance at Sethan. He's seated back in his saddle, though I don't fail to notice the hooks still aren't secured to his waist band.

He nods, on the brink of disappointment as I stop moving. With another quick breath and shaking hands, I unhook one of the straps on my thick leather belt. Another glance at Sethan, and he gestures, implying his waning patience.

"You're doing great," Daeja whispers, sensing my new spike of nervousness.

As my fingers brush the second hook to undo it, A'nala dives straight into us. Her body slams into Daeja's, and Daeja tucks her wings to cut away from her. The sudden motion throws me clear off the saddle as I pathetically scramble for something to hold onto. Each swipe for a horn, strap—*something*—slips. I slide down and off the saddle and slam into Daeja's shoulder.

Upside.

Fucking.

Down.

I have absolutely nowhere else to look but at the ground. The forest is but a splotch of various shades of greens far below, and a thin blue river snakes through the valley. I swear the one single strap holding me from falling to my death rips slightly, and I slip an inch down. Drawing out my inevitable demise.

"Can you get back up into the saddle?"

I squeeze my eyes shut, my heart in my throat as I fumble for the one lifeline holding me to the saddle. But even trying to pull myself up is useless. *"What the fuck was that?"*

"Apparently A'nala and Sethan were getting impatient. I'm sorry!"

"I can't even get back up!" Panic creeps underneath my skin. My head is heavy and tingling with all the blood rushing to it, a heavy constriction of terror gripping my chest in a vice.

"Unhook yourself!"

"Are you out of your godsdamned mind?"

"Do it!" she roars.

I open my eyes, my vision beginning to blur and blacken. The landscape below begins to fade in and out of view. Fuck. My head pounds, drowning out any reasonable line of thinking.

"Trust in me!"

I suppose it makes no difference if I die hanging upside down from Daeja or splattered on the ground far below. As a last-ditch effort, I heave myself up, fighting gravity itself as I grip the strap with one hand. With all my lasting strength, I push down the locking mechanism with my other hand and release the hook. My stomach recoils as I slip from the one thing holding me to Daeja.

And free-fall.

TWENTY-TWO

A LESSON IN FREE-FALLING

Daeja's black figure shrinks at an alarming pace, along with the rest of the dragons and their riders. The wind whistles around me, ripping an endless scream from my throat. As I fall, my stomach is somewhere between two feet and two miles above me. The speed of my descent forces my eyes closed, the muscles in my body bracing for the eventual impact. The wind and terror drown out my every sense.

And when I have nothing left…I surrender to the fear.

Something snags me, snapping me out of the air. My eyes flash open, my head whipping back violently at the sudden stop, causing a screaming pain to flare in my neck. Black as shadow, swift as the night, Daeja has me clutched in her claws, her thick talons piercing my cloak and shirt, the tips having scraped my chest.

She caught me.

"I want down…I want down, I want down, I want down!"

"Understood," she says gently.

I hang pathetically from her claws, clenching my fists into my shirt to give me some sort of control. She pulls me closer to her dipped head, gently picking the fabric of my clothes between her daggered teeth and transferring me from her talons to her jaws. Twisting her neck, she places me back on the saddle.

My hands and entire body tremble as I latch the hooks onto my belt, before lowering my head and keeping my eyes shut. Every nerve and muscle in my body screams and swirls, my heart threatening to burst out of my chest.

I don't know how long it takes until we land back in the forest. But as soon as we do, I rip the hooks off my belt and jump off Daeja's back, folding to my knees onto the ground and brushing my hands over it. Reminding myself how much I love being on the ground, with the earth steady underneath my feet.

A'nala and Sethan land seconds afterward, the ground thundering underneath her heavy landing, and my hair swirling with the gusts. I whip a glare at Sethan as I stand, and he waves at the rest of the dragon riders above us to land further away.

I stomp toward him, anger bubbling in my veins and likely the only thing keeping me going at this point. "What in the fuck was that! Were you trying to fucking kill me?"

A'nala snakes her head toward me, her lips curling up in warning and revealing her yellow-stained teeth as I approach. Daeja shifts close behind me, her own anxiousness wafting over me as she shadows me, her eyes trained on A'nala as she growls. As soon as I'm within reach, I shove Sethan's chest. A'nala lunges forward, snapping at the air inches from my forehead. Daeja lurches, snapping back at A'nala despite being half her size.

A'nala's mouth parts, a deep rumbling hiss emitting from her throat. Strings of saliva drip from the top of her rows of teeth. Her hot, rancid breath washes over us. And those golden eyes narrow to slits.

Sethan whips a wordless look at A'nala. She shifts back a few paces, closing her mouth, slitted eyes still locked on Daeja.

Sethan holds out a hand to me. "Calm down. Did you forget you and I forged a blood pact?"

I'm two steps away from him, my body shaking as if I were freezing. "So what? I die and it takes you out for breaking your oath, but it also kills the King. The Vitalans win. Seems easy enough of a solution to me."

"If I truly thought that, then you would have been dead long before you made it to the Dragon Lands. I don't think the prophecy meant something as simple as killing you. In doing so, it would kill your dragon."

Great, so he's keeping me alive for Daeja. I flip my ring finger up, partly wishing I had placed Cole's ring on my middle finger instead. "So, you've known about this ring linking me to him, all this time, haven't you?"

"Yes," he answers flatly.

"Who else knows?" I lower my hand to my side.

"Most of those here in the Dragon Lands have heard of the rings from their grandparents' generation. But it's impossible to know how many might glimpse it and know what it actually is. No one has seen it in well over a century. And it looks as simple as any other metal ring but with imperfections that may come across as the workings of a juvenile jewelist, rather than an ancient artifact."

"And so the only reason you aren't killing me is Daeja?"

"Told you I was scary," Daeja purrs in my mind.

I toss her a glance, the wind whistling over her tail as she swishes it back and forth with her white, narrowed eyes still fixed on A'nala.

"She's the only moon dragon to ever inhabit this earth in over a century. The Gods wouldn't put her here if they wanted her to live a short while. Besides, I think…" Sethan laughs, shaking his head and dragging a hand over his face.

"What? What's so fucking funny to you?" I growl. "You asked me to trust you, and then you pull some bullshit like that!" I flick my hand up to the sky.

He turns a heavy stare onto me and sighs. "It's foolish, really.

But I think the Gods intend for you to lead. For you to rule over all the lands."

My mouth drops open, completely gobsmacked out of my anger for a split second before I shake off my expression.

He clears his throat and the half-hearted humor from earlier. "So, if that's their plan, who am I to interfere? In fact, they might smite me if I don't do what it takes to keep you safe—to keep you on track for that destiny. And despite how much I may detest the thought of the kingdom falling to their knees for such a young, incompetent woman—"

I narrow my eyes.

"—if my daughter believes in you, then so shall I. Many of the other rebels may not agree, but I've been chosen to govern this realm, and I will spend my last breath protecting these people. Which means, in exchange, I must protect you."

"By letting me fall out of the fucking sky?" I flick my hand back up toward the heavens.

"Once you lose your fear of falling is when you will really learn how to fly."

I glower at him. Sounds like some roundabout bullshit way to inspire me. But I'm still seeing red and struggling to push down the trembles snaking up and down my spine.

"You need to trust her," he says gently, his expression softening slightly.

"I do trust her—"

"No. No, you don't. I don't mean to be crude, but you looked like you were going to shit yourself up there. And that was when you were still hooked in *and* had your hands wrapped around the horns."

I open my mouth to respond, but nothing comes out.

He holds out a hand as if to calm me. "It's alright. We all start off that way. Us humans have a preference for our feet on the ground. Just as the dragons have their preference to take to the skies. The beauty of our bonds is that we work as a team, each trusting the other for our own strengths. Together, we make something formidable. We start training all our dragon riders this way, and you aren't an exception. Once you learn to fully trust her—to fully let go—you'll be able to actually fly. Now, we are but a short flight away from Driftmond—"

"Flight? Ha. Suppose we'll walk, then," I state. My stomach flips and churns at the thought of being any more than two feet off the ground. There's no way I'll be flying again anytime soon.

"You can't walk. If you two stay down here, people will get suspicious about a lone black dragon with a rider. You'll have no one to defend you against any Vitalan rebels if they're lurking around Driftmond."

"Then I suppose we can take our chances, huh?"

"You're being ridiculous. You don't even know what Vitalan rebels are capable of."

"You just said it yourself. If there are rebels lurking about Driftmond, who's to say they won't attack even if I stay with you and the other dragon riders?"

"Because I'm a symbol for peace and for the good of Vitalans. There's a percentage of the population that opposes my rule, but most people are cowards. Us dragon riders go by 'dragons of a scale' instead of 'birds of a feather,' because we have strength in numbers. They won't strike if they have the disadvantage. The rebels here are quiet, working within the shadows. If you stay here by yourself, you're out of my protection and an easy target."

"Tell him I said if anyone threatens your life, they'll be the ones needing protection," Daeja grumbles.

A'nala hisses at her, and Daeja snaps at the air in defiance.

"We can manage on our own," I retort.

Sethan stares at me, waiting for me to falter, before finally dipping his head and mounting A'nala. "So be it."

A'nala and him take off into the sky again, her flapping wings stirring the pine needles and grasses around us. I turn to Daeja, her white eyes dilating as I stretch my hand up to scratch her under the chin.

"I'm sorry. I didn't intend to throw you off, but A'nala cut into me—"

"Don't be." I smile. *"I know it wasn't you. Thank you for catching me."*

I know she hadn't had any ill intent. Sethan was just forcing my hand over what he thought was necessary. If I'm pissed at anyone, it's him. She bumps her forehead to mine, and even though she means to do it gently, I stumble back a step.

"Always," she purrs.

After patting her cheek, I throw myself up and over her into the saddle. As Daeja lifts onto her four legs and begins to stalk through the forest, I glance up to the sky above the treeline. The other dragons and their riders join back into formation with A'nala at the front. The seven dragons shrink to spots of red in the vast blue sky.

My eyes narrow.

I latch the hooks back onto my belt, wrapping my hands around the saddle horns until my knuckles groan in withered protest. My stomach churns at the thought of lifting off the ground. The vision of falling flashes in my head in short, terrifying spurts. A dizziness swims in my skull, and I begin to slouch to the side, trying to fight my body's responsiveness by closing my eyes.

I rip the hooks back off my belt, half-sliding, half-falling off the saddle and collapse to my hands and knees. A bitter heat creeps up my throat and out of my mouth as I vomit bits of my breakfast and bile several times over. Something whizzes nearby. As I lift my head up, I swear I see a flicker of shadows through the distant trees. A glimmer of sunlight on metal flashes for a split second between the trees before it's gone.

Daeja nuzzles my back, her exhalation billowing in my hair. **"If you'd prefer, you can take your own two legs."**

"No." I wipe my hand across my mouth, eyes still fixed on the spot where I thought I saw something. *"Fuck it. If Sethan doesn't believe I trust you, I'll show him he's wrong."*

Daeja lifts her head, stilling as she scans the forest. ***"Did you hear that?"***

I slowly rise. *"No, did you hear something?"*

She tilts her head to the side, unblinking, her wings unfolding out to the side. Something like a branch snaps, and we whirl to the left. The horns on Daeja's head and neck bristle, her lips peeling up into a growl. I reach up onto the saddle and pull out my sword from its sheath and turn to face the sound as Daeja curls her body in front of me. Approaching footsteps whisper in the undergrowth.

"Get on my back. And don't you dare argue."

"What if it's someone from our group walking ahead of the wagons?"

"It's not. Whoever this is has an odd scent I don't recognize."

Sheathing the sword, I climb onto her back, feeling even weaker than before now that I'd dumped everything in my stomach out onto the forest floor. Fastening the hooks once more to my belt, I scan the trees around us. For any movement. For any of those stray rebels Sethan threatened might be out here.

A masked figure slinks through the shadows, and that glimmer of metal in the sunlight flashes again. Daeja growls harder, her wings extending out to her sides.

Slink. Something slices through the air toward us.

"Get down!" Daeja roars and drops to the ground.

I fling myself forward, flattening myself to her spine as something whizzes behind my back. Daeja jumps to her feet, and I rock forward as I glance at the masked person. The glimmer isn't from a blade. It's metal-tipped arrows in a quiver. The masked person pulls back a newly notched arrow. More shimmering metal sparks throughout the forest behind them, with shadows crawling out of the underbrush.

"Daeja, get up! Go, fly!" I wrap my fingers around the saddle horns, ignoring my brain and nerves screaming at me to get the fuck off.

She clambers forward, and I keep my head down as I work through each roll of her body threatening to dismount me.

"Hold tight!" She launches into the air and ascends at an angle which tips my stomach back out of my body.

I squeeze my eyes shut, hanging onto her for dear life as I'm shifted back a few inches in the seat, suspended by my belt. Wind whips at my face, pulling at my cheeks. When I peek open my eyes to see how far we've risen, the masked person watches us below with a cold threat in their eyes. More shadowy figures slink out from the forest behind them.

TWENTY-THREE

HYDRA'S KEEP

Holy hells if this ride isn't the most difficult one I've had yet. After we've put a healthy distance between us and the masked person, Daeja slows to a rhythm of flapping only enough to keep her at a glide.

"Are you alright?" she asks.

"Mmhmm," I answer with my eyes closed while I focus on settling my racing thoughts and queasiness. Each breath I pull in through my nose and push out through pursed lips.

"Let's ummm…not tell A'nala and Sethan they might have been right?"

"Agreed."

When we land, my entire body aches from all the built-up tension. I slide off Daeja, rolling my head and shoulders. The other dragon riders dip their heads at Daeja and me as we stride toward them, and Sethan turns his attention to me. They've stopped on a hillside overlooking a town bustling with people throughout the cobblestone streets. Rows and rows of buildings with angled, brown wooden roofs stretch into the sky. I glance behind my shoulder like the masked person might show at any second.

"Welcome to Driftmond." Sethan motions toward the town. "Considering rebels can be hiding anywhere in the Dragon Lands, I suggest you keep quiet and to yourself. Do not speak of the ring, nor the King. The rest of our people should be showing up soon. We flew slow and looped around so they weren't too far behind. In the meantime, we owe you a drink. Come."

The thought of anything in my stomach makes me cringe. But I push it away, unwilling to admit my mental, emotional, and physical state to Sethan. He and the other dragon riders lead us to one of the buildings on the outskirts of Driftmond, with a wooden sign hanging above the door that says *Hydra's Keep*. One of the male dragon riders swings the thick wooden door open, and cheery bubbling conversations spill out, followed by music.

I smile. I'd heard a fiddle once before in Padmoor when a musician was traveling through to get to Groveden. Cole took me by the hand and at the time, we were only friends. But the way he spun me about, out in the sunny crowded streets while passersby glared, I knew he'd become so much more than a friend. I think that moment was when I first fell in love with him.

Sethan tosses a silent look to A'nala, and she folds her wings at her sides, then leans hard into Daeja, herding her away toward the back side of the building. The other dragons follow suit, disappearing around the corner. I'm really missing the days when she was small enough to fit inside a door.

We humans pile into the crowded tavern, torches lining the walls and bustling with loud patrons. Despite the fact I'm still wearing the black leather gloves Marge gave me, I slide my hands into the pockets of my winter jacket and scan every person we pass. My mind wanders to the thought of how many of these people might try to kill me if they knew I wore the Blood Ring. Sethan leads us into the farthest corner, and a group of people settled at the table quickly rise once they see who's approaching them. They dip their heads and motion to their table before disappearing into the throng.

I suppose being the leader of the Vitalans has its perks.

One of the dragon riders breaks off from our group to the bar. Sethan has me sit nearest the window in the farthest corner of the room and takes a seat next to me, his shoulders facing the tavern door. It doesn't surprise me when I see a flicker of movement outside the window and spot Daeja settling herself on the other side like my own personal guard dog.

"They should have installed a drawbridge here," she calls.

"That's never stopped you," I chuckle.

She wiggles her body, tucking her front legs under herself. A'nala sits next to her with her head held high. Daeja's tail slides back and forth on the ground, knocking into A'nala's tail repeatedly. The red she-dragon bares her teeth at Daeja, and Daeja opens her own jaws. A'nala mirrors it, and they both clash into what can only be described as sparring with their jaws and teeth as the other dragons watch.

"Relax. A'nala won't draw blood if she has to put Daeja in her place," Sethan says as a stein slides in front of me.

I catch it with my left hand before it can tip over and spill. I lift the heavy mug and take a sip before grimacing. "Her *place*?"

"Don't forget, she's still a juvenile with much to learn. Dragons tend to work in hierarchies, similar to wolves."

I glance outside, and A'nala snorts at Daeja, the two of them concluding the sparring and settling back down. The other dragon riders sitting at the table with us dive into their own side conversations. Four of them are men, two are women. All are at least in their forties.

I clear my throat to distract myself from the bitter taste of the ale and ask, "You mentioned earlier training all of your dragon riders… as if there's some formal process?"

Sethan takes a sip of his own drink. "Yes, we have an academy for dragon riders in the northwestern part of the continent."

"So…it's not just the seven of you?"

"No. Many have gone through the academy. Though, our numbers have dwindled significantly since Cyrus's death."

"Why?"

"He led the academy. And while he never had a dragon of his own, he trained all the cadets in how to bond them. After he died, no one was able to train cadets as well as he had. And since we lost the lesser rings when King Aaric took the throne, people have become less inclined to become dragon riders."

I glance sideways at him. "What lesser rings?"

Sethan sighs, but when we make eye contact his exasperation wanes. "Lesser rings were created to manipulate dragons' magic by their bonded riders. Back before Aaric ruled, if you graduated from the academy within the top ten percent of your class, you'd be immediately placed in a position of whatever field you were studying. The leaders of those fields were ones who bore lesser rings. But Aaric destroyed all of them in the Great War, and the dragon riders who wore them. Nobody knows how to remake them."

"So, if lesser rings manipulated a dragons' magic, you could essentially control dragonfire? Just like how the Blood—"

He gives me a look and I fall silent before I finish my sentence. *Right.* No need to mention the Blood Ring in such a public place. Even if the chatter is a dull roar, with music tinging, and the patrons' eyes are everywhere but us.

"Exactly," he whispers. "So, for example, A'nala's a typical fire dragon. She can produce flames and sustain dangerously hot temperatures. She'd be able to bask in a volcano if she was so inclined. But if I had a lesser ring, I'd be able to do those same things using her magic as a source, rather than conjuring it up myself from the ley lines like the one you have. One of the other fire dragons in our group used to be able to lift earthly matter. But…he's getting quite close to retirement. I don't think he'd be able to lift more than a stone the size of your palm."

"Would that mean his rider, if they were wearing a lesser ring, also couldn't lift more than a stone? Even if the rider is much younger and stronger than their dragon counterpart?"

"In theory, yes. Because a dragon's magic isn't infinite. Which is why the lesser rings are called that specifically—"

A flash of silver slices through the air between Sethan and me then sinks into the wall behind us. Sethan grabs the back of my jacket and throws me to the ground, knocking the stein clear out of my hand. I land sideways on the ground as beer streams off the table and pelts me in the side. The otherwise normal buzzing of conversation turns into a tense clamoring of panicked shouts. The music cuts.

"Get down!" Sethan snaps, hunching his body over me protectively.

The boots of the dragon riders sitting on the other side of our table rush into the crowd, and the smashing of glass explodes over the chaos, showering remnants of the window over the nearest bodies. Daeja's roar combines with several others, all differing in timbres and pitches.

I unsheathe a dagger from my side, and Sethan mirrors my movements, his eyes trained on the crowd beyond the wooden table's legs. A familiar black, scaly muzzle reaches through a broken window. Daeja's mouth parts with saliva dripping off her teeth in long strings as her nostrils flare. She snatches the back of a patron's hem and tears them back off their feet, revealing a masked person.

My stomach drops. Fuck, I should have told Sethan about the masked person back in the forest.

The masked person scrambles to get loose with a scream. But it's no use. Daeja whips them up out of view like they're nothing more than a ragdoll.

"Tell her not to eat them," Sethan whispers. "Some dragons can become addicted to human blood."

"Daeja, do not eat—"

"I know. I know," she sighs. **"Though, I'm not sure if they're playing dead or actually are. I didn't bite that hard."**

"Guess that takes questioning out of the picture."

"There's more of them, though. At least ten from what I can see."

A new explosion of glass shatters over the sound of patrons fighting, and Sethan tugs me up and shoves me back into the corner, my shoulder blades flush with the wall.

He shifts in front of me, balancing his weight on the balls of his feet with his hand outstretched in front of me in a protective stance. "We need to sneak you out the back. A'nala and the other dragons are plucking them out through the windows, but there's too many of them."

"Who are they?" I glance up at the dagger in the wall above us. "Trying to kill me? Or you?"

"Rebels. Could be both. Though…if you haven't taken off those gloves, I imagine it's me they're after." He points over to the bar top where the tenders are missing. Beyond it is a wooden door. "Go through there, and it'll take you out to the alleyway. A'nala and Daeja will meet us there. I'll watch your back."

"But what about—"

"Go!" He shoves me. "I'll be right behind you."

Crouching, I slink against the wall to the bar top and slip behind it to find a woman lying dead in a pool of blood, a dagger sunk hilt-deep into her throat. Her blank eyes stare up at the ceiling. Guilt swarms me, drying out my mouth. If the masked person followed us here, this is all my fault.

Shoving my fear and sadness aside, I tiptoe over her body. Blood wets my boots, and I creak open the door before sliding through it. Clenching my hand around the hilt of my dagger at my side, I make my way through a dusty, dimly-lit storage room until I find another door. Tossing a glance over my shoulder, Sethan nods from behind me. I unbolt the latch, and we spill out into the cobblestone street, sunlight flashing over us.

Daeja's shadow looms overhead, blocking out the sun, and she lowers her muzzle to sniff the side of my head.

"I'm fine. Unharmed," I assure her, wiping off her

blood-smattered maw. I turn and ask Sethan, "Where are the others? Has anyone been able to get the civilians out?"

A'nala lifts her massive red head and freezes. Sethan looks up and follows her gaze to something in the distance, before he swings his brown gaze back to me. "They're working on it, don't worry. We need to…hey! Where do you think you're going?" He snatches my forearm.

I swallow against the tension in my throat. "I have to go back. I have to help. The reason they're here is because of me."

"You don't know that. More than likely, they were feeling daring with some ale, saw an opportunity to kill me while I was unsuspecting, and took it."

"No…because the one Daeja pulled out of the window was the same one who tried to shoot us back in the forest after you and A'nala left."

He drops my forearm. "What?"

"I'm sorry. I should have told you, but I didn't want to admit I was wrong, and you were right."

"What happened to not telling them?" Daeja grumbles.

"If I told them, perhaps we could have avoided this. Perhaps no one had to die. Not being honest was a mistake."

Sethan sighs, rubbing a hand over his face. And I swear A'nala has the same exact expression.

As I retrieve the sword sheath on Daeja's saddle and withdraw my blade, I mutter, "I made a mistake. But let me correct it, let me go back and save those people."

"I can't. If you die, those people die in vain. And the rest of the realm will suffer a similar fate."

"And I can't just stand by waiting!"

"You can, and you will!" he roars.

I lurch forward. "When are you going to understand I am not yours to command!"

"When you take your head out of your ass and realize this is much bigger than you!"

Clenching my teeth to silence my rage, my breath comes out of my nose in loud puffs. I stare him down, tightening my grip on my sword and about ready to brush past him.

He continues, a touch softer, "As a leader, you'll make mistakes. Mistakes that will hurt the people around you, and you'll have to live with that burden the rest of your life. But that is the vow we make when we step into a role like this. You have to look outside of yourself and what you want. Do you think I ever wanted to leave Melaina and her mother? Do you know how many nights I spent breaking over the fact I had to leave them in Arterias? How sometimes I felt like I needed to tie myself down from running back to rescue them?"

My breathing slows, and I tear my gaze away to look down toward the side of the building. Where the snapping of dragon jaws, shouts, and blade against blade rings out.

"It is not easy…" His voice lowers. "And it's not fair. This isn't a role I wish on anyone. But if you don't, then no one will."

I look up at him as he places a hand on my shoulder.

"This was my mistake, too. Gods be damned, I shouldn't have given into your stubbornness and left you out alone. And I shouldn't have pushed you so hard on our first riding lesson," he says.

"Is that an apology?"

His head snaps back toward the building, mirroring A'nala. When he sweeps his attention back to me, he says, "It sounds like they've captured the last rebels."

"How many casualties?" I say as we stride around the tavern toward the entrance, Daeja and A'nala hot on our tails.

"One bartender, and several of the rebels. Quite foolish of them to think they could take us down, considering our entire thunder is here."

"Thunder…?"

"A group of dragons," he answers.

We meet the rest of the dragon riders near the front entrance of the tavern and find them exchanging three masked rebels with soldiers dressed in their metals. Sethan commands the Driftmond guards to escort the rebels to the northeastern most part of the continent to a city called Millton, where they'll be interrogated before deciding their fates. Depending on the vote of the council there, they'll either be executed by dragonfire or thrown into the prison there to live out the rest of their lives as traitors.

Once the remaining rebels are whisked away by the Driftmond guards, Sethan orders the other dragon riders to dispose of the bodies. Daeja with her round pleading eyes begs me wordlessly to participate with the rest of the fire dragons in burning the bodies. I swear her tail quivers when she almost bounces off after them behind the tavern.

Sethan and I work on cleaning up the shattered glass from the inside of the tavern with brooms from the storage room. He encourages the rest of the remaining patrons to leave, despite their willingness to help clean the place up. To me, it feels like a small way of apologizing for being the catalyst of an attack. I can't help but glance over at the bar top, where the bartender's body was. How those she knows and loves will have to mourn her death—all because I was too proud to warn Sethan about the rebels Daeja and I saw in the forest.

"Her family will be sent an allowance," Sethan mumbles, not looking up from plucking a shard of glass from the floor. "Whenever someone is wrongfully killed, part of our taxes pay the family so they don't have to worry about finances. It was a policy I installed knowing I might have put strain on Melaina and her mother when they thought I died."

I pull my attention off the bar and continue sweeping the glass.

"If you're going to feel guilty, use it as power. Don't let it eat at you," he says.

I stop from sweeping a pile of glass to look at him. "You could use more practice, if that's your attempt at making me feel better about it."

He shrugs and says something, but all I hear is Daeja warning, *"Incoming in three…two…"*

As I swing my attention to one of the busted windows where she is outside, the tavern door swings open and slams against the wall.

"What kind of shit were you trying to pull?" Cole roars, gunning straight for Sethan. "You could have fucking killed her!"

Before he can close the space between him and Sethan, I drop my broom and slide in front of him, blocking his path. "Stop. It wasn't his fault the tavern was attacked—"

"I'm not talking about the tavern," he growls, eyes still burning into the man standing behind me. "I'm talking about him knocking you out of the sky."

"How did you possibly see that?" I hiss half under my breath and shove him back. I can't imagine his terror if he watched me free-falling from the sky. But now is *not* the time.

Sethan calls cooly, "But I didn't kill her now, did I?"

That sends Cole into a frenzy, another crack splitting through his uncontrolled anger.

I slam my palms against his chest and push him back step by step. "Knock it off!"

His molten hot glare tugs off Sethan for a moment to meet mine. That unfiltered, raw rage burns inside his irises like fire. I flinch under the intensity, as if caught in a wild inferno that might consume me if I don't douse it. His eyes float back up to Sethan, hooking into him.

I seize his collar in a fist and growl, "Get out. Now."

He has to physically tug his chin away to tear his gaze off

Sethan. Leading him by the shirt, I yank him out and away from the tavern, out of the town, and closer to the trees.

Once we are completely alone, I let go of him and turn to face him head on. "You need to get a grip on yourself, Cole. You can't keep having outbursts like that. Not when we are already walking on eggshells with our own squad trying to keep them here in the Dragon Lands!"

"He put your life in danger."

I rub a hand over my face, exhaustion wearing on me. "It's not your place to defend me like that all the time."

"I will defend you until my last breath, Kat. Stop faulting me for it!"

"I am not some simple, fragile little girl anymore!" My blood rushes in my ears, nearly drowning out any voices of reason in my head. "When are you going to learn I don't need your protection?"

"When I feel like you're able to defend yourself!"

I freeze, stunned at the confession. Though the truth of it has always lingered in the back of my mind that he doesn't trust I can take care of myself.

His voice dips dangerously low. "The truth is, if I hadn't protected you all those years ago, you might not have survived."

I crinkle my nose. "What the fuck is that supposed to mean?"

"It means before you actually let me help you rebuild your fishing trap years ago, *I* was the one who snuck over to the river in the early mornings before the sun was up to put fish in the trap—"

"What are you talking about? That was *years* before—"

He flicks out an expressive hand gesture. "Exactly my point!"

"Why would you do something like that?"

"Because you're incredibly stubborn. You don't ask for help when you need it. And you especially don't like to be seen as weak—"

"Because I'm not weak!" I slap a hand to my chest.

"No…you're not…" His eyes soften slightly, holding my gaze in a headlock. "But you have this twisted idea that you can't ask for help when you need it, and *that* is what makes you weak."

"*That's* your excuse for practically tackling Sethan to the ground?"

"To him, you are a tool!" His fury spikes again. "You are nothing but a means to an end to him, and it would be wise that you remember that. He doesn't care about you—he only cares about what it's going to take to save his people. And he needs to be reminded you are a person. People break. And if he pushes you too hard—"

"No, you're misguided. You've always been the one to take it too easy on me."

"What is it you want from me, Kat? You want me to back off? You want me to step away and leave you alone? Then just come out and say it. Because I'm not going to stop until you do."

The thought alone tears at my heart, an echo of pain rippling inside of my chest. As the pain recedes like a tide, it summons the betrayal from learning of his engagement with Celeste. "I want you to stop lying to me! Stop trying to protect me and tell me the fucking truth!"

"The truth?" He thunders closer, staring at me down his sharp nose. "You can't handle honesty—"

"Fucking try me!" I throw my hands out to the side, completely careless about who might hear us at this point.

"Alright. You know what? I *had* lied to you, you're right. I omitted the truth about Celeste. About being engaged. I also lied to you all the times I was late meeting you at the river back in Padmoor. It wasn't because I was caught up playing tea parties with Arabella. And I didn't go days without seeing you at times because I had to help my father in the forge. It was because my father beat the absolute," he spits the next words out on the ground, *"shit* out of me when he found out I was using our coin to help you."

My breath catches in my chest like a trapped bird, fluttering inside my ribcage begging to be freed. *"What?"*

He continues, "Vivian never hated you—she hated the *idea* of you. The effect you had on me. She hated that I loved you so much, I would give anything just for you to survive another day. I would put you above my own life. And when she walked in one day and found me unconscious, bleeding out at the hands of my father, she begged me to leave you. Cried for me to let you go."

His anger subsides, his breath still heavy but his eyebrows pinch together as he shakes his head. "But I couldn't. I couldn't…because you were and are everything to me." His voice cracks. "My heart *runs* to you. Why can't you see that?"

Rushing in like a current, flashes of memories flood me. How I would sometimes wait hours by the river for him to come. How mussed and flustered he looked when he finally did show. I thought maybe he was only stressed from being late. And the occasions where he would go days without meeting me had always angered me. All this time, I thought he had other matters to attend to, and perhaps I wasn't a priority for him. But the dark rims around his eyes weren't from lack of sleep in the times he did show up late.

They must have been *bruises.*

His chest heaves up and down, eyes burning into mine. "So… forgive me for not telling you about the engagement. Forgive me that I love you. Forgive me that it shatters me to know I'm the one who fucked this all up, and I have *no* idea how to get back to you. Forgive me that I fucking *hate* myself for pushing you so far away you fell into someone else's arms—"

"It was nothing…"

He blows out a heavy breath, eyes dragging away from me to take a break before they're back. "I don't believe you. You're not that kind of person."

"And you know what kind of person I am?"

"He will hurt you, Kat," he croaks. "And I can't stand the thought of seeing someone hurt you again. He will break. Your. Heart."

"There's not much more to break." I push past him, avoiding his eye contact. "You made sure of that."

TWENTY-FOUR

STUBBORN ARROGANCE

Sethan leads our group of Vitalans and Arterians deeper into Driftmond, Cole at the back of the line with Archie. I can't bear the sullen look on Cole's face, so I keep my eyes focused on the town around us. Colorful ropes with dragon symbols swoop across the street, anchored to tall, sharp-angled buildings. The cobblestone streets are wide enough for dragons to pass through. Townspeople dip their heads in respect as we pass, their eyes wide as they behold Daeja—the only black dragon anyone has likely ever seen.

And Daeja eats it up.

Her lips twitch up into the look of a grin, her chin held high as she struts through the town. Though, she accidentally knocks over a kid crossing the street behind us with the tip of her tail. I swear it's the highlight of the kid's life as he gawks at Daeja. He dismisses my concern before scampering off and chattering about it with another group of kids across the street.

Sethan leads us to the northwestern part of the town and stops near the outskirts where the buildings give way to a hillside. Daeja grumbles beside me.

"What is it?"

"Apparently, dragons usually stay out here. A'nala is commanding us all to settle here for the night."

"You're…you're nervous about something?"

She shakes her neck like a horse shooing away a fly, avoiding my question. As I scan the bare land, dusted with grass and blocked in by the city against the hillside, with trees far out in the distance… *"You don't like sleeping out in the open, do you?"*

She blinks at me, confirming what I already suspect. She's spent almost her whole life under the cover of the trees. And I understand it on a personal level—because I feel the same way. The Northern Forest was always a sanctuary for me. The smell of sap, the whisper of the wind through the trees.

I run my gloved hands over her muzzle, looking her in the eyes as I say, *"You can always admit to me when you're nervous. Or scared. I'll do a better job of telling you, too."*

She snorts, silently challenging my statement before closing her eyes as I rub underneath her chin.

"I sent notice to the council of our travel plans, so Driftmond has already been made aware of our needs for accommodations," Sethan says as he sweeps up beside me. He turns his head over his shoulder. "Corvin, please take a few soldiers and check in with the Driftmond council to confirm when the rider sector will be ready. Then take a pass through town for any rebels."

Corvin dips his head and gathers several other soldiers before heading off back into town.

"In the meantime…" Sethan murmurs and opens his hand. "Let me see your blade."

Giving Daeja one last pat on her nose, I unsheathe my sword and hand it to him. He takes it, inspecting not the intertwined circles embedded in the hilt but the blade itself. Holding it near his ear, he flicks the blade a few times and then draws the tip across his palm, watching the blood seep from the fresh wound with careful fascination.

He shakes his head and hands it back to me. "It's what I thought…dragonblade."

The dragons all around us shift uncomfortably, one of them grumbling until A'nala snaps at them to quiet.

"Dragonblade?" I murmur.

He withdraws his own sword, then slices his opposite palm, before sheathing the blade and showing me both hands. The one he sliced with my sword has speckles of light glimmering in his blood. The other palm has a coin-sized collection of blood without shimmering light refractions. "A few of the King's Close Circle members have dragonblades. They're forged with dragonblood and bone. Have you ever seen this one glow blue?"

"Erm…no?"

"Well…I suppose that's a good thing. It'll only glow blue once in contact with dragonblood. That blade contains a magical energy just like the ley lines. It won't necessarily siphon the magic, but it can either paralyze or kill a dragon."

I freeze, staring down at the blade in my hand. My grip loosens until I drop it to the ground. I swear as it lands and the sunlight gleams off its edge I see a shimmer of brilliant blue. All this time I've been carrying a weapon that could potentially harm or kill Daeja?

Sethan grabs it off the ground and holds it out to me. "Don't worry. It's not immediate death to a dragon with a dragonblade. A lot of factors determine how many stabs it will take to bring down a dragon: age, strength, and overall health. Think of it as…an enhanced blade."

"I don't want it."

"But you might need it. Dragonblades are our best defense against other dragonblades. And you never know when we might run into a wild dragon. Just…try not to stab your dragon with it."

Daeja snaps her head into my direction with a 'hmm?'

Hesitantly, I take the blade back and sheathe it at my side.

Archie jogs up to us and claps me on the shoulder with a goofy grin. I don't miss Sethan's narrowed glance of irritation.

"Hey! How was the flight? Heard you fell out of the sky, that was super badass!" Archie laughs, then tosses a wink at Daeja.

Melaina follows close behind, exchanging a look with Sethan that borders on the line of discontentment before she looks back at me and her expression softens.

"Marge make it here okay?" I peek over the other soldiers' heads toward where people are hopping out of the wagons.

"She was a little ornery with all the bumps and sitting for so long on a wooden bench. I tried to give her my jacket to cushion her seat, but she refused." Archie shrugs. "Anyway, she went off into town."

I raise an eyebrow. "By herself?"

Archie holds up his hands. "Well, I wasn't going to stop her."

"Should we be worried? Can you send someone after her?" I ask Sethan. I can't imagine what Marge is doing wandering a town she's never been in on her own. And as a Spoiled.

Sethan directs two of his soldiers to search Driftmond for Marge. While we wait for Corvin to return with word from the council and assessing Driftmond, the dragons settle into spots in the grass up against the hillside. Daeja's black figure is a shadow against the green backdrop, with the other menagerie of fire dragons curled in on themselves, most of whom watch us with yellow eyes.

I settle into a spot by Daeja, throwing one ankle over the other and leaning back against her ribs. My eyes are heavy, and my stomach grumbles. As I'm about to lose to fluttering eyelids, Archie walks up to us.

"You've had a long day…" He crouches and pulls out a chunk of wrapped bread, then offers it. "…hungry?"

I lean up. "You brought that from Midkeep?"

"I always come prepared." He smiles. "Food is just as important as weapons."

"Couldn't agree more," Daeja purrs, then sniffs his hand and recoils. *"On second thought, I'm not that hungry."*

Without waiting for a response, he tears it in half and hands it to me. Tossing a glance up at Daeja, he points to the spot next to me. "May I?"

Daeja blinks at him, and he slowly slides up next to me, and we both lean back against Daeja. My stomach feels better once I've swallowed the last bite.

"Don't take this the wrong way but…you look spent. Are you alright?" he whispers.

"It's been a long day to say the least…" I sigh. "I don't know, Arch. Sethan's adamant I'll save the realm because of the prophecy."

"The one about the sun and…death and stuff?"

"That's the one."

"My ma used to say when you're angry, you should eat first. And when you're sad…you should sleep first." He tosses me a smile and pats his shoulder.

"Won't…Melaina get jealous—"

"No," he chuckles. "She knows who you are to me."

When I hesitate, he prompts, "Kat, get over here and just close your eyes. I'll wake you up when Corvin gets back. It could take them a few hours, and you need to rest."

With a small smile, I lean my head on his shoulder and close my eyes.

It's nearing sunset, and I wake to the sound of blade against blade. Flinching forward with my heart leaping out of my chest, I reach for my sword at my side.

Archie grabs my shoulder before I can get to my feet. "Shh, you're alright. Just sparring."

Arterians and Vitalans are gathered in a circle, watching a pair of soldiers spar in the middle. After stretching out my aching bones against a dozing Daeja, Archie helps me up off the ground. We watch the spar for a few minutes until it ends. And then Archie playfully taunts Melaina until she gives into a match. Melaina beats him, and the two of them come to sit next to me.

Sethan turns his attention to Cole sitting over with his back to the dragons. "My father used to always tell me fighting your way out of a problem could be just as successful as talking it out. Care to test the theory?"

Cole's eyes darken despite his hauntingly calm expression. Wordlessly, he stands and begins to withdraw his sword at his side.

"Ahh, ahh," Sethan clicks. "Wouldn't want us to get too carried away. Let's start small, shall we?" He snaps at his men, and they retrieve two wooden rods from one of the wagons.

They hand one to Sethan. The second rod goes to Cole, who snaps his gaze back up to Sethan before accepting it. The two of them stalk out into the makeshift circle of people and begin to spar. They spin and lunge, swinging and striking like two angered snakes. Each contact of the rods is a heavy, hard smack. After a quick minute, Cole disarms Sethan, and the rod flies off several feet away. Cole drops his rod and turns his back to Sethan, returning to his previous spot on the sidelines. Not a drop of sweat on him.

Darian snickers from the crowd, still manacled and held between two soldiers.

Sethan drags a lethally slow glare over to him. "That funny to you?"

Darian's lips tug up into a coy grin. "Hilarious. Would have never guessed you were in the King's Close Circle. Though, I suppose you've always been lousy with lifting your weapon any higher than your knees. Explains why you were always second in command next to Jurrock."

Sethan narrows his eyes. "You mean your *father?*" He kicks Cole's wooden rod toward him. "Seems to me you never had that stubborn arrogance beaten out of you."

Darian tilts his head to the side, watching as the wooden rod rolls and bumps into his boot, before glaring up at Sethan. "Is that you asking for a chance? Because I assure you, if it'll be anyone getting their ass beat, it's you."

Sethan snorts. "I'd be glad to finally put you in your place, boy."

The two guards at Darian's side step away after Sethan gives them a nod. Darian snatches the wooden rod off the ground, his eyes trained on Sethan. When he rises, he snaps the rod over his knee, the crack splitting through the clearing and creating two wooden rods with jagged edges. "Let's see if your legs run as fast as your fucking mouth."

My pulse leaps into my throat as Darian strides into the center and everyone else falls away silently.

Archie watches with wide eyes. "That…doesn't seem like a fair fight? Darian's still manacled—"

Melaina rests a hand on his arm, as if he might spring into the circle himself. "Don't. You might be surprised. My father might not want to admit it, but age has slowed him. It might be as fair of a fight as any. Let them work it out."

It still doesn't convince me. Because while Sethan agreed in the blood pact not to kill him, we never specified he couldn't *hurt* him. But as Darian strides closer to Sethan, confidence exuding from each step and swing of his shoulders, I begin to question my concern. If the chain connecting Darian's wristlets were only a foot apart instead of a generous two feet, it might be enough of a limitation for an easy loss. But it's not a one-foot-long chain.

And it's Darian.

Considering the way Darian glowers at Sethan, I can't find any guarantees Darian won't try to kill him. The cracking whip Corvin drove down against Darian's back the night he was held in the dungeon replays in my mind. At the time, I thought Sethan was only desperate to get answers. And maybe he was. But there's an extra layer to it. Something that has soured with time. A hatred rooting deeper and deeper from both sides. It's impossible to miss now.

Darian swings out first, though his range of motion is limited due to the chain connecting both of his manacles. Despite the disadvantage, he moves with confidence, grace, and lethality. Sethan catches Darian's strike with his rod before sweeping it to the side and stabbing toward Darian's chest. Darian blocks his attack with his opposite hand and then twirls his other rod to thwack Sethan on the side of the head.

Sethan seethes, thrown off a few steps as his lips twitch up into a silent snarl. They explode into whips and spins, striking and swiping. Darian ducks, dodges, and jumps, avoiding each of Sethan's attacks. A few moments in, and Sethan's heavy panting is nearly as loud as the wood cracking as their poles connect. Darian's only wearing him down. Playing with him.

Darian finally smacks Sethan's pole down from his chest with one hand, spins, and rears back onto one leg, kicking Sethan straight in the chest and sending him flying back. Sethan lands and skids across the ground a few inches. Darian tosses the poles at Sethan whose chest rises and falls quickly as he fights to regain his breath.

"You're lucky I don't fucking kill you," Darian spits at the ground and stalks out from the circle.

TWENTY-FIVE

A LESSON IN BARGAINS

Later that night, after we join the town in their community hall for dinner, we're led to our own quarters. The residence designated for Cyrus in this town is no different than the last. Lush, intricate stonework on the outside and lavish furnishings on the inside. And a peculiar set of restraints adhered to a far side of the wall.

He *really* must have had anger issues.

Sethan's soldiers escort Darian into the room and hook his restraints into the wall, before leaving the two of us alone in an awkward silence. I swallow the memory replaying in my mind of a shackled Darian fighting against Sethan and *winning*.

"What?" Darian grumbles, his eyes narrowing in on me.

I clear my throat, shifting my attention to my feet and tapping the bedpost with the tip of my boot. "The way you fought Sethan…"

"Go on."

I sigh, looking up at him and crossing my arms over my chest. I can't admit I was impressed or that such a theatrical event nearly gave me a heart attack. Even with the blood pact, it only meant Sethan couldn't kill him. But what if he injured him enough to knock him into an indefinite state of unconsciousness? What then?

Darian's eyes darken, and a smug tilt lifts his lips. "Ahh, you were impressed, weren't you? Or were you scared for me? Either way, I appreciate the sentiment." He laces his fingers together behind his head and leans back against the wall as he watches me.

"No. It's just…" I duck my head, fighting to get the words out and debating about dropping the conversation entirely. Gritting my teeth, I take a full breath before asking, "Do you think you could train me?"

He snorts. "What's in it for me?"

"Well, what do you want?"

His gaze floats up to the ceiling in a playful thought before he tilts his head to the side, regarding me with that haunting, predatory gaze.

"Within reason," I blurt before he can get ahead of himself.

He rolls his eyes. "You're no fun. I was about to request a bathtub full of gold—"

"As if the royal houses don't have enough?"

"It's a joke." His voice dips to something lethally quiet. "Like I give a shit about money."

"Well then, what *do* you give a shit about?"

He watches me, jaw working in a calm fidget as if he's waiting for me to falter. Or run away.

"Well?" I prompt again. "If this is a test of my patience, I assure you we won't get far."

He rolls his neck as if the mere existence of me in the same vicinity of him is exhausting and emotionally challenging. "You let me out of these chains."

"Absolutely not."

"You let me out of these chains every night we're in here."

I cross my arms over my chest. "No."

"You let me out of these chains for two hours—"

"I said no." Though, I have to give him the unabashed credit for his persistence.

He mirrors my body language, folding his arms over his chest. "What kind of bargain is this if you're not willing to compromise *something*?"

"Releasing your shackles is off the table. What else would you want?"

He sits in silence for a few heartbeats to mentally run through some sort of list. Finally, he says, "Letting me free."

"Forget it," I grumble, shuffling into bed, and wrapping myself in sheets.

I wait.

After what feels like forever and doubt trickling in that Marge won't come, a knock taps on the door. Darian shifts a suspicious look to me. I ignore his questioning gaze, pulling my boots and cloak on and slipping out the door. Marge and I walk silently through the quiet, dark streets and out to the hills where the dragons rest. Daeja perks her head up, watching Marge and me from a distance, her white eyes almost glowing in the darkness.

What are you doing?

"Marge said she'll be training me."

Training for what?" She shifts in her spot, and the other dragons open their eyes.

"She calls it pulling. Basically, controlling magic. Don't worry about me, go back to sleep."

Daeja lowers her head to the ground but keeps her eyes trained on me. She lifts her chin off the ground a few inches to turn her head every time we stride out of her vision.

After we've left the dragons behind and venture further into the forest, I turn to Marge. "Why is it only you and I can hear the humming?"

"I can't hear it. I can only feel it."

"Okay, well, how come you and I can both sense it? Does it have anything to do with the fact you're a Spoiled?"

"No. Well…possibly," she mutters.

"So why can I hear it now?"

"Most riders can sense it due to their magical bonds with their dragons. But you are likely extra sensitive, especially the longer you wear the Blood Ring, and now that you know what to look for."

"Can the dragons sense the rings as well?"

She shrugs. "I'm not sure. That might be a better question for your dragon, but I imagine they do, just as they sense Spoileds."

"So…let's say I manage to master pulling. What can I do with the magic? Sethan said before I entered the blood pact that the ring holds power, but what kind?"

"They say the most powerful magic can be done with blood and bones, but I'm not sure anyone alive today knows its extent other than the King himself. I've personally seen King Aaric shatter another person's bones without doing so much as lifting a hand. I've seen him raid people's memories and transform his own form to look like someone else. Since he couldn't locate the Blood Ring, he's been attempting rituals with blood to mimic it, but he's been unsuccessful."

I shiver, not wanting to ask, but doing so anyway, "What kind of blood has he been using? And for what kind of rituals?"

"Mostly dragonblood. But humans and anything else he can get his hands on, too. As for the rituals…nobody is quite certain what he's trying to accomplish. That's why it's so important you don't take the ring off under any circumstance, Katerina. He needs it. And if it falls into the wrong hands…if he gets hold of it…" She shakes her head. "There's no telling what he'll do. But in the meantime, if we are to stand any chance, you need to learn how to power it. How to use that magic for good."

"Even if it'll bind me to it?"

She sighs. Already knowing what I'm implying. Because if I bind to it, then the only way to kill the King is to kill myself.

"Yes. Even if it binds you to it," she answers. "But that is exactly why we need to get to Vitalis. We need to find answers because the prophecy speaks of you and Daeja. You're destined to restore the balance, so there must be a way to end him without killing you both."

"And if there's not?"

She stops walking, and I mirror her.

Finally, she swings her gaze to me. "We don't have room for 'not.' So, let's not even entertain that reality."

She continues, and I watch her go. Then, realizing she won't wait for me, I catch up to her. We come to the southern part of Driftmond where a patch of trees encircle a small clearing. She crouches with a grunt, her body creaking as she lowers to the ground. One hand braces herself against her staff, while the other stretches out before her, grazing the tips of grass on the ground. "Can you sense it now?"

I close my eyes, settling into myself as I listen to the sounds around me. Second by second, the humming rises from the chatter of the forest sounds, lifting like an audible fog. "Yes."

"Good. Now…feel it."

Crouching down beside her, I remove my gloves and take a deep breath before I let my fingertips skim the ground. Something underneath the surface jolts to my touch like a shot of electricity. I push my palm down flat against the surface. The euphoria of it steals a gasp from my lips, and I rip my hand off the ground, my eyes flying open as I stare at Marge.

I swallow hard, a lurking danger prickling my skin. "I can't."

"Yes, you can. It's a little stronger tonight, but channel it like you did last time. Don't let it override you. You are in control—remember that."

But how much is a little stronger? A new spike of fear rises within me.

"Go on," she encourages, nodding to the ground.

Slowly, inch by inch, I press my fingers down into the ground again and close my eyes. The energy beneath the earth rushes toward me, and this time I don't pull away. An agonizing pain spiders up my fingertips, webbing out through my hands and slinking up my arms. Despite my every effort to control my panic, my pulse quickens, and my breath rattles in my lungs as I curl forward to tuck my chin into my chest. The pain—the power—it floods me. And I can't contain it.

"Slow down," Marge warns. "You're pulling too fast!"

"I can't!" I scream, beginning to writhe against the growing agony slipping up past my elbows as if I were dipped in hot oil.

"You can! Focus! Channel it!"

Squeezing my eyes tighter, tears leak from my eyes and jet down my cheeks, and yet I still can't escape the pain. A liquid fire fills every crevice, every vein and drop of blood. With every inch it gains, I fall closer and closer to the ground, succumbing to the raw power, subject to its endless torrent of anguish.

"Help…please!" I gasp out, opening my eyes only to discover my field of vision is clouding in white.

"Katerina, lower it!" Marge calls again somewhere, buried deep within the earth. "Lower it back down!"

But I fucking can't.

I can't pull any last bits of strength out. Not when every nerve in my body screams against the drowning power. Pulling me into the earth, as if I belonged there amongst the dirt. Calling me to return to what I once was before this life.

I slip.

And everything fades to white.

I'm lost in an endless abyss of white. Emptiness. It overrides all my other senses. I can't feel my fingertips or the beat of my heart. All is silent. The chaos and overwhelming sensation of life is gone.

Even as I blink, the white is blinding, leached of all color and texture. A thick, creeping tingle races up my spine, raising every hair on the nape of my neck. An invisible tug pulls my attention to my right, and I turn to follow.

Out of the deafening white, a shadow shifts, so subtly as if to convince me nothing is actually there. I can't tell if it's seconds, minutes, or hours, but as I watch, the shadow darkens. Growing closer and firmer until it finally takes on the silhouette of a person. I realize then that the shadow isn't getting closer. I am. My feet appear in the haze of white beneath me, carrying me to the figure. By the time I look back up, I'm a few feet away from the silhouette, and I stop, unable to urge myself further. A swallow rolls down my throat, thick and tight, as recognition overwhelms me.

My brother.

He's facing away from me, but I would always recognize that dirty blonde hair and the cowlick sticking up near the back of his head.

"Aiden?" I call, but the words won't leave my tongue.

My fingers tremble as I stretch a hand out, desperate to get his attention. The longing to see his face overwhelms every bit of my heart. To erase the memory of the last time I saw him: terrified, ashen, and frozen before he was swept into the freezing depths of the river back in Padmoor.

"Kit?" Aiden calls, though the rest of his body is eerily still, as if encased in stone.

His voice alone shatters something painful inside my chest. How long has it been since I heard his voice? Since he called my name?

Aside from that fateful day at the river, I couldn't recall what his face looked like. As if the painful flashbacks of his death created a dam, holding all of our other happy memories together hostage.

"Look at me!" I scream inside my head and out loud, the sound nearly foreign.

He still won't turn to me. Instead, he takes a few steps away. I reach out again, swiping more frantically for him, but I can't step any closer. My legs are locked into place.

He just needs to look at me. Just one. Simple. Look.

"Look at me!" I cry, tears blurring my vision of him. "Aiden! Please! Please, look at me!"

But the white creeps in like a hungry fog, disintegrating the sides of his arms, his legs, and spilling over his back.

"No, stop! Don't go! Hold on!" My voice is raw, unrecognizable with the fear and desperation that has me in a vice grip. And there's those two little words again. The two words that haunt me. The last words I ever spoke to him.

The rest of his silhouette is drowned out by white, and I'm left alone.

"Look at me! Please!"

As if all the white fog were sucked out of the room, everything snaps to black and a bone-chilling cold explodes through my body. At once, all my sensations roar back to life.

"Look at me! Please!" The words I said in my head in an unfamiliar tone repeat. But the fog of disillusion lifts, and the words ring inside my mind like a bell, each echoed repetition shaking off my uncertainty.

"Kat! Please, Gods. Kat!" Someone shakes me.

My eyes flash open, the black melting away to texture and shades of blue. A dizziness swarms my head like an angry mob of bees. The blurry glow of amber eyes, warm in the cold night, meet mine.

Cole.

"Look at me! Please!" His whisper is strained.

My vision sharpens. His broad torso is curled over me, my head resting against his chest. Even with the layers of his clothes deafening the noise, his heartbeat slams against his chest, dying to escape. One of his arms is tucked underneath my neck, holding me to him, while the other hand brushes my cheek with his thumb.

As our eyes connect, a fissure cracks through his pained expression, relief flooding his eyes. "You're going to be okay, alright? I've got you." He darts a look over his shoulder to where Marge is staring. "She opened her eyes!"

A shadow shifts behind Marge, and I recognize Daeja in the background. Her eyes lock onto mine, and she grumbles, ***"Perhaps the Spoiled isn't the best person to be training you."***

"I have no one else," I respond weakly.

Marge races toward us, shaken out of her awe and nearly falls to her knees next to Cole, her scarred, withered hand coming to slowly rest on my shoulder. "What did you see, Katerina?"

A severe chill drowns out my nerves, and my teeth chatter uncontrollably in response. I squeeze myself closer into Cole's warmth, my muscles groaning in protest. *Gods, I feel so weak…*even keeping my eyes open is nearly impossible.

"I…" My head swims again, as if I'll be lost to unconsciousness once more.

Marge squeezes my shoulder. "Don't close your eyes. Tell me. What did you see?"

"My…my brother," I manage between shivers.

Cole's eyes flash wider, and he rips off his jacket and wraps it around me before drawing me closer into him. "She's cold, Marge. We need to get her warm—"

Marge shushes Cole and tugs at my arm. "What did he say?"

"N-nothing but my n-name…h-he didn't even…l-look at me."

"Did you touch him?"

"No…why are…you asking me th-these th-th-things?"

"Do you feel alright?" She pats my cheek and forehead, nearly flinching when she touches my skin. Her breath whooshes out in a single blow. "Gods and heavens, you're freezing."

I nod, each second draining more energy to keep my eyes open.

Cole presses a hand to my cheek again before whipping a pointed look at Marge. "Why is she so cold?"

"Because she visited The White."

"What in the hells is that?" he asks.

"The White is what many of the elders called the afterlife. When we die, our souls go to The White—"

"And you just let her fucking pull until she died?" Cole growls.

"Well, I alerted you, didn't I?" she bites back. "Don't get mad at me. There wouldn't have been anything I could have done to stop it. And besides, she didn't actually die. She just visited it, you overprotective buffoon."

I can't seem to form my thoughts into words past my trembling lips. *The afterlife? Where was everyone else? My mother, my father, the little girl I failed to save back in Hornwood?*

Cole continuously rubs the side of my arm firmly, narrowing his gaze at Marge. "We need to get her inside and warm. Are there other repercussions we should be wary about?"

"Not that I know of. As long as she didn't touch anyone…she should be fine. She'll just need rest."

Numbness seeps throughout every inch of my body. Just as I'm about to curse Marge for not warning me of the risks, I slip back out of consciousness.

TWENTY-SIX

CUTTING LOSSES

My muscles groan in protest as I work to wake them. With a yawn, I turn to my right, feeling like bags of sand lie on my eyes as I drag them open. The heaviness in my body turns out to be from the weight of blankets piled high on top of me. I shove them down to my knees and sit up as someone's snicker pulls my attention to the stone wall.

"So cold-blooded, you needed that many blankets to keep warm?" Darian taunts.

I glance back to the pile of blankets and recognize a jacket draped over them. And it isn't *Cole's…*

I side eye Darian. "Why is your jacket up here?"

"They stripped it off my body to keep you warm, of course." He flicks something off his knee.

"Liar."

He sighs with an eye roll. "Fine. I threw it over to you in case you froze to death. You're no use to me dead, you know."

"How charming of you," I mumble as I get up and toss his jacket back over to him. This is now the second time I've woken up in the morning with a poor recollection of the previous night's events and his jacket draped over me. Though, I guess I should be happy this time around I didn't wake up in his bed. *Wearing* his jacket.

"Just as I wouldn't be so useful to you if I were dead either…" he starts, glancing over to me slyly.

I tie my boots up my shins and pause, still bent over as his voice tampers off. "Yes. As you already know."

"I have a proposal," he says rather plainly.

I perk up, straightening my back and staring at him from the other side of the bed. "I'm listening."

"I'll tell you what the King is planning…" He drags his gaze away from mine, lazily examining his fingernails before he clenches his fists and cracks his knuckles.

The sound alone makes me flinch. Triggering the memory of those two prisoners back in Arterias forced off the outlook tower, their necks snapping as they hit the end of their ropes. How he had been the one to sign off on their deaths. At the time, I didn't recognize the full meaning when he announced 'in the name of the King' at the execution. But now I do. Because he's the heir to the throne.

Gods, I feel so stupid I didn't piece it together sooner.

He drawls on, "Aaaand how you can defeat him…*if* you kiss my ass."

Narrowing my eyes, I snag the closest thing to me—my father's journal—and chuck it at him. It misses his face by an inch too low, smacking him in the shoulder. His eyes flash wide in surprise, then he settles into a wicked smirk of amusement.

"You really think you're funny, don't you?" I challenge.

"And you really think you have all this sway. I'm not fucking helping you until you release me."

Is his voice tipping into…desperation? I root myself in self-composure, deciding not to give into his antics. "Well, that's not happening. I'm not releasing you until you prove yourself trustworthy—and you give me what I want."

"Trustworthy?" he laughs. "And how do you anticipate I do that? I think you and I both know there isn't a world where I could do anything to gain that from you. So, let's cut our losses with that one."

"I know how much Edith means to you," I blurt. And as soon as the words slip off my lips, I'm ripped back to the night he held me in his arms and carried me to his room. When I told him I wouldn't use Edith to manipulate him. But it's too late. The words have already left.

His expression ripples into something deadly serious.

But godsdamnit. That look tells me enough—it works. The one thing I know can convince him to do the right thing. Something more powerful than torture or bribes. Would it be so terrible of me to persuade him, on the behalf of all humans and dragons? When thousands and thousands of lives hang in the balance?

I continue, treading cautiously, "And…I know she's in a coma. I know you'd do anything to help her. To save her."

His face is still, his lips barely moving to let the words slip out as he glares. "You are so sure of yourself, aren't you?"

I stalk closer to him. "I am sure of myself, because I've been where you are. Twice. And let me tell you, Darian, being on the side I'm on now where they're already gone is not something you can come back from. So, if you want to avoid that reality, then you need to work with me."

He holds my gaze, his chin tilting up toward me as I stop a few steps from him. "There is nothing you can do to stop him."

"Then why are you so against helping me, hmm? If you think we're such a lost cause?"

He hesitates, his eyes falling away from my face and down to my hand. To the Blood Ring. I flick a look back up at him, my mouth parting. Realization floods me, rushing through my fingers as I struggle to grasp onto a single thought. "You…knew what this was all along, didn't you? The King wants this ring. He *needs* it for something. And so *you* want it."

"I don't know what you're talking about," he sneers.

I lift my hand, facing the ring toward him. "Celeste never wanted to marry Cole, did she?"

Holy *fuck*. When Cole confessed all that happened between the time we had split up in Padmoor to when I arrived at the outpost, he mentioned he was sent down to Arterias for a trial with the King for deserting the military. He should have been executed for abandoning his post when he left to find me in Padmoor. But if Cole had his mother's ring and had seen the King…

Marge said he was searching for it for years. And if Cole showed up with that ring, he had to secure it somehow. Being promoted to a military captain was already a feat in itself. But to be promoted following such a serious transgression? Cole's words back in Arterias ring inside my mind:

And then I was offered a proposal. If I married Celeste, I would be wed into a wealthy family. I'd have a handsome dowry, and I could send that money back to my family. My life sentence would be lifted so I could be with her.

The King proposed a betrothal to Celeste because, naturally, Cole would have given her his mother's ring in marriage. And she would have had possession of the Blood Ring. Willingly. Easily. Which begs the question…why wouldn't the King just forcibly take the ring from Cole in the first place?

A smile splits across my face. "The King is scared, isn't he?"

Darian rolls his eyes. "Of a puny, incompetent woman like you? Not likely."

I grab his chin in my hand and turn him to face me, getting awfully sick of men implying I'm any less capable than them. "Then I'll become something he can be scared of."

He twists his face out of my grasp, fury edging his expression. It all makes sense. The way Darian easily flip-flopped back and forth between kindness and brutality. He was only trying to get the ring. Everything I experienced in Arterias with him?

Wasn't real.

A cloud of anger rises in my chest, blotting out the rest of the thoughts rushing into my mind. "The only reason you fucked me in Arterias was because you thought I had the Blood Ring, wasn't it?"

"Don't sound so disappointed," he purrs.

I smile at him, sickly sweet. "Oh, don't get confused. I'm not."

I rip the chain from his shackles up, forcing him off the ground. Unlatching his chain connecting him to the wall, I grab my belongings and put them in my satchel. Leading him out of the room, we head toward the western part of Driftmond, back to the grassy clearing where the dragons lie in wait for us.

Out of extra precaution, Sethan instructs that the Driftmond guards will be delivering us breakfast out here in the open, rather than having us gather in the community hall. Once we've eaten our fill, we'll move on from Driftmond to the next city of Kilamber. Archie exchanges freshly cooked chicken for Darian's chains and leads him off to get food. Marge checks in on me, and based on Cole's gaze across the crowds, my presence is enough to convince him I'm alright after last night's events.

Daeja's still lying on the frost-tipped grass, and I take a seat right on her massive wheelbarrow-sized paw after I've secured my satchel to the back of the saddle. She stretches her neck forward and sniffs the back of my head, stirring my hair into a gust of wind. Leaning back onto her foreleg, I look up at her and offer her a piece. *It's your favorite.*

Her pupils flicker back and forth between rounds and slits, her nostrils flaring as she inhales deeply before shaking her head and wrinkling her nose. ***I'm not hungry.***

"But…" I don't finish my thought…*you're usually a bottomless pit?*

"I don't like it anymore."

I lean up off her foreleg. *"What? Since when?"*

"Since A'nala got mad at me for raiding a chicken farm…"

"Daeja!"

"…and when I told her it wasn't me, she saw a feather I missed stuck in the scales beneath my chin."

I can't help but laugh as I glance over at the red she-dragon. She's lying in the grass with an assertive posture most military soldiers wouldn't be able to emulate. A mirror image of her rider just twenty feet off speaking with some of his men. Those yellow eyes narrow. Her lips lift into a growl as Archie approaches her, with Darian towed behind him, and tosses her a casual wave. She snaps at the air as Archie passes her, and he stumbles a step before continuing on his path. Darian doesn't miss a single step.

"I would have brought you food if I knew you were hungry then—"

"It wasn't so much that I was hungry. Just that it was fun. Besides…A'nala said dragons of my size should be eating something with more sustenance, so we can go longer without food. As we get older, our metabolism slows down. And being a dragon with a rider means we need to be able to go months without food if we're in the skies traveling. We can request deer or elk from Sethan whenever we please, though."

"Well…while I agree raiding a farm isn't the best practice, I'll always find a way to get you chicken if it's your favorite. And if I need to speak to Sethan about it—"

"No, no. Don't. I don't need you to step in on my behalf."

"Then don't let them dictate what you like and want."

"After she let me try elk, there wasn't much room left to dictate anything." Her tongue flicks out across her lips like she's still savoring it.

"I'm sorry I was never able to provide something like that for you." I stare up at her massive head as she tilts her face down to look at me eye-to-eye.

"You gave me everything I needed. Don't even try to feel guilty."

Smiling, I reach up and brush my hand across the side of her jaw. Curious, I tap two fingers against the side of her muzzle.

She blinks out of view for a few seconds before flickering back into existence. *We need to keep working on that. And we need to test what other abilities she might have.*

I glance over to the saddle and the bags sewn into the back half of it to carry extra cargo. It's freeing now that I can wander these lands without having to worry about hiding Daeja or my father's journal. Taking a bite of chicken, I fixate on the spot where I know his journal is, trying to recall his notes on the sun dragons. If a sun dragon could control the position of the sun and channel solar power, what can Daeja do? As far as we know, she can turn invisible. At least, for a second or two.

Daeja shifts her folded wings, aware of me zoning out on the saddle.

"Is it uncomfortable? We haven't removed it since we put it on."

"The saddle?" She rests her head on the ground between her forelegs beside me. **"I imagine it's something like wearing boots on your feet. It takes some getting used to, but I don't really notice it much now."**

Minutes later, Sethan rounds us up with the dragon riders.

When I sling myself up into the saddle, Cole appears and double-checks all my buckles. "I trust you're feeling well enough to ride?"

"As well as I'll ever be."

As soon as he tightens a strap, he dips his head and pats Daeja. "Be safe."

I can't help but watch him walk back to the wagons, my heart sinking with each step he takes away from me. I haven't had a full conversation with him since our argument outside of Driftmond. Nor much of a chance to tell him I'm sorry.

"He'll get over it. Don't you fret."

"I sure hope so…"

"He's in love with you. And I don't think anything will ever change that."

Sethan and A'nala say their peculiar little stars and skies motto before launching into the sky, the rest of the dragon riders on their tail. Once I lean forward and have my hands wrapped around the saddle horns, I narrow my eyes and chase away the queasy anxiety with determination.

"Don't forget to breathe," Daeja rumbles, and then breaks into a few strides before launching into the sky.

We lift higher and higher until Driftmond becomes a small cluster of buildings in the expansive landscape below. My stomach roils, threatening to upheave my breakfast. *Perhaps it was an oversight, eating right before we fly. I won't make that mistake again.* I tear my gaze from the ground below and focus it ahead on the other dragons dotting the horizon line.

"A'nala is calling us to the front of formation for your second flight lesson."

I sigh but clench my jaw. *"Here we go again."*

I fell three times.

Three.

Fucking.

Times.

Daeja swooped up and grabbed me every time, long before the ground could be a threat. But it still made every fiber of my instincts scream. On the third fall, I found myself able to peek my eyes open and watch as Daeja descended upon me with outstretched wings and extended claws. Her grab was gentle. And I realized, this was training for her, too. She's just much, much better at it than I am.

I will say, I didn't manage to upheave my breakfast. I'll call that a win.

By the time we land with Sethan and the rest of the dragon riders, my nerves tingle with exhaustion and adrenaline. Throwing my braided hair over my shoulder and out of my way, I work on unclipping my hooks and removing the waist belt before sliding off Daeja. Gods, the ground feels so steady beneath my boots. I didn't realize how much I take it for granted until it's hundreds of feet beneath me.

Sethan dips his head in a half-assed sign of approval, and his posse regards me with long glances before they turn their attention back to their dragons.

"Was that better?" I ask Sethan weakly, fighting against the urge to brace my weight on my knees.

"I suppose so."

"How long do the riders at the academy usually train for?"

Sethan grins and slides his gaze over to the other riders in an open invitation to answer.

"Six years for me," a man with a burly, brown beard says. His build is stocky, his head completely bald.

"Three for me," a woman with black hair cropped to her jaw answers.

"Show off," another woman with half her head shaved replies.

A man with black braids down to his abdomen interjects, "Generally, it takes about four years. But it mostly depends on your classification and ranks."

My gaze bounces from person to person. "What do you mean by classifications and ranks?"

The man with black braids answers me first, "Each classification is broken down into the elements: fire, water, earth, and air. And from there, each classification has its own set of ranks: scouts, combat, messengers, healers, assassins, breeders, strategists, mages, and guards. Some of the ranks and classes take longer than others. Unless you're Lexi."

"At least you tell the truth, General," the one with short black hair—Lexi—responds as she crosses her arms over her chest with a flirtatious grin.

"Enough, let's keep moving. We'll walk the rest of the way to Kilamber," Sethan says, his gaze fixed on the city in the distance.

"Why didn't we fly closer?" I ask.

"Kilamber has one of the several dragonblade forges in the continent. It's been shut down since Aaric took the throne. As you witnessed yesterday, we have our own rebels, and I'd rather not risk any more run-ins if we can help it. Jerome." He tosses a glance over to the man with long braids. "Take Lexi with you and scout out ahead. Find any guards and alert them we've arrived and have them report back if the dragon rider sector is ready for us."

Jerome and Lexi dip their heads and walk off together, their fire dragons close behind them. The tremors of their footsteps fade into the distance.

Marge stands before Daeja, tapping her staff on the ground several times.

"What are you doing?" I ask, coming to stand next to her.

Daeja lifts her head from where it was tucked underneath her wing and growls.

Marge takes a few steps back and holds out a hand in front of her, as if it would actually stop a dragon from attacking her. "We need her for tonight's training."

Daeja rises from the ground like a menacing shadow, and the other dragons huff their irritation at the late-night intrusion. The three of us, led by Marge, walk further away from the other dragons and the city of Kilamber. Marge stops at a spot void of trees and shrubbery, marked only by a cluster of boulders set against a barren hillside. Without trees to mask the night sky, it's a beautiful expanse of stars and dark clouds racing across the heavens.

Marge snaps her fingers, pulling my attention away from the sky. "Focus…what do you remember from that night back in Arterias, when Daeja lit the forest on fire?"

"Umm…well…"

"If she's alluding to the fact she'd like to ride me again, she might as well start digging her own grave."

I toss a glance to Daeja, who sits back on her hind legs and folds her wings against her sides, curling her tail around her front paws.

"Think, Katerina," Marge pushes. "Do you remember what happened with the dragonfire?"

"It…" I stare off at Daeja, locking into her white eyes and waiting for the answer and memories to flood me. "…it sort of…moved? I-I don't know. It sounds ridiculous—"

"No. It's not ridiculous. Go on."

"When I moved my hand, the flames seemed to follow. Almost like they were alive?" I turn to look at Marge over my shoulder, like she'll confirm where my thoughts are heading.

She nods, then hobbles forward. "Dragonfire is magic. That's why it's more destructive than regular fire. The Blood and Bone Rings were created to channel magic, which is why you were able to move it back in Arterias. It's a similar practice to pulling directly from the ley lines. Just at a smaller, more diluted scale."

She shifts her attention to Daeja and prods her tail with the end of her staff. "Test your rider."

Daeja's lips curl up, her teeth flashing in the moonlight. *"Tell her if she touches me one more time, she won't be here to witness the outcome of your so-called test."*

"Shhh," I whisper aloud, and then direct my question at Marge. "Is the blade within your staff a dragonblade?"

"Yes."

I flick my hand to encourage her to back up. Daeja lowers her head a few inches above the grass, her jaw parting, and a warm glow collects within her broad chest before traveling up her long, serpentine throat and through her mouth out onto the ground. But rather than a small flame, it blasts out in a wide circle that has the grass blackening and curling in on itself.

"Stop!" Marge barks at Daeja. "Before it spreads far beyond her control!"

Daeja snaps her jaws closed, ceasing the shower of flame. Most of the fire dissipates, with some remaining embers glowing hot like ruby jewels in the dirt.

Marge jerks her chin at me. "Good. I think you can work with that. Take it slowly. Otherwise, you risk your control slipping."

And I don't want to do that again. Sucking in a quick breath, I lower to one knee and press my hand into the earth. That rushing sound of energy hums around me, and I lock in on those wispy flames threatening to disappear. My mind wanders beyond my control to thoughts of Hornwood. Of the little girl, and the doll I buried near the river. The painful memory of not being able to save any of them. My heart clenches. I normally try to push it all away. To sweep it under the rug and ignore it.

But I can't—I need this.

I need to feel angry that I didn't have the tools to defend them at the time. I need the overwhelming determination to not allow it to happen again. And if I need to hang on to the memory that tears open the stitches in my heart, then I'll do it. I'll bleed myself out to promise I won't let it happen again.

"You don't have to touch the ground when it's already surfaced, only when you're pulling from the ley lines. Try to move it," Marge directs me.

I lift my hand off the ground and reach toward the flames. Palming the air between us as if I'm trying to draw the magic to my hand. The flames hiss, stubbornly clinging to the blackened spot, until I jerk my hand to the left, and it follows. I sweep my hand back to the right, and as I do so, I loosen its grip on the earth.

"Good…" Marge whispers.

I sway the flames back and forth, until I pull them toward me. It crawls across the ground, inch by inch, and grows more and more receptive to my call. As soon as the flames get a few inches from my boots, I take a step back and slam my hand down to stop them in their tracks. But instead, the fire zips down into the earth and disappears.

A clapping sound pulls my attention off the ground, and Marge is grinning at me.

"I meant to stop it—"

"You did. You returned it to the ley lines." She taps her staff on the frozen earth. "Now, let's up the ante."

She draws the hidden sword from her staff, the moon behind her outlining the blade in a brilliant blue. Daeja shuffles back, her eyes flicking back and forth between Marge and the sword as the horns on her head bristle.

"She won't hurt you." I caress the bond between us.

Marge lowers her sword and draws a lop-sided circle around herself. Breathily, she says, "This time, your job is to keep the flames from reaching me—"

I snort. "Definitely not that advanced."

"Well, you'll have to be."

As I open my mouth to argue, she flicks a side glance over at Daeja as she finishes the circle.

"Again."

TWENTY-SEVEN

COLD REFUSAL

I damn near drag myself through the door back at Cyrus's old residence in Kilamber. Darian's at the farthest wall, sitting against the bricks and shackled.

"I see you've been up waiting for me?" I ask, trying not to sound as breathless as I feel. As I close the door behind me, I freeze when I notice how violently he's trembling. His jaw is clenched, fists balled into the pants at his knees.

For once, he doesn't respond. He squeezes his eyes shut.

I scan the room, only to find no windows are open. And it's not like it's any colder than outside. I walk across the room and stop just outside the perimeter his wall chain will allow him to reach. "Are you…cold?"

His breath comes out through gritted teeth and pursed lips, his body rocking back and forth slightly. "No."

I begin to shrug out of my cloak. *He's that damn stubborn to deny something as simple as being cold?* Taking a few steps into his space, I hold out my cloak for him. "Here."

"I. Don't. Want. It," he grits out, opening his eyes to glare at me.

Sighing, I toss it over his boots anyway. As I turn and take a few steps away, he grabs it and chucks it off to the side.

Stubborn, prideful, and *an asshole. What a combo.*

I make my way to the wall where the hearth is, remove my gloves, and slide my fingertips across the cool marble mantle. Finding the flint and steel, I crouch down and begin to strike, again and again. As soon as a spark bounces off and flares into a soft ember, I reach my hand out with a steady breath. And pull.

To my surprise, the ember grows brighter. Then flames begin to rise out of the small kernel of heat. Until seconds later, fire snakes up through the logs and a tide of warmth washes over me. The fire fills the room with a sultry light, casting long shadows across the grand room and illuminating the gilded bed frame.

Darian has his head leaned back against the wall, his eyes screwed shut. I place the flint and steel back on the mantel and grab my cloak off the ground. At least this way he can't deny the heat of the fireplace.

Good luck refusing that one.

The next morning, I find Daeja near a massive oak tree, attempting to mimic the chirping birds. Cole relays the information that Sethan and the other dragon riders are about to take to the skies. He helps me into the saddle then checks all the buckles and straps before heading back to the wagons.

We take another half day flying to the city of Vathstone. As we approach the far western part of the continent, a blinding glimmer of the endless ocean expands out beyond what the eye can see. It's stunning, an almost seamless blend of sky and water in the distance.

I've never been to the ocean. Never even seen it outside of a map. I'd heard countless stories from Aiden when we were little, but it was mostly big brother intimidation of why I should never venture away from home. Massive water dragons could shatter the King's ships in a matter of seconds. Guaranteed disappearance if you dared any further than knee-deep waters.

The smell of saltwater whips over my face, and my mouth parts the lower we glide toward the shores. Smaller bays of water line the stretch of almost-white sand. And a bit further inland, likely no more than a fifteen-minute walk, is the towering cityscape of what I imagine is Vathstone. All around the city are lush, tropical plants and trees. Sethan and the other dragon riders land on the sandy shore between the ocean and Vathstone. I brace myself as Daeja glides into a running landing. Tightening my knees around her, I fight to keep myself upright until she slows, her body sliding forward slightly in the thick sand.

"Ooh…" she purrs and flexes her claws in it. ***"I think I like this."***

I unhook myself and jump down, pleasantly surprised to find my landing softened by the sand beneath me. Reaching down, I brush my fingers through it and revel in the gritty, foreign texture.

"It's much better during the summertime," Sethan calls from ten yards away.

I walk toward his direction, my steps slower than I'm used to. When I glance nervously toward the water's edge, a breeze picks up, carrying my cloak out behind me like a waving banner.

"It's winter. Past water dragons' mating seasons. Just stay out of the water and you'll be—hey!" Sethan's eyes widen at something behind me.

As I turn, I find Daeja running in quick, jerky, enthusiastic circles in the sand. Each time she turns, she sprays a shower of sand, one of which shoots into the side of A'nala. The red she-dragon snaps at the air a few feet away from Daeja and growls.

Daeja pivots back and slams into A'nala, bowling her over into the sand. The two become a tangle of scales and claws. A'nala slips over top of Daeja, pinning her underneath until Daeja's form disappears, gaining herself a flinch from A'nala. An unseen force shifts A'nala sideways, and Daeja blinks back into existence as she throws A'nala back down.

Sethan gawks. "They're…"

"Playing." I smile.

Though, A'nala looks more annoyed than anything. Daeja keeps teasing her with nips to the side of her neck and half-hearted paw swipes. The other dragons look on with craned necks and twitching tails.

The people of Vathstone have been nothing short of cheerful and kind. Every person I met in the community hall last night smiled and welcomed us with a warmth that mirrors what I can only imagine is what the summers feel like here. I ended up removing my cloak halfway through the evening after I found myself too heavily dressed.

After dinner, we all split off to our own private quarters for the night. Archie helps me hook Darian's chain into the wall. Darian, surprisingly, is still quiet. And still trembling. Despite his attempts to ignore my offers of help, I light the fireplace for him again, anyway.

Throughout the night, I dream again of my brother in great detail, and the river that pulls him under every time. When I wake in a cold sweat, I can't help but wonder if it has something to do with my nearness to the ocean. And how similar the currents of a river mirror the tides of an ocean.

By the next morning, the fire is still going in the hearth while I braid my hair back and dress, preparing for another day of travel. Just as I sit on the bed and bend over to lace my boots, an alarm rings out. An alarm that sounds an awful lot like…

A carnyx.

TWENTY-EIGHT

FIRE INCARNATE

The sound shakes the walls of the room. Both Darian and I watch the roof tremble above us, followed by a cluster of roars echoing outside.

"Wild dragons!" Daeja roars. *"Where are you?"*

"In my room—"

"They're attacking the city! Get your ass out here now!"

If I wasn't so alarmed, I might laugh at her use of vulgar language—perhaps I should be more mindful of how I speak around her.

Screams explode outside, and Darian pulls against his shackles as I race toward the door.

"Wait—wait! Don't leave me here!" he calls after me, fighting against the chains.

I hesitate, eyes locking with his. But I can't. I can't trust him. This would be his best opportunity to escape under the distraction. And I still need him—I need to crack whatever wall he's putting up to protect the secrets that could be the key to freeing this realm.

"I'll come back, you'll be safest here," I whisper and slam the door closed on his protest.

Screams and roars mix in a manic orchestra outside on the

streets. A massive shadow a few blocks away glides above the cobblestone street toward me, following a throng of screaming townspeople. A gigantic red dragon bursts through smoke, soaring above the roofs of the buildings, its jaws parting as it rears its horned head back and its nostrils flare. Fifty feet from us.

Thirty feet.

"Take cover!" I scream, bolting toward a mother cradling a newborn baby to her chest, and lifting my hand to block the flame.

I wrap an arm around her shoulder and lead her through the people scattering in opposite directions, their shoulders and arms hitting us as they sweep past. Going against the grain, I pull her down an alley away from the main street as the dragon blasts a fiery bolt of flame down the road and up the middle of a three story building seven streets down.

The newborn baby's cry rises as the sound of the dragon's thunderous wings and roaring fire fades, the chaos of alarmed townspeople quieting. I turn to the woman as she glances down at my hand resting on her arm. Her eyes widen as she looks at my fingers and the rings on my hands, before dragging her wild gaze up to me. Shit, so much for keeping a low profile. Especially while wearing the Blood Ring. *And I left my gloves back in the room.*

"Do you have somewhere safe to go?" I whisper.

She nods, her mouth still parted in shock. "We have an underground bunker near the center of town."

"Good, can you show me where?"

She nods again, and we race back out to the main street. As I scan the skies, I see a glimmer of multiple other shadowy figures in the distance, dipping and gliding, blasting shots of fire down at buildings.

"Where are you?" Daeja growls.

"Helping some townspeople to a bunker near the center of town. Where are you?"

"Helping A'nala and the others try to lead the wild dragons away from town. Or expend all their fire preserves. Sethan's pissed you're not here."

"Tell her and Sethan I'll join you soon once I'm done. But ask her if Sethan can send someone back to get Darian out of the room."

"Got it."

The woman and I skirt left down a crossroad alongside a crowd of other townspeople. Several buildings bursting with flames groan in the crackling fire, the heat radiating even at this distance, warming an otherwise chilly winter morning. Tall, skinny trees sway back and forth, their large green leaves glowing aflame.

"We're almost there!" the woman pants, her steps slowing as she points to a stone building off a few streets ahead, where a group of people surround it.

We join the back of the crowd and shift as the people fighting to get to the front are pushed back. Panicked cries rumble within the throng. Turning my head back into the direction we came, I watch another dragon dip low over the town.

Relief rushes over me as I pick out someone strapped to its back. The dragon and its rider glide toward the southern part of the town toward another red, riderless dragon. The first dragon with a rider slows as it approaches the wild one, flaring its wings out as it roars. The wild dragon spins to face it, and the two slam into each other midair, barreling down into the buildings in a mash of teeth and claws until they disappear below the roofline. A boom claps in the distance.

"There's not enough room for us all!" someone screams at the front of the group, trying to squeeze into the entrance of the bunker. "Only women and children!"

An old man hunched over a cane lifts his head, wrinkles weathering his brown skin.

A younger man rests a hand on the man's back and shouts, "My grandfather! Please! He can't run like the rest of you!"

More arguments burst out of the group, with others coming to their own conclusions about who should be saved and who should have to run for their lives. The crowd rushes forward, shoving past whomever had been baring the entrance, and squeezing through the double stone doors. I grip the woman's elbow more tightly.

Her face is ashen, as she turns to me, lip trembling. "Please. Please take my baby. You can keep her safe."

I shake my head. "No. You're taking your baby." I pull her behind me as I shoulder my way through the crowd. "She has a baby! Let us through! Let her to the front!"

Everyone turns to me, angry until they realize who I'm towing and edge out of my way as I pull her through to the front. I usher her through the stone doors with several others. When she turns to look at me over her shoulder, she holds her baby closer to her chest. Her eyes say it all. *Thank you.*

I shuffle back out of the way, ready to run back and find Daeja. The rest of the townspeople continue to squeeze through, the mass dwindling as they manage to make their way inside. As I get to the back of the crowd, I freeze.

Marge stares at me, her hand resting on her staff as she stands still. Her expression is calm and serious.

"What are you doing out here? Get your ass in that bunker!" I reach for her, about ready to drag her to the entrance if I need to.

Instead, she lifts her chin to the skies as another riderless dragon off in the distance turns in our direction. "They won't all fit. And if you don't do something about it, they will die, Katerina. All of them."

I swallow, flicking my gaze back and forth between the quickly approaching dragon and Marge. "What do I do?" I ask, panic lacing my voice.

"Remember what I told you about the ley lines and magic?" She draws half an invisible circle with her staff around her, stirring my memory of blocking the flames from reaching her two nights before. "Channel it. Don't let it overtake you."

I take a few steps back from the approaching dragon, whose yellow eyes find mine. "I'm not ready," I squeak.

"You never will be," she murmurs behind me as the dragon

roars, the sound traveling down the alleys and streets in a tidal wave of sound.

Widening my stance with my eyes glued to the dragon, I crouch down, my fingertips brushing the cold, dusty cobblestones. My breath kicks up a pace.

It's down to me.

I'm definitely not ready, but I have no choice.

I can't close my eyes. Not with the dragon gunning straight for us. With some internal part of me, I search the earth for that hidden river of magic, summoning it to me. But it doesn't come, avoiding my call as if it's an evasive wild animal. Or we're too far from a ley line.

"You're running out of time, Katerina!" Marge's voice kicks up a pitch.

The dragon parts its jagged jaws, a glowing heat collecting in the back of its throat. Those wild, slitted eyes trained on me. It wants me dead. I can *feel* it.

"Now! Now!" Marge cries.

My grunt becomes a scream as I try to pull the magic underneath the ground through my fingers, like a master moving its puppet. But this puppet has a mind of its own. As I lift my hands off the ground a few inches, a soft wisp of blue rises through the cracks of the cobblestones.

The dragon blasts a stream of fire that barrels down the street in our direction, a cloud of heat threatening to consume us. My grip slips, and the magic falls back out of reach. I'm too weak.

"Katerina!" Marge's scream chills my blood.

I fall to my knees with a roar, digging back into that magic as I ready myself for the rush of flames racing toward me. That roar transforms into something else. Something deep, throaty, and animalistic.

A shadow falls over me, and a black figure dives from above my head. Daeja lands with a hard *thud* in front of me, cracking cobblestones underneath her feet as she rears up, stretching her wings out to take on the flames. They slam into her chest, pushing her back until her talons scrape at the street.

"Daeja!" I cry aloud, scrambling onto my feet.

Her body absorbs the fire until she glows almost white. As the flames fade, she lowers her body back to the ground as the wild red dragon bursts through the remaining flames and tackles Daeja to the ground.

She's outmatched.

She's nearly half the size of the other dragon. And she just took a chestful of fire. She could be injured, though no pain radiates through my body. She twists underneath the red dragon, slipping from its grasp and rearing back with a ferocious snarl.

"Get them inside!" she tells me, her eyes still locked on the red dragon as she snaps forward in warning.

I turn to Marge, who watches in awe and terror. Pointing back at the entrance to the bunker, I realize there are only three people left trying to fit. The entrance is jam-packed with people who peer out from the double-wide doors, their terrified gazes set on the two dragons snarling and circling one another. I usher Marge and the remaining three people near the entrance.

"Please! A few more! Shift back, let them in!" I shout into the bunker. They manage to squeeze enough to let the four of them in, with Marge at the front. Though, there are so many of them the doors don't close completely, despite how fervently people try.

"Get them out! You'll kill us all!" a man shouts somewhere inside.

Some mutter agreements, and the crowd surges, trying to force people back out of the bunker.

I slam a fist against the door to get their panicked attention. "No! If you push, you'll forfeit your right to stay here, do you understand? Stay, and do not move!"

Daeja roars behind me, and I turn and watch as she slithers

around the dragon to be between it and me. The wild dragon snaps forward, latching its jaws around Daeja's throat as she claws at its face.

My blade sings as I unsheathe it, my eyes focused on the wild dragon. Daeja and the dragon fling and snap, swipe and strike, each fighting for the upper hand. Despite her smaller stature, Daeja is quick and still presents a challenge for the other dragon. I slink forward, raising my blade, and ducking under a swinging red tail.

Daeja slips out from the red dragon's jaws, flinging herself on top and pinning the dragon on its back, before it throws her off into a building. The building groans and folds, showering brick and wood onto Daeja. She ducks under the impact, dust billowing out from the fall. When her eyes flash open, they are pure white with a raging fury.

The red dragon is facing away from me as it snarls. I creep up and stab my sword down into the beast's tail, straight through its thick muscle until I sink the blade hilt-deep. The dragon roars, spinning toward me with a live fire burning inside its small beady eyes.

I hold its gaze. "Stand down."

Its lips curl up, revealing decades-old teeth, cracked, stained, and jagged. As it hisses, its rank breath washes over my face, but I refuse to flinch.

"Stand…"

Daeja slinks out from the rubble toward the dragon, shaking off any excess wood and bricks as she approaches the dragon from the other side.

"…down."

A voice nearly as old as the Gods whispers inside my head as the dragon narrows its yellow eyes, *"You housssse Ssspoiledsss. Wear and sssssummon the great magic. Wield dragonbladessss. A ssssinful ssspeciesss you are. Why ssshould we let you live?"*

I remove the sword from its tail in a show of good faith, the dragon roars in pain as I do so. Its orange blood seeps from the wound, trickling down its shiny red scales and pooling on the pale cobblestones.

As I look the dragon in the eyes, I sheathe my sword and speak aloud, "We are a sinful species, that much is true. But many innocents live here. Children who haven't yet been tainted."

"You take our young, too. Sssstole my eggsssss." The dragon's voice tilts more into something feminine as it stalks a few steps toward me, lowering its head to look me in the eyes.

"We are not the king of the south," I explain. "He is the one who steals your eggs. And we do not condone such actions."

Daeja growls as she sides next to me, ready to lunge if the she-dragon threatens. The fire dragon drags her gaze from me up to Daeja, locking on her eyes as a silence falls between them. Whatever they discuss, both of their pupils blow out and then narrow before the red dragon retracts her head, taking a few steps back from us. Daeja stretches her neck forward, lowering her head over mine. The movement alone conveys an entirely universal meaning.

Mine.

Daeja's jaws part as a deep grumble vibrates in her chest, shuddering the blood in my veins. The red dragon dips her head, staring at the ground as she backs away from us. Her hind quarters back up into a building, and she pauses before looking up at me. *"Ssssave our kind,"* she whispers inside my head, before launching into the sky.

I squint through the wild dragon's gusts up at Daeja towering over me. *"What did you say to her?"*

Daeja finally tears her gaze off the dragon disappearing into the distant clouds and angles her head to touch her nose to my forehead. **"Something along the lines of, 'if she takes another step closer to you, I'll destroy her.'"**

"Leading by fear, I see?" I rest a hand on the column of her throat.

"She knew who I was. Most of the dragons do. But they think because I'm younger than them, they can sideline my requests. But you are mine. And I will not tolerate someone threatening you."

I smile and turn to face her. *"Are you hurt?"* I brush my fingertips gingerly across her midnight black scales. But they shine as they always do, free from any blemish or wound. *"You…you don't have any injuries? You absorbed that fire?"*

Daeja lifts her wings, glancing at the perfect webbing. Well… aside from the single hole when she saved me back at the battle in Arterias. She shakes her wings and spine like a dog ridding itself of water. ***"Felt warm. But aside from that, I'm fine."*** She lifts her head, eyes snapping to the distance. ***"A'nala says they're running the last wild dragon out of town. I think we're safe."***

"Katerina!" a familiar shout echoes in the town square.

Daeja and I turn back to the bunker where Marge emerges. A little at a time, more and more people spill out of the bunker, scanning the skies.

Marge's eyes widen, pointing at something in the distance. I follow her stare. Massive flames stretch into the sky, engulfing buildings and razing several of them down to the foundations. A wooden beam falls, swinging across the street and slamming into the base of another building, transferring the fire to more homes and shops across the road. As the townspeople cry out, witnessing the rapidly spreading fire, I spin around and find every direction bursting with flames. And not just any flames—dragonfire.

"A'nala and the others are going to evacuate people. She's saying we need to head south out of town—it's the path of least flames," Daeja rumbles. ***"But we need to go now, before it cuts off the path and we're trapped."***

Godsdamnit. We might have chased off the wild dragons… but this is different. We can't ask for the flames to recede. To spare these people who built their entire lives here. Where generations grew and died. Where memories lived and breathed.

In the distance, where flames meld with the buildings, a shadow flickers within the blaze. The startled shouts of the crowd behind me fade away, until the only thing surrounding me is the sluggish, painful pulse of my heart. The sporadic dance of flames slows as that shadow of a person turns sideways.

It's her.

I can't make out the details of her clothes, nor her expression. But I know it's her all the same. And hanging from her hand is the small doll I know has a tear in its arm. The very one I buried back in Arterias. She takes one small step. Then two. Until she disappears out of view and into the burning city.

As soon as she's gone, alarmed cries and murmurs snap into the background around me. As I swing my attention over to Marge, she's already watching me. Her eyes say it all. *So, what are you going to do?*

A new group races down a street and spills into the town's center with Archie, Melaina, Gavin, Nolan, and the Arterians. I recognize Cole at the head. His gaze sweeps to Daeja before he finds me.

"Everyone retreat to the south!" he calls out across the chaos. Something about the calm determination on his face convinces the crowd, and they follow his lead as he points down a specific street. He pats people on the back, ushering them to go. "Stay calm, but move fast."

The throng of townspeople shift and sway as they all move toward the street Cole suggested. Marge squeezes my shoulder before hobbling over to join the rest of the crowd, Archie leading her away. I watch them go, creeping fear and self-doubt racing through me. Daeja stands next to me, her wings still stretched and ready for the moment we need to fly, but her attention focuses on the townspeople disappearing into the distance.

Even if they all survive, they'll have nowhere to go. And in the thick of winter? It could be an even more painful death than dragons. And a slower one.

This is up to me.

I *can* do it.

Dipping my head to stare at the ground beneath my boots, I drop down to a knee on the street. I press my left hand to the stones. With all the pleading I can summon, I beg for that magic to come to me. Trying to pull the pulsing energy from the fire surrounding me.

But each teasing flick of the unseen magic beyond my vision taunts me. Gods, I swear I almost sense it *laughing* at me.

A heat crowds my body and sweat trickles down my neck and back. But the flames around me don't falter. When I pull my hand off the stone, my handprint leaves a wet mark on the ground.

It's not working.

I slap my palm to the street again, gritting my teeth as I attempt to suck the magic surrounding me to my hand. But that spine-tingling sense of magic doesn't flood my veins like it should.

Still. Not. Working.

"Fuck!" I cry out, as the precious seconds tick by. Ripping my hand off the ground, I look up at the buildings around me engulfed in an ever-growing flame. It bleeds over to the buildings lining the pathway Cole suggested the townspeople take south.

No…no!

More homes burst into flames. I push up to my feet, standing to face the raging fire. My hands tremble. The screams of that little girl back in Hornwood resurface, along with the distant chanting of a nightmare.

Fire incarnate.

Flame in flesh.

Blood of power.

I failed. What good am I if I'm destined to save this realm? To save these people? My thoughts begin to spiral into something dark. Into an unclimbable pit—

Something wraps around my hand. Stilling the rush of racing thoughts and whispers pulsing in my brain.

I look down at my left hand and find strong fingers lacing through mine. The rough calluses brush my skin with a distant comfort. Flicking my gaze up from our hands, I find Cole's warm amber eyes staring down at me, the flames dancing in the reflections.

He doesn't say anything. He doesn't need to. He only squeezes my hand.

It's okay. It'll all be okay.

The meaning of it alone chases away the storm breaking inside my head, clearing a path for me to take.

"I believe in you," he whispers, so softly I almost question whether he was the one who actually said it. "You are the strongest person I know."

He slips his hand from mine, his eyes still focused on me as he takes a step back. I look at the flames, my heart slowing in my chest as I come down from my own panic. I had practiced manipulating Daeja's dragonfire with Marge. And while it was at a much smaller scale, I have to try again. I have to try until I have nothing left. I take a step forward, stretching my left hand out with Cole's mother's ring in the direction of one of the closest buildings on fire.

"Yield to me," I whisper inside my head, eyes locked on those wicked flames as I take another step. Another. And another.

The heat blasts me in defiance, warning me to get back. I stop a few inches from the flames, narrowing my eyes as sweat drips down my forehead. The salt stings my eyes and blurs my vision, but I can't blink. Gritting my teeth and fighting the trembling in my arm, I bend my fingertips toward the fire as if I were digging into it for a stronghold. As heavy as if I were moving the building itself, I swing my hand across my chest.

The flames, shrieking in protest, reluctantly follow my hand, sending a blast of embers off into the sky. A small smile tugs at my lips. It's all the confidence I need.

I stretch out both of my hands and focus on hooking my influence into the flames before swinging them back and forth to break them from their own volition. As I find a steady rhythm, the flames surrender more and more to me as I swing them. With a strangled grunt, I slam them down into the ground, forcing them to join the magical ley lines beneath me. A soft smoke rises from the building, but at least it's free from dragonfire.

"Well done," Daeja purrs. ***"I knew you could."***

A soft laugh rumbles in my chest, a flare of her pride bleeding into my subconscious as I pant. I *can* do this.

I turn my attention to the rest of the buildings surrounding the square. I can't wrap my head around how much effort it'll take to return it all to the ley lines. But if anyone can do it, it's me. And if I have to do it one at a time, if it drains every bit of my strength, so be it. I sweep my hands across the town's center, spinning myself in slow circles as I coax the flames out away from the buildings and toward me.

Marge's voice whispers inside my head from the last time I slipped into The White. *You are in control—remember that.*

Sucking in a quick breath, I spin in slow, staggered circles, arms outstretched and summoning the flames closer to me, pulling them in as if I'm the center of gravity. As I spin, the fire twirls with me, becoming a cyclone of heat and flame.

Yield to me!

The flames grow larger and larger around me, spinning faster and faster and teetering on the edge of my control, waiting for me to slip an inch before it bursts and explodes.

But I won't. I can't.

"Yield to me!" I scream as my head begins to catch up with my body, my skull pulsing with an uncontrollable dizziness.

The flames roar, desperate not to give into my control. The tips of the inferno spike, as if racing toward the sky to escape my grasp. I stop spinning, though the lingering sensation still has me staggering, my head lolling as I fight to regain my balance. I pull my elbows into my sides, dragging the flames closer and closer to me, to where the wall of still spinning flames surrounds me.

I should be scared.

If I were in this exact situation a few months ago, I would have already pissed myself. Or passed out. The temptation to let go of the flames and rest flirts with me. But those two little words echo in the back of my mind: *hold on.*

My determination overrides any of the alarm bells, and I

scrunch my eyebrows down tighter as I fight to keep my eyes open in the blinding whirl of flames.

Yield!

Trembling and shaking, I rake my fingers down from the top of the fire tornado as it screams with almost human objection.

To!

Just a little further to the ground. But it refuses to bow before me, as if I'm not nearly worthy enough.

Me!

With a guttural scream, I fall to my knees and slam my hands down onto the heated cobblestone street. The deafening circle of flames roars as it swirls down and around in a whirlpool-like motion, as if sucked into the abyss beneath the streets. The fire disappears into the ground, and a bitter coldness snaps in with the lack of overpowering heat.

"You've done it." Daeja's grin is palpable. **"That's my two legger."**

Panting, I stare at my hands splayed on the ground before me, my arms shaking beneath me and threatening to collapse as I fight to catch up to my racing pulse. The Blood Ring glows with a soft blue before fading to its normal gray sheen.

My vision snaps black, and I collapse forward onto the ground, face first. But I can't care about the slamming ache that meets my face. Only the exhaustion tearing at my bones like a vulture stripping a carcass. As my consciousness fades, something slides underneath my belly.

I peek open my eyes. Daeja has her nose underneath me and lifts me off the ground. My feet flail weakly beneath me as I fight to regain my balance. My arms are strung limply over her snout as I try to lift my heavy head. My boots meet the street, and she freezes, allowing me to slowly pull myself up off her muzzle, my legs shaking underneath me.

When I turn around to assess the damage to the buildings, my head spins. Cole dives to me as I fall forward, catching me in his arms before I can smack face-first into the ground again.

"I've got you," he whispers into my ear, lowering to his knees.

"Did everyone…everyone make it out okay?" I croak into his chest. "Did I save them?"

He pulls my head back gently, a small grin splitting his beard as he motions behind him with his chin. The buildings around us sizzle, a light gray smoke rising from the foundations and clouding the air. The bases of the homes are stained with black scars, but the wooden beams and brick columns still stand. And down the smoky street where the crowd slipped away, their distant silhouettes return.

I fucking did it.

A laugh breaks from my chest, tears misting my eyes the harder I smile. For once, I made a difference. For once, I saved them.

The street shakes under the heavy landings of A'nala and the other dragons with their riders. Sethan dismounts A'nala, who flicks her golden gaze between Daeja and me. Her expression is free from annoyance and could be mistaken for something resembling pride. The other dragon riders dismount. Sethan looks at me wordlessly, a serious calm drowning his features as he unsheathes his sword, stabs it down between two cobblestones, and kneels, dipping his head low.

One by one, the rest of the dragon riders follow suit, removing their weapons and kneeling. Each red dragon bows, with A'nala being the last, her eyes closing as she dips her maw. A swarm of pride and sheer amazement swallows me as I watch them all.

For Daeja.

And for me.

A patter of rapidly approaching footsteps steals my attention, and I turn to the sound. Corvin races up to us like a bat out of the hells from one of the side streets. Almost tripping over his own feet by how hard he runs. Once he reaches Cole and me, he hunches over, coughing as he tries to catch his breath, before looking at me with wild eyes.

"I…couldn't…" He gasps, sucking in a large breath of air. "…get…Darian…out."

TWENTY-NINE

THE DEATH IN SYMPATHY

Corvin's round eyes convey all the shock and fear I'm already swimming in. "I went back to set him free, as Sethan commanded, but didn't have the key. I don't think he has long—"

Fuck, how did I forget about Darian? I funnel my strength into lifting myself up out of Cole's arms.

Cole scans me, his hands on my waist and bracing me as I rise. "Wait, where are you going?"

"I have to get to him."

"You'll get there faster if you let me carry you."

I slide my gaze to Sethan who begins to direct the dragon riders and returning civilians into groups. Then to Daeja, who nods.

"Don't be prideful," he whispers so only I can hear. "Just let me help you."

I nod, and he sweeps me up into his arms. Corvin leads us back through the streets torn up by dragonfire, the smoke stinging my eyes and nose. Several buildings we pass are a blur of smoking rubble.

Oh Gods, did my room catch fire?

Once we turn a corner and find the building is still standing, I pat Cole's chest, requesting he let me down. As I stand on shaking legs before the structure, I notice half of it is dusted in black. I stumble for the door handle and burst into the room.

A fresh waft of smoke overtakes me, and I cough, waving it away from my face and leaving the door open for it to escape. As the black cloud dissipates, my gaze falls to Darian's body on the floor. Something I can't quite pinpoint crumples inside of me, growing cold and tight.

I should have trusted him. Had I listened to him and let him go, he would have lived.

He died on *my* watch.

I race across the room and sweep his limp body up into my lap before fishing out the key to his shackles from my brassiere. Darian's chest rises with a wheezy, tight shake before falling again and stilling. I brush a hand over the soot staining his cheek, waiting for his eyes to open. Steps sound at the door behind me.

Corvin whispers at the door frame, "I'm so sorry."

Cole brushes past him into the room and crouches down beside me, resting a hand on my shoulder. "I can carry him to Marge. She… she might be able to do something?"

"He won't survive—not after sitting in smoke for that long," Corvin interjects softly.

"I have to try…he can't die. Not yet…" I murmur, watching his face like he might wake. *But if Marge isn't able to save him…*the seconds tick by, heightening my sense of panic. "Leave," I grit out through my overwhelming guilt.

Corvin whispers, "But, ma'am—"

I turn to glare at him over my shoulder. "I said leave."

With a flustered nod, he bows his head and disappears, leaving the door still parted a few inches.

Cole brushes a thumb over my shoulder, staring at me and waiting to look his way. "Tell Daeja to alert A'nala that we need Marge, and Sethan can send her."

"No." I finally turn to face him. "I need you to go, too."

He flinches, pain sparking his pinched brows.

"I need a moment alone with him," I whisper. Because I can't tell him what I'm about to do. He might not agree with it—he might stop me. And witnessing it will crush him.

But rather than pushing against my wishes, his face falls and he stands. Squeezing my shoulder once more, he slips out the door. I swear I can hear his heart breaking at the thought I'd need a moment alone with Darian. Like he *means* something to me.

Pushing away my guilt, I look down at Darian in my lap. His skin is abnormally pale, drawn tight over his angled features. The only hint of color is the dark circles splotched under his eyes. He takes a wheezing, shaky inhale that gets stuck at the peak and releases it slowly, until he falls silent. Seconds tick by, and my skin prickles. He has to be breaths away from death now, based on his appearance alone.

"Darian?" I whisper and tap his cheek gently, like it'll force him to open his eyes and tell me he's only faking it. Like this is just another ridiculous stunt to escape. But he doesn't respond. Doesn't even flinch.

I press two fingers against the side of his scratchy stubbled neck and shift them every few seconds across his throat, searching for a pulse—

Thump…thump. There it is. Weak and brittle. Slowing by the second.

"Darian, I need you to get up."

Still, no response. His eyes are sewn shut, cracked lips parted slightly.

"Hey. Get your stubborn ass up." I shake his shoulder gently. Waiting for him to fight against death with the same vigor he did everyone else.

He's limp. Too far gone to respond, if he can even hear me.

I open the top of my shirt, fumbling for the necklace holding the vial Marge had given me. Without a second thought, I rip the cork open and inhale all the dragon's breath. Holding it in my lungs, I scoop his head into my hands and press my lips against his. I exhale into his mouth, the burn of the dragon's breath lingering in my lungs. My eyes flutter closed. I'm begging the Gods it'll be enough to save him.

Hold on.

A hand gently scrapes my cheek, dragging my hair back from my face and holding it behind my ear. My eyes flash open at the same time his eyelids drag open. His dark lashes frame his green irises, his pupils abnormally dilated.

His chest heaves with a sharp inhale, sucking the breath out of my mouth until I break off his lips. He coughs, his shoulders hunching in on himself as he fights to regain his breath.

Once he steadies his coughing, he drags a wary glance to me through half-lidded eyes. His voice is smoky. "What did you do to me?"

"I saved your life," I murmur as I shift away to leave.

He snags my wrist. "You *what*?"

He doesn't have to remind me how foolish it was. His tone conveys enough. And knowing how much shit I'll be in if Marge finds out? Perhaps I can keep it a secret that I used it on someone other than myself.

"Why did you do that?" Darian croaks, his fingers still wrapped weakly around my wrist.

I can't ignore the slight shake in his hand, trembling around my forearm caught in his grasp. "Because I still need you—" I swallow.

I need the information he isn't willing to share. The information with the potential to save all dragon and humankind. I know somewhere, deep down, there must be something to convince him. Something to shift his perspective. As far as I've gathered, all that matters is his sister, Edith. I can tell by how sensitive he is whenever she's mentioned—to the point I expect him to snap at the mere mention of her name.

He releases my wrist, his eyes fluttering closed as he sags back into my arms and rasps, "You should have let me go. It would have been the merciful thing to do."

"I—" I pause, stupefied by his response. Swallowing, I stare at his closed eyelids. I whisper weakly around the guilt still filling my throat, "I'm sorry I left you here."

He doesn't respond. The shallow rise and fall of his chest is the only confirmation he isn't dead. I glance over my shoulder at the door and then the bed. With a grumble, I slowly lower him back to the floor.

After flicking the last wisps of smoke out of the room, I close the door. The trembling in my muscles has ceased, and a new surge of strength lines my steps. The dragon's breath must have worked on me a bit, too.

Tug by tug, I pull the bed closer to where Darian's shackles are. Each squeaking scrape against the stone floor has me certain it'll wake him. But either he's a damn good faker, or he truly is stuck in a deep sleep. As soon as I get the bed close enough to him, I pull his limp body off the ground and slouch him onto the bed.

Curse him.

Even with the lost weight and muscle over the last several weeks, he's still a challenge to lift. He stirs slightly with a grunt as I pull him up onto the bed, inch by inch, with the chains clinking from each movement.

Once I finally get him on, his head flops to the side, his eyes still closed. I check his pulse. It's still a dull drum in his throat. A spike of pity pricks me when I glimpse the discoloration of deep bruises on his wrists. I can't even recall if they were there before today or not. Unsheathing one of my daggers, I slice off strips from the bed sheets and wrap the fabric gently around his wrists before securing the restraints back on.

I press a hand to his forehead, his skin icy cool. It's enough of a drastic difference to remind me of how cold I'd been when I went to The White. I brush the strands of brown hair spilling onto his forehead back away from his face, before pulling blankets over him.

"He still alive?" Daeja questions from somewhere off in the distance.

"Yes. Well…for now, anyway." I slide off the bed and undo my

braid, dragging my fingers through the crown of my head to loosen the waves as I stare at Darian's solemnly still figure on the bed.

"And you're alright? Last I saw, you couldn't even stand on your own."

I pause with my fingers in my hair. *"Can you keep a secret?"*

The bond wiggles between us in excitement. **"Does a dragon not hunger?"**

"I…used the dragon's breath Marge gave me on Darian. And…part of it worked on me, too. I'm feeling much better."

"I'm not even going to ask you how you also used it…"

I change the subject. *"Any casualties?"*

"None that have been reported. Those that lost their homes in the fire are being housed in the town's community hall. A'nala says they want to throw a feast for you."

"For me?"

"Yes, for you. Because you saved the town. If it weren't for you, the entire place would have burned to the ground."

I allow myself a small smile as I lean my back against the stone wall and slide down. I stare blankly ahead, exhaustion tugging at my eyelids and body, begging me to rest.

"And if it weren't for you, I would have been dead anyhow. Whether it was today or long ago."

"You know it goes both ways," she purrs. **"Get some rest. Your exhaustion is bleeding over to me. It's quite annoying."**

Chuckling, I allow my eyelids to finally close as I doze off. Sometime during my slumber, I sink to the ground and rest my head on piled hands. The cold, hard stone digs uncomfortably into my hip.

As I shift, I open my eyes and peek at Darian. How funny that we are here with him in my bed, as I lie on the ground. I can't imagine how he slept comfortably for the nights he spent here on the floor. Or…perhaps he never was comfortable.

Gods, did it really take me this long to realize it? Did it really take me experiencing it to sympathize?

Each time I begin to doze off, I snap back awake, woken by the lingering worry that the dragon's breath wasn't strong enough. What if he had been too far gone and it only prolonged his inevitable death?

After an hour of fighting against my intrusive thoughts of finding him dead, I push off the ground with a grunt and slip into the bed next to him, my eyes trained on his face. I don't even bother to settle under the sheets with him, figuring it far too intimate. Resting my fingers on the side of his throat, I search for his pulse. Once I find it, I leave my fingers there. Beat by beat, I anchor myself to the pulse, allowing it to carry me into sleep.

THIRTY

Back to

"Good morning."

My eyes flash open, and green eyes stare straight into me.

For a moment, I don't even recognize Darian's voice, still gravelly and rough from his previous night's brush with death.

My hand still rests on the side of his stubbled neck, the tips of our noses mere inches apart. Before my mind can catch up to why I'm in bed with Darian, I scramble backward frantically.

My cheeks heat, and I pull the sheets up over my chin. "The hells are you doing here—"

Oh. It all swims back to me. The dragon's breath has clearly settled within his body. Color blooms in his cheeks, chasing away the ashen color into his hairline. Even his eyes are a brighter shade of green, the rise and fall of his chest mellowed to a simpler rhythm.

"Not like I have anywhere else to go," he whispers, pulling a fist up to rattle the manacles encircling his wrists.

My grip on the sheets relax, and I let my arms fall into my lap.

He pushes up to lean his weight onto his elbow. "Who knew you'd become *so* fond of your roommate."

I turn my back to him, sitting on the edge of the bed braiding my hair as I mumble, "I'll soon be requesting your transfer to someone else's room, so don't hold your breath about being my *roommate* for much longer."

"I'll hold my breath if it means stopping my heart to kiss you again," he whispers as his hand rests on my upper back and slides over the top of my shoulder.

I spin with a glare, the bed jumping underneath us at how vigorously I turn. I suppose there's no hope he might have forgotten that little detail in his delirious state.

"Good," he purrs, locking eyes with me. "I have your attention."

His hand travels down the front of my shoulder, skating across my collar bone and edging dangerously close to the swell of my breast. I'm frozen, my heart thudding painfully in my chest as I watch his lazy movement. He cuts toward the center of my chest and plucks the necklace, then turns the vial over in his scarred fingers.

His eyes snap back up to mine. "Where did you get this?"

I hold his stare and flick his fingers off the vial. "I don't think that's any of your business."

"It is my business if you forced it down my throat. So, you're going to tell me exactly where—"

I laugh in his face. "You're cute if you think—"

"Ahh, so finally you admit your attraction to me." He tilts his head to the side, his hair sweeping down into his brow.

Guess he's back to his regularly scheduled bullshit. He must be feeling much better now. "I'm not telling you anything. At least, not until you tell me what I need to know. That's the only reason I'm keeping you alive. Now you owe me."

"Pfft, I owe you nothing. You did me no favors. I wanted to stay dead, and you took the choice from me. If anything, you owe *me*."

"I'm sure another opportunity will present itself." I push off the bed, stalking across the room to gather my clothes and changing into them.

He falls quiet. When I turn back to him, fully clothed, his

head rests on a fist, hair a flustered mess and a coy smile on his lips. He doesn't even bother to hide his lazy infatuation.

"Your turn." I throw him a set of fresh clothes.

One of his eyebrows raises in question, and he pulls the clothes that landed on the bed toward him, eyeing it for a second before looking back at me. "How do you expect me to change myself? Not sure if you noticed, but my wrists are a bit..." He lifts a hand and shakes the chains.

"I didn't see you complaining about your restraints limiting your capabilities when you fought Sethan."

"I have no problem taking my clothes *off*, kitten. If you remember, I fuck as well as I fight. But getting my clothes back on will be difficult."

I cross my arms over my chest. "You've never backed down from a challenge before."

"If you really want me to change, you'll get your stubborn ass over here and undress me. Unless you'd rather call on someone like Nolan or Archie to help. In which case...they might ask how I managed to survive so miraculously. And I might tell them Katerina Ashbourne—"

Cole's last name on his tongue makes me fidget. He still thinks we're related.

"—pressed her *luscious* lips to mine, forced dragon's breath down my throat, and *begged* for me to not stop kissing her. Considering you don't want to disclose where you got that vial from...I'm assuming you don't want anyone to know you used it. Especially on little ol' me. Am I right?"

Gritting my teeth, I stare him down. *Manipulative asshole.*

"Clocks ticking, kitten. And I'm feeling less inclined to keep my mouth shut..."

I mumble a string of incoherent words under my breath and storm toward him. Not wanting to look him in his stupidly smug face, I train my eyes on his chest. I pull cord by cord loose in the crisscrossed tie down the front of his shirt. Grabbing the hem, I tug it up an inch, then realize it'll be far too complicated to remove while he's shackled. I grab one of my daggers and place the tip at the bottom of the V in his shirt and slice it down his abdomen.

"Oof," he hisses playfully. "What a disappointment. I was quite fond of that one."

I sheathe the dagger at my side and freeze when the fabric splits into two pieces. My eyes flick to his naked, bronze chest—I can't help it. *Good grief, am I so simple as to be distracted by a set of perfectly muscled abs?* As I consider shifting my attention to something less damning like his shoulder, my gaze wanders down to his navel.

Damnit. *Yes…yes, maybe I am.*

He clears his throat. "Like what you see? I have a pretty simple rule of if you look, you touch."

"Nope," I grit out, accepting the fact I have to remove his shackles. Working quickly, I unlock them long enough to pull the sleeves off before securing it back on his wrists. Then remove his smoke-stained shirt. Adopting the same strategy of unlocking and locking, I tug the new shirt over him, pulling perhaps a little too roughly to cover his naked skin.

"I don't believe you. I can see it in your eyes. Can tell by how quickly you breathe—"

"You're delusional," I say as I lace up his new shirt, still avoiding his eye contact.

"And you're pathetic at hiding the things you want."

Finally, I glare up at him. "And what is it you think I want?"

"You don't want someone to be gentle with you. You want rough. Raw. To be tossed around. You're tired of being treated like you're some frail thing. You're not breakable. Or…maybe you're so broken, you don't feel like you can break any more. And maybe, there's a freedom to that. Knowing there's nothing else you have left to lose."

I pat his chest with a little force, signaling the end to our conversation now that I have him dressed. "I should have just let you die."

He grins. "I know."

During the morning, the townspeople report the damage to Sethan in the community hall. Apparently, the reason the bunker wasn't large enough to fit all the townspeople is because wild dragons haven't come this far in almost half a century.

They weren't prepared.

I say to Sethan, "Before she left, the fire dragon mentioned we stole her eggs. And that's why they attacked?"

"Likely was the King's Close Circle. Since he took the throne, he's had a special operations group designated for extracting dragon eggs and bringing them back to Arterias to destroy them."

Damn. So, the King's Close Circle could have been here in the city? "My father wrote that during his time spying on the King, he found a locked room of eggs. Why not have his Close Circle members destroy the eggs immediately? Why risk bringing them back to the castle?"

Sethan's lips twitch into a frown. "I'm not sure. There were many peculiar things the King did. While I was there, I tried to keep my head down and nose out of things."

We sit in silent contemplation, before he says, "But…thanks to you, the city is still standing today." He dips his head, swallowing. "Thank you."

I nod, clearing my throat. "I couldn't have done it without Daeja. She had taken a full blast of fire to the chest and saved me and the civilians before she fought off a fire dragon."

He twists his head. "Really? Only fire dragons are tolerant of flame. She shouldn't have been able to take such a hit without major damage. But…I suppose being a moon dragon, there's no telling what she's capable of. Perhaps she can reflect other elemental magic? Have you noticed any other peculiar powers?"

"She used to be able to turn invisible. Though, it seems to have faded since she grew."

"Hmmm…perhaps just a hatchling power, then. Or one that may resurface once her mind matures enough to catch up to her body. A dragon of her size should easily be a juvenile. At least several years old."

"Don't let her hear you use the word juvenile in reference to her." I grin.

A guard steps in, whispering into Sethan's ear, before Sethan straightens and looks back at me. "We'll stay one more night here in Vathstone to recover and assess our supplies. Tomorrow, we'll press on to Ashfall."

THIRTY-ONE

"Whiskey," I announce later that night, before I lift the flask in my hand.

"Sorry?" Darian raises an eyebrow at me from across the room, sitting on the floor with his back up against the wall and restraints hooked into the bricks.

It was an easy request to ask Sethan. One that wouldn't raise any warning. "I remember that silly little flask you had back in Arterias—"

His eyes flash with something I can't quite place. Excitement? Hunger? Desperation?

Fear?

"—here's the deal. If you train me how to fight, I'll sneak in a drink for you."

This has to be a step in the right direction. I always saw him drinking and pushed it to the back of my mind. But earlier today it struck me as I watched the townspeople roll barrels of the strong liquor down the bumpy cobblestone streets.

Darian's back to watching me with that laser-focused gaze. "How am I supposed to trust there's anything inside it?"

I shake the flask, the liquid inside sloshing. "That enough proof for you?"

"As far as I know, you could have filled it with water or piss."

Arching an eyebrow, I take a few steps toward him as I uncork the flask. "Fine, then as an act of good faith, smell it—"

He rips the flask straight out of my grasp, and before I can even try to fight him back for it, he throws the liquid into his mouth, gulping it down feverishly as it drips from the corner of his lips. He lowers the flask, then swipes the tip of his tongue to catch the excess, his eyes still burning with an unsatiated hunger.

"We didn't even agree to any terms," I hiss.

He tosses the empty container over onto the bed without a care in the world, then lowers his head and holds out a hand to me, ushering me forward in a silent challenge by bending his fingers. I ball my hands into fists, then pause. I'm still uncertain if I can actually trust him. He might have confirmed he can't kill me, but it doesn't mean he won't beat the absolute shit out of me. And while I might have saved his life, that only seems to have annoyed him more.

His eyes narrow with impatience. "If I'm anything, I'm at least a man of my word. But you're trying my patience here. Do you want to learn how to fight or not?"

With a shaky breath, I take another step into the circle I've mentally drawn around his vicinity, breaching the invisible border into the perimeter of where his shackles will allow him to reach.

His metal chains clink as he stalks forward, then stops two steps from me. "Throat, thighs, and head are the most critical spots if you can slice through them. But if you want a quick take down and don't have a weapon—" I flinch when he lifts his hand to motion toward each spot on me, "—eyes, nose, or crotch. But you stay away from here while we're practicing, got it? That's rule one." He motions down to his groin.

I look away quickly before my gaze lingers, trying not to laugh when I recall the one time I won in a sparring match against him. At least I had a good instinct on where to strike. "Got it."

"Second rule…you'll need to get closer if you want to learn anything useful." He grabs my waist and sweeps me toward him, taking his hand off me once I'm toe-to-toe with him. A coy smirk stretches across his face. "Third, I get the drink before I train you in these sessions. Not after."

I open my mouth to protest.

"Ah, ah, ah!" He wags a finger at me. "Don't test my tolerance."

I narrow my eyes and nod reluctantly, sweat dripping down my neck as he holds me hostage in his green eyes.

Thank Gods he breaks our eye contact, glancing down at my arms. "Let me see your stance."

I raise my fists as I power my core, setting my right foot in front and readying myself to throw a punch. He circles around me, his chains rattling on the ground with each step in his wake.

He stops behind me, then taps my left elbow with two fingers. "Throw a punch with your arm farthest away from the poor bastard trying to fight you."

My eyes flash, and I crinkle my nose at his mocking tone.

He whispers behind me, "Go. Show me."

I throw a left hook.

He continues, his voice close to my neck, "Alternate jabs for a rapid succession."

I punch again: left-right, left-right, left-right. I feel stupid for swinging at the air. Is this seriously going to be our training? I may start to reconsider having made such a deal with him.

He circles around to the front of me and raises his own fists. "Hit me."

A ripple of intimidation flutters in the pits of my stomach. I throw a punch with my left fist, and he slaps it away with one hand. Within that same motion, he throws a fist with his opposite hand and stops half an inch from my chin before pushing his knuckles into my skin in slow motion.

He doesn't bother to hide his boredom. "Keep your other hand in front of your face so you can block your opponent if you need to."

I swipe his fist away from my chin, and he drops his hands to his sides.

Stepping to my left, he ghosts a touch near my waistline. "Stand to the side so they have less of you to try and hit."

Obeying, I twist so I lead with the right side of my body.

He brushes a strand of hair out of my face, taking my breath with it, before he sinks his fingers into my hair and then yanks my head sideways to look at him. "Never let your guard down."

I snatch his forearm right underneath the metal band on his wrist, anger boiling in my blood as I unsheathe the hidden dagger from my waistband and stab it toward his ribs. He spins out of the way, releasing my hair with a surprised chuckle, then blocks my advance with his shackle. My blade glides off the metal with a sharp scraping sound before he palms my hand hard enough to smack the weapon straight out of my grasp. The blade goes flying, clattering to the floor a few feet away from us.

When he flicks his green eyes up to me, he smirks. "That's your biggest problem. You use your anger like an explosion in your fighting. When you do that, you'll either get your ass kicked or get yourself killed. You're far too easy to manipulate. Use that anger as fuel. You release a little at a time to sustain you."

I take a few steps away from him to try and swipe my dagger off the floor, and as I stretch my hand out to grab it, he kicks it a few inches out of the way with his black boot. I glare up at him.

"Once you figure out how to fight hand-to-hand, we can graduate you to weapons," he supplies.

I rise to my full height. "Are you just saying that to milk this whole getting a drink every night?"

He chuckles. "I guess you'll never know, will you?"

"You forget who's in control here—"

"Oh, do I?"

I lift my chin. "You train me tonight. Now. Consider me graduated. I don't have time for a ceremony."

A small smile warms his cheeks. "Such a demanding little thing, aren't you? You aren't ready for weapons."

"Watch me," I growl, snatching the dagger off the ground and pointing it directly at him. "New term. If I beat you at any point, you tell me what the King wants."

"That'll never happen—"

I chuck the dagger at him and miss his head by two feet. The blade sinks into the bed behind him, straight into a pillow. His rigid stance tells me he's considering that I might be bad enough to hit him by accident.

Good. Let him be scared—even if it's not for exactly the reason I want him to be. I stalk across the room and rip the dagger from the pillow, pulling out white goose feathers with it and leaving a trail of them in my wake.

"Fine," he purrs. "I'll play. It's only fair I get some sort of incentive, too. If you want to train with weapons, you remove these shackles from me."

"When are you going to give that up?"

"When are you going to give *in*?" He takes a few steps into my direction and cranes his neck to look at me. "If you want to train with the best—"

I scoff. Though, his arrogance shouldn't surprise me in the least. He closes the space between us, and I watch him with uncertainty as he grabs the wrist of my hand holding the dagger.

"—then that is my requirement. You know I can't kill you at this point, even if I might want to. And I wouldn't be fast enough to escape if you called your oversized black lizard for backup. But if you're so concerned about me fleeing…block the door. It'll give you more than enough time to keep me trapped until your scaled beast arrives."

Flicking my attention down to where he grips me, I spot blooms of purple and greens peeking out from underneath his shackle.

The strips of the bed sheets I tied around his wrists to create a barrier between his skin and the metal are gone.

Swallowing against the sympathy rising in me like an ocean swell, I lift my chin to look him in the face. "Fine."

I stalk over to the dresser and, push by push, shove it in front of the door. Once I've got it blocked, I return to Darian and unlock his shackles. As soon as the metal drops to the floor, his shoulders relax an inch. He brushes a thumb softly over his bruised wrist, looking like he can't believe I've actually done such a thing.

"But I don't trust you with a weapon, yet," I state.

While rubbing his wrist, he snorts, acknowledging that we both know he'd be more than capable of taking my own.

"Think you can make do with what you've got?" I taunt, powering my stance with my dagger and waiting for those wicked eyes to look back up at me.

His dark lashes snap up to reveal those sage-green eyes. That signature bastard smirk pulls his features into all the lines that should make me feel wrong. But they don't.

"You're on," he purrs.

I lunge toward him, stabbing the dagger forward with one hand and keeping the other near my face, taking into consideration his tip from earlier.

He glides with a ghostly technique, evading each plunge and swipe of my knife and muttering out words with each dodge. "You're… making this…too…easy."

Striking like a snake, he grabs my arm wielding the dagger and twists it behind me, pinning it to my back as he sweeps me toward the closest wall and slams me against it. My breath puffs out from my lips, my hand springing open in shock and dropping the dagger. I blink against the ringing in my skull.

At least he's not holding back.

"So easy," he taunts again, leaning his chest into me.

Sucking in a breath, I kick my head back as hard as I can and slam into his face. The grip on my forearm disappears, and I slip out of his grasp before he counteracts. When I spin to face him, blood trickles down from one side of his nose, over his lips, and drips off his strong, stubbled chin. He wipes the blood off with a hand, successfully smearing half of it across his face menacingly. His brows lower over his eyes, darkening his expression into a mix of hunt and play.

We explode into a series of swipes and strikes, ducks and dodges.

He eventually pins me with my back against the wall with a hard *thump*, my wrists locked above my head by his commanding hands. "Easy," he purrs.

Gritting my teeth, I kick out at him, slipping from his grip with an ease that flirts with the idea he let me. We're back to a new set of spins, kicks, and punches.

He pins me next with my face down on the ground. "Easy."

I snarl in frustration, swatting at his hands, and he lets me up. As soon as I get to my feet, we're back at it. Not even a minute later, he slams me backward into the desk, his hand seizing my throat.

He smiles. "Easy."

Every time he pins me, I fight the urge to scream, especially as he finds a way to do it harder and harder. Like he's trying to get me to relent. We knock things off the desk and slam into the wall with a force that rattles my teeth. He swipes my feet out from under me, and my elbow cracks on the floor as I attempt to catch myself, a scream ripping from my lips as I glare up at him. "Fucking asshole!"

"Lower your voice!" he snaps, dropping down to his heels in front of me and bracing a hand against the wall behind me. "Do you want the whole godsdamn town to hear you?"

I squeeze my eyes shut to block out the pain. "Of course not!"

He slaps a hand against the brick inches away from my ear to snag my attention. "That's not lower!"

My breath rises and falls in quick succession in my chest, rage nearly blacking out my vision as I cradle my elbow and slowly, shakily, move my arm to loosen the stiffness. When I look back up at him, my heavy breathing through my nose is the only sound between us.

"Better." He holds my glare, nodding his head. "Now calm the fuck down before someone thinks you need to be rescued."

He has a point. I'm not necessarily in the mood to explain why I'm having secret training sessions with Darian in the middle of the night.

As soon as I slow my breathing, I whisper under my breath, "Asshole."

"I know," he mutters, then offers me a hand to help me up off the ground.

Ignoring the help, I stand and brush off my knees and back, straightening my spine as I look him in the eye. Aches pulse through my body like hotspots.

"I think that concludes our training for tonight. Unless, of course, you'd like to owe me an entire barrel. Though, best of luck requesting that one from Sethan." He sweeps back the long brown strands falling into his eyes.

At least they look damp enough to prove he had to work for his wins. *Damn…am I getting good? Or is he just rusty after being a prisoner for weeks?*

When I move to reattach his manacles, he taunts about his ability to overpower me. That he doesn't have to have them back on. I remind him of the risks of pissing me off. Dungeons. No whiskey. As much as he doesn't want to admit it, he needs me more than I need him.

Finally, we part ways, and I change into my nightgown before sliding into bed, my joints and muscles groaning. I'm unable to keep my thoughts from wandering to the night I spent on the ground where Darian currently is. At least I have a warm, comfortable bed to sleep in. I take the pillow I sank the dagger in earlier and toss it at Darian.

Feathers fall like snow in the space between the two of us, and he catches the pillow before it can hit the ground. He watches me with a questionable side eye.

Without another word, I turn my back to him, close my eyes, and settle into sleep.

THIRTY-TWO

ASHFALL

My morning starts with aches in places I didn't realize I have. A dull fire lies within my bones. Marge must have decided after I saved the town from burning, I could take a break from training sessions last night.

As Darian and I step out onto the street of Vathstone and close the door behind us, a middle-aged woman steps out of the home beside ours. Her eyes sweep over into our direction, then widen, her cheeks reddening by the second before she hurries down the charred cobblestone street in the opposite direction.

*Oh Gods…*my own cheeks flush in heat. *Did she hear me screaming? All the thumps against the wall? Did she think we were—*

Darian snickers next to me, clearly thinking the same thing. I smack his arm to quiet him, but it does little to quell his smug grin.

We gather with the rest of Sethan's soldiers, our dragons, and our squad on the western outskirts of Vathstone. The salt air wafts over me, and I glance out at the ocean in the distance. Sethan warns the group we won't be flying on dragon back until after we pass Ashfall. It's too risky.

We riders mount our dragons and lead the wagons with the

rest of our people. We pass over rolling hillsides, across small creeks, and through wooded areas until the land slopes down into a soft crater walled over by a gray mist. At the front of our group, A'nala and Sethan pause.

Daeja growls beneath me, and I pat her neck. *"What is it?"*

"Something doesn't feel right."

A'nala spins her head toward us, staring directly at Daeja and narrowing her eyes. I don't need to know what she says because her expression alone conveys she wishes Daeja to silence herself.

Sethan turns in his saddle toward the several wagons behind us chattering and holds a finger to his lips. An eerie silence settles over our group, the previous muffled conversations dying out. Some of our squad members lean out of the wagons to peek at why we've stopped.

But there's nothing to see. A blank, looming wall of gray that stretches from the ground to the sky, void of texture or shade. The faded path dips down a gentle slope and disappears from view.

Sethan locks eyes with me, his full lips in a tight line, before he dips his head and faces forward. A'nala and Sethan slip down into the mist, disappearing. The rest of the dragons follow suit, each fading one by one until it's our turn. The horns on Daeja's neck bristles as she steps through it.

A cold, otherworldly chill washes over us, and the sunlight is swallowed by the mist. Every which way I turn is a cloud of gray. I tighten my hands around the saddle's horns, waiting for the moment we'll need to turn back or fly out of this thing. A few shadowy figures slither in front of us, and the only reason I know it's the other dragons and their riders is because of the sparks of red glimmering in the mist.

Something dark on the ground appears in the distance, and the other dragons skirt around it. As we approach, the stench of rancid flesh washes over me. Daeja's heavy footsteps chase away the mist, blowing it out with each footfall. We get closer. And I realize it's not just an object.

It's the rotting corpse of a massive blue dragon. Its maw is twisted at an ungodsly angle, the eye sockets picked clean, with vicious tears ripping down across its face and throat. A dark stain spills out from beneath it, shadowing the dusty ground.

"Look away," Daeja commands.

I squeeze my eyes shut like it'll wipe it clear from my memory and tug my face away, holding my breath to avoid the smell.

A screech rips through the mist, disrupting every grasp I have of time and sound. A rippling pain dragging out a buzzing in my nerves. I clap my hands over my ears, but it's no use. I'm caught like a butterfly in a windstorm, unable to fight against the atrocious sound and succumbing to the torrent.

"A ripple," Daeja's voice cuts through the scream. She pauses midstep, tilting her head and sinking down low to the ground.

It's close. Back when Sethan first showed us a ripple, it was miles away. But now? Now it echoes like a haunting song around us. I squint open my eyes, curling into myself as the cry pitches louder and nearly cracks my eardrums.

"Can you tell what it's saying, Daeja?"

"No." She cringes as she tries to tuck her head into the side of her throat. *"They're just…screaming."*

Screaming as if stuck in a perpetual state of torture. Reliving their last moments before death, over and over, unable to ever settle into the afterlife.

I glance behind us toward the wagons, but the few faces I glimpse don't seem to be bothered. Whipping my attention back to the other dragons, Sethan catches my gaze with a painful pinch of his features and hands gripping the sides of his head.

"A'nala says this is why no one dares into Ashfall. The ripples are far too great here for us with magic," Daeja's voice is strained, as if every few words took a heavy amount of focus to form. *"Those without ties to dragons and magic cannot hear it directly, but they'll get lost in the mist."*

Which is why nobody in the wagons looked pained. They just swing their attention around them to the same colorless, blank walls.

"So then how do we know where to go?"

"A'nala says that's our one advantage as dragons. We can see a path through the mist, but the ripples are quite…" she grunts, **"…distracting."**

Sethan dismounts and walks toward Daeja and me, scanning the mist around us as he approaches. I slide off the saddle and onto the ground, the mist scattering from my boots as I hit the dirt. Sethan grabs me by the shoulder and leads me back to the wagons. He scans several of them until he finds Marge and motions her out. She hobbles off the wagon, squinting and cringing as the next wave of screams rolls over us. The three of us break off from the group and follow Sethan deeper into the mist, A'nala and Daeja following close behind.

"This is worse than I thought it would be. We need to turn back. The wagons will slow our pace, and if we stay in this for too long, we may succumb to madness," Sethan explains loudly over the high-pitched shrieks.

"How much farther do we have to go until we're on the other side?" Marge asks.

Sethan tosses a look over his shoulder at A'nala, who prowls through the thick fog and sends it scurrying. Her yellow eyes are narrowed, her tail swishing behind her with feline annoyance.

"At least an hour. Probably more," Sethan finally answers. "I don't want to risk any of us losing our sanity. Especially since we have greenhorns when it comes to this type of raw magic."

"Greenhorns?" I repeat.

Daeja growls, **"He's calling us novices. And last I checked, I have black horns instead of—"**

"Then let her free it," Marge interjects. As Sethan starts to shake his head, she takes a step toward him. "She can do it."

Sethan's still shaking his head. "We don't know how many of them are on this path—"

"You saw what she did in Vathstone. She's more than capable

of releasing them. And as you've said previously, we don't have time to tip-toe around her power."

I still as they both slide their attention to me. Marge didn't witness me putting out the fire back in Vathstone, but I imagine she was told. Though…I flick my gaze back and forth between the two of them…since when did they start talking to each other?

Marge grabs me by the elbow and pulls my attention toward her. "Can you pinpoint where it's coming from?"

"I—" I pause, closing my eyes. The scream rings around me, as if I were stuck in an iron bell. The sound ricochets in confusing directions, making it almost impossible to determine where it's coming from. The more I strain, the more confused I become. Slowly, I pull my hands off my ears to listen for the humming layer underneath the screaming. As I find it, like sifting through a lake for a single rock, I snap toward the northwest and point.

Marge flashes me a proud grin. The three of us head in that direction, allowing me to lead the way. We pass by more carcasses, shattered human and dragon skulls, along with large stains in the dirt resembling the wavy pattern of old, puddled blood.

My skin explodes in goosebumps as we draw near, and somehow the screaming pitch lowers to something more manageable. As if it knows we're coming.

I pause and hold up a hand to Marge and Sethan, signaling them to freeze.

The mist nearly sighs and sweeps out into opposite directions from a set of withered and shattered bones lying in a pool of dust. Violent gashes rake across the pieces still left whole. The only thing still discernible is a skull. One of the eye sockets is a cavernous expanse, busted into the skull from whatever unspeakable acts were committed against the creature.

I swallow back my queasiness, my imagination running wild at who and what could have done such a thing. Even without the evidence of flesh and blood, the bones tell a gruesome story.

A hand rests on my shoulder, and I turn to meet Marge's gaze.

"Pull it. Channel it, and return it back to the earth," she whispers, though her face is still contorted in discomfort.

The screaming dies down to silence, as if the trapped souls hear Marge's words, giving me more space to focus. Only my strained breath echoes in my ears as I draw near and drop into a crouch in front of the skull.

Removing my gloves, I reach out, my fingers trembling as I rest my hand against the ancient bone. "I'm so, so sorry," I whisper to ears no longer listening.

Closing my eyes, beyond the cold bone beneath my fingertips, I feel the familiar thunderous hum rise around me, pulling me into several directions at once. But I cut through it, solely focused on the creature left here in eternal agony.

I have the power to release it—to free it from these monstrous bindings, trapping it in its last living moments.

As if it were my own memory, the dragon's last seconds of life flash before my eyes, repeating again and again in a dizzying whirl until it slows enough for me to decipher it.

Men, women, and dragons clash into a chaotic sea of battle around me with dragonfire raging in hotspots throughout the valley. Dragonblades glimmer and glow with bursts of blues as they strike, while other dragons and soldiers fall to the ground with a deathly stillness. A man, dressed in silver with swirling circles on his breastplate, races toward me, a club poised and ready to strike. My eyes narrow, and I rear back my head, calling upon the fire within my chest as the man runs into my range. A shot of pain slices through my back, and when I turn to see the cause, I realize it was only a distraction. Another man sinks his dragonblade through my wing, straight into my spine.

I can't fly.

I can't even run.

As I snatch the man's head who impaled me and throw him back into the fray, a new blow shatters my jaw. I turn. Another shot explodes in my snout, caving in the ridge of my nose with a sickening crunch, and I gasp out a strangled breath. I can't breathe. Can't move.

The man with the club strikes again, bashing me in the eye. Half of my vision goes black, and I fall to the ground. But he doesn't stop. Walloping me, again and again, as if it were nothing but a game to him. My flesh squelches under the strikes. Bones shattering. Muscles screaming in agony.

Help, help me please.

But not one human or dragon can hear me. They're all suffering the same fate.

Before the blackness overtakes my senses and the scene and agony repeats, I watch as the man beats his club into my skull. Again. And again.

Tears streak down my cheeks as the images haunt me, replaying over and over in my mind in a dizzying stream of memories, even as I open my eyes and stare at the fragmented remains of the creature. A sickening heaviness settles in my stomach. Not only did it suffer it once but thousands of times over being stuck within this limbo, for however long it had lain here.

"I will help you," I whisper into the screaming void, closing my eyes as another tear trails down my cheek, and I press my other hand to the skull. *I'm here. You are not alone…*

Summoning every bit of my strength, even as my arms tremble, I reach for the creature's soul, pulling it into my palms as if I can cradle it. Daeja's presence hums around me, anchoring me to the earth so that I won't get lost in the chaos and tempting madness. I suck in a breath, pulling more and more of the creature's lost soul into my arms until I have every piece.

Without opening my eyes, without letting my focus slip, I break my contact from the dragon's skull and slam my hands down to the cold dirt before the soul can escape my grip. As soon as my hands make contact with the earth, I force it back into the ground, as if I had to physically shove something as tangible as the skull through the layers of dirt.

"Rest…find peace." My arms shake violently, tremors snaking up through my chest. Hanging my head, I curl over the ground and clap one hand over the other on the earth, putting all my weight into my palms to ensure its successful transition. To release it back to what magic it came from.

The trembling in my body transforms into something else. Into a quaking beneath my feet, the very existence of the earth seeming to rattle. The dragon's screams fade slowly to a peaceful hum, and even though I have my eyes closed and see nothing but black behind my eyelids, a burst of white flares in my vision before fading to a comforting black.

I wait a few moments in the darkness, my hands still braced against the ground as I fight to regain my panting breath, my heart slamming into my chest and threatening to burst.

But it's gone. All that remains is peace in the absence of its tortured presence. I slowly open my eyes, staring at my hands and dragging my attention to Sethan and Marge staring at me incredulously.

"You…you did it," Marge breathes.

Sethan watches me, a hint of a smile on his lips as he crosses his arms over his chest. "Well, I'll be damned."

After I've released two other nearby ripples, we return to the group and continue through the ruins of Ashfall in silence. A silence just as calming as it is unsettling. The energy in my body is exhausted, and I hook myself into the saddle just in case. Every sway of Daeja's body beneath me has me sliding a little too far to the left and right, and I fight to keep my head up. When we finally break through the mist, a collective sigh whispers amongst us—or is it from the mist itself?

The sun dips beyond the horizon, leaving behind orange and red streaks in the sky. Sethan announces we'll stay at the town of Silkwood a bit farther north, and we only need to keep pushing for another few hours. Somewhere between sunset and night, I slump forward onto Daeja, and despite the two saddle horns digging into my chest, I fall into a heavy sleep. Every once in a while I shift to relieve the pressure in my chest from the saddle.

We arrive at Silkwood. A thick, jungle-like forest stretches out north beyond the town. The humidity is significantly higher here, and I swipe sweat off my brow as the other dragon riders dismount. Once Sethan has spoken to the outside guards of the city and ushered us into its barricaded perimeter, we are led to the city's main hall. We spend the next hour acquainting ourselves with the citizens who've been waiting for our arrival.

I'm so drained, though. I sit at the table tucked back in the farthest corner of the grand room. Daeja sits behind me, watching the crowds like a hawk. My forehead rests against my crossed arms lying on the table, my brain drifting to somewhere between wakefulness and sleep.

Someone taps a finger on the table.

Blinking away the grogginess, I lift my head to find Marge. She walks around the table and slides in next to me. "You look dreadful."

All I can muster is a snort, and I fall back into the comforts of my own arms. I flinch when I feel her hand rest on my back.

She rubs in small, gentle circles until I relax. "You did very well today. Very well every day. You always continue to surprise me."

I lift my head to glance at her. "Careful, Marge. You might start to sound like you're proud."

She snorts and pats my back before her eyes flick down to my chest. I self-consciously pull my arms a little closer to hide the necklace containing the dragon's breath I already used. I plan on telling her at some point. But that point isn't right now. Especially with an audience. That, and I don't feel like I have enough of a reason yet to share why I saved Darian.

Instead, I work to divert her attention to something else. "First time I pulled too much, you mentioned I slipped into The White."

She tosses a wary gaze around us, ensuring no one else is in earshot. Or at least, no one she doesn't trust. But all the Arterians and Vitalans mingle with the citizens of Silkwood out toward the center of the room. I catch a glimmer of red hair above the rest of the crowd.

I continue, whispering, "When I returned those dragons to the earth, was that where they went?"

"Yes. All creatures go to The White. Unless their souls are tainted beyond saving."

"Why did you ask if my brother had said something to me when I went into The White last? What would have happened if I touched him?"

She blinks, as if weighing her answers carefully. "If you touched him…you could have essentially brought him back to life."

The shock alone steals my breath, followed by the next one stolen from the idea of being able to see my brother's face again.

"And you can't do that, Katerina. You're walking a very thin, very dangerous line. Not many can dip into The White like you have without already being dead. And certainly not without taking what their heart desires most. If I ever had any doubt you were the chosen one, it's long gone now."

Silence falls into the space between us.

"How do you see the spirits you want to see in The White?" I ask slowly, thinking of how close I'd come to seeing my brother's face again. How I could possibly see my mother again and my father for the first time. Gods, is it so wrong of me to long for my family? How I would give nearly anything to see them again?

Her eyes are trained on our surroundings before she responds,

"You can't quite control it. It's a fifty-fifty chance because it has to be desired from both sides. A spirit won't show itself to you if it doesn't want to be seen."

I sag at the thought. Had my brother not wanted to see me? Was it all just some fluke? "Why…why wouldn't they want to be seen?"

"Magic like this is old, ancient, and dark. Many of the spirits are well aware of the temptation to revive someone familiar. Especially when it's someone you love. So rather than showing themselves, they avoid contact entirely."

"So…" my voice dies off. *Aiden didn't want to be seen, and that's why he didn't turn toward me? Because he was afraid I might make a wrong decision?* "Then how come I could see my brother? His back was to me, and he called out for me—"

"Have you ever heard of the saying 'the eyes are the windows to the soul?' Perhaps he was trying to communicate with you without tempting you to bring him back. No one should even toy with this forbidden magic…but you?" She turns her attention back at me. "You're not no one. I believe you can harness it, without losing control."

I smile slightly at her vote of confidence, even if it terrifies me.

THIRTY-THREE

DEAD SERIOUS

"Exceptionality requires you to trust all of your senses," Darian states matter-of-factly. He snatches my nightgown off the dresser, and now I'm seriously regretting my agreement to release his shackles if he'd train me.

"Excuse me," I hiss, still in my daily blouse, corset, and pants. I move to take back my nightgown from him.

The first night we stayed here in Silkwood, I was so exhausted from returning the ripples back to the earth that I slept almost a full twenty-four hours. A bone-tired exhaustion still weighs on me, but I brush it aside, unable to give into it with how close we are to arriving at Vitalis. Sethan gave me a questioning look when I asked him for a flask of whiskey, but he didn't push me further on it. Only stated we need to stay here in Silkwood a few days while he waits for extra soldiers coming in from Bayrock to escort our group through the mountain range to the old castle ruins.

According to Melaina, our next stop is Pinepoint, and within the last few weeks there have been rumors of undercover rebels settling into the surrounding cities to recruit more members. A secret rebellion looking to overthrow Sethan and hunting for one person.

Me.

Now that the King knows without a doubt someone wears the Blood Ring, word has been spreading throughout the lands. The Vitalan rebels want me dead. The King's Close Circle who've snuck over the border lie in wait to kidnap me. Outside of the people within our group, there's not anyone I can trust.

Darian waves me off and ties the nightgown around his forehead, successfully shielding his eyes. "Need I remind you I've seen you naked. You don't need to blush that I've touched your nightgown. It's not like I've grabbed any of your little unmentionables."

I stare at where his eyes would be beneath the nightgown. "You can't be serious."

"Oh, I'm dead serious." His stupidly sculpted lips lift in a tempestuous smile.

I palm his chest like it'll actually prompt him to change his stubborn mind.

He rolls his shoulders back and rotates his head around his neck, stretching his arms across his chest before he shakes his hands out at his sides and powers his stance. He lifts his fists underneath his pointed chin. "Let's go."

A blind Darian should be easy enough to beat. *Right?* With a soft inhale, I raise my own fists, testing his vision in case he's peeking. I slide to the right, and his head follows me. Slide to the left, then duck down. He still follows my motion.

"You're cheating," I whisper, loud enough to draw his attention back to the right.

"No, I'm not. I can just sense where you are."

As he speaks, I tip-toe far to the left. His head is still pointed toward the last spot I whispered.

I swing a quick left hook toward his waist, and he snatches me as quick as a frog catches a fly. His strong fingers grip my wrist until I relax my hand open.

He rips me into him, lowering his face so we're nose to nose.

At least I don't have to look into those unforgivable, endless green eyes. Then he pushes me out of his grasp, and I fumble backward, barely catching my balance before I can topple over. As I circle around him, he stands rigid. Still facing away from me. I lunge for his back, and he spins toward me as he drops low. Avoiding my attack completely, he seizes my arm and twists his grip to spin me into submission. I throw a punch, and he glides left, releasing me. Another punch, and he glides right. I snatch the collar of his shirt and throw all my weight into him until I pin him against the wall.

My forearms rest against his strong chest, my legs pressed against his as I trap him between me and the wall. As I smile in victory, he swoops an arm around my waist and rips me up off my feet. I kick pathetically at his shins as he spins to shove me against the wall.

"And here you thought you had me. Next rule. Don't assume. And don't…" His voice drops as he skates a hand up to my ribs, leaving shivers in his wake. "Let…" He leans in, his sharp nose brushing against the side of mine. "…your…" He stops a hair's width from my lips. So close that if I breathed, if I even could in such a scenario, we might touch.

"…guard down."

Something touches my ribs, and I retreat from his face to look down. He somehow managed to find the dagger hidden at my side and now threatens me with my own weapon, tapping the razor-sharp tip against me.

I flick my glare up at him, and even though he's still wearing the nightgown tied over his eyes, I hope my gaze is hot enough to burn through the fabric.

"I've been merciful and tolerant. Patient, even. I think I deserve something extra special after this session, don't you think?" He smiles as he presses the blade gently into the side seam of my shirt and drags it down with a cautious precision until a few of the threads pop, and the fabric breaks open an inch.

"What do you want?" I grunt and shove him away from me.

I cup a hand over the hole he's created. Thank the Gods Marge taught me how to sew, otherwise it might be an awkward explanation later on.

He takes his blindfold—my nightgown—off, then brings it to his nose with a clenched fist. With dark, hooded eyes, he breathes in deeply. "I keep this."

I snatch it out of his hands. "In your dreams."

"You're not wrong."

I grab for my dagger in the hand at his side, and he lifts it up and out of my reach.

His voice dips into a scold. "Ahh, ahh. You rely far too much on your weapons, rather than yourself. You need to think outside of the box in instances where you don't have a simple dagger or sword. Next lesson. Anything is a weapon if you're creative enough."

Snatching the plate with cheeses off a bedside table Corvin brought earlier today while I slept, he smashes it over his knee like he's done it a thousand times before. He takes two of the biggest pieces in his hands, tossing one of them up in the air and catching it several times over in an arrogant show.

Just as I'm about to scold him for breaking an item when the town of Silkwood has been so generous to let us stay, my eyes narrow in on one of the wall sconces, blazing with fire behind him.

Fine. If he wants creative…

I race for it, and he's after me, hot on my tail. Snatching the torch off the wall, I spin toward him, swiping out with the fire to warn him off. A flicker of pride warms my chest when he lets out the smallest gasp, his eyes wide as he jumps back, the flame nearly catching the front of his shirt on fire.

He freezes with his legs shoulder-width apart, then flicks his eyes to me, a new grin twisting his expression into something sinfully playful. "Bravo."

As I swing the torch at him, he ducks and lunges for my leg. I jump sideways out of his range and throw the sconce at him. His eyes flash as he somersaults forward and out of the torch's path, then whips toward me. Sparks and embers scatter across the floor.

With a wicked smile, I reach a hand out and lock into the flame, curling my fingers to latch onto the fire and drawing it up off the tiled floor. Darian's face looks like I smacked him as he watches me lift the flame from the torch up into a curling ball of fire waiting for me to release it. Up, up, up it floats, until it's eye level with him.

Finally, he flicks his gaze to me. "Fuck." He drops the plate fragments to the ground, shattering them into small splinters of porcelain. "You…you can pull?"

"Scared now?" I purr with a smile. *Good luck fighting this.*

He swallows, then takes a step back, eyes still locked on the flame.

"Tell me something about the King. Per our agreement." I push the flame closer to him and chase him back against the wall.

He breathes heavy, his jaw working as he debates what tidbit of information he'll share. "He can pull, too. Just like you can."

"Why does he want the Blood Ring?"

He narrows his green eyes, the flame flickering in the reflections. "We agreed to one piece of information. You'll have to beat me again if you want more."

With a frustrated growl, I throw the ball of flame at him. He covers his head and ducks, the fireball missing his head by a foot and exploding onto the brick wall above him. He snaps his attention up to me as the flames disappear, leaving us in darkness.

After another half-hour or so of fighting in hand-to-hand combat in the darkness, he seizes me by the throat with mild pressure and forces me back until the edge of the bed bumps my hamstrings. As I fall back onto the mattress, my heart skips a beat when he presses himself between my legs.

His grip on my throat is steady, his forearm resting between my breasts. That long brown hair sweeps down and tickles my forehead as his eyes burn into me. Those irresistible, curved lips hover inches from mine. It's too easy to picture how warm and soft they'd be, compared to the last time I kissed him on the brink of death. How could something so gently curved deliver words that cut and split and slice. Gods, does the lack of space between us stir some wild idea in my mind of wanting to—

Don't.

Sweat glistens on his forehead in the dim moonlight spilling through the windows. Even his breathing is laborious. I can't help the smile pulling up at my cheeks…he's tired. He's tired because of *me.*

His gaze flicks down to my lips, and he wets his own before he rasps, "What are you smiling for?"

I tip my chin up, staring down my nose at his mouth. "Are you letting me win?"

All he'd have to do is reach down a single inch. Just a stupid inch to touch me. To kiss me.

He leans slightly off me, but his hand is still wrapped neatly around my neck. "Is your definition of winning being choked?"

Fighting against the raging disappointment, in both him and myself, I smack his forearm off me and rise to my elbows.

He backs up off me. "I think we've trained more than enough tonight." He grabs the shackles we left on the floor, clamps his wrists in, and readies himself for another night on the cold, hard floor.

"Wait…" I whisper.

He whips his head to me like I screamed it—or he imagined it.

I stand, shaking my head. "Not tonight."

"What are you talking about?"

"Get up."

He snorts, his eyebrows pinching at the authority in my voice.

"Get," I growl and thunder to him. "Up."

Once I stop two steps away from him, his features fall still. A painful, long silence ticks between us. He finally grunts and rises to his feet, towering over me.

As I stare up at him, I swallow back the tension collecting in my throat. "There's no reason for you to stay on the floor."

A small grin lifts his lips, but it doesn't touch his eyes. "Oh, are you going soft on me, kitten?"

Clenching my jaw, I grab the long chain leash connecting his shackles to the brick wall. I swivel back to the bed and secure the chains to the headboard rails. Ripping open the sheets, I pluck the pillows off from the top of the bed and place them in a line to split the mattress down the middle.

Turning to him, I motion to the left half. "Your side." Then I gesture to the opposite side of the pillow wall I've constructed. "My side."

"What about…" He takes the pillows and shifts them until the line splits the top half from the bottom. With that wicked grin, he mockingly gestures to the top half of the bed. "Mine." Then he gestures down to the bottom half where someone's feet would go. "Yours."

I snag a pillow and smack him with it as he snickers. Quickly rearranging the pillow line back down to split the left and right side of the bed, I glance back at him. "Now get in before I change my mind."

We both settle into the bed. It feels far too intimate to face him, so I turn my back to him and close my eyes.

"Remember that night when you moaned my name in your sleep?" he chuckles.

My eyes flash open. "Is this you asking for a death wish?"

Silence. He takes the hint. My eyes flutter closed again.

Marge and I stand in the darkness a few hours later, staring out at the shadowy figures of trees stretching into the starry sky. My mind wanders to Darian, second-guessing if I properly secured his chain around the iron-wrought headboard before I left with Marge.

Marge nods at me, encouraging me to begin our training session. I crouch down, staring at the dirt, not quite touching it. Exhaustion has become my constant state, lingering over me like a blanket. I can't recall the last time I've gone without training with Marge, flying with Sethan, or fighting with Darian. I hesitate as a soft breeze carries my hair off my forehead and brushes it across my face.

"What's wrong?" Marge asks.

I stare at the ground, already sensing the energy humming beneath the surface. Without looking in her direction, I murmur, "What if…what happens if I lose control?"

"You won't."

"You have so much confidence in me." I turn to look up at her. "How do you know I won't?"

"Would you die for the ones you love?"

It's not a question in my mind. "Yes."

"Would you kill for someone you love?"

I flinch at the thought, and my mind immediately drifts to Daeja. I would gladly kill the King if it meant she was safe. Does that make me a terrible person? What if it meant having to kill Darian, Melaina, Marge, Archie, or even…Cole? Where can I possibly draw the line?

"I…I don't know," I admit in a whisper.

She nods, as if she already knew my answer long before she even asked the question. "Maybe you won't ever know. But the world we live in today is not one to make that decision lightly. You hold the entire fate of the realm in your hands, Katerina. Make sure you make the right choices."

I blow out a breath. "Is that supposed to convince me you trust in me?"

She shrugs nonchalantly. "No. But it's the truth. And sometimes you need to hear the truth, no matter how painful and hard it may be." Her eyes are soft, concealing something painful and raw behind them.

"What are you hiding from me, Marge?"

Her lips form a tight line.

I stand up, refusing to practice channeling until she tells me. "I can see it in your face. Tell me. I'm not pulling until you do."

She shakes her head, then turns, attempting to leave.

I snag her shoulder, keeping her from taking another step. "I mean it. If you truly trust me, then trust me with the whole truth. What have you not been telling me?"

"You persistent girl…" Her gaze falls to my hand wrapping around her thin shoulder.

I give her a gentle shake. "I'm serious."

"The reason I know you're capable of all these great things is because I once was you. You were not the first one rumored to be the savior. That's why some of the rebels don't entirely believe Sethan's choice in making a blood pact with you. Because the ones before you failed. And I was one of those failures."

I drop my hand from her shoulder. "You…you've been in The White before?"

"No, I never could channel like you. It nearly killed me."

"And you survived? How?" My gaze falls to her hands. To the wicked scars wrapped around them, angry and haunting. My voice lowers, if only slightly. "Were those scars actually from when you were sick as a little girl, or was that a lie?"

Her expression stills. "A lie."

I flinch, even though I knew deep down her story wasn't all it seemed. She was hiding things. The depths of those secrets were unknown, but some intuition told me they were there. Lurking beneath the surface.

I whisper, "What were they from, Marge?"

Silence.

"Answer me!"

She flicks her gaze down at her hand and clenches her fist. "They were from taking dragonblood. I am a Spoiled—that much is true. When I was your age, I fit the description of who they thought the savior would be. I was young, with long icy-blonde hair so much like yours. I knew far too much of dragons, and my grandmother taught me the secrets of medicine and magic. When a Close Circle member got wind of it in my town, I was taken to the King. The King thought I was the chosen one. He dragged me through the halls and demanded I try to hatch the dragon eggs he had been collecting. But it didn't work. He beat and tortured me, pulling me back from death every time with dragonblood. And when that didn't work, he raided my town, pulling people to use against me and force my hand into helping him. He killed friend after friend in front of me. My eldest brother escaped to the Dragon Lands, while my other brother stayed behind. For me. But my eldest brother was killed in battle. The King tempted me to pull the ley line magic so I could see my brother again and raise him from the dead if I tried hard enough. Eventually, the King realized I wasn't who he thought I was. He knew I couldn't do it. So, he sentenced me to a life as a healer for the throne, figuring he could at least make use of my knowledge. Just as you are bound to your blood pact with Sethan…"

She flips her hand open, exposing her palm and a sliver of white scarring her skin. "I am bound to the Arterian throne. To heal those in the royal family, regardless of whatever my reservations may be."

"You…you signed a blood pact with the King? That's why you always gave Darian alcohol?"

"No. Well…sometimes he might have swiped some. But what he was really after was dragonblood."

The confession smacks surprise across my face. "Darian's a Spoiled? That's why he's so much weaker now without it? Why he has so many scars? Why…"

Why he's been shaking. It was never the cold. It was *withdrawals*. Was that also why he was so damn aggressive in the early days?

"Yes…go on?" Marge urges.

"I've noticed him shivering. And I thought maybe he was weakening because of the lack of training. He's always been a bit of a temperamental man. But…it's withdrawals, isn't it?"

"Yes."

"So…what happens if he doesn't get more dragonblood? Will he die?"

"We all die eventually, do we not?"

"Will you just give me a straightforward godsdamned answer?" I hiss.

"Fine. It's possible he could die a slow, painful death the longer he goes without it, yes. Though, it's hard to say how long it would take. He's been taking it since he was a boy. Could be months, could be decades. Side effects and long-lasting repercussions vary depending on each individual."

My stomach twists as I recall one of the last few nights in Arterias. "I drank from his flask one night. And I thought perhaps my alcohol tolerance was lacking but…I hallucinated. And one night when Archie and I swiped a bottle from the healer's quadrant, I had a similar feeling. Was it all dragonblood?"

"Indeed. Though, the dragonblood I kept in the healer's quadrant was much more diluted, and a different strain than Darian normally carried. The unrefined blood was designated for him only."

The crates. The night Darian and I slept together, I turned the corner of his room and kicked a crate with liquid. Not wine, but dragonblood.

I take a small step back. "So, the times you used medicine on me…you were using dragonblood? You've…you've essentially tainted me to be a Spoiled? And everyone else you've treated?"

"Now, now, Katerina. Consuming diluted dragonblood a few times will help speed up the healing process. It won't automatically make you a Spoiled. You need a strong dosage of dragonblood and at a consistent rate for it to taint your blood permanently."

"So then if you're a Spoiled…you're still taking dragonblood?"

"No," she answers softly.

"Then how did you survive coming off of it?"

"It was no easy feat. The withdrawals alone can drive you insane. But I slowly reduced my intake over months, until I was only taking a drop a day. Mixed with a softer dragon's breath, eventually, I was able to completely stop. There were times I slipped, but what mattered is I kept pressing on. But Darian…that boy has been taking it almost his entire life. I'm uncertain if he'd be able to do the same."

"How could you not tell me all of this before?" My voice pitches in irritation. All these revelations rocked me, throwing me off balance as I scramble to grab hold of the truth. What if this information could have changed the course of things if I had known earlier? "I thought you trusted me?"

"Sometimes there is a time and place for everything. You weren't quite ready to know of that yet—"

"And so you use the excuse of time as to why you never told me?"

"Katerina," she warns. "There are many things you need to learn, but at the top of the list is controlling your anger. Being angry doesn't constitute the right to be rude."

"What else do you think I'm just 'not ready' to hear, Marge? As you've alluded to several times, the days are ticking by. Every wasted moment is time taken from what we can be doing to stop this war. To stop King Aaric!"

"And yet, things must be done in order. You cannot rush this, Katerina—"

"It is *so* easy for you to say these things, Marge, when *you* aren't the one responsible if people die!" I flick my hands up to the sky, my chest heaving with each angered breath.

"I know. I understand. You seem to forget I was the one who was in your shoes not long ago. Except, there was absolutely nothing I could do. I was misled and misguided. And yet, I still paid the price for hundreds of innocent lives."

"Then if you understand me so well, cut the bullshit and tell me the Gods-honest truth. If you keep thinking I can't handle it, then how do you expect me to grow enough to be able to? I have proven myself again and again to you that I can!"

"Let's not get carried away here. You haven't been entirely forth-coming with me either, so let's not pretend you're the shining example of honesty. Don't think I didn't notice the dragon's breath I specifically commanded you to *only* use on yourself is now gone. And, miraculously, Darian seems to have made a full recovery after he should have been *dead*," she bites out.

My mouth parts, my breath coming out in an audible pant.

"Exactly. So don't pretend you're any better than I am. I know you have your secrets, just as I have mine. When I feel it is imperative for you to know, then I'll share. But until then, you just respect my advice." She looks me up and down in irritation. "Now. Are we going to stand here and argue all night? Or are you going to put your coin where your mouth is and pull?"

I narrow my eyes, holding her stare until I relent and drop back into a crouch. I brush my fingertips across the ground, stirring the magic lying beneath the surface. It tugs at me with a familiar magnetic pull, calling to me with a desperate urgency.

As I press my fingers down into the dirt, welcoming the call, a zap of energy explodes into my skin. I tip away from reality. The environment around me is drowned out in bursts of light, fading in and out as they grow larger and form into one.

The last thing I see is Marge; her eyes trained on me and expression fading into the light. "When you get to The White, don't touch anything or anyone. Just listen."

A wave of pain ripples through me, my eyes roll back into my head as it nearly takes me over. The next wave hits, and my control slips, the energy shooting up my fingers and through my arms like liquid fire, unlocking a guttural scream from my lips. The pain is so blinding I can't even silence myself. I swim in an endless abyss of agony, until all at once, the instant stretches into eternity. Like the snap of a finger, everything falls silent.

I'm stuck in an endless expanse of white, waiting. But nothing calls or whispers to me, and nothing shifts in the blank, colorless sheet surrounding me. My heart calls out to see my brother, mother, and father.

But no one comes.

THIRTY-FOUR

BAIT

After spending most of the next day resting, I stalk into my room after dinner and find Darian already sitting with his head leaned back against the wall. Stopping a few steps away from him, I toss out the wrapped canvas square I've brought toward him. It lands on the ground with a soft thud a few inches from his right foot, ripping his attention away from me to it.

Watching me suspiciously the entire time, he drags the fabric package toward him and flicks open the top flap before looking up at me. "What's this?"

I nod toward it. "Just open it."

Earlier this morning, I made the request with Corvin, hoping he could find the materials without alerting Sethan since he seems to be his right-hand man. I can't take any questions from Sethan. Or even Marge. While Corvin was quite confused as to why I was requesting paints, brushes, and several rolls of parchment, he didn't press me on it. Figures he probably thought due to the state of peril this realm is in, and how much pressure it puts on me as being the chosen one, I deserved the fulfillment of a small, easy ask.

Darian tilts his head to the side, his brown hair sweeping down into his eyes as he reveals the small set of brushes, simple coin-sized paint containers, and rolled sheets. "Why are you giving me this?"

"The morning I woke up in your room back in Windmere, I saw all the brushes and paints by your windows. I saw the night sky painting and the one of you, your mother, and your sister—"

"That was *private*," he growls, finally looking up at me. "And you think I'm the one who painted those?"

I shrug, taking a small step back. "It was a guess."

I thought such a gesture could instill some peace into our relationship—*no,* partnership. If we have to tolerate each other and share a bed, perhaps we can at least be amicable. And maybe, just *maybe*, it can lead to me learning more about all the secrets of Arterias. Judging by the way he fails to deny it, it must be true he painted those back in Windmere.

With the tip of his boot, he pushes the canvas rucksack away from himself. "I don't paint anymore."

My jaw relaxes as I watch him. I need to get to him. I have to figure out a way to crack his impossibly hard exterior. Because trying to win against him in a fight is near impossible without magic. Mentioning his sister is far too risky and sensitive of a topic. Paints don't work. I could try to get him really, really drunk and see if he slips. But…he's too cunning for that. And I can't quite let him out of his manacles to do anything else. What will it take to get an answer out of him?

Just a *sliver*?

A thought strikes me. Perhaps I can seduce him…manipulate him into giving me the information we need. *No, Gods, that's a stupid fucking idea.* I slink forward a few steps anyway, staring down at him as my pulse quickens and I swallow.

Don't even fucking think about it, Kat…

He side-eyes me, glancing from my face down to my feet. "What do you think you're doing?"

I drop into a crouch two feet away from him, regarding him through lowered lashes.

He leans forward and snags a paintbrush from the materials I brought him, flicking it expertly in his dexterous fingers before pointing it a few inches from my chest.

I scoff, and wordlessly, both of us slowly rise to our feet, my hands splayed out to the side as he stands half a foot over me. Considering how well he fares with a sword, I imagine he can do plenty with even just the brush. He could stab me in the eye with the blunt end, shove it down my throat, snap the wooden handle in half and slice my neck with the sharp, broken edges. He only has to want to.

"Why are you looking at me like that?" he growls.

I flick my gaze from his lips up to his eyes. "Looking at you like what?"

"Don't come any closer," he warns quietly, pushing the paintbrush's soft bristles to my chest to keep a few inches between us. "Or you might not like the outcome."

I stare at him in challenge and step closer. "Are you seriously threatening me with a paintbrush right now?"

"There's more to life than threatening, kitten."

"I hope you don't forget that…" I whisper.

Never faltering from breaking our eye contact, he slowly drags the brush up my chest between my breasts, and it glides over the surface of my shirt up to my naked collarbone. *Good, he's taking the bait.*

"Can I ask you something?" he mutters and pulls the brush up my throat until I tilt my chin up to him.

I'm unable to keep myself from swallowing against it, a flash of heat creeping up my chest. This…this is easily becoming a mistake. I can see the flashing warning signs as bright as a strike of lighting. But I'm already struck.

Unable to move away from him, I whisper, "No."

He leans toward me, his nose brushing a few strands of hair

off my ear as his warm breath tickles at the corner of my jaw. "Well, I'm going to ask you anyway."

As if against my own will, I lean my head away from him to angle my ear into his lips.

His voice lowers to a whisper dripping in seduction, "Is the only reason you decided to let me live because you wanted answers?"

"Yes," I breathe, only able to get out single words as I struggle to contain myself. My eyelids become heavy.

His laugh chuffs against my ear, and my eyes flutter completely closed. I need that vibration. Need it surrounding me, touching me, inside of me. Gods, all the places his mouth could be other than sitting near my ear. Like between my legs, where I dreamt he'd be. The memory of his sensual threat flickers in the back of my mind: *I fuck as well as I fight.*

He drags his thumb across my lower lip. "Liar. You know you want more than that."

The accusation makes my eyes flash open, ripping me out of my moment of delirium. I push him away from me, my breath abnormally heavy in my chest as he snickers. *Snide, arrogant, pompous—*

My glare flicks down to his lips. For a moment.

A fucking *moment.*

I don't know who moves first. And quite frankly, I can't be bothered to care. We crash into each other like the sea against a rock, my lips on his feverish and torrid. I grab the collar of his shirt, throwing my weight half-haphazardly into him to get closer as I swipe my tongue across his lips, and he groans. Groans with a sensuality that heats every fiber in my body. We clamber back until his body shudders as I slam him up against the wall. The paintbrush in his hand falls to the ground.

The rush of adrenaline from the battle in Arterias, in Blackfell, and against the wild dragons in Vathstone is no comparison to this. I chase after the same thrill with each kiss, each grab of his hair, and each roll of my hips into him. Despite knowing he can't kill me, I can't help but feel danger with each touch. With each kiss, as if it may destroy something even more precious than my life.

Don't I deserve this? Don't I deserve *something* to make me feel good, even if for a moment, while I hold the weight of the world on my shoulders? I just need a moment to forget about it all—to be lost in something else. Any desire I have for Cole is selfish. Painful. But this? This is nothing but lust. *Right?*

It doesn't matter.

Because Darian's holding me, touching me, kissing me, and matching my own ferocity and desire. Every caress clears the thoughts straight out of my head and brushes them off into the wind. His lips explore me more frantically, as if he's slipping into an abyss of his own desires, and I'm his only tether to reality. He holds the sides of my face in his hands, like I may disappear if he lets go. My desire chases away all my sanity and replaces it with desperation. With a hunger for him to demolish me until I've crumbled and rebuild me back with each kiss.

Foolishness. This is all so foolish and yet…I can't stop. I don't want to stop. Fuck him for being such a godsdamned good kisser.

He pulls his mouth off mine, the absence of his warmth a shock of cold air. I gasp as I realize I haven't been breathing.

"Don't touch me like that if you don't intend on letting me fuck you senseless," he growls.

I glance down, and my hand is wrapped around his cock straining against his pants. I should be racing back across the room or, *shit*, out of the room at this point to stop myself from touching him. But I can't. Slowly, I shuttle my hand up and down his length. His eyes explode into full dilation with shock, adrenaline, and arousal.

His hand flies to the nape of my neck, capturing my hair at the base of my skull. Ripping my head back, he grazes my throat with his teeth as he growls, "Normally, I wouldn't be the one in handcuffs. But I suppose for you I'm willing to make an exception."

He latches his mouth onto the column of my neck, sucking and licking his way up to my ear. He gravitates toward that sweet spot between my ear and the corner of my jaw, as if he's done it a million times before. As if he knows what makes me melt. His hot breath warms my skin, dragging his tongue across and behind my ear until he sucks my earlobe into his mouth and nibbles.

I flinch forward, closer into him. My hand around his length quivers as I fight to regain my composure. His mouth moves over my jaw, my cheekbone, down to my lips. He kisses me. Claims me. Taking me as his own and whispering to some wild, untamed part of me that he's in control. His hands grip me steady, fisted tight in my hair, as I work my hand up and down his length until I need more. I need him to moan. To need me as much as I need him. My mouth waters, begging to taste him.

I break off our kiss and suck on the side of his throat as I use both hands to rip his pants down. As soon as I do, I retreat from his neck. My jaw goes slack at the view. Before I can change my mind, I get down on my knees before him. Looking up to watch his reaction, I flick my tongue across the head of his cock.

He grunts as he throws his head back and smacks it against the stone behind him. His breathing gets heavier, and it teases my fantasy of wanting to hear all the sounds he makes. All the sounds I can pull out from him. I wrap my fingers around the base of his shaft as I lower my mouth over his head, taking his cock into my mouth.

"Oh fuuuuck," he hisses.

I begin to bob up and down on him in time with stroking my hand over his shaft, sucking him farther and farther into my throat. He grabs me by the hair and slowly begins to direct the motion of my head onto his cock. Until he's pushed me deep enough I gag.

"You're so pretty when you're gagging on my cock," he purrs. "Next time you open your lips to insult me, remember how much I fill this tight little mouth of yours."

He begins to pull my head off him, but I grab his wrist with a spit-soaked hand, not wanting to take him out of my mouth. Saliva dribbles out the corner of my lips, and his length is glistening. I begin to work on him again, my hand gliding along his length with ease. The entire time, I look up at him. Watching his lips part, his jaw relax. A gratified growl rumbles in his chest, encouraging me to keep deep throating him, even if it nearly cost me several breaths. I adopt a corkscrew motion, up and down and twisting around him as he pants and groans. The long chain connecting his two wrist swings and smacks against my chest as he fucks the back of my throat. I remember the intoxicating control I used to have over Cole. How I loved the sounds he made as he spilled himself into my mouth. That I was the one who earned it.

I suck Darian's dick greedily, near desperate for him to fill my mouth with his cum. Needing to hear him break. He rips my hair back hard enough my mouth pops off his cock.

His hazy, lust-filled eyes meet mine, his lips open as his breath saws in and out of his mouth. With his thumb, he smears the drool on my lips. "As much as I love fucking your mouth, I want your cum on my cock. You either take your pants off or get your ass out of this room before I break through these godsdamned chains, bend your ass over, and fuck you like you're mine."

Watching him with panting breaths, I slink back, never taking my eyes off him. His eyes flash with a mix of simmering disappointment and frustration. The space between us is unbearable. It takes a fuck ton of effort to increase it until my ass bumps the edge of my bed. Eyes still locked on his, I sweep a hand back over the sheets, then slide it underneath the pillow and into its case before pulling out the key.

As soon as the light catches its golden gleam, Darian straightens. "What are you doing?"

I strut back over to him and unlock his manacles. Now, he has full free reign. I toss the key back over onto the bed, my eyes glued to him.

"I don't want you to stop," I admit in a breath, grabbing the sides of his face in my hands and pulling him to me.

He snaps forward with an animalistic grunt, his hands and

mine fumbling at my waistband, scrambling to strip me down. Once I'm naked, he tosses my clothes off into the corner of the room. His turn. I revel in gliding my fingertips across his hot, muscled skin.

As soon as the both of us are naked, Darian skates his gaze up and down every curve and length of my body. "Get your ass up on that desk and spread your pretty legs for me."

My heart thunders in my chest as I back up with every menacing step he takes toward me. Gods, seeing him stalk toward me naked has my pulse doing somersaults in my stomach. Each step is outlined in pure confidence, exuding sensuous, sinful temptation. My ass bumps into the wooden desk, jolting me out of my trance for a moment. I hop up onto the desk, watching as he closes the gap between us.

He stops before me. "Open them wider. Show me how wet you are."

I obey, spreading my legs open for him as I watch him through heavy lids. He's so damn hot as he marvels at my naked body. Especially as he lazily brushes a hand up and down his length, his gaze heating my skin with all the unspoken things he wants to do to me. I dip my fingers down between my thighs to test how wet I am. "Is this to your satisfaction?"

His tongue flicks out across his bottom lip. "It's a start."

Smiling, he grabs my left ankle and lifts it straight into the air, then lowers his mouth to the inside of my shin. Kiss by kiss, he inches down lower and lower, his other hand pressed against my lower abdomen and snaking up to my chest and gently pushing me back to lie down. He sets my left leg down on his shoulder. With a thumb, he swipes down from my clit to my entrance, and I instinctively buck against the sensation.

"Gods, look at you," he groans, almost pained. He slips two fingers inside of me until they're as deep as they can go, his thumb resting on my swollen clit. "So wet…" He removes his fingers from me, and I whimper as he starves me from his touch. "So messy for me." He takes his fingers and sucks on them, one by one, ripping them out of his mouth with a hungry groan as if he's complimenting a chef's dish.

He drops down to his knees in front of me. "Put your feet up on the desk and show me that pussy. Yes. All the way, that's it. Just like that," he praises. "Gods, you're aggravatingly fucking sexy."

His hands grip the inside of my thighs, keeping me spread open, and his devious smirk lights up as his darkened eyes meet mine. Slow, as if he owns all the time in the world, he drags the tip of his tongue from the bottom of my entrance all the way up to my clit, watching my expressions from between my legs the entire time.

Sinful bastard.

I should hate him for how wicked he makes me feel. My legs clench instinctively around his head as I arch off the desk.

He groans, delectably pleased with tasting my arousal. The hot, wet press of his tongue against me disappears as he pulls back slightly to speak. "You're going to come on my tongue. I will lick, suck, and swallow every drop you will give me, and I will not stop until I've had enough. Then, and only then, will I stretch you out with my cock, and fuck you so hard the only word you remember is my name. And I will not stop until you ask me to. Do you understand?"

I nod, nearly breathless as I absorb his words, almost shaking at the thought of all the things he'll do to me. "Show me you're a man of your word."

There's his sinful, one-sided grin that curls my toes.

He releases one hand from my thigh and with a thumb, firmly presses right above my clit and tugs the skin up, tightening the pressure. Leading with his nose, he traces his tongue just after it, rocking his face into me as he licks my pussy. Slow at first. Building that need. His stubbled cheeks and jaw scrape the skin on the inside of my thighs as I fight myself from trembling around him.

Holy fucking Gods and dragons.

His strong tongue slips up to where my throbbing clit is, rubbing in deliberate, strong circles. Up and down, round and round with a localized pressure that has me arching off the desk, my toes curling to the point of cramps. My breath sticks in my lungs.

Maybe he has a reason to be as cocky as he is. He's had his mouth on me for maybe thirty seconds, and I already feel the danger. There's no coming back from this. Not now that I want it. That I *need* it.

As if he couldn't max me out at this level of pleasure, he rockets me into the next bracket as he adds in two fingers back inside me, pumping them in rhythm with the circles as he sucks and licks my clit. He's steady and consistent. Rather than trying to race me to an orgasm, he takes me step by step, allowing me to relish in every flick of his tongue, every plunge of his fingers.

But it doesn't matter because the tight coil of pleasure winding within my core steals my breath as I rip his hair into my fingers like he'll save me from the inevitable fall and blissful crash.

I come undone.

Biting down on my lip to try and silence my cry, my eyes squeeze shut as I tremble and ride every scorching hot wave of pleasure rocking throughout my body. And he doesn't let up—just as he said he wouldn't. Licking, sucking, swallowing, and rubbing. As soon as I catch my breath, I edge up onto my elbows, waiting for him to remove his mouth. But he flicks up a warning glare and gently pushes his fingers into my chest, pinning me back down onto the desk.

He unlatches his mouth from my clit, switching spots with his fingers and plunging his tongue inside of me with a delectable moan. He glares up at me from between my legs, a hint of a smile at his lips. Fucking me with his tongue, shaking his head back and forth as if it'll allow him more access to dive deeper inside of me, devouring every bit of my flesh, sweat, and arousal. Each move exudes an innate drive to please me, to serve me.

It doesn't take long until I crash again, crying as I throw my head back against the desk and gripping his head between my thighs. My breath saws in and out of my chest, my legs shaking so violently the desk trembles underneath me.

He lifts his head up, licking his lips, his entire face soaked. Before he can even think about returning between my legs, I force his head up toward my face, a pained growl rumbling in his throat as he follows my grasp to avoid tearing his hair out.

"Who said I was done with you?" he grumbles. "I was perfectly content watching you writhe on my tongue."

Tease. I tug his head back to reveal his proud throat.

"Me." My next string of words comes out desperate. Breathy. "Darian…I need you to fuck me."

A smirk splits his lips at the simple word. "Need, huh? Need is a funny little thing…"

Probably shouldn't have admitted that. I'm sure it'll bite me in the ass.

He leans forward and kisses me, slipping his tongue between my lips so I can taste myself on him. His mouth moves over mine as he slides his tongue with mine, a salty taste washing over my mouth.

When he breaks our kiss, his voice is husky and tight with failing restraint as he speaks against my lips. "You wouldn't have your way…but I need to fuck you hard enough to forget my existence."

He grabs my hips in his hands and slides me across the desk against him, then sweeps me up into his arms. I wrap my wrists around his neck, holding myself to him as he fumbles around blindly, mouth locked on mine. He slams me back into the wall, barely breaking my concentration on his mouth. He fists his fingers back into my hair as he breaks away from my mouth and kisses down my jawline. I roll my head back against the wall to give him full access to the sensitive parts of my neck. And he takes it. His hot tongue caresses my skin, coupled with soft sucks that have me bucking my hips into him.

"Enough with the teasing already. Just fuck me," I grunt through tight breaths, trying to school my aching need for him. "Please."

He chuckles. "So impatient. As you wish."

He sets me on my feet, spins me so I'm facing the wall, and pushes me against it. With my cheek flush against the brick and my hands braced on either side of my face, I slide my legs apart as he taps the inside of one of my thighs. He presses one palm against my lower back, encouraging me to arch more for him, before he grabs one of my asscheeks and pulls me open. He brushes the thick head of his cock against my heat.

"Remind me of my name when you scream," he whispers roughly into the back of my neck, sending goosebumps down my spine.

He slides himself inside of me, choking out any response I'd been thinking of. Slow, inch by inch, he stuffs himself inside of me, waiting for me to grow accustomed to his length and thickness before he pushes farther. He stops once he's fully inside of me, his hips set flush against my ass. That full pressure of him inside me is mind-tingling. I'm burning for more friction. I glance over my shoulder at him, waiting for him to give me the movement I so desperately need.

He grins. "You're holding your breath."

I blow it out, heat escaping my face, and instead I wiggle my hips against his groin, wordlessly asking for him to fuck me. He tangles his fingers into my hair to gently pull my head back, before he leans in close, his lips trailing whispers of kisses down along my temple until he reaches my ear.

His voice is soft and sultry. "I want you to…"

He pulls out a few inches, then plunges deep inside of me with a forceful grunt, my legs quaking beneath me, and I gasp out.

"…beg for every inch." He pulls out again lazily.

"Beg for every kiss…" He gingerly pecks my shoulder. "…beg for every touch—"

He slaps my ass, and I jolt forward into the wall with a muffled cry, the sting of it delicious and startling all at once. The pain rings in ripples across my skin, contrasting against the wicked heat collecting in between my thighs.

"Beg for me," he growls as he kisses against the back of my neck and bites down into my skin with a softness that conveys nothing but possessiveness.

I groan, the sensation of pleasure and pain an entirely new concept to me. And one that takes me by surprise with how much I like it. There never would have been a world where I begged from a man, let alone for a man to fuck me. But here I am, pressed up against a wall and needing him. Craving every bit. He turns me into an absolute animal—hungry and focused on the overwhelming and all-encompassing need for only one thing.

Him.

"Please…Gods…fuck me like I won't break," I say with my eyes closed.

"I am not your god."

The next string of words come out in a jumbled, breathy mess. "I don't care who you are, give me your cock. I want you to touch me. Kiss me. Fuck me. All of it. Take it all and make me yours."

"Mmmm, I like the sound of *mine*," he growls.

Something snaps, and he uses a hand to pin the side of my face against the wall as he fucks me hard and fast. So much so that I'm spreading my legs wider so he can reach those irresistible spots that have me trembling and whimpering for him. Each thrust is harder than the last, and a tight grunt escapes his lips. A loud clap sounds every time he slams into me, filling the room with a rhythmic applause that matches my pounding heart.

Every attempt at saying something is stolen by the roll of his hips, every inch of him drowns out my thoughts in euphoria. I whimper, sensing the inevitable new wave of pleasure rolling in. Understanding exactly what I need, he begins to smack my ass. Not hard enough to sting but enough to grab my attention.

He whispers breathily near my ear, "You gonna come on me like this?"

"Yes," I moan. "Please, don't stop. Please let me come."

He listens, continuing to work himself faster, chasing that next climax until I shudder, clenching around him again with a force that seals my eyes shut.

"Atta. Girl. You. Take it. So. Well." He punctuates each word with grunted thrusts while gripping my ass so hard I'm sure it'll leave bruises.

We descend into pure, mad lust. He fucks me over and over, pinned against the wall, until my ears ring from coming so hard, so many times. It's almost as if with each thrust, he discovers exactly what makes my body tick and melt, adjusting his tempo and speed to what my body calls for.

"Darian…I…" I pant, my entire body shaking as if I were left out in the cold, sweat drenching my skin and my hair plastered to everywhere it touches. "I…can't…stand…"

He slips out of me immediately, sweeping me into his arms just as I collapse. He carries me over to the bed, laying me down and flipping me onto my stomach. He plunges back inside of me and continues to pound me. I melt into the bed as he fucks me into the bouncing mattress, just as he said he would.

"Darian," I cry and shatter once again.

"That's right. Make a mess on my cock."

I'm struggling to find a single breath. My bones are an aching, blissful mess. Perhaps I'm in way, way over my head. Here I thought Darian might have been all talk…but now that we're here, in a room with just him and I, things are different.

We rock back and forth, the bed squeaking in appreciation, our sweaty bodies slapping against each other. I push up to my forearms, glancing back at Darian. His eyes are trained on his glistening length gliding in and out of me. Sweat plasters his brown hair to his forehead, his brows lowered as he concentrates on the task at hand. His strong fingers pull my ass apart, stretching me wider to accommodate him as he fucks me.

His eyes begin to flutter, his head lolling back as he thrusts again and again. Gods, from this angle he's devastatingly beautiful. Each carved muscle shifts with every snap of his hips, sweat dripping and rolling down his bronze skin. Even his staggered, panting breaths spike a desire within me. He looks vulnerable, basking in every touch and sensation. Losing himself to *me.*

I look away as he hunches over me, tucking his hard cock deeper, and I gasp. His lips brush my shoulder blade, up to the back of my neck, and bites me as he rocks both of our bodies back and forth.

"Come…come for me…one more time," he rasps near the shell of my ear. "Remind me who I am. Remind me who's fucking you."

Gods, even his voice sounds so completely desperate and unlike him. It unravels something in me, this vulnerability in him I've never seen. As if on cue, he slaps my ass, jerking me out of my fascination and reminding me of whom I'm dealing with. Reminding me this is just a nasty, good fucking.

A screaming high of ecstasy and pleasure peaks and explodes into an array of sound and colors, until it rips out of me into an audible cry of his name.

He matches my vigor, slamming into me with a ferocity that makes my body shudder. With his own deep, delicious roar, his thrusts become erratic as he fills me with his cum. He slumps forward and catches himself with his hands braced on either side of my head while his cock pulses inside of me. His chest presses into my back with a comfortable heaviness, barely keeping himself from completely crush-ing me. His heavy, panting breaths stir the hair near the nape of my neck, and he rests his forehead against the back of my head. I'm still lost in the sea of rippling pleasure, my mind buzzing until I sink into something quieter and stiller.

The weight of him disappears as he pulls himself out of me. I flop onto my back, my chest still rising and falling with the rush. When I glance over to Darian, he's also on his back, eyes closed as he works to slow his breathing.

I sit up as he mutters, "Don't worry. I'm barren."

The statement stuns me, and I slowly look back over at him. I open my mouth to ask if it's because he's Spoiled, but instead I ask, "How am I supposed to believe that?"

His eyes are still closed. "You can still take pennyroyal if you don't. I just thought you should know."

Uncertainty clouds my thoughts, and I lower back down, pulling the sheets over my body as I stare at his profile lit by starlight. The hard line of his stubbled jaw, the strong bridge of his nose, up to his dark full lashes. And those undeniably soft lips.

Before I can do a second stupid thing tonight, I turn away from him.

And sleep.

THIRTY-FIVE

SECRETS AND SHAME

Darian's face is the first thing I see when I wake, his eyes still closed and breath slow as he slumbers. I glance down to the rest of him underneath the sheets. Still naked.

A knock sounds at the door and all my blood drains from my face at the same time Darian's eyes flash open. I scramble off the bed, frantically pulling on a shirt and pants. Then gloves onto my hands. I flatten my hair on the sides of my head as the knock sounds again.

With a quick inhale and swallow, I inch the door open, positioning my body in the gap so no wandering eyes can glimpse a naked Darian sprawled out on my bed.

"Sethan is requesting you this morning for—" Melaina pauses, eyeing me up and down suspiciously. Her nose wrinkles. "You... umm..."

"Yes, we'll be there shortly." I slam the door quickly before she can finish, and before I give myself away by the rapid blush of my cheeks. I flinch as soon as the door is closed, mentally noting I'll need to apologize for that later.

Darian snickers from the bed, propped up on his elbow with his hair a stupid mess of brown. His other hand rests on his thigh, where the sheets just barely, *barely* cover everything I shouldn't be looking at. "You know, most women I've been with flaunted the fact they spent a night with the prince. And now you've spent *two*."

I snag his clothes off the ground where we discarded them the night before and chuck them in his direction.

He continues, not reaching to clothe himself, "I wouldn't be surprised if the entire town heard how loud you screamed last night. I'm surprised they didn't come check in on you. They could have thought you were dying."

Gods, I'm dying right now from embarrassment, a new heat rushing to my face. I avoid his eye contact, braiding my hair back out of my face and adjusting my clothes before pulling on my socks and boots.

"Last night was a mistake." I glance over at him. "We'll pretend it never happened."

He gasps, pressing a hand to his chest in over-exaggeration and falls to the mattress with a smug grin. "How she wounds me so."

He rips the sheet off and I look away, before remembering I'd unlocked his shackles and tossed the key on the bed.

Shit. *He didn't…he wouldn't have grabbed it. Right?*

I can't figure out a way to ask or search without making it obvious—staring at him while he's naked leans a tad too intimate. Besides…I don't need to tempt myself. I already proved last night my own self-restraint is much weaker than I hoped.

Thankfully, he dresses himself quickly, slips his manacles back on, and stalks toward me before stopping a step away. "Here. You'll probably want this." He grabs my hand, opens my palm, and places the key there.

I don't have time to mask my shock, our eyes locking for a split second before he brushes past me for the door.

"Are you coming or not? I wouldn't keep a man like Sethan waiting for long," he calls.

Sethan's a bit wary of crossing the river twice to get from the eastern side of Silkwood to Pinepoint. The Bayrock soldiers who've traveled in to escort us the rest of the way to Vitalis noted a surge in water dragons and suggest we avoid the waters where we can. No one knows why they're breaching so late into winter. Water dragons are seasonal, with more activity during the warmer months. So, the plan is to skirt the eastern part of the Forbidden Forest to avoid the rivers. Sethan mentions earth dragons are easier to deal with since our entire thunder is fire dragons. And given the fact the Forbidden Forest is teeming with earth dragons, it's imperative we don't fly overhead and disturb them. We have to walk.

Melaina pulls me to the side and out of earshot of the rest of the group.

I begin, tripping over my words, "Look, I'm sorry about this morning I swear I didn't—"

"Don't bullshit me. I could see it all over your face."

I blink. "See what all over my face?"

"The look of someone who just got laid or got damn near close to it. I don't think I've ever seen you so embarrassed and flustered. And I've seen the way Darian watches you. Anyone can see his eyes follow you as a starved man would. How he has the audacity not to care that anyone notices is beyond me."

I suck in a quick breath, unable and unsure how to respond as I shake my head.

Her brown eyes meet mine as she crosses her arms over her chest. "Tell me I'm wrong."

My mouth parts, but the lie won't come.

Luckily, she doesn't let me suffer long. "Exactly. Don't lie to me. You don't have to be ashamed—"

"I'm not ashamed…"

"Yes, you are. I've seen the way your cheeks redden when he's near you. And the way you always cross your arms when he comes within your vicinity. You constantly dart your gaze away, but it always goes back to him."

"Fine. He's not bad to look at. Is that what you want me to admit, Melaina?" I grumble.

She smiles mischievously, and I roll my eyes, beginning to cross my arms before I stick them down. I can't admit more than she might already think she knows.

She bites her lip. "If…I can give you one piece of advice, though. Don't let that secret out. If someone finds out, they might use the information as a weapon."

I blow out a breath, imagining all the potential scenarios if the Vitalan rebels discovered I was fraternizing with the heir to the Arterian throne. While wearing a ring which could single-handedly take down the King if they killed me. Yeah, she has a point. "Then that means you'll keep it between us?"

"Archie—"

I shake my head. "No. No, I'll be the one to tell him. But… can you do me a favor in the meantime?" My cheeks heat, preparing for my next ask. "Is…there any way you can get me pennyroyal?"

She coughs, pounding her chest before looking up at me. "If my father finds out and thinks it's for me…"

I grimace, realizing at the same time she does. "If he finds out…tell him it's not for you. Tell him it's for me and Cole."

She shakes her head like she's been slapped. "I'm sorry, *what* did you just say?"

Swallowing back the creeping fear, I answer, "He'll understand. Cole's not my brother. We've been lying to you all."

Her jaw drops open, and I squeeze her arm gently as I eye our surroundings. Signaling her to hide her shock.

"Who else knows?" she whispers.

"Your father and Marge. That's it."

"Archie…?"

I sigh. "No. He doesn't know. But I'll have to let him in on that, too…it's just…"

"How could you have gone on this long lying to all of us?"

"Because we didn't want the truth to shake our group's trust and confidence in us. There's too much at stake and—"

"And you couldn't trust me or Archie to keep it a secret?" She takes a step out of my grasp. "We're supposed to be your *friends.*"

"You are! It has nothing to do with how I feel about either of you. I trust you."

"Then why not tell us?"

I blink. Then shift my gaze to the floor as I consider an answer. "I'm…I'm not sure. Honestly, I just wanted there to be one less thing you had to worry about. And keeping a secret felt like piling more on top of everything else going on and…I don't know…I'm sorry, Melaina."

"You know what…fine. Your love life is really nobody's business, anyway."

I flinch, taken off guard by her response.

She continues, "I won't say anything to anyone about it. You have my word."

"That's…kind of you—"

"No. Don't think it's *kind* of me. You're right. Nolan already doesn't trust you, and Gavin is too quiet for me to discern what he thinks. But the fact of the matter is, if this prophecy really is about you, we need to make sure nothing else throws off our plans of getting to Vitalis and finding answers. And if we do ever get back to Arterias…" her eyes narrow, "you'll come to clean. To everyone. And that includes Celeste."

The words stick to my throat before I force them out, "Cole and I aren't together, if that's what you're implying—"

"No. It's not about love. She was never in love with him. But she was in love with the *idea* of him. She gushed about how elated she was to have you as a sister, since Darian never loved her. She has no one, and Cole was the answer to her prayers. To having a family of her own. She deserves to know it's no longer an option."

Before I can answer her, she brushes past me. "I'll get you that pennyroyal."

THIRTY-SIX

The Forbidden Forest

The Forbidden Forest is thick with humidity and sprawling with every green flora I've ever seen. Soldiers at the front of our group lead through the thicket, tapping aside vines that hang like mangled curtains.

Archie is in front of me, his gaze sweeping left, right, and up to the canopy. He stumbles over a vine on the ground, and I catch him before he can fall. When he turns his beaming smile on me, it twists that pain in my heart of how I need to come clean to him about Darian and Cole.

A soft song of crickets chirp near and far, while distant birds whistle in the trees. Most of the forest is shrouded in shadow, sunlight choked out by the overgrown trees above, but streaks of golden sunlight leak through, casting enough of a glow for us to see.

Daeja walks beside me, snorting and then shaking her head as dragonflies attempt to land on her neck, then buzz around her snout. When they still linger, she blows a breath out of her lips and the two bugs tumble away and flit off.

"Wow…are you alright?" Archie mumbles in front of me, his attention stuck on Darian. "Did you fall or something?"

Darian is to his left, with Melaina holding his chains on the opposite side. Both of which meet Archie's wide, concerned gaze.

Darian's lips lift into a smug, arrogant grin before he tugs his collar down to reveal a set of purple bruise-like markings decorating his strong throat. "Oh, this? You should see her."

I swear all my blood rises to my face, and I might pass out from the mortification. And the asshole turns his head only slightly over his shoulder to wink.

To fucking *wink* at me.

I stop in my steps a split-second before Daeja bumps me with her shoulder as she passes, encouraging me to ignore it and keep moving forward.

"Oh…I see…" Archie drags his rounded eyes back ahead to the path, his spine straightening. "Hope…hope she's…okay…"

"I'd argue more than okay," Darian tosses back.

I'm going to fucking kill him.

"Please do. No one is stopping you," Daeja chuckles.

I toss her a wary glance. *"Stop doing that."*

"Not my fault you're a little loud with your thoughts. Shut the door if you don't want me to hear."

Grumbling, I internally search for the pathway between us. But as I reach it, I leave it open. Not wanting to close it off.

"So I thought," she snickers. **"But if you keep blushing every time that man opens his mouth, everyone's going to catch onto you."**

I clear my throat, roll my shoulders back, and grumble, *"Thanks for the advice."*

She swings her head back to look at me and snorts with affection. The hot blast sends my hair back from my face.

After a few hours of silent trekking, we stop at a massive tree covered with tangled moss and vines. Long, wispy, lime-green fronds drip from its branches, swaying back and forth in a light breeze inches above a pool of green. A toad leaps into the water, causing a small ripple before it's gone. Daeja stiffens beside me, and I pat her shoulder.

Though, I'm unable to stop my laughter from spilling over into my consciousness. *"Don't you worry. I'll protect you from the toads."*

She narrows her eyes into slits at me, but she doesn't deny the fact they still intimidate her.

"And don't worry. I won't let the others know your…reservations." I rub her foreleg playfully.

The soldiers turn, looking back at the end of the line past me at Sethan. We all step aside as he strolls forward, then joins in some hushed conversation with the front of the group. I catch 'which way' and 'left' versus 'right,' along with a small squabble between two soldiers.

"Wow, look at this!" Archie snags a brilliant emerald off the ground where it had been perfectly nested in a bed of grass.

The ground glimmers with more of the green jewels, casting sparks of dazzling light as sunlight leaks through the trees above.

Archie turns a wide smile into my direction and holds the emerald up for me to see it. "This alone could get my family out of debt!"

"Stop!" a rough whisper cuts through our group from someone behind us.

As I turn, Corvin races forward with wide eyes and his hand outstretched as he barrels past me. "Archie, put that back now!"

At the same time, a low rumble trembles somewhere deep within the forest. Corvin bumps into Archie, and Archie loses his grip on the emerald for a split-second before seizing it mid-air and scrambling over himself to set the jewel back where he found it.

But it's too late.

The leaves of the undergrowth shake, the movement drawing closer and closer. Yellow eyes flash open in the darkest part of the forest. Emerging from the thick shrubbery is a jade green dragon the size of…*a cat?*

"Lower your eyes! All of you!" Sethan commands, dipping his head low.

Oh, shit. Those aren't emeralds—they're dragon eggs.

We all lower our faces, eyes glued to the ground. But not fast enough, as the small jade-green dragon screeches and races toward Archie and Corvin. Several more small green dragons leap out from the undergrowth. One toward Sethan and A'nala, both of whom slide in front of Melaina holding Darian's chains.

"Do not let them bite you!" Sethan draws his sword. "Hold them back!"

Another one, the size of a dog, lands in front of Cole, its scales glimmering underneath years of undergrowth blanketing its back. Roots rise from beneath its talons and snake toward his boots as he unsheathes his blade.

A fourth wingless dragon that resembles a snake slips toward Gavin and Nolan. Its black beady eyes flashing while its forked tongue slithers out from its crooked jaw.

Three more dragons varying in shades of green spring toward the dragon riders.

Seven dragons. Seven *small* dragons. It shouldn't be a cause for concern…except the fear in Sethan's voice spikes my pulse.

The first small dragon flings itself and barrels into Corvin, knocking him clear off his feet. The two of them turn into a wrestling match of teeth, claws, and fists. Corvin's metal armor screeches as the dragon rakes its claws across his chest plate, then sinks its teeth to his face. Corvin screams with a terror that chills my blood.

The rest of the group explodes into havoc. A'nala and Sethan work at guarding Melaina and Darian from one dragon. Marge shifts behind Cole and removes her sword from her staff, while Cole swings his blade at the roots tunneling toward his feet. Gavin and Nolan work at keeping the wingless earth dragon at bay. And the other riders and their dragons circle to fend off the last three. Spare soldiers split to defend the horse-drawn wagons at the back of the group. The horses throw their heads back with panicked squeals.

Daeja and I race toward Corvin where he writhes on the ground, as Archie snaps forward to grab the dragon by its long, skinny tail. He pulls the dragon off Corvin, and the creature whips to snap its needle-like teeth at Archie's hand. Archie dodges just in time. As the dragon rears back, I close the gap and shove Archie out of the way and raise my blade in front of me.

The earth dragon pauses. Its gleaming, yellow eyes narrow, Corvin's blood still dripping from its maw. A gurgling hiss emits from its throat.

Heat barrels over my shoulder and fire blasts the grass between me and the dragon. Within the blink of an eye the fire ceases. Leaving behind a circle of fire no bigger than a spinning wheel.

A warning shot.

A *successful* warning shot, followed by Daeja's thick growl.

The earth dragon backs up, squealing in terror at the flames. I know it's fear all too well. The difference is I've overcome it. Forged myself new from the flames.

The earth dragon scampers away and disappears into the underbrush, and I turn my attention back to our group. Archie falls to his knees next to Corvin, and Marge joins to help.

Roots wrap around Cole's shins. Despite slicing through several branches crawling up at him through the ground, they multiply and conquer inch by inch.

"Get down!" Sethan roars to everyone before he rips Melaina to the ground, and Darian drops, too. A'nala stretches her wings out to cover the three of them. The green dragon near them has its jaws parted to reveal rows and rows of tiny sharp fangs. Like the blooming petals from a flower, part of the green dragon's skin fans out around its face.

Everyone drops to the ground. I only have enough time to fall to my knees and send the dragonfire back down through the earth before ten splinters explode from the dragon's mouth. Daeja rears up in front of me and flares her wings, blocking Marge, Archie, Corvin, and me behind her. The small barbs puncture her wings, and she lands on the ground with a monstrous thud. Parting her jaws, she roars until the trees sway in a chaotic dance.

Oof. Now they've pissed her off.

The rest of the earth dragons pause before snapping their attention to Daeja. Air hisses as Daeja pulls in a long breath through her fangs, and she pushes up onto her hind legs. Her throat glows orange as she gathers the next breath of fire.

The earth dragons turn tail and bound back into the forest, disappearing into the thicket. Daeja lands and blows out a breath of smoke, watching the bushes quiver then still. Everyone else rises to their feet, and Cole brushes off the roots tangling his legs before he's helped up by one of Sethan's dragon riders, Jerome.

"Are you in pain?" I ask as I rush to Daeja.

She twists her head to pluck a two-inch-long barb from her shoulder and spits it out with a scowl. ***"No. Bunch of yappy little things. Lucky I didn't torch them."***

"Pull the barbs out, and she should be fine," Sethan says. "That earth dragon was far too small to be poisonous enough to take down a larger dragon. Though, the side effects may be uncomfortable—"

"Help! Please!" Archie calls.

Corvin convulses on the ground with his eyes bulging and hands clawing at his face, smearing blood across his paling skin. Marge brushes a hand over his forehead, while Archie tries to still Corvin's hands.

"Katerina!" Marge snaps. "Earth dragons can be poisonous. He might only have minutes left!"

I run over to them and drop next to Marge as Corvin begins to gasp for a solid breath. Sethan ushers people back to give us space, while muttering commands to the other dragon riders.

"No—wait, no!" Archie whips out a dagger, slices off part of his shirt, and holds it to Corvin's bleeding nose. "There has to be something we can do! Can we…can we tie a-a…tourniquet? Or something!" He whips around to look at the group, eyes wide with desperation. "Please!"

Marge drags her gaze to me. "There's nothing anyone else can do for him but you. The poison's magical composition is similar to dragonfire, just in a different form. Just like how you set those ripples free, pull it. Control it."

I rip off my gloves finger by finger as I look up at Daeja. Cole's at her side and gives me a small nod as he works to remove several of the poisonous barbs from her scales and wings.

Corvin gurgles beneath Archie, his legs twitching as he sporadically thrashes. Archie watches me with glassy eyes as I stretch a hand out to Corvin's cheek. I rest my palm against his face, wet with blood. My eyes lower to the rapid rise and fall of his chest. We don't have much time—and Gods…if I fail. I feel every stare burning into my skin. The inevitable humming energy sings around me, as if from a hidden world just beneath the surface.

This is where it matters. Where I matter.

"You've never let me down," Marge murmurs gently.

Summoning all my strength, I shut my eyes and focus on Corvin's body. I picture his muscles. His bones. I fixate on the veins in his body and sink my concentration into the rivers of blood, following each curve and flow as I pinpoint the black, sparkling fluid pulsing throughout him.

As if I were sucking it out with my breath, I draw it closer to me through my fingers with each inhale. Calling it to me. The liquid trembles, fighting against me. But slip by slip, it edges back toward the center of the wound in his nose, until I feel it collect in my palm. My body shakes as I fight to keep it from escaping. My breath comes out in ragged pants. The poison burns and freezes my skin all at once as it sits in my palm. With a strained roar, I flash open my eyes and fire the handful of poison away from Corvin. The liquid flies from my hand as if it were a spear, splattering against a tree and running down its mangled bark in dark rivers.

Corvin's eyes fall closed, and his body stills to a peaceful calm. The tension in his expression melts away.

"Move!" Sethan barks and pushes Archie out of the way.

"Did it work?" Archie's voice twirls into something almost distant and incomprehensible.

"Katerina?" Marge's voice echoes as if some underwater call.

The colors of the forest around me whirl, and my breathing slows. An icy burn spiders up from my hand, through my arm, to my chest.

"Kat?" Archie turns his bewildered gaze to me, his face beginning to spin. He lurches forward to catch me, but I can't remain conscious long enough to see if he does.

My sense of gravity slips away, like I'm falling. My skull crunches against something hard.

Even in the depths of whatever existence I'm in, she's there. A sparkling onyx orb promising peace and home.

"Where are you?" she calls out to me, the orb constricting and expanding with each inflection.

"Here," I groan, but I'm too far for my voice to carry. I reach for her, only to find my nerves tingling as if I slept on them for too long and just woke. But my hand is outstretched before me, and I wiggle my fingers. Something about the sensation tells me this isn't The White. I'm not dead.

Or at least not yet.

"Katerina?" Daeja calls again, her voice tipping into fear.

"I'm still here," I croak.

An invisible breeze brushes against my skin. And a foreign, sultry voice whispers in my head. *"Let me help you…"*

I flinch. Raking my gaze around the blank wall of white around me to pinpoint the call, I stop at a green orb.

"Here. Yes. Come to me." It echoes out across the vast nothingness.

When I turn back to the black orb where I felt Daeja, she's gone.

"How do I know I can trust you?" My voice echoes loudly around me.

"You either trust me or die. Which shall it be?"

I glance down at my hands, and while I still have the dark stain around my middle finger where the bond marking is, the Blood Ring is gone from my left hand.

"The clock is ticking. And if you die, so does the Moon One."

As I open my mouth to respond, something crawls over my face. A solid wall of heat blasts me off my feet. My mouth is ripped open by the unseen.

The voice distorts into something sinister and menacing, *"Breathe…"*

My eyes snap open, and I gasp for breath like a fish out of water. My vision floods with blinding greens and yellows. I claw at my mouth, pulling off roots hooked into my teeth and tossing them off me with a cry.

A pair of wide, gold-glittering eyes regard me from above. Long strings of ivy cascade from the antler-like horns on the green dragon's head. It retreats from me. The sunlight behind it outlines the overgrown moss strung like curtains from its wings. Every square inch of the dragon's scales is covered in growth, as if it surfaced from the earth itself.

Daeja crowds into my vision next to the green dragon lurching over me. ***"You're here."*** She nuzzles her scaly nose under my chin, her breath heating my neck.

"What…happened?"

"You passed out. When you drew the poison from Corvin's

body, you absorbed a lot of it through your skin. So, it kind of took you…"

"To the brink of death," the foreign voice rings in my head.

So it wasn't because the magic overwhelmed me. When I try to curl up off my back, I find a numbness blocking my limbs. I'm unable to do anything but move my head and blink.

"Careful," the earth dragon warns, somehow sensing my struggles. *"Let the breath chase out the poison."*

"The breath?" I ask.

"Dragon's breath," Daeja answers. ***"He was gracious enough to come to our aid and heal you."***

I lock gazes with the green dragon with vines curling around its body. *"You…you were in there, weren't you?"*

It blinks long and slow at me. *"Yes. I heard the Moon One's roar. The forest has been quiet for over a hundred years, so I knew there was trouble. Though, I never expected to find you."* As it turns its head slowly to Daeja, I hear the creaking of wood. *"Take your humans and fire dragons and leave. This forest does not welcome outsiders. And others may not be as forgiving as I am."*

Daeja looks up to the earth dragon, dipping her head in appreciation. ***"Thank you for sharing your breath."***

The earth dragon settles me with one long look, then it turns and leaves, disappearing and becoming one with the forest.

THIRTY-SEVEN

POISONS

I'm lying on the ground, my muscles still paralyzed from the poison, but at least I'm alive. Turning my attention away from Daeja, I find Sethan and Archie still crouched at Corvin's side, with more soldiers gathered around them in a half circle. Marge hobbles over to me, her legs and staff blocking my view of Corvin as she nears.

She crouches down in front of me, my vision filled with her warm, wrinkled face as she stretches out a hand and presses it to my forehead.

Cole's right behind her, also dropping to his knees in front of me. His mouth moves quickly, but no words come out. Marge turns to respond, but I still hear nothing.

"Why…why can't I hear you?" I mumble, the words feeling like a mess on my numb lips.

Marge and Cole turn their attention to me, eyes wide with concern. Cole says something, but I can't read his lips. I try to glance around them to where Corvin is.

"Is he…is he okay?" I ask.

Cole lowers his gaze and tosses a quick look over his shoulder as Marge frowns and shakes her head.

"I'm sorry…he was too far gone," Daeja whispers.

I strain against the invisible block, gritting my teeth as I fight to sit up. But it's no use. A heaviness blankets my body from my neck down.

Cole leans forward, sliding his hand underneath the small of my back and my head before lifting me up off the ground into his arms. Daeja turns a pointed glare at him, and I can feel the vibration of his deep voice rumble in his chest.

"He wants to carry you until the poison fades from your system."

I slur the words out loud, unsure if I'm making much sense, "When will that be?"

When Marge answers, Daeja relays the message, *"She says it could be an hour or two, depending on how much leaked into your bloodstream. But since that earth dragon gave you its breath, it's likely to speed up the process."*

I nod, sighing and sagging into Cole's arms. When I glance up at him, he meets my gaze and mouths, "It's going to be alright. Rest if you can."

An hour or so later, the numbness fades from my nerves. I walk alongside Daeja and the rest of our group, a sad silence settling over us. Cole is with Archie, rubbing his back and murmuring to him. Daeja informed me they strapped Corvin's lifeless body onto A'nala's saddle to transport him to the next town, since the wagons didn't have quite enough room.

By the time we make it out of the Forbidden Forest, the jagged spires and rooftops of Pinepoint reach into the sunset. The other dragon riders fly ahead of us, their thunderous beating wings are the first sound to bubble up through the silence blocking my hearing. Melaina relays that they'll check in with the city council, then loop around Pinepoint to ensure the city is safe for us to stay overnight. And to find a proper burial site for Corvin.

We stop a few miles out from Pinepoint out of caution—the size of the rebellion against Sethan is building, though no one knows the numbers. We sit on the grassy hills and watch the clouds race by in vibrant bursts of pinks and yellows. I flop down, and Daeja takes a seat next to me, her hip touching mine.

"It wasn't your fault," she murmurs, swinging her gaze to me.

Shaking my head, I wrap my arms around my knees and stare down at the grass swaying in the wind. *"I should have saved him. The only thing I knew about him was his name, and I should have saved him."*

Archie plops down next to me and wraps his arms around his legs before whispering, "Thank you for trying."

I turn my face toward him and find his eyes lined with tears.

"It should have been me. I was the foolish one," he croaks. "Gods, I feel so fucking stupid sometimes."

"Hey…" I grab his shoulder nearest to me and shake him when he won't look my way. "Hey, it was an accident. You didn't know they were dragon eggs."

He shrugs out of my grasp, his face settling into a somberness. "It doesn't matter. Sethan already hates me and thinks I'm not worthy of Melaina. I can't imagine this will do anything in my favor. And maybe I'm starting to agree with him."

"Sethan doesn't think a lot of people are worthy. Even me sometimes."

He blinks, then glances sideways at me.

I press on, "You are the most eligible man I know. You are kind, brave, strong, and all the things me and any other woman would dream of having in a man. And I'd be next in line for your hand if I didn't already know you belong with Melaina."

"You're ridiculous." But a distant smile winks at his lips.

"Ridiculous or not. It shouldn't matter what he thinks of you."

"But it does…" His voice breaks. "Because I'm in love with her, Kat."

I bite into my lip to stop the creeping smile and nod. "Then that's all that matters. Don't get hung up on what he thinks. He's not the one you're in love with…unless you're in love with both of them, which would just make things awkward—"

He chuckles and shoulders me. Firmly enough it knocks me off my balance and I tip over into Daeja's side before she nuzzles me back into my spot. Warmth returns to his expression, and it distracts me from the guilt sitting in my chest.

"Have you told her yet?" I whisper.

He shakes his head. "I haven't been able to find the right time. And part of me is scared she doesn't feel the same way."

"We all feel like that. The first time you say it is always the scariest. It gets a little easier after that."

"What was he like?"

I snap my head in his direction. "What?"

"O-or she?" he covers.

"No…he umm…" I break eye contact with him, trying to trudge through all the emotions I can't quite decipher in my heart. Daeja leans gently into me, silently reminding me she's there.

My gaze floats up to Cole speaking to Marge, far enough away I can't hear what they're saying. They're backlit by the sunset. With that soft, golden glow outlining their silhouettes. Cole brushes the auburn hair at his forehead back as he looks down at Marge. When he nods and lets his hand fall to his side, he has a soft smile. The one that's like daylight.

And it fucking kills me.

"He was everything I wanted. Everything I dreamed of. He was like daylight…" My throat tightens, and I clear it before I continue, "Like when you wake up for the first time after a long night. Everything's a little blurry at first, and you can't quite…figure out what's around you. So, you blink until your vision corrects. And then it's like seeing everything for the first time. Eventually, it becomes all you've ever known…"

Cole, mid-conversation with Marge, glances my way. A tidal wave of yearning rushes over me, and I can sense he's drowning in it, too. Time fades. And I can't tell if we've been looking at each other for seconds or hours.

Marge whacks the side of his arm with her staff, and he shakes himself out of his distant longing. Finally returning his attention to her.

I glance at Archie. And he's shifting his gaze from me to Cole and back a few more times.

"W—wait. Wait. This isn't…what did I just see? What was that?" He flicks a finger between me and Cole.

"Cole isn't my brother, Arch," I whisper.

His mouth drops open as he pushes up to his feet. I follow and grab his shoulders as he runs his fingers through his sandy blonde hair.

I say under my breath, "Let's talk about this. Away from everyone else—"

"What the fuck?" he mutters.

"Archie, please. No one else can know."

He lets his arms fall to his sides, his hair strewn from raking it with his fingers. Without waiting for permission, I grab him by the elbow and tug him with me until we are so far out of earshot, we'd need to scream to get someone's attention.

Daeja follows us closely behind and puts herself between us and the rest of the group. She unfolds her wings and stretches them out to the side to block us from view.

"Thank you." I toss a grateful glance at Daeja.

She settles into a comfortable seat with a nod. Forced front row tickets to what's about to be anything but entertaining.

Archie whirls out of my grip. "What the actual fuck, Kat?"

Hearing him use such vulgar language is like a dagger to my lungs. And even though we are a healthy distance away, I can't help but whisper, "Listen—"

"No, you listen! I have been nothing but honest with you. I have told you all my secrets, even if it was hard for me to admit. And when I found out about," he whips a hand up to Daeja, "her, I kept that a secret from *everyone*! Even when it could have lead to my execution!"

"I know," I whimper. "I know—"

"No. You don't know. Because even after all this time, it's still not enough for you to trust me with the truth! Who all knew about Cole not being your brother before I did, huh?"

I shake my head, my pulse racing. It feels unfair to put Melaina in such a situation—

"Answer the question, Kat." His voice is an unsettling amount of seriousness.

"Why? Why does it matter?"

"Because it'll show me all the people you've trusted over me."

"But that's not why they kno—"

"Answer the Gods. Damn. Question."

Letting go of a breath, I sag my head. "Sethan…Marge… and…Melaina."

He tips his head back to look up at the sky and turns his back to me.

I reach forward and grab his shoulder. "Marge put it together herself. Sethan caught Cole and me kissing. And Melaina…don't be mad at her. I asked her to let me be the one to tell you. And because of this sick, twisted prophecy, she was forced to comply to my wishes."

He turns to glance at me. "It doesn't matter. You still told her before me."

I swallow. Here comes the next blow. "Because I slept with

Darian. For a second time. The first time was in Arterias when I almost left in the middle of the night after I found out Cole was engaged to Celeste. And the second time was last night. Melaina just found out this morning when she came to my door, and I asked if she could get me pennyroyal from Sethan."

"And you couldn't have asked me?"

"Arch…" I pull him to face me, angling my neck to try and look him in the eyes. "If I asked you to get pennyroyal from Sethan, he would have had your head put on a spike before you could explain it wasn't for you and Melaina."

He turns his brown eyes on me.

"And…and…" I pull my glove off my left hand. The words pour out of me like a floodgate. And now I'm just desperate to tell him everything, if it means he won't hold me at arm's length. "This ring? The Blood Ring? It links my life to the King's. But long before I knew what it was, I wore it as Cole's fiancé. Before he came to the military, before he was engaged to Celeste…"

A tear slips down my cheek. "He was mine. He was mine first. And I loved him. All I knew was him. All I wanted was him. And…and now I don't know what I want anymore. I feel like things are slipping from my fingers like quicksand. And I don't know how to stop it. I am so sorry I kept it from you. It wasn't because I don't trust you. A secret like this would destroy the trust the rest of the Arterians have in us, and we had to get to Vitalis first. And I know—I *know*—you wouldn't let it slip. But I didn't want to add pressure to everything else you're carrying. I've never had a friendship outside of Cole before you. So I—"

My vision gets blurry as I shake my head. "You don't deserve my dishonesty." My voice wobbles. "I'm the worst friend."

The silence stretches between us. His eyes are narrowed, his jaw set.

Finally, he mutters, "Best. The worst *best* friend."

He pulls me into his arms, and I *sob*. And just when I think he can't hug me tighter, he does.

"I'll forge a blood pact with you. I'll swear to never keep secrets from you again." I sniffle into his shirt, now damp with my tears.

He pulls me back to look me in the eyes. The small smile on his face warms my chest. "No, Kat. You don't need to do that."

"I'll never be secretive again. I want you to know it's true when I say that."

"Then I suppose you'll need to make it up to me." He squeezes his hands on my shoulders.

"Whatever you want. Name it."

He glances over his shoulder at Daeja, who's watching us in silence.

"Why is he looking at me like that? Whatever it is, tell him no."

Archie continues, "Melaina has always wanted to ride a dragon…A'nala is far too big…"

Daeja snorts. ***"Excuse me? I don't like where this is going."***

"…and Sethan wouldn't allow her to ride anyway."

I raise an eyebrow. "And so, to the wind with Sethan's reservations?"

"As you said…it's a good thing I'm not in love with him, right?" Archie smiles.

THIRTY-EIGHT

Sit down

Later that night, after the sun has set and the moon is high in the sky, Sethan returns to lead us all to our individual residences in Pinepoint. With the promise of two elk carcasses reserved just for her by the end of the week, Daeja agreed to fly Melaina and Archie later in the night.

As soon as Sethan's soldiers hook Darian's shackles into the wall and leave, an awkward silence falls between us.

I sit on the bed with my back to him, unlacing my boots.

"Did you bring me any whiskey?" Darian asks.

"No."

"Why not? Are you not wanting to continue your training?"

I ignore him, biting down into my lip to keep the sadness at bay. Perhaps it was only luck that I was able to save Vathstone from burning down. And returning the ripples back to the ley lines in Ashfall. What good am I if I can't save a life? Can't save more than just buildings or souls already passed?

And while I'm relieved I came clean to Archie, admitting my feelings out loud only opened the hole in my heart where Cole is. It's simple. I still love him.

"People die all the time. You better get used to it," Darian says with a casualness that stings. "No need to mope about."

"Stop talking," I mutter, removing one boot with quick, angry movements.

"You're pissed. Good. Remember what I told you last? You use it as fuel. Slowly. Deliberately. If you explode, you'll only hurt yourself."

I rip my second boot off and throw the pair of them near the door. "Oh, fuck off. Like you know anything about me."

He lifts his chin with a broad arrogance. "Take it out on me. Come fight me."

"I said fuck. Off," I growl.

He taps his chest, then splays his hands as wide as his long chain connecting his wrists will allow him. "Get your ass over here and make me."

I storm across the room, snatching my sheath from where it leans against the wall and drawing my sword with ease as I meet his eyes. Hoping it's enough of a show to shut him up, and he'll actually leave me alone. "I mean it."

He presses on with a smirk, adamant to push me off the edge I'm teetering on. "And *I* mean it. Come over here and make me fuck off. We can even pretend you can actually fucking hit me."

Shaking my head against the mounting rage, I close the distance between us and swing the sword in the direction of his chest, and when he jumps back, catching my blade with his chains, something flashes in my heart when I miss him—relief.

"Good," he purrs. "More."

I swing again and again, channeling my frustration slowly with each swipe, as he's suggested. Each move grows dangerously close to slicing him, until he stops with his back against the wall, his chin still lifted high.

I prowl toward him, keeping the blade pointed at his throat as my chest rises and falls. "I've got you pinned."

"So, it seems." He slowly spreads his fingers open in a silent surrender.

"Per our agreement, tell me about the King. Why does he want both rings?"

His eyebrow raises. "Per our agreement, you were to owe me whiskey before our little scuffles."

I lean forward, inches from his face as I grit out, "What does the King want?"

"The same thing I do."

"And what's that?" I hiss.

"You," he breathes, then leans forward despite the blade slicing into his skin and kisses me.

Gasping, I shove his chest back so it breaks our kiss. He leans his head back against the wall, a stupid, lazy smile on his face. A small trickle of blood races down the column of his throat to the top of his shirt. He's fucking toying with me, and I'm not in the godsdamned mood.

"Here's the thing…" he whispers, then wraps his hand around my right wrist, the hand holding the sword to his throat. "You've been wrong all along. This?"

He peels my fingers off one at a time from the hilt, never breaking eye contact. And for some fucking reason, I don't fight him—I'm just stuck in his sea of green.

He takes my left hand off his chest, then places the sword in it. "Is the reason you're so shitty at weapons. Because you're actually not right-handed…"

I tear my gaze away and look down at my left hand as he squeezes and lets go, the weight of the sword heavy and oddly comforting. I've never been the most impressive with weaponry, and my experience has been less than stellar. But the longer I sit with the familiarity of the sword in my left hand, the more I believe his theory. How easy it is to balance the weight in my palm.

"I should have noticed it sooner," he mutters.

I look up at him, flexing my hand around the sword's hilt. "How? What makes you think I'm left-handed?"

He taps the blade low, down and away from his direction. "You grab door handles with your left hand."

"So?"

"So, you grab with your left hand. You always put your right foot first when you start to walk. When you get heated in conversations, you use your left hand to gesture. And whenever you pet your oversized flying lizard—"

I narrow my eyes.

"—you always touch her with your left."

He's been watching me. Even in all the times I didn't even realize he was around. A small warmth creeps to my cheeks, spreading across my face and down to my chest.

"Wipe that smile off your face," he growls. "The only reason I've noticed it is because if you die, the King dies. And then I have no chance at saving my sister."

"I'm not sure if I believe you," I murmur, a swell of hope rising within me.

"Then trust me."

I snort. "I don't trust you, either."

He sighs, then slides with his back down the wall to sit and look up at me. "You're impossibly difficult. Especially so when you're pissed off."

"Sounds like your problem, not mine."

He smirks. "Funny, I tend to fuck my problems. Or, I guess, they fuck me."

Crouching down to his level, I place the sword behind me out of reach and snatch the front of his shirt in my fist. "Listen. If you so much as hint about our little mishap outside of these four walls one more time—"

"Mishap?" His eyebrows shoot up his forehead before he shakes his head with that agitating bravado. "I'd prefer the term *stroke of luck.*

Or I suppose if we're getting technical, many, *many* strokes of luck. And I wouldn't call my study of your pleasure luck. I work damn hard to figure out what makes you quiver and come—"

"Stop talking before I fucking kill you," I growl.

"Then I suppose you won't get those answers you need, will you?"

That godsdamned smile of his triggers a crest of heat within me, and I tighten my grip on his shirt.

"I noticed something about you," he whispers and snatches my hips in his strong hands.

My breath slips out in a soft gasp. This is dangerous. I already can sense it. And yet, his hands on me are too tempting to do anything but freeze. His thumbs rub a gentle circular pressure in front of my hip bones.

"But you're going to need to..." He pulls me forward and positions me over his strong thigh and plops me down. "...sit down."

"You bold bastard—" I'm interrupted by a shot of pleasure exploding up my spine.

He shifts my hips back, rubbing his thigh against me with a jaw-clenching pressure. I fight to keep a moan behind my lips.

"Sorry, what was it you were saying?" he rasps, eyes locked on mine. He guides me, pulling my hips back and forth into a tight rocking motion. "Tell me if you want me to stop. But I know it feels good, and you need to take your mind off everything for a moment. Feel something else for just a second. Let me be your distraction."

I fight against the pleasure rising inside of me as it threatens to drown out the logical side of my brain. But he has a point because my anger begins to melt away. My sadness. Everything but him.

I find myself grinding harder into his lap. Chasing the beautiful friction against my clit.

He looks at me with hooded eyes and parted lips. "If you want to keep pretending you don't think about me fucking you...fine. Mistake or not, take what you want from me. You've come on my fingers, you've come on my tongue, and you've come on my cock. You want to be a good girl? You don't want me to fuck you? Fine. You don't need my touch. You can make yourself come instead and not feel bad about it."

He takes his hands off my hips and holds them out to the side, testing me. "I'll sit here for you and let you take whatever it is you need."

Our movements still, his eyes locked on mine. The longer the seconds drag on without that friction, the colder I grow.

It…technically wouldn't break my new rule about sleeping with him.

Gods. What is it that makes me so pathetically stupid with him? That I'm dying to grind myself on his fucking thigh for a climax? But I don't care.

All my worries are gone.

Before I can stop myself, I slowly roll my hips forward up his thigh, grazing myself over his muscled leg. His parted lips turn into a grin. He threads his fingers together and places them behind his head, his chin tilted up to watch me lose myself.

I rock my hips again and again, faster and faster until I'm grinding myself greedily against him. My fingers find his shoulders, digging into them to steady myself as I race toward an orgasm. My breath comes out in pants.

"Fuck," he mutters, eyes dancing up and down my body. "Even clothed you are so godsdamned sexy."

I glance down at where the heat collects between my thighs and admire the growing erection in his pants. All I'd have to do is ask. My thoughts drip into a fantasy of ripping his pants off and riding him until we both come. But this is a good compromise, and the closest I can get to him without giving myself completely.

"Eyes up here," he snaps.

"I want you to touch me," I breathe, sweat dampening my brow.

"How? Like this?" he asks, one hand sneaking around to grab my rear. His fingers sink into my cheek, gripping me hard as he gives me a good shake. "Or this?" He smacks my ass with a delicious sting, and I stumble forward, nearly sharing his breath.

"Both," I moan and whimper. "Just don't take your hands off me."

Wordlessly, he grabs my ass and spreads me wider as he helps grind me against his thigh, his expression tight with wicked determination. I edge closer and closer to my climax.

Staring at his mouth, hungry to kiss him, I ask, "Will you make me come?" He opens his mouth, no doubt to taunt me, but I whimper, "Please."

He grabs me by the hips and spins me away from him before plopping me down on the ground between his legs. Angling me back to lie against his chest, he pulls my legs up until they're bent at the knee. He slips his right hand down between my thighs.

Despite not being skin to skin, his tight, controlled circles against my clit have me arching back into him. I spread my legs wider and watch him rub me, my lips parting as desire floods me. How gods-damned obsessed I am with his possessive touch. With his left hand, he slips it underneath my shirt and fondles my breast, kneading my nipple. Knowingly, he presses his lips to my neck, grazing his teeth up the column until he gets to the spot behind my ear.

Moaning, I lean my head back onto his shoulder as my eyes flutter closed. My legs quake, and I grab onto his thighs as he works me like putty.

Sucking on my earlobe before he pulls at it with a soft bite, he whispers, "Come in my arms. Break for me. Let it all go." Then he rubs my clit faster, biting into the spot above my collarbone. His breath is hot on my skin, and Gods, he *moans* into my neck.

Surrendering, I tip over into euphoria.

My mouth parts as I cry, my climax ricocheting like a wave of echoes spasming my limbs. His fingers on my clit draw the rest of my pleasure out, his mouth still devouring my skin.

As the hazy tingling of my orgasm subsides, a heat flushes over my cheeks. Darian removes his hand from between my legs and my shirt. I lean up off him, and as I turn to face him, he smiles. Wicked and handsome.

Holding up a shiny key.

Guess I'm not the only one who's using our sexual tension as a manipulation.

Gaping, I swing forward to try and snatch it from him before he evades me, chuckling. He unlocks the shackles and stands, before he adjusts the erection in his pants.

"Remember what I've told you?" He taps the key against the side of his head and slips it back between my brassiere and my breast. "Don't let your emotions control you."

He fucking pats my breast, kicks off his boots, and flops into the bed, stomach down.

Did I just get bested by a fucking thigh ride?

Shaking my head against the rolling wave of vexation at myself, I walk over to the other side of the bed and pile the pillows into a barrier between us. I shift down beneath the sheets as he lifts and turns his head to face me. His cheek is pressed against his crossed forearms underneath himself, a sly smile on his lips.

"Goodnight," he chimes.

I take a pillow at our feet and pile it on the one already between our faces, blocking him from my view.

THIRTY-NINE

THE EGO AND THE ANGER

Marge doesn't come in the night to fetch me for training. And for the first time in a long while, I'm able to sleep uninterrupted for more than a few hours. Though, my dreams are still haunted by flames, blood, my mother and brother, and this time, Corvin's bug-eyed gaze. The tendons in his throat bulging as he gasped for breath.

Lucky for me, when I wake sweating, Darian's undisturbed next to me. One less thing he can taunt me about.

"How was the flight yesterday?" I ask Daeja in the Pinepoint community hall at breakfast.

Taking a bite of cheese, I glance up to where Archie sits a few seats down, bumping his shoulder into Melaina's with a grin. Based on how she glows around him, she must know he loves her. And it would be foolish to think she doesn't feel the same.

"Next time you commit me to a ride like an oversized show pony, you'll be owing me more than two elk carcasses," Daeja grumbles.

I grin, keeping a laugh to myself. *"Would three suffice?"*

"…"

"Come on, was it really that bad? You love Archie?"

"I'd argue he's a better rider than you."

"Going for the heart today, are we?"

"Fine. It wasn't terrible. But tell him next time if he tucks a flower in one of my horns, I'll bite his ass."

"You temperamental, merciful thing."

She snorts with a snide amusement. **"Odd way to say thank you, but I'll take it."**

The forest surrounding Pinepoint thins out to long stretches of plains. A snow-tipped mountain range quadruple the size of Dragon's Back Ridge—the Serahaven mountains, Sethan explains—spans out across the northern horizon. Rather than flying on dragonback to Mossmead, Sethan instructs us to walk along with the horse-drawn wagons, since Mossmead is a town built on an old, shallow lake. While the water may only be hip-deep and well-trafficked enough the water dragons never venture to it, it makes the fire dragons uneasy.

As we come to the outskirts of Mossmead, the sunset bathes the waters around the quaint, stone town in golden ripples as small boats cut through the waters. Sethan leads us to the northwestern part of town where the streets and bridges are extra wide leading to the dragon rider sector. As we venture farther into town, I quickly realize why they call it Mossmead. Every stone archway, building corner, and bridge is dusted in moss.

Sethan mentions all of the Dragon Lands source their mead here, with Driftmond producing the most ale. And after I try a stein of mead at dinner, I quickly realize it's not for me. We all turn in early with the buzzing anticipation of starting an early morning scouting Vitalis and, day after next, we begin the last stretch to the castle. We're so close. The apprehension and hope stirs like an itch I can't yet scratch.

After Gavin and Nolan deliver Darian to my room and secure his shackles, the door falls closed behind them.

Darian eyes me with his arms crossed over his chest. "I don't take it you decided to hold up your end of the bargain and have a flask hiding somewhere underneath that blouse of yours, do you?"

"I'm not really in the mood," I retort. But really, what I don't want to admit to is the fact that if I fight him, if I get close enough to touch him…I'll be tempted into a repeat of what happened last night. Or into something further. Every time I think of how he touched me, how he drew out every moan and shake of my legs, I blush. When Sethan asked me a question, Daeja had to whip her tail into my boot to warn me I was zoning out—replaying the moments of last night for a *second* time today. It's enough to convince me I'm letting things get out of hand.

Darian smirks. "In a life-or-death situation, nobody is going to give a shit if you're in the mood."

I snap my attention to him. "Do you have to be such an asshole all the time?"

"I'm not a coddler." He pushes off the wall. "Come take it out on me."

Oh, no. I know what that means. Because it's is *exactly* how things started off last time. I walk over to the bed and pull back the sheets. "No."

"You're still upset even though your pathetic friend wasn't the one who died?"

I snap my gaze up to him at his disrespectful mention of Archie as I ball the sheets in my fists. He knows exactly what to say to tempt the fantasy of me gutting him. Testing, poking, prodding every angle of my self-composure. And I'm about to break it just to teach *him* a lesson to shut his godsdamned mouth.

He smiles, finding my weak spot. "He should have, though."

"Shut. The. Fuck. Up," I say through gritted teeth and rip my eyes off him before I do something stupid.

"Why? Because you know it's true?"

I blink, and somehow I've cleared the space between us. Rearing my left arm back, he opens his hands and stretches back, exposing his chest. "Come on. Hit me. Show me what you can do with that left hand."

I swing, and he catches my arm as if I'm nothing but a toddler on the offense.

He taunts, "Is that all you have?"

Throwing my next punch with a grunt, he boils my blood with a mocking laugh. I erupt into a typhoon of swings, punches, and kicks. Anything that will land me a blow. But each of my movements is halted.

"Hit me," he grunts with each missed strike. "Hit me!"

I fake him to the right and slap him on the cheek with the left. As soon as I make contact, the collision stings my hand. A horror spikes in me, and I shrink back as soon as I've hit him. He swivels to me with a red-hot handprint outlined on his face.

His eyes burn, his lips pulled up to reveal his teeth. "Good. But slapping a foe isn't going to do much other than piss them off."

He jerks his chin toward the opposite wall. All of hell's wrath simmering behind his eyes, and he visibly struggles to maintain composure, spitting out each word through gritted teeth. "Grab your fucking sword. Before I change my mind."

Without turning my back to him, I retrieve it from the wall and walk back to him.

He taps underneath my elbow. "You're getting lazy. Keep it raised."

"It's heavy," I admit, stuck in his gaze and watching the fury recede.

"Would you prefer a knitting needle, my lady?"

I narrow my eyes. "Need I remind you who's holding the sword here?"

He laughs, crossing his arms over his chest in defiance. "A toddler with a sword would scare me more."

"I could kill you if I wanted to."

"You don't scare me, kitten. Try me."

As soon as I swing, he swats the sword out of my grasp, and it sails off a few feet before landing on the ground. He tilts his head in a gesture that says, *see?*

Good Gods, am I relieved we're doing this in the privacy of my room. I'm not sure I could stomach embarrassing myself in front of an entire crowd entrusting me to save the realm.

I throw a punch, and he deflects. A second punch, and he grabs my arm and twists me into submission as he always does. He laughs, my ears ringing from the sound. I glare back at him and slam the heel of my foot down on his boot.

He grunts and shoves me to the ground, pinning my back with a knee as he still holds my arm. "Say you relent."

I growl in stubborn protest. "No."

He pushes me harder into the ground. "Re*lent*."

I wiggle underneath him, fighting for space to free myself.

"I could break your fucking arm right here," he hisses, and throws my arm out of his grasp, the pressure spiking my spine disappearing.

He walks around to the front of me and stops, his boots filling my vision. "Your problem is you lead with your emotions. If you go into a real war, with a real battle, your ego and your anger will be the death of you if you don't learn to control it. I keep telling you, and you're not listening."

I push up to sit, glaring at him as I spit, "Then stop taunting me."

"How else are you going to practice if no one else is challenging that side of you? When you're weak, you train until you're strong. Just thinking you'll be strong will do jack shit. You have to put in the effort, the time, the blood, the sweat, the tears. I've trained until my tears ran dry and my body was beat to a pulp, every day, for *years*. You're fucking lucky I'm easy on you." He turns his back to me and begins to stalk off.

"Why? Because your father didn't take it easy on you?"

His back is to me, and he stops mid-step. "We don't talk about him."

"And why's that?" I stand up, lifting my chin to him. I use his same words from earlier. "I'm not a *coddler*."

"Remove my chains from the wall."

"Or what?" I challenge.

He swivels to me, anger blistering in his expression. "I don't need to answer that. Just listen to me, and fucking do it."

I hold his glare. A chill runs down my spine as calm lethality washes over his features. I've hit a soft spot. I undo his shackles as he asks, and he kicks his boots off and slides into bed.

Constructing the pillow wall between us, I mutter, "You want to talk shit about Archie all day long and push me until I'm pissed off. You think you're so much more composed than I am. And now look at you."

"I'm not the one who needs to be trained," he growls, flipping his back to me. "Watch it. Or I won't hesitate to remind you of your place."

An awkward burn crawls up my throat. Perhaps I shouldn't push him so hard. But it feels like I'm teetering on the edge of something monumental. "Why don't you refer to him as your father? Why do you call him by his first name?"

"Get to your point," he grits out.

"Sethan…mentioned your stubborn arrogance. He said it was never…" my voice grows smaller.

"Beaten out of me?" he finishes for me. "Yes. Jurrock had a short temper and rough hands. Terrible drinking problem. Sethan has known me since I was a boy and had been best friends with him for longer than I can remember."

My breath escapes me in a single exhale, a coldness spreading throughout my limbs as I stare at the back of Darian's head. "So, he… he knew?"

"He more than knew. He saw," Darian tosses out plainly. "Now, will you be quiet so some of us can sleep?"

Anger bubbles inside me at the thought. Where Cole had a similar experience, Darian had an adult witness it and still not stand up for him. I fight against the temptation of letting my horror win and storming off into the night to find Sethan for answers.

But I know what I'm doing first thing in the morning.

"Fine. Let her in," Sethan's muffled response sounds from behind his thick, wooden doors.

After a soldier slips back out, he invites me in past the two guards posted outside of Sethan's quarters. As soon as Sethan's eyes connect with mine, he recognizes my fury and dismisses the other guards inside the room.

"We aren't leaving for Vitalis until tomorrow, and the dragon riders aren't to scout ahead for another two hours. Why are you in here at the crack of dawn?" he asks.

As soon as the door closes, I explode. Even training with Marge last night wasn't enough to channel my horror into something productive.

"You watched Jurrock beat Darian, and you did *nothing*?" I

nearly snarl. "How could you do that? He was a boy. And to throw it in his face like you have in front of everyone back in Driftmond?"

"That happened weeks ago, and you're just now wanting to talk about it? He's a grown man—he has no excuse to act the way he does now. That all happened a long, long time ago." Sethan turns his attention to writing a new sentence on his paper, as if I were simply sharing what the weather was like outside.

"Something like that follows you, Sethan! What the fuck is wrong with you?"

His head snaps up, glaring at me through his lowered eyebrows. "I know that. And I've had to carry the fact I didn't step up to help that boy my entire life. But he has so many other skeletons in his closet he's responsible for, that part of me doesn't feel so bad anymore."

"Do you fucking hear yourself right now?" I bubble over and close the space between me and his desk. Gripping the edge of the wooden piece of furniture, I lean over it. "He was a child!"

He raises an eyebrow, watching me with fascination, before something clicks. He tilts his chin up in recognition, tosses his pen onto the table, and leans back into his chair as he crosses his arms. "You care about him."

"No. But it doesn't mean he should be subjected to torture or ridicule! No matter how long it's been!"

He shakes his head, jaw clenched. "He's a dangerous man, Katerina. You'd be wise to not involve yourself with him."

Too late for that, though I won't admit it to him. Besides, it was only sex. Only something to distract me from the oncoming war that could only mean death and destruction.

"We're all dangerous people, Sethan. You involved me when you started beating the absolute *fuck* out of him back in Midkeep!"

"It was necessary."

"It was not *fucking* necessary!" I slam a fist into the desk.

He smirks. And I'm so godsdammned furious I'm ready to throw myself over the desk and throttle him.

His voice is quiet. "You're quite angry. Tell me, have you gotten those answers from him you were so confident you'd get?"

Not backing down from his gaze, I hold my anger behind clenched teeth. His quiet tone alone prods the fire within me. Testing me.

He stands from his chair, never breaking eye contact. "That's what I thought. Because for men like Darian, you will not bend him. You have to break him."

"Have you ever stopped to consider people like you are the reason why he is the way he is? That maybe if you had stepped up to help him, if you'd shown him kindness, he might have turned out to be someone else entirely?"

"It doesn't matter now. You need to keep a comfortable distance from him, Katerina. If he had no problem killing his father, he surely would have no problem killing you."

All the blood drains from my face. "Wh-what do you mean killing his father?"

Sethan dips his head slowly, confirming his statement. "Darian killed Jurrock."

"No. No…Celeste said Jurrock died in battle—"

Sethan shakes his head, his brown eyes sad. "I told her that because I was trying to protect her. She loves Darian, and if she knew he killed her father, it would have destroyed her. I had to create a cover that Jurrock died in battle, but it wasn't the truth. The truth is Darian was young, and he possessed the same temper his father had."

"I don't…I don't believe you," I mutter, taking a few hesitant steps back.

"Then ask him. But you keep it between me, you, and Darian. You do not tell anyone else."

"Why would you tell me such a thing and ask for me to keep it a secret?" I ask angrily. I didn't ask for this. I didn't need to know such a heavy secret.

"You weren't going to take my warning seriously, otherwise."

FORTY

LIS FOARTH GASH DINNEN

We spend one more night in Mossmead. After dinner, I practice sparring with Darian in my room, becoming more and more confident with using my left hand for sword fighting. Darian was right—there's a certain natural ease to using my left hand. I also manage to improve my resistance in keeping myself from tipping into his seduction again—thanks to Sethan's lingering warning.

After sleeping for a few hours, I slip out with Marge and spend another two hours channeling the ley lines. The goal is to pull the small blue wisps up from the ground and form them into a sphere. I get them maybe two inches off the ground before they slip and fade.

As encouragement, Marge reminds me the ley lines are the hardest to pull from with how deep they're buried in the earth. What I've done with the ripples, the fire back in Vathstone, and the poison that killed Corvin is easier. I only need to keep training.

Days after Corvin's death, we arrive at the base of the massive Serahaven mountains.

"Is…there supposed to be a castle here?" Archie asks beside

me, leaning heavily from one side to the next like he might be able to peek around the mountainous terrain in front of us.

"It's on the other side of these mountains," Sethan grumbles.

Melaina tosses Sethan a look, warning him to mind his attitude. Archie nods. "Right…right."

"Considering the majority of us haven't seen a map, I think it's a fair question," Cole levels at Sethan. He's been spending a lot of time with Archie as of late, especially during the travel days. It warms my heart to know they get along so well. How Cole always looks after him.

Sethan ignores Cole's stern look. "Us dragon riders will scout the perimeters, just to make sure there are no rebels and the castle grounds are clear." He looks at me. "You and Daeja will stay in the middle of the formation, just in case."

I nod, and as the rest of the group moves to mount their dragons, I turn to Daeja. A set of footsteps behind me catches my attention as I braid my hair back for the flight. Cole strolls toward me. His auburn hair swept back from his rugged, handsome face. As soon as our eyes collide, my heart skips a beat.

I've been so wrapped up in training and my own guilt, I can't recall more than a few words exchanged between us. The only times I've seen him have been in passing, at dinners from across the tables, or the times he checks all my buckles and hooks to make sure it's safe before I take off. Except normally I'm already in the seat. Buckled in and ready. Where we only take it as far as a casual nod and 'thank you.'

How heavy it hits me, knowing it's easily something out of the norm we've created between us over the last several years. The distance just…doesn't feel right.

He stops a few steps away from me. His fingers twitch nervously at his sides. "Hey."

"Hey," I breathe. I motion up to the saddle. "I can…umm… get up there, first. If—"

"I wanted to see you."

My hand drops to my side, my jaw relaxing as I glance back

at him. Daeja takes a few steps to turn her body to block Cole and me from the rest of the groups.

He tilts his head partly to the side. "I...I wanted to come check in on you after the Forbidden Forest. I just wasn't sure if I'd be the one you wanted to see. I wanted to give you space, if you needed it from me."

I swallow. Stuck in his gaze. Unsure if the space between us feels uncomfortable because it's new and something I have to get used to or if it's because it's unnatural. Like trying to drift upstream. And I can't tell if I'm doing it as a defense mechanism, or if I actually, truly want it like this between us.

"Are you alright?" he whispers.

"I mean…alright as I'll ever be, I suppose…"

"I miss you…" he breathes. So softly, I almost wonder if I hallucinated it. So genuine, it breaks my heart when it drifts off into the void between us.

Gods, I miss him, too.

Before I can respond, he shakes his head and says louder, "Can I, umm…show you something?"

After I nod, we both stroll over to Daeja. He rests a hand on her scales near the strap wrapped around her ribs. He inches his fingers to try and slide them underneath the belt, but it won't budge.

"I need to loosen these," he says quietly.

"Loosen?" Daeja turns her head to puff at him.

He wraps his hand over the back of mine and traces it up the strap. My finger dips with each hole we pass. Until we get to the metal prong slipped through the second to last one. He gives me a quiet look.

She's getting bigger. And fast.

He drops my hand to loosen the strap and slide it to the last hole, tossing me a glance.

I nod. She's about to outgrow this saddle, and who knows how and when I'll be able to get a bigger one. But we can't stop our journey to Vitalis now. Not when we're so close.

Daeja turns her head to snort at us. ***"What? Why are you two so quiet?"***

I clear my throat, looking for the next thing to divert attention. "Sethan isn't the only one who knows about our past now. I told Melaina and Archie. And Marge has known for some time, too."

"Yeah, I know Marge knows." He nearly blushes, a shy grin lifts his face. "She and I have had plenty of conversations about it. Or…I suppose it's been more her scolding me."

"She scolds me all the time. I'd venture to say it's part of her love language now."

Both of us chuckle and look at the floor. Daeja grumbles a reminder the others are waiting for us.

"Anyway…let me help you up." He jerks his bearded chin toward the saddle.

I open my mouth to decline it, as I've done it on my own countless times before. Granted, Daeja normally has to crouch down and I half-climb, half-scramble up. But I surprise myself when I nod with a small smile. We walk to Daeja's side, and he laces his fingers together into a makeshift foothold.

I slide my arm around his brawny shoulder until I've wrapped it around the back of his neck for security. Stepping into his hands, he lifts me up until I grab the stirrup and pull myself up and over into the seat. I strap on the waist belt. He checks the straps as he always does. And once I'm hooked into the belt, I look his way.

"I'm always here for you. You know that, right?" he whispers.

I smile and nod. Without another word, he pats Daeja's shoulder and stalks off to join the rest of the group.

Daeja turns her head to side eye me. ***"Ready now?"***

With a sigh, I lean forward, settling my weight back into my hips. *"What do A'nala and Sethan say? 'To the skies?'"*

"'And the stars,'" she snickers, leaping into the air with hearty flaps, lifting us higher and higher.

Our squad below us, all gathered in wagons or walking, turn

into tiny specks as we rise. The air is crisp with a winter bite, numbing my hands and face.

Sethan, A'nala, and the rest of the dragons and riders take their normal positions in a V formation, and Daeja takes a spot directly behind A'nala. We find a steady flap-flap-glide, the air slicing under Daeja's wings and cut in half by A'nala's figure blocking the wind in front of us.

"I'm surprised Sethan and A'nala haven't complained about us taking a few extra minutes to get to the skies."

"Oh, they have. But I think Sethan's a little more understanding. Or…approving of you talking with Cole rather than Darian."

Of course he is. *"And what do you think?"*

She snorts in my head. **"You're asking me like who you do or don't love should be at my discretion?"**

"Hold on. I do not love Darian. I simply mean…talking."

"Riiight. But you do love Cole?"

I swallow. *"I don't know…"*

"I think you do. I think you just don't want to admit it to yourself because it hurts."

"And since when do you have any idea what love does or doesn't feel like?"

"Since you just asked for my opinion?"

"…Fair."

"And sometimes loving you is a pain in my scales."

I laugh and pat her neck. *"Do you always have to be so discerning?"*

"Do you prefer me to lie?"

"No."

"Didn't think so. And one day when I have a mate of my own, you can have these little pep talks with me, just as I do with you."

"Considering you should still just be a hatchling, I think that conversation is so far in the future we don't even need to consider it."

"Hatchling?" she grumbles underneath the seat. ***"Mind you, I am far bigger and more advanced than any hatchling. I might have only been in this realm for half a year, but I have lived for centuries, several times over. Maybe you should start taking notes from me."***

"Quite the arrogance." I chuckle. *"Do you…remember anything from your previous lives?"*

"No. Only that this one with you has easily become my favorite."

My heart fills to the brim. A giddy smile on my cheeks. *"I love you, too."*

We pass over the front of the Serahaven mountains, soaring over snow-dusted peaks, and find the other side is even more breathtaking.

A masterfully designed stone castle sits in the rocky face of a gargantuan mountainside, lush with greenery. Waterfalls pour from the tops of the mountains, snaking down the slopes behind the castle and pooling in a massive lake between us and the fortress. And from that lake, several rivers branch off and meander their way through the mountain ridge. Bridges span out from the grand citadel, stretching long over the lake until they touch land.

A thunderous hum rises from the earth, vibrating the blood in my veins as we fly closer.

"There's magic here…" I murmur to Daeja. *"A lot of it."*

"A'nala says we'll land on the outskirts. There's a magical barrier at the end of the bridges nearest the castle. That's probably what you're sensing."

"Can you sense it, too?"

"Yes…it feels like I've been here before. It feels like…"

"Home," I finish for her, and warmth spreads the bond between us.

A'nala dips down, and Daeja follows with the rest of the dragon riders on either side of us. We turn left, circling around the back half of Vitalis as the wind rips my braids back from my face and threatens to force my eyes closed. My stomach tips, warning it'll plummet to the ground at the dizzying speed and angle we're gliding, parallel with the mountainside. Luckily for my own pride, we even out before I throw up.

Minutes later, we circle back and land at a southern bridge, each chaotic flapping of wings stirring dust and overgrown vines and fronds. Sethan dismounts, and I unclip myself from the saddle and slide off.

The rest of the dragon riders follow suit, and we all gather a few feet from where the bridge arches over the sparkling, turquoise blue lake below. Sethan's eyes are glued on the water, scanning its surface before he plucks a loose cobblestone from the street. Before anyone can ask what he's doing, he chucks it into the lake below, taking a few steps back and bracing his forearm against my chest.

And waits.

A bubble of water turns into a rush, and a hiss emerges from the depths below. Daeja flares her wings, as do the other dragons, tails whipping and talons scraping against the cobblestones.

"Get back," Sethan whispers.

I obey, slowly walking backward until I bump into Daeja's chest.

"Water dragons," a woman next to me growls, withdrawing her blade.

I follow suit, unsheathing my own and tossing it to my left hand—while pushing back the thought of who exactly taught me I was better with it.

A long, skinny, blue muzzle with white whiskers rises from the edge of the street near the bridge and scans us in a flash of turquoise eyes. Two rows of webbed horns start at the crown of its head, then slip back and down its neck. As it parts its dripping muzzle, it reveals a mouth as black as the oceans.

According to my father's journal, water dragons could have a myriad of abilities. And while I'm praying this one might only be capable of the less dangerous ones—echolocation or camouflaging— the possibility of the other powers has me sliding Sethan's outstretched arm away from my chest. I take a step forward. If this one is capable of blasting boiling water or producing electric shock waves, we might all be doomed if we don't play our cards right.

But I have the Blood Ring. And it was me who was able to stop the dragonfire from completely ruining Vathstone. Me and Daeja. What's to worry about but one single water dragon?

Daeja follows me like a slick shadow, her chin a few feet above my head, clearly attuned to my thoughts. Slowly as to not spook the water dragon, I slide off my gloves and tuck them into my waistband.

"What are you doing?" Sethan hisses each word from behind me.

"Taking the lead," I whisper without taking my eyes off the dragon.

Its vibrant eyes watch me, narrowing. Water creeps up over the edge of the street and snakes through the cobblestones. Collecting quickly enough that it begins to bleed out from the grout lines and merge into one wave of water rushing toward us. The wave is maybe three inches deep when it gushes over the tip of my boots. But the water rises more rapidly, more furiously from around the water dragon.

I'm not willing to chance the powers it holds. Today is not a good day for drowning. I rip my right hand up. Rather than pulling the magic as I've practiced with Marge, I push it. Slamming a wall against it to keep it from venturing farther than a few inches behind me. As I force the water back, inch by inch until it's dammed out in front of me, the water dragon hisses.

Just as the fire dragon spoke in my mind back in Vathstone, I reach, calling out into a cavernous void in the event it might hear me. *"We mean you no harm. We only wish to pass to Vitalis."*

The water dragon rises and leans forward until the tip of its glistening blue snout is a few feet away from me. Daeja smashes her heavy feet on either side of me in a protective stance, a growl rumbling in her chest behind me.

"Vitalis is no longer for humans," a gravely deep voice booms in

my mind, and the dragon flicks its gaze at my sword in disgust. *"You are not welcome here."*

I whisper back, gently, *"Vitalis is not only yours to guard."*

It roars, *"It is when your species desecrated this ages-old pantheon! Leave, and do not return."*

I shake my head, then sheathe my sword at my side in a show of good faith. Though I still hold the waters at bay with an outstretched hand. *"We do not wish to fight you. Only to find answers about how we can save this realm from destruction. Please."*

The dragon focuses on the sheathed blade at my side before it drags its attention to me. *"As if it hasn't been destroyed already. Why should we allow you? You are no different from the rest."*

The water sloshes up against the invisible dam I'm magically holding between us and the dragon. The water level is equal to my waist now. Adding a slow but sure pressure against the force I've created, two other water dragons rise from either side of the first one. The three of them a glistening cerulean threat.

"Because you will allow me," Daeja's slick as velvet voice chimes in. ***"And I will not be challenged."***

The dragons turn their attention to her. A flash of recognition, of fear, *something,* waves over their faces. The water around them stills, allowing me a slight break at keeping it dammed.

The first dragon rumbles, *"You side with the ones who stole your future? Who've destroyed the Gods' plan?"*

"She is my future. And we have only come to restore it."

"You know not of which you ask, Moon One. You are far out of your depths."

"Lis foarth gash dinnen," A'nala's hiss echoes around us.

I whip my attention to her, the water leaking out of a crack I allow in the dam before I shove it back. All three water dragons' eyes narrow. The horns lining their necks and spines, connected by webbing, fan out.

The first water dragon speaks again, *"We do not converse with fire dragons. How dare you use the ancient tongue."*

A'nala's snapping at the air makes me flinch. *"Gilltha fintike meesh notak!"*

"Stop," Sethan warns her.

Pride trickles into my skin because A'nala should be scared shitless about not one, not two, but three water dragons before her. They could potentially take out all of our fire dragons if the situation gets worse.

Daeja slides her body in front of me, lowering her head to look at the water dragon eye-to-eye. All at once, a wall of silence slams down between me and the rest of the dragons. Daeja and the main water dragon stare each other down, their eyes dilating as if announcing each silent exchange.

One of the water dragons retreats. And then the other. As Daeja and the first water dragon converse, the water recedes until it's gone, leaving the cobblestones a darker shade than the rest of the street and bridge.

The first water dragon slides its gaze to me. *"Find him in there. Set him free."*

It retreats and slips back down into the waters below. With a relieved sigh, I let my hand fall to my side. I smile up at Daeja.

She meets my gaze. ***"Why are you looking at me like that?"***

"Because I'm proud of you. You hold your own, even when others doubt you."

"Tell A'nala that." She jerks her muzzle back toward the rest of the group. ***"I'll get an earful later of how I shut everyone else out."***

Sethan grabs my shoulder, turning me toward him. "What did you do? What did it say?"

"You…you couldn't hear it?"

"No. Dragons do not speak to others unless they want to. It's far too risky of them to do so."

"Why would it be too risky for them? A'nala spoke to me." And the fire dragon. *And* earth dragon.

Sethan drops his hand from my shoulder. "Because it could establish a two-way connection. And they prefer not to get entangled in the problems of humans. That's why most of them do not want to bond us. A'nala knows you will not manipulate her."

"So, if they speak to us…it establishes a bond?"

"Not quite. But it makes it much easier to do so. And in previous generations, humans have been known to exploit magic to bond a dragon."

"Like through the Blood and Bone Ring?"

He shrugs. "I'm not quite sure how. The ways have been lost to translations. But that's beside the point—what did it say to you?"

"It said for us to *find him in there and set him free.*"

"Who's he?"

I peer up at Daeja. "I have no idea."

FORTY-ONE

BLOOD MAGIC

The horses whinny, throwing their heads back and scraping at the ground with their hooves, refusing to move further than the entrance of the bridge. Sethan scans the skies, the water, and the mountains around us.

"What is it?" I ask. "Why won't they move?"

He shakes his head. "I'm not sure."

The handlers attempt to get them to move, kicking into their sides, bribing them with apples, and hopping off to tug their reigns forward. But nothing works.

"Commander?" one rider asks Sethan.

"They must sense something…" Sethan glances up to A'nala.

A'nala speaks, her voice echoing inside of my mind like a slippery snake. "*A great tragedy has happened here. The horses can sense it, and they will not move forward. If you force them, you'll spook them.*"

Sethan directs two finger points at all of those aside from the dragon riders. "You all stay here with the horses and wagons. The rest of us will continue. If we aren't back by tomorrow evening…"

All of them dip their heads, while our Arterian squad's faces twist in disagreement. I turn to Sethan, tossing him a look until he rolls his eyes.

He groans. "Fine. Arterians may come with us, but we only have enough provisions to take ten into Vitalis."

Easy enough for me to weigh in. "Marge, Cole, Archie, Melaina, Gavin, Nolan, and Darian."

It's Sethan's turn to whip a pointed look at me. "That gives me only one other person to take with us."

I shrug. "That's who I choose."

With a grumble, he motions to one of the dragon riders and we all gather at the edge of the bridge. Nolan seizes Darian's shackles, and I help Marge to Daeja.

"I am perfectly capable of walking on my own," Marge sneers.

"Yeah, but we won't get there for another three days at your pace, Margie," Darian taunts as Nolan tugs him by the chains past us.

I have to hide a laugh, because he's right. Marge is the slowest one in the group, and at her pace we won't have enough provisions to last us that long.

Marge swings out her staff, smacking Darian in the calf with mild effort. "Wretched boy."

I pull her away from Darian before he decides to retaliate, and Daeja's slight annoyance ticks in my side as if it were my own. Cole joins in to help Marge up into the saddle. After Marge is settled, he lifts me next, and I slide in behind Marge and clip her into the belt. Her narrowed side eye peers over her shoulder at me. But before she can try and decline the extra support from the belt, she faces forward, her old, withered hands gripping the saddle horns.

"If she falls off…I'm not stopping," Daeja quips and begins to walk forward.

I snort, smacking Daeja's shoulder playfully. *"Stop it. Why do you hate her so much?"*

"It's not that I hate her. I just don't necessarily…enjoy her company."

"It's because she's a Spoiled. You're not supposed to like her because of it, but it's nothing she can change now. It was forced upon her. Just as you don't like Darian—"

She snorts. "**No, I don't like him because he's threatened you so many times that if you asked me to put him on my back, I'd roll over and crush him.**"

"Well, I suppose it's a good thing I'm not asking you to." I glance over to Darian and Nolan who leads him by the nine-foot-long chain.

Something about riding a dragon and not flying has an awkwardness to it. We sway and slide in the saddle with each step Daeja takes, and I hook my fingers into the back of the waist belt on Marge to steady myself. We cross over the bridge, my eyes glued to the lake below with every step and holding my breath in the event the water dragons, or any other dragons lingering about, decide to attack us. And as Daeja accidentally bumps her tail into the bridge wall, crumbling some stones off the top ledge, my stomach twists at how long it takes for them to crash into the lake below.

Luckily for us, we make it across to the other side. Though, we get about twenty feet across the northern side of the bridge and into the main street surrounding Vitalis before Sethan, Melaina, and Archie all abruptly stop ahead of us.

Sethan calls back to me, "This is where you come in. Only those with a direct bloodline can enter."

I unhook Marge and dismount Daeja as Cole comes up to my side to help me get Marge down.

Archie presses a hand to the invisible wall, then a second one, and scales it like he might find a secret gap. "How are all of us supposed to go in with her?"

I flex my hand with the Blood Ring, ready to siphon magic to pull the wall down if I need to. Though, I haven't quite yet mastered pulling.

I glance over at Marge who brushes away Cole as she steadies herself on her feet. "What do I need to do?"

Marge glances up to the castle spires stretching into the sky. "I don't think you'll be able to pull enough to take down the barrier without severe consequences. They likely have it warded from top to bottom."

"But only those with a direct bloodline can enter…" As I sweep my attention back to Sethan, my gaze gets caught on Cole. Who is already staring at me with that stern tension to his jaw. That shake of his auburn hair already warning me not to propose the idea of using my own blood. He knows me too well.

"We can try to hold hands?" Archie pitches. "If we're touching Kat, maybe we can breach the wall?"

Darian tosses him a glare like he'd rather jump off the bridge and call it a life.

"While that seems like a warm proposition…" Sethan grumbles, "I don't think it'll work."

"We should try it nonetheless." I pull my attention off Cole and don't miss the slight sag to his shoulders at a tamer solution than what I was originally considering. "What's the worst that can happen?"

Marge's gray-blue eyes are still on the distant angled rooftops of Vitalis. "Depending on how strong the magic is—who set the barrier and how long ago—it could rip you apart from the inside out if we try to force it…"

Archie gulps and turns his attention back to prodding the invisible wall with less enthusiasm. "Think I'd like to keep my insides just the way they are…"

Daeja joins in, nudging the barrier alongside him.

If Daeja can't get in either…

"I have a better idea." I remove my glove and unsheathe one of my daggers. I slice a three-inch cut along my palm. "You said only those with the direct bloodline can pass the barrier, right? What if I cut through the wall with my blood so we can pass through?"

"You won't have enough blood to cut a big enough entrance to let the dragons through," Sethan responds.

But leaving Daeja isn't an option. I fold my fingers over my palm to keep the blood welling in my hand contained as I take a few steps toward where Daeja and Archie are. "I have to at least try."

Melaina slaps an arm out across my chest to stop me. "Wait. Do you understand how much of your blood it would take?"

Daeja is the smallest out of the three dragons, and I'd need a solid fifteen feet wide gap to get her through. Maybe ten feet high if she ducks her head and crawls in. And the other two fire dragons? They'll need close to double.

"Melaina's right. By the time you cut through half of what you would need for the dragons, you'll pass out," Cole warns like he's been fighting himself from chiming in. He withdraws his sword and slices open his palm. "Here. Let me mix my blood with yours—"

"Wouldn't that null her blood's effect on the magic, though?" Melaina interjects before we can decide.

"No," Marge says.

"Yes," Sethan responds at the same time.

We all bounce our attention back and forth between the two of them, but my gaze settles on Marge at last. "How sure are you?"

She hobbles over to Daeja and prods her side with her staff. Daeja growls at Marge over her shoulder before lowering her side to her. Marge retrieves a flask from one of the bags attached to the rear of Daeja's saddle.

Flicking the lid off, Marge tips the flask over and looks up at me as the water gushes out of the container onto the gray stone street. "There's only one way to find out. And we don't have the luxury of time."

When I glance over at Cole, he nods, then the two of us walk to Marge. I go first, squeezing the blood from my hand into the flask. As soon as the flow slows, I step back and allow Cole to also drain his blood. A hiss catches my attention, and I find Archie wiping his bloody dagger off on his thigh before sheathing it. Once Cole steps back, Archie joins in, followed by Melaina.

As Sethan drips his blood into the flask, he glances over at the other dragon rider. "Bristol? Care to contribute?"

Bristol joins in. Then Gavin. Marge hands me the morbidly full canister of mixed blood, and I cork it before swirling it to mix the contents.

"So, what? You're going to just pour it over a wall that nobody can see?" Nolan calls from behind me.

I stop a foot away from the invisible wall and everyone takes a step back to give me space. I fixate on the crimson liquid after I pop off the cork. *It has to work. Otherwise, we've come all this way for nothing.*

"No…" I murmur. Slowly, I pour a small strip of blood along the length of the dagger, before tipping my blade down so it'll coat the tip. A drop slides off the front of the dagger and drips on the floor. Before more can slip off, I press the blade forward and sink it into the air in front of me with slow caution.

The invisible barrier in front of us wavers. The castle on the other side of the wall ripples like a reflection in a pond being disturbed. A buzzing energy bolts up the dagger and rings in my arm like struck metal, but I grit my teeth and push harder into it.

The barrier fights against me but relents inch by inch until I've sunk my dagger hilt-deep through it. With a quick inhale, I slide the dagger down until the red streak runs out. Pulling the blade out, I pour more blood on it and cut until I've hit the ground. More blood, then back up until I can't reach any higher.

"Allow me," Daeja purrs.

She edges her nose into my heels and when she pushes too hard, it knocks my feet out from under me. I catch myself back on her snout as she lifts me up higher into the air. Straightening myself, I'm perched on the tip of her snout and continue cutting through the barrier. Pour, slice. Pour, slice. Once we finish the top part of the frame, I hop off Daeja's muzzle and cut down the right side until the blade hits the last half inch. The pressure between the dagger and magical barrier vanishes. Like slicing through a curtain, the glimmering space in between the frame I created falls to the ground.

Panting, I rise and take a step back. The air surrounding the rectangle I sliced still moves with a liquid-like sheen. The shapes and colors behind it swirl like oil in water.

I reach out, stretching my fingertips through the sliced frame, and find…nothing.

Smiling, I take one step. And then another. Until I'm well past the barrier and turn to face everyone else. Daeja bumps Archie's back with her nose, and he fumbles forward, catching himself on his hands. Half of his body is past the barrier.

Cole steps forward and helps Archie off the ground, prompting more to come through. Then, our entire group steps inside. Daeja is at A'nala's side like a shadow, slightly leaning into her shoulder as they breach the barrier to this side. A'nala's lips twitch up in a silent growl as she glances down at Daeja, and Daeja snorts playfully at her before she breaks off and walks toward me.

"What's that dragon's name?" I ask Daeja as Bristol's fire dragon is the last to enter.

"Nadja. She's quite…ornery. Apparently, it's rude to ask how old she is."

I chuckle, and before I can even respond, she continues, **"And before you ask—no. I didn't ask the other dragons the same question. Though I'm starting to think the attitude may be hereditary with fire dragons."**

"Just fire dragons, huh?"

Daeja narrows her eyes at me, and as she passes me, she swipes her tail into the side of my thigh, and I take a few steps just to keep myself upright.

Sethan stares up at the castle towering above us with a parted mouth. Overgrown ivy and ferns drape over the elegant stonework in green curtains. Yet, golden accents still glimmer in the sunlight like it's never been abandoned.

"It worked…" he murmurs, as if he hadn't quite believed it would.

The rest of the group mirror his wonder, eyes wide and mouths open.

Marge hobbles over to one of the massive stone arches leading into the inner courtyard of the castle. When no one follows, she turns, looking over her shoulder. "Well? What are we waiting for? As Sethan mentioned, we only have enough provisions for ten of us. I imagine those won't last us too long if we dally."

For being the slowest walking one here, she sure is fast.

FORTY-TWO

VITALIS

We walk through the courtyard in silence, our soft footsteps echoing about the stone walls. Leafy green ferns burst through the stone floors and walls, threatening to overtake what once was man-made. The sunlight spills through parts of the crumbled walls six stories high, casting beams of dusty light across the floors. Every story of the castle is layered with deliberate curves, arches, and lines that create a picturesque fortress. Every which way I turn is a set of steps leading up to hallways and doors through archways. We pause in the middle of the courtyard, with Sethan and Marge at the front.

Sethan turns to Marge. "Any idea which way we need to go for the libraries?"

Marge shakes her head. "No. But if it's built similarly to the castle in Arterias, the library would be in the northwestern part."

"We can split up?" Archie offers.

Sethan whips a disappointed glare at Archie. "No, we aren't splitting up."

"Why not?" I step forward. "If we split up, we can cover the grounds quicker. And if we separate into three groups, with a dragon in each, we should be able to communicate via them."

Sethan's jaw works, clearly not wanting to give Archie a single lick of recognition, before he glances at Marge.

She snorts. "Don't look at me. They make a good point. Especially if we haven't brought enough provisions to last us more than a night."

Sethan scans the group, taking a mental headcount and working out some plan. His eyes settle on Melaina, his expression softening. "Melaina, you take Archie and go with Bristol and Nadja to explore the northern sections. Katerina and Daeja will take Marge and…"

He scans the group, his eyes falling on Cole. "Cole. You four will search the western quarter. Gavin, Nolan, and Darian, you're with me on the east. If we can't find anything, we'll all reconvene here in the courtyard by sunset and search the southern section tomorrow. With it normally being dedicated to the guard rooms, towers, and armory, I doubt we'll find anything there."

"What are we looking for?" I ask.

"A book," Marge answers plainly, as if I should have already known the answer.

"What kind of book?" Melania prompts.

"We're looking for Queen Elara's journal," Sethan responds.

Archie scratches his head with a nervous smile. "You want us… to find the dead Queen's diary?"

"Something like that." Sethan's voice is flat. "The castle might not be built for dragons to access all the rooms and hallways. The walls are built thick enough that they should support any of our dragons' weights. If they cannot follow you into a section, do not go too far. While it's been over a hundred years since Queen Elara died and this castle was attacked, there's no telling what else might still be here. If you find yourself in trouble, alert your dragon rider so we may come to your aid."

The courtyard we've come to discover is bordered all by storage rooms and hallways leading to the guard towers and outside barrier walls, with only the northern part of the courtyard leading out through the rest of the castle. A massive tower with arched columns spanning its width sits at the northern part of the square. Marge mentions it was likely where the King and Queen would address crowds from above, looking down into the courtyard. As we pass beneath it, I can't help but look up and wonder how many lines of royalty spoke from the platform.

On the other side of the rounded tower is a wall of stone with four sets of thick wooden doors, wide and tall enough to allow a dragon through. Nadja steps forward, nudging the door with her muzzle, before she rears back and headbutts it. The door swings open with a rusty creak.

"I suppose they didn't lock it," Daeja murmurs.

"Maybe they didn't have time…" I whisper back, a chill running down my spine.

We all step through the door into an enormous room with an endless expanse of marble floors and thickly carved stone columns holding up a five-story-high, curved ceiling. Hanging from lines of black, rusted chains, wound painfully tight, is a massive dragon carcass.

Melaina turns her head, tucking her nose into her elbow and gagging.

The stench of rotting flesh fills the grandiose room, burning my eyes and flipping my stomach over. Below the dragon carcass are rows and rows of ornate tables, and the ones directly beneath the dragon have dark stains. I drag my gaze back up to the lifeless dragon, its blue scales muddy with old blood and muted with death.

"Fuck," Cole mutters, swinging his gaze down and away.

"At least it's not a ripple," Marge murmurs. "Whoever left it must have preserved its corpse with magic—as a message."

"That's…disturbing." Archie grimaces. "Poor fella."

Sethan sweeps his attention back to me. "If for some reason we cannot meet back in the courtyard, this room will be where we reassemble."

I nod, and Sethan sends pointed gestures to separate directions for all our groups before we split up. I watch the dragon carcass, its flesh and scales torn at agonizing angles, as Cole, Marge, Daeja, and I stroll silently across to the back left corner of the room. Gold plates, cups, and cutlery with silk-spun napkins lie peacefully still on the tables. Several human corpses lie hunched over the tables, some half-in and half-out of their seats, while more bodies lie face first on the ground. More dragons are hung from the ceiling throughout the room like macabre chandeliers, all different colors: blue, green, and red.

I drag my attention away before a new wave of nausea rolls over me and before my fear coats over my limbs. Cole grabs my hand for a split-second and squeezes me, before dropping it again in the event anyone notices. I glance at him sideways, and he keeps his gaze set ahead on Marge. Daeja snorts, confirming she saw the motion.

The back corner of the ornate dining hall leads down a hallway, capturing our footsteps and amplifying the sound to an uncomfortable and eerie degree. Daeja tucks her wings in tight and dips her head to squeeze in after us. Thankfully, she's half the size of the other dragons, otherwise she wouldn't have been able to fit.

The end of the hallway leads to a door, which then leads to another outdoor courtyard. In front of us is a towering stone keep, its windows peering out in every which direction. Marge leads us along its southern half, and we pass a gargantuan well. I peek over the edge and find only darkness, before stepping back into line behind Marge.

"In Arterias, the library is built there," Marge whispers as she pauses in front of a wall of various doors, archways, and dust-coated windows.

The first door I try is locked, and Cole's first door swings wide open with a creak that grabs all our attention.

"That was almost too easy…" he mutters, and peeks his head inside.

Marge, Daeja, and I all slide over to him, and he backs his head out before turning to us. "You're right, Marge. Looks like this was the library."

He pushes the door open for us to peer inside, and my heart sinks.

The room, unsurprisingly, matches the rest of the rooms we've encountered here at the castle. Lavish furnishings faded with time sprawl about the cavernous room, along with curtains framing the windows spanning from the marbled floors up to the arched ceilings, so high above us I have to tip my head back just to look. Rows and rows of shelves line all the walls.

But every single one is empty.

We all slip inside to double-check, and Daeja grumbles when she tries to squeeze in but finds she's far too wide.

"They probably were hesitant to have dragons in here with paper…"

"I'll stay back and keep watch," she mutters, her wings sagging at her sides.

"We won't be long," I promise, patting her neck.

Marge gravitates toward the farthest wall, hovering her fingertips along the shelves, like if she moves slow enough, one might appear. Cole and I exchange an awkward look before we split up to search the walls at the opposite sides of the room. After scanning all the bottom shelves, I find an old wooden ladder and take a step onto the bottom platform.

The wood shrieks. I flinch, looking over my shoulder to Marge, who only diverts her attention away long enough to make sure I haven't broken an ankle before returning to her own shelves. Cole stops what he's doing and strolls over to me. Before he can reach me, I brace my weight onto the step, testing its limits before I begin to ascend.

"What are you doing?" Cole whispers.

"I have to check the top shelves." I test the next step. Lift. Test, then lift.

The ladder groans underneath me, its wooden frame trembling more the farther up I get. Until it suddenly stops quaking. I stop and glance down about fifteen feet to find Cole gripping the sides of the ladder to still it. He gazes up at me, his forearms locked and jaw tight.

Taking a soft breath, I keep my hands on the sides and pull myself farther up the ladder. Checking each row as I go, my hope sinks deeper with each dusty, empty shelf I pass.

I'm almost to the top of the ladder when I notice a stray piece of paper on one of the shelves. Face down. Just outside of my reach. I glance back down at Cole, and my stomach swings as I realize how small he is below me.

"I found something," I call out.

"Great. Grab it and come down," Marge responds from across the room as she walks to join Cole at the bottom.

Gripping the side of the ladder harder with my left hand, I stretch to my right. The corner of the page is still a little over a foot away. Sliding my other hand over to give me extra reach, I lean farther until my chest is past the ladder's width.

So…close…

The ladder groans. Warning that this much pressure on one side of it will snap it in half.

"Get down. Quickly," Daeja growls.

She doesn't have to tell me twice. I snatch the paper and, to free my hands, stuff it into my waistband before securing a two-handed grip on the ladder. I work my way down, trying to keep my weight dispersed and balance centered. Four stories left. Then three. Two.

Snap.

The ladder swings to the right.

"Kat!" Cole cries.

Daeja roars.

I lean left and grab onto a shelf with both hands as the ladder drops to the right, and the steps beneath my feet disappear. Swinging back and forth from my momentum, I kick out for the shelves beneath me to steady myself. Then pull my knees up slightly until I find a shelf I can rest them on. It does little to solve the current dilemma. It's only a break from the inevitable fall.

My palms grow sweatier, my fingers weakening. If I weren't wearing Marge's gloves, I would have instantly slipped.

"I will…break…down…these…walls…" Daeja grunts, followed by thuds as if she's trying to shoulder her way through a door.

"Don't! You break them, you risk the room collapsing!"

"Kat, jump to me!" Cole calls.

Breathing out of my mouth, I glance down behind me. Cole's arms are outstretched to me. Fifteen feet down. Maybe a little less. But enough of a fall that all of us are nervous it might lead to a broken ankle. Or worse.

"Fall! I'll catch you!" Cole pleads. "Trust me!"

Sucking in a quick breath, I let go of the shelf. And fall back. The rows and rows of empty shelves zip past me, until my back hits something solid. Cole grunts and wraps me in his arms. The two of us fall back until a tremor works its way through his body and out of mine.

I curl up and flop onto the floor next to Cole. "Are you alright?"

His eyes are closed, teeth clenched as he's lying on his back. The tile beneath him is cracked. He blows out a tight breath through his lips and inches up onto his forearms. "Yeah…I think so."

I jerk forward to slide my hand behind his back to help him up.

"I see you trust him more than you did me the first time we flew."

I toss Daeja a look. *"That was also at double the height."*

"Over water," she retorts.

"Are you hurt?" Cole whispers, his fingers brushing the tips of mine.

Marge taps her staff to get our attention and breaks the lingering gaze between us. "You broke her fall. Any broken bones I'm sure she would have felt by now."

Cole gets up first, the tension in his jaw and posture telling me he'll be feeling that one for the next few days. He offers me a hand and helps me rise.

"What did you find?" Marge asks.

I fish out the page from my waistband. Then flip it over, only to find both sides are blank.

Marge rolls her eyes, and I sigh. Cole silently asks to look at it, and with my permission, he folds it and pockets it.

"Can you pass along to A'nala and Nadja that we've found the library, but nothing else?" I ask Daeja as the three of us exit the library.

"Too embarrassed to admit you almost fell to your death for a blank piece of paper?"

"…Don't sound so concerned."

She nudges me with her muzzle as we close the door to the library. Sniffing at me and assessing me in her own way. If I felt pain, though, she would have likely already felt it.

She nods, then tilts her muzzle to the sky, before turning her attention back to me moments later. **"A'nala says they're still searching the kitchens, though it sounds like they don't have much hope in finding anything. Nadja reports Bristol, Archie, and Melaina are still searching the northern quarter. They've found the King and Queen's rooms but haven't found anything yet to garner excitement."**

Marge hobbles over to the next door farther down, attempting to twist the handle before stepping back and prodding it with the end of her staff. Cole joins her, twisting the handle and opening it with ease.

Marge narrows her eyes at him. "I must have shaken some of the dust loose."

"Or maybe your muscles are loose."

I smack Daeja's shoulder playfully with a snort, even if Marge can't hear it.

Cole nods at Marge, fighting a small smile. "Definitely."

The three of us enter the room, Daeja standing guard outside. A humming sizzles underneath the marbled floors. A massive set of three windows, sparkling with dusty, colorful stained glass, stretch above us to the beamed ceilings at least a hundred feet high. Streaks of color bounce off the floor and warm the room in a muted collision of light and color. In front of the windows are a set of shallow steps dressed in thick carpeting.

My breath leaves me in an audible gasp as I stare up at the magnificent stained glass windows. "What is this?"

Marge follows my stare. "Must be the chapel. King Aaric had the one in Arterias destroyed, as he no longer believes in the Gods…I imagine it must have looked much like this one." She hobbles over to the windows, brushing her fingers across the glass and leaving a clean streak.

A chapel. I've never been in one. But I used to dream about the day I finally would with Cole. With his mother's ring on my finger, him beside me, and his last name on my tongue. Bitterness coats my throat—parts of that dream came true. Except the reason I'm wearing his mother's ring is because it's a weapon. He walks the room with me, and I can't recall the last time I told him I love him. And the only reason I can say I'm Katerina Ashbourne is because almost everyone thinks he's my brother.

I swing my attention to Marge, then to the floor beneath my feet where a rumbling vibrates my boots. I follow Marge and whisper, "Can you feel it?"

Cole calls from the other side of the room, scanning sets of marble figures perched on stone podiums, "I do. Though…" He drops down and presses his fingertips to the marble tile, before glancing up at us across the room. "What do you think it is? If the castle is built on a mountain, surrounded by the lake and waterfalls…"

He knocks against the tile with his knuckles, listening carefully, before lowering his face and pressing an ear to the floor. He lifts his head again. "I think there's something underneath this room."

I follow suit, dropping to the floor and pressing my hand to the cold, grimy tile. What I thought was a rumbling of magic is something else entirely. I glance over my shoulder at Marge, who's watching the two of us with knitted brows.

"Underground dungeons, perhaps? Or…" she trails off, scanning the room for a hint before she taps her staff against the ground.

"Or what?" I stand at the same time Cole does.

Her blue-gray eyes meet mine. "Or…they're hatching grounds."

"A'nala and Sethan's group are on their way back to the main dining hall. They've tried all the doors in the kitchen and servers' quarters they can, but just about everything seems to be locked," Daeja calls.

"Weird…why lock the kitchens and servers' quarters but not the library or chapel?"

"I don't know. I suggested they try to break down the doors, but apparently it didn't work."

"What about Nadja, Bristol, Melaina, and Archie?"

"Still searching."

"Got it." I turn to Cole and Marge and relay the message before the three of us agree to head back and meet them. As we leave the chapel, I swear I see one of the marble statue's eyes shift to follow us out, but as I spin to face it head on, its glazed eyes are set on the stained-glass windows.

We meet the rest of the group back in the dining room. Where Melaina's group disappeared is an inset room that overlooks the massive dining hall. Two elegant throne chairs sit in the center, their golden frames twisted into intricate circles, swirls, and dragons of every shape and kind.

Behind the chairs, a door is propped open a few inches by a dagger—Archie's dagger—with light leaking through and casting the throne chairs in a backlit glow of warmth. The door swings open farther, and Archie appears on the other side with a smile, holding it open for Melaina and ushering her in, followed by Bristol and, as Archie opens it wider, Nadja. Archie plucks his dagger from the ground then sheathes it before their group joins us near the throne.

"Any luck?" I ask.

All of them shake their heads.

Sethan turns his attention to Darian. "Now's your chance to make a difference, boy. Tell us what you know."

Darian sneers, staring Sethan up and down. "I'll die before I tell you anything, you fucking slug."

"Hey, watch your mouth!" Bristol snaps, jolting forward like he'll fight Darian.

Archie moves forward, following Cole, and everyone swarms in to stop a fight before it breaks out. Darian shoves Cole, forcing him back, and his heel hits one of the throne chairs. Before he can topple over it, he regains his balance and slingshots back into the throng. Archie withdraws a dagger from his side, and as he's shoved by a scraping Darian and Bristol, he accidentally slices Cole.

"Shit, sorry, Cole!" Archie calls.

"Sheathe your weapon!" Cole hisses, brushing Archie away from the throng. "Nobody needs to get hurt!"

"No, fucking cut me if you think you actually can," Darian growls, before Cole seizes the chain to his shackles and tears him away from Bristol.

Their squabbling dies out as I focus on the chair. Magic buzzes beneath my feet, breathing and living. But also rising out of the hum comes a rushing current of whispers, growing louder and clearer as I step forward to the closest chair. As if led by some invisible force, I reach out, brushing my hand along the chair's golden arm, and following each intricate curve, over dragons' elegant figures, and swirls with rings.

Rings.

Two of them. Joined at the center.

I turn, scanning the room beyond our group where rows of tables with corpses lie, and the slain dragons hanging above them.

"What is it?" Marge whispers.

Two rings…two chairs. Marge said the rings were worn separately to disperse the natural flow of power. But why position the throne room here, of all places? Yes, perhaps to overlook their citizens and any out-of-town guests. But there had to be some other reason…more than just some gathering room. I look back down at the throne chair, moving my hands up the arm and over to the back as Marge watches me with mild curiosity.

Without looking up, I ask, "Cole mentioned he noticed something underneath the chapel. It may be an underground dungeon, but you mentioned hatching grounds?"

"Yes…? And?"

I drop down and touch the tile to confirm my suspicion, then smile. Something is definitely underneath this throne room. I stand, circling back to the front of the chairs—and freeze.

There, set into where the two chairs' arms touch, is an inlay of two rings. With a shaky inhale, before I can second-guess myself, I remove my gloves and tear the Blood Ring off my finger and place it into the inlay on the left. When nothing happens, I move it to the one on the right.

The ring snaps inside of it like something magnetic, and then the humming grows louder. Loud enough everyone fighting stops and turns. Thin lines like rivers hidden in the golden frames of the throne chairs glow an iridescent blue. My breath fills my ears, and I reach forward as if I've done it a thousand times before and turn the ring to the right. The ground trembles beneath our feet, shaking loose dust from the ceiling and showering us in a thick cloud. After the dust settles and we wave away our coughs, the platform with the throne chairs we all stand on is sunken ten feet deeper than before. A dark staircase spirals down into the depths below the throne room.

"Well…that wasn't weird at all," Archie laughs, then scans our group before his face falls. "What?"

I snag the ring back from the chair and slip it onto my finger before meeting Marge's wide gaze. It's a silent confirmation I haven't been sealed to the Blood Ring…yet.

"How did you know how to do that?" she whispers.

I shrug. "It was a lucky guess."

"I believe you're more than just lucky, Katerina. You are brilliant."

Smiling, I walk to the edge of the platform and peek down over the side, only to find the steps shrouded in shadow, not telling me much else. Like how many stairs there are and what it leads to. But one thing is for certain.

I turn to everyone already watching me. "We have to go down."

FORTY-THREE

Down below

After realizing the dragons won't fit down the winding staircase, we split up. Despite Daeja and the others' grumbled protests; Bristol, Darian, Gavin, and Nolan stay back with A'nala, Daeja, and Nadja.

I pat Daeja's muzzle as she curls up near the entrance to the stairs, her head flat on the stone floor looking up at me. *"If they fight again…you have my permission to bite."*

She perks her head up. **"Really?"**

"Don't draw blood though."

"Well then where's the fun in that?" She sinks back down.

Chuckling, I rub her snout a little firmer. *"We'll try to come back quickly. I'll keep you updated if things are looking scary."*

She might as well have rolled her eyes. **"You're never scared."**

I sink to my heels to look her in the eyes. *"I'm always scared when you're not by my side."*

"Remember that next time you try to go somewhere without me."

"You know I wouldn't ever want to go somewhere I can't take you.

But this…" I motion to the stairs. *"I have no choice. This isn't just about me and what I want."*

"Fine…" she sighs. **"Go do your chosen one thing."**

"I'm sorry. I don't like this responsibility, but I have to live with it." I kiss the tip of her nose. *"I'll be back as soon as I can."*

"I better see you running up those steps when you come back! High knees and all!"

I laugh and follow Sethan and Melaina down the stairs. We descend farther and farther into darkness, relying solely on the light leaking in from the throne room above us. The lower we get, the colder and wetter the air becomes. As the shadows grow larger and darker, I graze my fingertips against the side wall for extra balance. The rest of the group slows our pace, and a smack pulls my attention behind me. Marge waves Cole off with glaring independence and descends another step to put space between the two of them. Cole watches her, rubbing the elbow still held out for her to grab onto.

Marge flicks her irritated gaze to me. No matter how hard she tries to mask her fatigue, her voice is heavy and breathy. "Don't you get any ideas, either. I'm perfectly fine handling myself."

I nod and allow her to pass before Cole slides in next to me, and I can't fight my smile. Stubborn thing. Half the time she'd rather push herself past exhaustion than ask for help. I throw Cole a playful eye roll, and he snorts with a grin. We continue our path down the circular staircase in silence. His shoulder brushing mine all the way, comforting my nerves.

"Do you think we're almost there?" Archie asks, his voice bouncing off the walls.

"Shh," Sethan hushes.

"Do you think we're almost there?" Archie asks again, this time whispering.

"I said silence," Sethan grumbles. "We don't know what will be at the bottom."

After what feels like the thirtieth full turn, the staircase ends at a single archway. We all slip through it into a brighter room, and immediately a frosty chill wraps around me. Our group fans out to the sides, allowing me to step to the front of the line.

I gasp.

Dangling in front of us is a magnificent white dragon, its long tail disappearing into the depths of an endless black pit clouded with a still fog. A bridge stretches from the rocky cliffside we are on out to another platform, blocked by the massive dragon suspended from the immeasurably high, cavernous ceiling.

"What…is this?" Archie murmurs, then peers over the edge of the cliff plunging into shadow.

Melaina snatches his forearm and pulls him back from the edge, then laces her fingers with his as if to assure herself.

"I'm not sure. But let's agree to make sure we don't try and find out," Sethan responds, his voice carrying and echoing throughout the monstrous cave-like space.

My mouth stays open as I ghost toward the dragon, taking a few steps onto the bridge as I twist my head to survey the entire carcass. Despite how long it's been strung up here, it's the only one I've seen so far who's scales still shimmer and shine. I reach a hand out to its sparkling white muzzle—

Melaina smacks my hand down. "What are you doing?"

I turn my head toward her but place a hand on the scaled snout. Its body is a shock of cold against my palm, forcing my eyes closed, but beneath the wall of ice is a distant hum shifting in its depths.

It doesn't call to me like the other ripples, yet, I can still sense it—a soft glow of light buried in a chasm of cold and shadow. My eyes flash open, and I catch Melaina's bewildered gaze as she lowers her arm to her side.

Archie walks up behind her, awe and respect lifting his features as he notes every detail of the dragon. "Holy…shit."

I follow his gaze, my heart sinking lower as I trace the ridge of the dragon's back. Thick, barbed hooks bite into its skin and, judging by how deep they are—likely its *bones*. Its curved face emanates otherworldly beauty, hanging with the tip of its muzzle just out of reach from the bridge.

I brush stray hairs out of my face, gathering all my hair behind me and tying it back as I assess all of the hooks. "I'm going up. I'm going to free it."

"You aren't serious, right?" Archie laughs nervously, then looks at Melaina. "Tell me she's not serious?"

"Absolutely not," Sethan calls, stopping a few feet behind Archie.

Marge and Cole watch from the beginning of the bridge, standing side-by-side, both surprisingly quiet and watchfully still.

"It's still alive," I say, grabbing the closest chain hooked into the dragon's shoulder blade and testing its strength as if it isn't holding a several ton creature.

Melaina chimes in, "In that case, wouldn't we not want to disturb it? It would likely turn its wrath on us—"

"If you don't want to be here when I do, that's fine. But you aren't going to change my mind," I mutter and seize the chain with my other hand before heaving myself up. I curse under my breath as I try to gently find footholds on the dragon's arms, missing with a few attempts as the dragon's body begins to sway back and forth a few inches. I spot a lift in the dragon's scales and slap a hand over it to pull myself up and over its back. As I straighten and find my balance, I discover the lift I used wasn't a scale or part of the dragon's body at all.

It's a saddle.

Scanning the rest of the dragon's body from this angle, I find a saddle as white as the dragon's scales, wrapping around its torso.

"What? What is it?" Marge calls.

"It's…a saddle. A bonded dragon," I answer blankly, before turning my attention to the group. "Everyone get off the bridge."

"Why?" Sethan asks, then follows the chains up until it

disappears into the black ceiling, answering his own question and snapping his gaze to me. "You can't."

"I *can*."

"Who do you think you are to deny direct orders—"

"Remember what you told me the days before the blood pact? It could have been anyone else, but for some reason, it's me. I'm the chosen one, whether or not *you* like it." I turn my attention to the closest hook and inch over to it.

"Why is A'nala telling me you're doing something stupid?" Daeja growls.

"Just trust me," I whisper, then unsheathe my dagger with my right hand and grip the chain with my left hand.

"Hard to do that when she's saying you're putting yourself in danger."

"Do you remember when we were flying for the first time here in the Dragon Lands and you asked me to trust you?" I grunt, apologizing under my breath as I saw the blade between the bottom of the hook and the dragon's muscle.

"Yes?"

"And admittedly, I didn't?"

"And you're acknowledging this now…why?"

"Just reminding you that you're better than me." I grin, waiting for her to take the bait.

I swear I can envision her eyes narrowing. **"You think you can so easily manipulate me by stroking my ego?"**

I chuckle, and she interrupts, **"Do go on. You must have more to say. Examples aplenty."**

"We can continue this conversation later once we're together…" I slice through the last inch of the dragon's flesh, and the left side of the dragon's body swings down limply. I cling to the chain with both hands, waiting for the swaying to slow before moving to the next hook. *"But thank you for trusting me."*

She grumbles, ***"Not like I have much of a choice right now anyway."***

Sethan whispers something where he's gathered with everyone else, and Cole elbows him quiet, motioning to let me have complete silence.

I keep my eyes glued on the scales beneath me, slinking over from hook to hook and slicing them free. Every hook I sever makes the next exponentially harder to release, until I stop with two left: one at the nape of its neck, and the other at the base of its tail. I free the one at its tail first, and the back half of the dragon's body drops to the bridge, shaking it violently beneath us. I climb back up the dragon's back to the last hook between its neck and head. I saw through it until the dragon's head drops free, and I cling to the horns on the back of its head, praying I don't impale myself in the fall and tucking my head down into my chest.

We land. No horns through my torso, but then the next test starts.

The bridge jumps with a wooden shriek, shaking until it eventually mellows out. Releasing a breath, I drag my head off the cool scales and find everyone at the entrance of the staircase watching with a mix of awe, pride, and *I-damn-near-shit-myself.*

I hop off the dragon's neck onto the bridge, take a few steps, and freeze when a gust of warm air brushes against the back of my legs. I turn and backpedal in one swift motion, tripping over my own boots and falling back as the dragon's eyelids slide open to reveal eyes as black as any moonless night. Its shoulders rise in one solid breath, sucking strands of sweat-slicked hair forward off my head and blowing it back as it exhales.

A glimmer of light catches on one of the hooks hanging with chunks of the dragon's flesh. A blue shine gleams across the metal as it spins…

Dragonblade.

I flick my gaze back to the dragon and scramble backward. The dragon lifts its head weakly off the bridge, eyes burrowing into every inch of my soul, before it begins to stretch toward me. I freeze, lost to its soulless black eyes.

"Wait! I didn't do this to you! I only freed you," I call toward it as I throw out a hand as if to stop the advance, recognizing I won't be fast enough to run.

It proves me right, instantly closing the gap between us and pressing its warming nose to my palm. As if its name is wrung around me by an invisible bell, it's clear as day, echoing in the shadows of my mind.

Vue. The sun dragon.

"Katerina Blackwind…" it murmurs, voice like a whisper of wind. *"Thank you."*

Two hands snatch my shoulders, pulling me back and away as Vue rears back. A blinding light explodes from Vue, capturing every inch and crack of the cavernous expanse until we are drowning in an ear-ringing blast of white. I throw a forearm over my face, squeezing my eyes shut as if it'll stop the glaring brightness.

"Secrets never die, they're just buried in a grave," his voice melts from a whisper to silence.

The light fades as quick as it came, the energy and heat evaporating with it. When I open my eyes, Vue is gone. And the lingering veil of magic that hung in the air disappears, ushering in a sense of peaceful death.

"What was that?" Daeja's voice is tight with panic.

"Vue…the sun dragon…" I stare up at the dangling hooked chains. *"Are you alright? What's wrong?"*

"I don't know…I felt something snap in my chest. And now I just feel…cold? Out of place?"

My shoulders sag as I recall my father's journal entries about the sun and moon dragons.

At once, the two became the very first dyad. Bonded and inseparable. Endless as a ring, with no beginning and no end.

"He's dead. Isn't he?"

"I'm so sorry, Daeja…"

"It's…it's okay. I never met him in this life. How can I be sad about someone I've never met?"

"You met him in your previous lives. You're allowed to feel sad."

"Then I will see him in the next one. And in this one, all that will matter is you."

"Are you okay?" Cole's gruff voice is in my ear as he helps me to my feet.

"I-I think so…" I glance down at the spot where Vue just was, his words ringing in my head.

Secrets never die, they're just buried in a grave.

Marge claps me on the shoulder before hobbling forward to take the lead of our group. "Well done," she says as she passes me.

Cole brushes dust out of my hair. "That was the sun dragon, wasn't it?" When I nod, he turns his attention to Sethan who walks across the bridge toward us. "If that was Vue, and Vue was bonded to Queen Elara…is she still alive?"

"Not likely, now. Unless she broke their bond." Sethan whisks past us. "Let's keep moving. We need to check what lies on the other side of this bridge."

My heart breaks at the thought of Queen Elara severing her bond to Vue. Though if she did, I'd hope it was for a good reason. I can never imagine having to cut myself off from Daeja.

We cross the bridge and find at the other end is another archway, with a dragon-like gargoyle perched and snarling at the entrance below. A flickering warm light bleeds from the hallway on the other side, with several lit torches lining the walls.

"We aren't the only ones here?" Archie proposes.

"No, it's dragonfire. Dragonfire will stay lit as long as it's contained in some form of dragonblade. And those sconces are made from it." Marge squints at a wall, doing a double-take.

By the time Cole and I join them in the hallway, my skin is

crawling. Smeared across the walls in bright red blood, glittering with specks of gold, is a paragraph in a different language.

FORTY-FOUR

The calling

"What does it say?" I whisper.

Sethan strolls up beside Marge, squinting in the flickering light and scanning it as she does so for the fourth time. He presumably mouths the words and drops his head, staring at the ground before he lifts his head and mouths more.

"A'nala's fluency in the ancient language is a bit…restricted," he answers and then pauses, lifting his head again and listening. "But…I don't know what that's supposed to mean," he calls aloud.

"What? What is she saying?" Marge nudges him impatiently.

"The blood one is worth the blood of many."

Archie pats a thick stone door at the end of the hallway, tracing all the intricate swirls and patterns etched into it. "I think we need to go this way."

"Obviously," Sethan mutters. "But we won't be able to get that open. There's not even a handle. It might be an exit only. I think we should head back and call it a night. In the morning, we can check the perimeters around this area to see if there's another way in."

"Wait," Marge interjects and snaps her fingers at me. "Come here. Slice open your palm."

"What?"

"Just do it!" she barks. "We're running out of time."

I pull off my gloves and tuck them into my satchel before I unsheathe my sword. I cut open my palm.

"Press it to the door. Archie, stand back," Marge commands.

Everyone shuffles away as I swoop in, blood dripping down my hand and leaving dots of red on the stone floors. I turn my hand away from me and press it to the cold door. And wait.

And…nothing.

I glance over my shoulder at Marge, my hand still pressed to the door. "How long should it take?"

Her eyebrows pinch together. "It should have been instant…" She turns her attention back to the wall, tilting her head in consideration.

The blood one is worth the blood of many…my heart sinks into my stomach. Perhaps I'm not the one from the prophecy they've all assumed I am. Perhaps all along it's been a mistake.

"Would…a dragonblade taint her blood? Since it's magic, it might counteract with whatever spell is on the door? Maybe it affects her blood from opening it?" Archie mumbles as he slides a finger across his blood-spattered dagger.

Melaina nods slowly. "Earlier when we went through the invisible wall…we used a dagger instead of her sword, didn't we?"

Archie's avoiding eye contact with us in the event he's embarrassingly wrong. "Yes. We did."

Marge straightens the longer she sits with the idea before she smiles at him. *Smiles.* "Brilliant, Archie!"

His cheeks redden as he dips his head, then hands me his dagger. I take it with a grin, then slice open my opposite palm before returning the blade back to him. I press my hand back to the stone, a few inches away from the spot I had it on before.

The stone wall beneath my palm warms comfortably, and a glowing light seeps from cracks spidering across it as the walls rumble around us. The door trembles, then begins to inch open. All of us back up as it slides heavily to the left.

Marge's gaze connects with mine, and she gives my shoulder a quick squeeze. "I always knew it was you."

I don't have a chance to respond to her because my jaw drops at what's on the other side of the engraved door. Marble columns line a pathway, the tops of which flicker with flames as tall as I am that chase away the shadows. At the end of the path are two sizable, stone rectangles lying side-by-side, both carved with a strange language across the fronts and the same curving, elegant embellishments that adorned the throne chairs.

A thick, bitter cold falls on me like a blanket of wet snow, and I shiver. The soft rippling sound of the flames is punctuated by the splatter of water against the floors. Water trickles in from random cracks spread throughout the ceiling and walls, collecting in small rippling puddles.

Sethan throws a hand out to stop Archie, and Archie almost folds over his forearm, before taking a step back as Melaina collides into the back of him.

"What?" Melaina whispers.

Sethan scans the room, then without taking his attention off our surroundings, holds an open hand back to us. "Give me something I can throw."

"Why?" Archie asks.

"Stop asking questions, and just do it!" Sethan snaps.

Archie places the dagger I sliced my palm with in his hand, and Sethan probes the doorframe before tossing it far into the room. The blade lands a few feet in front of the two stone pieces, sliding into them.

The rest of us inch forward behind Melaina and Archie, peering over Sethan's shoulder.

After we hold our breaths for a few still moments, Sethan looks over his shoulder at us. "Whatever you do, do not touch anything." He drills his gaze directly into Archie. "Is that understood?"

"Yes, sir." Archie dips his head.

Sethan lowers his arm, and we slink into the room, all of us splitting up into separate directions to survey it.

"If that door was magically sealed…" Cole whispers, following me like a shadow. "Then something of value must be in here."

But I'm having trouble focusing on anything but the pull to the farthest side of the room, where a new archway awaits for us, leading into darkness.

"Wow, look at this!" Archie attempts to whisper somewhere behind me and Cole. "Such beautiful artwork…Melaina, come see this!"

I take a step up the shallow stairs leading into the shadowed archway.

"What…what is it?" Cole's voice is soft, a few inches behind me.

There's an unmistakable humming—a *calling* of energy—like I belong here, and it's been waiting all this time. The buzz increases beneath my boots, as if it may shake the very core of this earth and split it if I don't make haste.

"Something's here," I whisper back to Cole and take a few more stairsteps. Though, I can't quite tell *what* that is, yet.

Cole follows me up to the last step, and before I can venture further through the dark archway, Sethan calls out, "Wait. Shouldn't we explore this room first? It looks as if this may be the royal crypt."

"Not yet," I whisper, and without looking back, I step into the shadow and through the archway.

The light from the previous room dies off quickly, sinking us in darkness. I squint, waiting for my eyesight to adjust, then jerk toward a flicker of movement.

The room fades into more comprehensible details. Gargantuan marble statues are positioned along the side walls, each of their faces and figures differing in characteristics. Water slips from each statue's eyes and collects in a pool of water covering the entire room's floor and submerging all the marbled figures' feet. A thick overhang of ivy crowds the ceiling and drips water down into the pool below, sparking uneven ripples. On the other side of the room, rising from the pool, is another set of stairs leading through a two-piece archway.

And beyond that?

A soft, bluish glow.

I turn to Cole. "We have to get over there."

He dips his head and returns to call the others. I edge down the stairs, closer to the pool of water, side eyeing the colossal statues all the while. They're mirror images of the ones back in the chapel, and at least four times the size. Despite the lack of detail in their eyes, I can't help but feel their stone faces are staring at me, *watching* me.

As I stop at the last step and stare out at the dark water rippling with the dripping overgrowth, footsteps sound behind me. Cole helps Marge down the stairs, her breath heavy and hand shaky on her wooden staff. At least she finally has the sense to accept the help—there's no telling how many sets of stairs we took on the way down from the throne room, and I can only imagine how sore her knees are, based on my own.

She slips her arm out of Cole's once they reach the last step with me, and she ushers me aside, fighting to keep her panting behind her tight lips.

"Holy…shit…" Archie breathes from a few steps up from where we stand.

Marge thwacks the side of his leg with her staff. "You are in the presence of something sacred!"

Archie's cheeks flush, dipping his head in apologies and murmuring something under his breath.

"What is this place?" I'm unsure if I say it in my head or out loud.

"This must have been the main temple to the Gods," Marge whispers and bows her head.

Everyone else follows suit, dipping low in respect, and I quickly join them. When we straighten, Marge slams her staff into the water, watching the ripples break across the black surface to the other side of the vast room.

"What are you doing?" Cole asks.

"Shh," she warns, eyes trained on the water.

When nothing happens after a few tense moments, she turns to Cole. "The sword in this staff is made of specially cured dragonblade. If there were any dragons in the water, they would surface by now, sensing it."

"That's good then, right?" Archie chimes.

"Yes. Though…there's no telling how deep it is or if we can even cross it." She tests the depth with her staff, and it sinks lower and lower until it's mere inches below her hand, and she pulls it completely out. "I can't tell."

Cole nods, shrugging his jacket off and untucking his shirt before he takes it off.

"What are you doing?" I snag his arm. This is the first time I've seen him shirtless since we last made love. And even though everyone in our group is now aware of our true history, I heat at the thought of them noticing my blush.

"You said we have to get over there. And if there *is* something in there—" he gestures to the pool, his hair-dusted muscles working as he removes his boots, "—then I'm not letting you go first."

"He has a good point. You're the last person in this group who should go first," Sethan supplies cooly. "His death matters less."

I toss him a glare.

"And he's the tallest," Sethan adds. "If he can't walk across, none of us will be able to."

Archie wolf-whistles, and I turn as Cole throws his pants off near his boots, jacket, and shirt. In nothing but his undergarments.

I drag my gaze away before my cheeks redden again. "Well, couldn't we all just swim?"

Cole hesitantly glances at Marge, exchanging some silent

acknowledgment, before Marge admits in a defeated mumble, "I… can't swim—"

"It's fine!" Cole tries to interrupt quickly to cover her confession as he quickly wades into the water. "I'm happy to test the waters."

My heart thunders in my chest as he takes step after step. My hand on my sword. The water rises higher and higher on his brawny body until it reaches just below his shoulder blades, and then begins to recede.

He makes it to the other side of the pool and waves. "It's a little cold, but all clear!"

I release a breath I didn't realize I was holding. Most of us roll up our sleeves and pants, while Sethan just blazes through the water. Cole returns, water dripping down his carved body as he slides his clothes back on. He and I link Marge's arms between us, and the three of us cross the water together.

"You can't swim?" I ask quietly. "I didn't know that."

"It never came up," Marge mumbles.

I flick a look at Cole. But he knew. He mentioned having conversations with Marge about me. I'm curious as to how close they've gotten, if she's admitting things to him like not being able to swim. Something vulnerable she's never confessed to me.

We're last to ascend the stairs out of the pool, shivering in the cold air. With sloppy, wet footsteps, we all climb the staircase through the double-arched exit into the glowing room, the humming of magic growing louder and louder as we crest the top to a landing.

Waterfalls spill down from the rocky ceiling and collect into a new pool of glowing blue water beneath the cliffside we all stand on. All the previous rooms were clearly human-made, but this?

This is natural.

Raw, primitive, and yet perfect. Jagged rock formations spike from the floors, the walls, and the ceiling like angry claws.

The *ceiling*.

I've never seen anything like it—it reflects the pool below, and yet isn't a mirror. The water shifts and dances above us, glowing blue as the liquid whips back and forth. Shimmers sparkle in its depths like liquid stars.

Across the pool beneath us is a collection of black, sharpened rocks, formed to look like something between a nest and a throne. More waterfalls rush behind it, framing it with a blue glow and creating an island around the structure. But there, in the rocky shore of the island, are deep grooves. Carvings of the same ancient language we've been seeing, along with two intersecting rings, and two dragons. My father's journal snaps into my memory.

The ancient carvings in the hatching grounds of Vitalis depict two dragons: one of the sun, and one of the moon.

"Oh, my…" Marge whispers beside me, her mouth open in unfettered awe. "…The hatching grounds."

Sethan whispers, "This is where dragonkind began. With Vue and Daeja."

The sun and moon dragons. Gifted by the Gods.

"And yet, the staircase wasn't built to accommodate a dragon's width. How would they get down here?" I ask.

"Perhaps there are other access points deeper in the cave. I noticed drawbridges large enough for a dragon in the castle," Sethan responds. "So, I don't imagine they forgot to create an access point here."

"It's…it's beautiful," Melaina whispers, tears lining her eyes.

I nod, transfixed by the luminescent blue, the calming rushing of the waterfalls, the sparkling liquid suspended above us. Daeja should be here. She should be seeing this. *Feeling* it. Experiencing it just like the rest of us.

"I wish you were here…"

"You'll make it up to me," she purrs. **"I expect a full day's feast of elk alone."**

I smile. *"You deserve more than that."*

"In that case, hurry back to me. I grow quite tired of your

brown-haired friend here. I might bite him, even though he's been on his best behavior yet."

"He isn't a friend," I grumble, not willing to recall the heat he spoked in my desire.

"Oh? I don't recall all your friends causing such a stir in your blood when you think of them. Nor you zoning out when someone asks you questions as you think about whatever you two do at night—"

"Get. Out. Of. My. Head."

"When I'm dead," *s*he snickers.

I flinch at Daeja's choice of words. *Dead*…I swing my attention back to where we came from, in the direction of the crypt we walked through. Vue's voice, combined with my mother's, rings like a bell inside of my head, clearing out the cobwebs covering my comprehension.

Secrets never die, they're just buried in a grave.

When I turn to Sethan, my voice is clear with certainty. "I think I know where Queen Elara's journal is."

We return to the crypt, all of us still dripping from the second trip through the water. I see it now, clear as day. As I make my way down the steps into the room, my eyes are glued to the two stone rectangles in the center of the room.

Stone c*offins.*

We spill into the crypt, fanning out around the two coffins. I can make out two overlapping rings on both lids. Just like in the throne room.

Two rings to hold the power.

Archie clears his throat. "So…we just lift the lid and hope it's Queen Elara's?"

"No," Sethan says, arm outstretched. "Don't touch anything. Not yet."

Cole motions over to a wall dim with shadows. "What about that? Sethan, do you know what it says?"

Five panels span the wall, with the center having two circles joined, and the other four panels depicting carvings of the different elements: fire, earth, water, and air. Each panel has a small inscription, lined up horizontally with the other panels.

Sethan shakes his head. "No…no idea. But we've been gone hours at this point, and I'm not entirely trusting of Darian being in such little company for so long—"

"He's surrounded by three dragons, is restrained, and has three other men watching him. Do not worry yourself," Marge says.

Sethan snaps his attention to her. "I know him better than you do."

She snorts, the motion throwing her head back a few inches. "You know him as his father's weapon. I know him as a boy and a man."

I flick my attention down to one of the stone lids closest to me, reaching out a hand and hovering inches above it. "Shh, not the time right now…" I wave my hand over the lid and follow a tugging urge until I walk over to the other coffin. "Here. I think this one is hers."

I take the Blood Ring off my finger, then look each person in the eye. "Are we…sure we want to do this?"

"You have the gift and the curse of making the choice," Marge responds.

I'm caught in her gaze like a fly stuck in a spider web. "I don't want to make the decision. It's not up to me…"

I glance over to Sethan, and he shakes his head, clearly agreeing with Marge. Then to Melaina, Archie, and Cole, who all dip their heads.

I blink, returning my attention to Marge. "But I don't want to choose wrong."

"It doesn't matter if you don't want to choose wrong. You only choose wrong by not making a decision," she hisses.

"I—"

"Now's not the time for your indecisiveness. Choose."

With a shaky breath, I lower the ring into the coffin's groove, and after it snaps in, I turn it to the right. Invisible cracks burst from the lid before glowing with a pulsing blue light.

We all shuffle away from the lid, our splayed hands held in front of us as the stone lid scrapes sideways off the coffin, as if pulled by a pair of giant invisible hands. It tips over and slams onto the ground. The flickering flames in the torches surrounding us almost completely fizzle out before they flare back to life again.

We all exchange a wide-eyed gaze before we inch forward, peering into the coffin together.

My skin crawls at the vision before me.

Cobwebs are strewn across the eye sockets of a skeleton, its teeth completely missing and its bony arms crossed over a black book held to its chest. A rich, lavender dress trimmed with gold drapes over the body.

Her body.

Splashes of dark stains spread across the light fabric like a sinister ink, followed by one deep, angry gash slicing from her chest down to her hips, with her spine and ribs peeking through the tattered dress.

Mutilated.

She had been *mutilated*.

King Aaric killed her. Murdered her. Just to take the throne.

"So then…I suppose it's a merciful thing she's dead, right?" Archie murmurs softly. "If Vue was still alive before Kat freed him, she would have been stuck in this coffin. Alone for…well over a hundred years?"

"Which means the bond between them must have been broken. Yes," Marge answers quietly.

Cole leans over the coffin, squinting as he tips his head to the side to peer down at the black book. "Something's written on it. It must be her journal, right?"

Sethan slides in next to him, craning his neck to get a better view.

It feels incredibly wrong to be bursting into someone's tomb and plucking their belongings from their cold, dead fingers. But there it is, staring me in the face as bright as a sun.

Vue told me.

My *mother* told me.

Something deep within told me, like a flicker of a distant lifetime.

Secrets never die, they're just buried in a grave.

We need to read that book. This was what they all wanted—what they all tried to tell me.

Archie leans forward on the side of the coffin, he plucks the book out from the skeleton's rigid fingers.

Marge smacks him on the back of his thigh with her staff. "Foolish boy! What are you doing?"

He almost drops it back into the coffin, catching it midair, before whispering down into the coffin. "Sorry, Your Majesty!" Then he turns and holds it out to me until I take it. "Is this not what we came for? Are we not running out of time? With no disrespect, I imagine we may need it more than she does."

As I crack open the midnight black cover, a shot of energy ripples through my hand, down my body to my toes, and out across the room in an invisible wave.

"What was that?" Melaina asks, scanning the room.

Sethan withdraws his sword at his side, following his daughter's suspicious eyes surveying the room. "I'm not sure, but—"

A tremble quakes the ground and walls, shaking dust free from the ceiling above us.

Archie swallows, unsheathing his daggers. "That can't be good."

Cole follows suit by silently drawing his blade and shifting closer to me, his eyes set on the entrance toward the hatching grounds.

"Give that to me," Marge barks, snatching the journal from my hands. She hurriedly flips through the pages, her chest rising and falling quicker by the second. "Sethan, this entire journal is written in the old language—"

"We don't have time." His voice has a deadly frigid tone as he stares into the dark entrance through to the hatching grounds beyond, the ground still quaking. "Something is coming."

Marge is hit with a sudden thought, evident by her rounding eyes as she looks at me and tucks the journal into her side. "Give me your hand."

I offer it to her, still smeared with blood, the crimson staining the wrinkles of my skin.

She grabs my wrist and holds it out over the skeleton. "Do you sense anything?"

"No," I admit in a small voice, sweat trickling down the back of my neck.

"Close your eyes. Focus, just like you're pulling," she urges. "Hurry!"

Cole stalks up the stairs to the arched entryway of the hatching grounds, his blade raised and ready. Archie, Melaina, and Sethan follow behind him.

"Close your eyes, Katerina!" Marge barks.

I squeeze my eyes shut, and she removes her grip from my wrist, allowing my hand to hover. I fight to keep it raised as the ground beneath me continues to tremble, the force of which increases by each breath.

"We've got company!" Sethan shouts somewhere in the room.

But before I can open my eyes, a sparkle of energy whispers to me, far below and beneath the surface. I lean forward, partly nervous I might fall in if I'm not careful.

"Now, Katerina! Now! Follow your intuition!" Marge's voice wavers as if on a receding tide.

The hums grow louder, the black behind my eyelids transforming into a melding of blues until it shifts into a sparkling white. I reach toward it until my fingertips press against cold, brittle bone. I pull. And my consciousness is swept away, all my logic and thoughts vanishing in a single breath.

FORTY-FIVE

HER.

I'm in The White.

It's hard to mistake, with the blinding light surrounding me and lack of sensation. A black figure emerges from the mist. Her long, lavender-colored dress drags through the fog, sending it scurrying into various directions. But rather than having a rip as it did back in the coffin, the fabric is one. Free of stains.

Queen Elara.

The air about her is palpably regal. She holds out an open hand to me, a faint white circle around her ring finger where there should be one.

I flick my eyes back and forth between her piercing blue eyes and hand.

Marge warned me not to touch anyone in The White. But she also prompted me to follow my intuition.

I take a step forward and reach out, and as soon as my hand touches hers, her eyes flash into an endless expanse of white before my vision is sucked into a slate of black.

I race to the bathroom, my head swimming at a nauseating speed. Barely passing the gold-trimmed door frame into the room, I stumble, my knees colliding with the polished marble floors. My stomach tightens into a painful coil, a live fire burning in my throat until I heave vomit onto the ground, unable to quite make it to the sink.

My arms shake beneath me as I push myself up off the floor, then double back over at the putrid stench of my bile. I manage to drag myself to the sink and splash cold water over my face as I look up into the mirror.

My skin is as white as porcelain, my blue eyes dull and sunken into my skull, leaving behind deep bruised grooves above my high cheekbones. Every part of me is withering away, bit by bit. I'm starting to not look like myself…and the only thing that scares me more is other people noticing.

"Queen Elara?" Emerose, my lead maid, calls out from the bedroom.

I quickly brush my sweat-drenched blonde hair back from my face and suck in a steadying breath before turning away from the sink.

Emerose knocks at the door moments before she sweeps in, her dark eyes widening in shock and bouncing between the vomit and me. She rushes over, her small hands bracing me. "Oh, my Queen! Are you alright? You look—"

"I'm fine," I say with a small smile.

This is unfortunate if I'm trying to keep my illness a secret. I can't afford anyone else knowing I'm indisposed. It will only put a bigger target on my back, considering we're already starting to see a rebellion bloom after my brother, Aaric, married the Helmbrook southerner. Had he simply stuck to our original plan and been led by honor instead of love, we wouldn't be in such a predicament.

I see the hesitation in everyone's faces. Even as I pass them in the halls or share meals with them. They think I made a mistake. Think I'm too weak of a woman to command her own brother to fulfill his political duty. And my husband? Our relationship had already been one of tight conversations and brief meetings. But after my leniency with my brother, he's shut me out completely.

But I just couldn't. I couldn't force my brother into such a thing. Especially not when I saw the light on his face when he spoke of the woman he loves, the desperate adoration in his voice. The things I longed for from my own husband, and yet knew I would never get.

Aaric had never bonded a dragon, and therefore forfeited the throne. I spent so long trying to regain his love and trust, and when I was faced with the decision of shackling him to a loveless, political marriage or a lifetime with a woman who held his heart in her hands? I felt it was the best gift I could ever give him. I didn't need anything further to come between the two of us. And I only wanted to repair what was once whole.

"But…my Queen." Emerose motions toward the vomit.

I turn a stern look onto Emerose. "I am perfectly fine. It must have been the scones. Discard the rest of them."

She throws me a confused, hesitant look when I demand she leave, saying I'll clean up after myself. Lucky for me, being in such a grand position of power doesn't allow her to argue. Afterward, I fix my hair in front of the bedroom vanity and stare myself down in the mirror as I brush the wrinkles in my dress down my body. I pull a fierce mask of cold contempt over my features. They'll never know of my sickness.

They'll never use it against me.

Black swarms over the mirror until my entire vision is filled with it. When I blink, my eyes open to a new scene.

I sweep all the pages off the ornate wooden desk with an enraged growl, anger heating my face to a blistering level. The pages glide and flutter to the floor, and I knot a fist in the hair at my temple.

The family of Cordelia are going to pull their dragonblade

trade from us, as we rescinded their daughter's betrothal to my brother. While I hadn't had much use for it, I can't ignore how many they've produced. And if we don't have it, who will? The threat of rebellion has been simmering beneath the surface for years, and each week that passes flirts with the possibility we may see a civil war. And now the realm's biggest producer of dragonblade is cutting their trade relationship with us?

"Elara?" a voice calls.

I look up, my hand still clenched around one crumpled letter I couldn't quite let go.

Aaric stands in the doorframe, uncertain whether he should enter, his gloved fingers resting against the door. His sandy blonde hair sweeps back from his face in waves, accentuating his sharp, clean-shaven jaw. Those golden eyes regard me with a mix of respect and caution.

"Aaric, thank you for coming. Please, take a seat." I motion down to the chair opposite of me at my desk.

He dips his head, eyes down as he complies. His eyebrow tips up his forehead as he notices the papers strewn across the floor before sitting back in the chair and crossing his arms over his chest.

He already knows where this is going to go.

"The Baydens are going to revoke their dragonblades," I state.

He nods slowly, eyes scanning my office and looking anywhere but at me. "What use do you have for it, anyhow?"

"It's not that I have use for it, but a rebellion is only a breath away."

He snaps his attention to me. "There have been whispers of a rebellion long before you and I were born. Father told us of it many times." He pushes up out of the chair and stalks over to a painting framed in gold, regarding it with faux interest.

"Perhaps…but times are different now, Aaric. I can feel it. Something is coming, something is changing…"

He turns back to me, eyes a hard set of yellow. "Why have you brought me here, Elara?"

"Because you might be able to fix this…" I pause, eyes searching his.

He shakes his head, jaw clenched in determination. "No. No, I can't. I'm a perfectly happy, married man, Elara. And I refuse to go back on my vows to the woman I love."

I sigh, knowing that's what he would say but having to exhaust the option all the same. "This is just as difficult for me as it is for you. But I command you—"

Anger flares in his features, his lips peeling up into a scowl. "Don't you dare. Don't you do that again. This is not about you—"

"You're right. This is about more than me, because it's about our *entire* realm—"

"I don't give a rat's ass, Elara! I love her! What do you not understand? Just because you'll never experience what it's like—"

A new wave of rage washes over me, and I throw the crumpled paper back onto the desk before I push out of my chair and stalk forward, stopping a few inches from him. "How *dare* you."

He holds my stare, not backing down. "You know it's true."

"You've only known this woman for months—"

His nostrils flare as he inhales deeply. "That's where you're wrong. You have always been so focused on yourself, this throne, and your dragon that you have never stopped to pay attention to *me*."

"Are you so simple-minded you need my *attention*? Brother, look around." I motion to the room with both hands, though it does little to convey all that weighs on my shoulders. "I am the queen. I have a plethora of responsibilities all warring for my attention!"

"You are an aunt, Elara!" he roars.

I flinch, my breath caught in my throat, before I narrow my eyes. "You are not serious."

He continues, "She was born last year. The reason I was so desperate to go on the trip to Brookvale year after year was because the 'friend' I wanted to visit there was *Avice*. My *wife*. I have loved her since the second I laid eyes on her. Five fucking years ago."

My hand covers my mouth, and I stumble backward until I bump into the desk. Five years…five years he's been courting this woman? All this time I only thought he went to get drunk with a close friend of his. Maybe visit some brothels. "And why couldn't you have told me this years ago, then?"

"Because I knew you wouldn't bless our marriage."

"You have such little mind for me, brother," I growl. "Even if it puts me in the most precarious political situation, I still blessed your marriage."

"And now you're trying to break it."

The silence between us is filled with our heavy breathing as we stare each other down. I long for the simpler times, before politics tore us apart.

My heartbeat slows, and I whisper, "The…the girl. Where is she now?"

"Since you originally blessed our marriage, her and Avice moved here, just outside of the palace." His anger flickers, his jaw relaxing slightly. "You…you can meet her. If you'd like. She's been asking to meet you, but I was waiting for the right moment."

I shake my head, folding my face down into a hand and rubbing my temples, focusing on the black behind my eyelids.

This changes *everything.*

Seconds or eons pass with my eyes closed, and when I open them once more I'm in a massive library, columns of glinted marble supporting shelves and shelves of colorful books lining the walls. The same library Cole, Marge, and I were in earlier.

I flip the page of the book resting in my lap, studying the next set of passages, when a roaring sense of rage fills me. Twitching my head to the side with my eyes squeezed shut, I fight against the roll of blazing fury.

"*Vue?*" I call out.

He snarls, white-hot anger ricocheting in my skull, forcing

me to my knees as I wrap my hands around my ears as if it'll stop the sound. *"Vue, what is going on?"*

He doesn't answer me.

"Queen Elara?" Emerose calls in panic.

"Where…where is Vue?" I croak.

"Last I saw, he was in the hatching grounds, my Queen."

"Take me to him. Now."

We race to the hatching grounds, my head dizzy with the sound of Vue's fury. He isn't ever so ill-tempered, but something has changed recently. He's become territorial and moody…I can only hope I'm not rubbing off on him.

But as Emerose and I spill out into the Stone Gods' Garden with the hatching grounds in the next room, we find my brother. The second our eyes connect is enough to shatter my heart as I see the rawest agony drowning his features into something unrecognizable.

In his arms, limp and charred, is a small girl.

"If you have ever loved me," Aaric half-snarls and half-cries. "You will find her justice. You will honor her life, cut short by your savage beast!"

My niece had died a tragic death—caught in the dragonfire between Vue and the commander's dragon in the hatching grounds.

An accident. A heart shattering tragedy.

Aaric took his eyes off her for a few minutes before she wandered off from the Stone Gods' Garden to the hatching grounds. He didn't get to her fast enough, and by the time he did, she had already passed.

The missed opportunity to meet her before the incident has been haunting my every waking breath and every wicked dream. Everything's falling apart, right between my hands, and yet I can't do a gods-damned thing to stop it.

Tears creep to my eyes, and my throat constricts to a hard-to-breathe tension. But everyone in the room is watching me, so I swallow back all the things I want to say and force my heartache back into a box I can unpack in a private setting. Away from all the spectators waiting for me to break, hungry for more excuses as to why I don't deserve the throne. To usurp me.

I need peace.

I need order.

I need stability.

"Elara!" Aaric roars again for my answer. "A life for a life! Your dragon for my daughter!"

"He bites because he grieves," Vue rumbles. ***"I did not mean to harm the child, I swear it. Had I known she was in the hatching grounds, I would have protected her."***

"I know, Vue," I whisper sadly down our bond. She was caught in the crossfire.

I can't explain to Aaric why I can't kill Vue. Only those bonded to dragons know of how intrinsically linked we are as riders and dragons. Admitting it would only expose us. Nobody needs to know our lives are tied together.

So instead, I whisper, "It was an accident, Aaric—"

Avice—his wife—is at his side, her fingers wrapped around Aaric's arm. She whips around, staring at the people lining the room, her eyes wild and teary. "How can you all stand here and say justice won't be served? She wasn't even two!"

The crowd is still. Frozen in fear and horror and uncertainty.

Avice turns a deathly glare at me, pointing with a crooked finger. "You are a monster! It was on purpose!"

Aaric turns to her, stroking her arm and mumbling under his breath as he shakes his head.

"You know it!" Avice screams, batting Aaric off her as she lunges forward.

Several of my guards raise their weapons, pointing at them in silent warning. Aaric drags her back away from me.

"Tell them! Tell them it was all in retaliation!" Avice shrieks, still fighting Aaric to get closer to me. "If the Baydens didn't revoke their dragonblades, she would still be alive! This is punishment for our marriage! That we would not agree to your annulment!"

The crowd gasps, wide-eyed exchanges pass between the rows of citizens, soldiers, and nobles who've been invited here for a customary meeting.

This is only getting worse. My panicked breath rises, my skin bubbling hot and slick with sweat as I wipe the back of my hand across my forehead. The room spins slowly until it catches a rhythm, and I fall out of my chair to the marbled tile with a hard thud.

"Queen Elara?" someone calls.

"Oh, Gods! Someone, quick! Get the healer!"

More black swarms my vision, pulling me into the shadowed depths away from all other sensation and thought.

A new wave of mixed panic and pain washes over me before the black gives way to the pattern of stacked stones. I'm racing for my life down a set of stairs, using the handrail attached to the exterior wall to pull me down faster.

Faster. I must get there *faster.*

I clear the last few steps of the spiral staircase and dash across the bridge, through the dragonfire-lit hallways, the royal crypt, and the Stone Gods' Garden. Vue roars, though this time it shakes the walls. Bits of dust and rock pelt me in the head and shoulders.

"I'm almost there, Vue!"

"Don't bother. I'll take care of this quickly," he snarls.

"Don't hurt her! She can't die!" I command through our bond. It'll destroy Aaric more than he already is. *"I'll talk with her—"*

"She's not here to speak!"

I burst into the hatching grounds before screeching to a halt. Vue's scales gleam white against the shadowy cavern, his head low and teeth bared as his black eyes are narrowed at the woman standing several feet before him, her hand pointing a jagged blade straight at him.

Avice.

She slingshots forward, swiping the blade out as Vue dodges left. Her blade grazes Vue's tail, and he roars again. Black blood trickles out of the wound, and the sword flares blue.

Dragonblade.

"Avice!" I cry. Gathering my skirts, I race into the icy-cold pool separating me from the two of them. "Stop this! Stop this now!"

Mercifully, Vue listens. He could easily demolish her with a swipe of his claws alone. But instead, he slips farther back into the cavern. Avice affords me a glare and spits in my direction before she chases after him. Just as I climb up out of the water onto the rocky, black shore, Avice advances on Vue who's cornered. She swipes again, and Vue ducks out of the way, barely in time from getting sliced in the throat.

"Avice! Please, let us talk!" I cry, clambering across the hatching ground in a wet, heavy dress.

"We have nothing to talk about!" she screams back. "A life for a life. It is as fair as any!"

I race forward, pushing through the pounding in my head and all the whispers telling me to stop. Time slows, and I manage to clear the space between Avice and me as she lifts the dagger again, aiming for Vue. On her downward swing, I snatch her forearm, squeezing it tight and bracing all of my strength into stopping her. The raw power beneath our feet, vibrating in the walls around us, hums to me. Whispering to let it free.

Avice's hateful stare turns from Vue to me, setting fire to

something inside of me. She redirects the blade toward me, its menacing tip dipping lower and lower toward my throat.

I'm weak. Far too weak. I haven't been able to keep much food down for the last several months. Haven't been able to sleep with the stress, nor my niece's haunting death. Deteriorating my health even further. And I can't pull with the Bone Ring, either.

She throws her weight entirely into me and knocks me back onto the ground. My breath saws out of my lungs, and a sting like live fire splits through my chest.

Vue roars with everything he is and snaps forward, knocking Avice clear off me and onto the ground. But I can't breathe around the blade in my chest. Everything is on fire, and despite my multiple gasps, I can't pull in a solid breath.

The two of them turn into fighting spins of flesh versus scales until Vue swipes a taloned paw toward her, knocking her off her feet. Before she can escape, he pins her down and snaps his mighty jaws around her head before ripping it clean off her body. My slight relief is drowned out by despair.

Oh, Gods, Aaric. Aaric won't survive this—

"V-vue!" I manage to gurgle aloud.

"No!" my brother's scream ricochets throughout the cavernous expanse, breaking into a thousand pained echoes, followed by his hurried footsteps somewhere off behind me.

Vue slinks over to me, his black eyes filling my vision. ***"I shouldn't have listened to you…I should have killed her quicker. This would have never happened."***

The bond between us begins to thin as it tightens, like a thread being stretched near the point of breaking. One of Vue's front legs buckles before he straightens back up with trembling effort. His eyes lock onto something in the distance with a growl, and black blood seeps from the corner of his maw.

My vision grows dark at the corners, and the heat in my chest constricts. *"Break the bond…save yourself."*

"Never. There is no me without you."

I reach out for him. Longing to brush my hand across his warm, brilliant-white scales one last time. My own breath comes shallower and quicker with a spidering numbness crawling throughout my extremities.

It'll only be moments now.

"Tell Aaric to save the baby." I slip the Bone Ring off my finger, smearing blood across my hand. *"Break the bond, and give the babe your blood."*

Vue swings his attention down to me at the mention of the one I carry. ***"You trust your brother to keep it safe?"***

"Wait! I still need him!" Aaric's cry is loud. Close. Though, he won't be quick enough to save either of us.

Before Vue can respond, a single tear slips as I say, "I love you."

The bond between us snaps to an endless void as everything fades to black. And then…white.

FORTY-SIX

CRUMBLING

"We have to go! Carry her if you must!" Sethan screams, his voice ragged with fear.

A gasp rips through my mouth and I straighten, my sight twinkling back into vision from the endless black.

Through the archway leading into what Queen Elara referenced as the Stone Gods' Garden, a set of movements catches my attention. The water sloshes in violent waves. A massive, stone figure wades through the pool, with more behind it. They move for the stairs leading into the crypt we're in. All their faces are carved into otherworldly elegance and fury.

"Go!" Cole screams, breaking into a sprint and sweeping Melaina and Archie with his arm until the three of them race down the steps into the crypt.

Sethan waits at the bottom of the stairs, slapping their backs as they pass him before he takes the rear of the group and runs. I link my arm with Marge's, and we bolt from the other side of the coffins toward the exit. The walls around us thunder, with stones the size of my chest dropping from the ceiling. More threaten to shake loose. We all meet at the other end of the room and slip through the door. Archie grabs

Melaina's hand in his and pulls her faster through the blood message hallway to the bridge. Cole stops to offer Marge and me a hand, but Sethan growls and shoves him to keep running.

"Keep going!" I scream. "We are right behind you!"

He hesitates, but as Marge and I close the gap between us quicker than he anticipates, he races across the bridge. I don't dare look behind us. Already terrified by the ever-increasing thunder of heavy stone footsteps hot on our tracks. And the sound of crumbling walls.

The bridge sways beneath our feet with a vigor that would make me dizzy if I weren't solely running on adrenaline. Either side of the pathway drops to unimaginable depths. "Faster!" I grunt.

The rest of our group swats the hanging chains Vue was suspended in out of the way and clear the other side. Marge's staff taps faster and faster as we stride forward. The thunder of the Stone Gods grows closer behind us, and the end of the bridge stretches farther and farther away.

"Katerina, you must leave me," Marge pants.

"I'm not fucking leaving you," I growl, tightening my grip on her.

She glares at me, as if the profanity is the biggest of her problems right now. I smack the chains out of our way with one hand, but it slows our pace. One swings back and hits me in the side of the head. Another whacks Marge's arm, throwing her staff clear out of her grip. She falls forward, taking me down with her.

"Kat!" Cole yells from the other end of the bridge and races toward us to help.

I scramble to pull Marge up. The five towering Stone Gods burst from the hallway, spraying boulders into the cavity below. They fight to the front of the bridge, squabbling until one of them falls off the cliffside into the dark pit below, disappearing in seconds while the others advance without a second thought.

The bridge creaks with a sound dangerously close to snapping, and it whips back and forth beneath us with a dizzying speed. Pressure pinches in my ribs where my scar is.

I snap my eyes to Marge as I scream at her with an outstretched hand. "Get up! We have to move!"

Marge's expression is steadfast as she looks up at me, her unsheathed sword lifted in one hand as she places Queen Elara's journal in my outstretched palm.

As I take it, she stands and slices open her hand with her sword, whispering foreign words. Her blade flares like a blue flame. When I stand with her, I realize the pressure pinching my left ribs isn't from my scar, but from where she slipped one of the hooks under my corset.

"Hold on," she commands, her choice of words chilling my blood.

"Don't you *fucking* dare!"

Before I can stop her, she slices through the bridge between us in one swoop.

FORTY-SEVEN

HOLD. ON.

As the bridge swings down into two separate halves and my center of gravity leaps out from beneath me, I lunge. I snatch her by the wrist with a scream, "No, *you* hold on!"

I cling to her as we both fall a few feet, and our bodies snap as the chain adhered to the ceiling drops us as far as it'll go. Nearly breaking my grip on her, and her sword falls. The bridge and Stone Gods vanish into the thick fog below.

She looks up at me with her gray-blue eyes. "Katerina, you have to let me go."

"No!" I roar.

"It's me…" She slips an inch from my sweaty hand. I'm furious I'm not wearing her gloves. "Or the journal. And we both know what the right decision is."

I have Queen Elara's journal still tucked beneath my right arm as I hold Marge with my left. I can try to slip it into my satchel down at my hip, but I'm terrified if I move too much, I'll lose my grip on both.

Shaking my head, tears blur my vision. "No…no. I can't!"

She nods, a sad smile on her lips as she repeats what she said back in the crypt, "It doesn't matter if you don't want to choose wrong. You choose wrong when you don't make a decision."

"Don't! Please don't do this to me! I need you!" I cry.

She slips another half-inch. I'm not strong enough. Even with all the love I have in my heart for her.

"It's okay, you can do this," she whispers with tears lining her eyes and a warm smile. "You have never let me down, Katerina Blackwind."

She lets go of my wrist and slips out of my hand.

All sound dies out. Everything moves in slow motion as I watch her clothes ripple around her in her free fall. My heart plummets with her into the pitch-black oblivion below, the dark fog swallowing her whole.

"Marge!" my scream ricochets in my chest, tearing through my lungs. Every crack in my heart finally explodes into splinters.

The chain swings me back and forth, the metal hook hard against my ribs. My hand still extended as I stare at the blurry shadows.

"Kat! You have to get up!" Archie shouts from above.

I twist my head up to look at how far I've dropped. Only a few feet down from where the bridge was.

"Swing yourself to us!" Cole calls out with outstretched hands. "Come to me!"

Shoving the journal into my satchel with the swell of emotions beating in my chest, I tighten the strap crossed over my torso and grab the chain with both hands. Pulling a shaky breath between my lips, I swing my legs, pushing hard with my weight until I get momentum.

Closer. Closer. Closer.

Cole snatches me by the ankle, leaning dangerously close over the edge of the cliff to reel me in until my legs frame his waist, his fingers gripping my thighs, and my boots flirt with the edge. But I'm still held back by the hook.

"I can't pull her in any farther. Someone grab her arm!" Cole commands over his shoulder, never breaking eye contact with me. "Kat.

You'll need to remove your corset so we can free you from the hook. But we'll catch you, okay?"

I nod, not bothering to still the shaking in my limbs. Archie grabs my left hand with Melaina and Sethan spotting Cole.

"Ready?" Cole breathes.

I glance down at where the hook pierces through the dragon-bone corset. With my right hand, I quickly work to unclasp the front of the corset. Each snap I release tugs the pressure tighter and tighter against my chest. The tension holding me upright slips, and Archie yanks me by the left hand into Cole. Cole's strong arms hold me to him, and he takes a staggering few steps back. "I've got you, I've got you."

Once we're clear from the edge, Cole sets me on my feet. I hunch over, bracing my hands on my knees.

"Do you have the journal?" Sethan asks.

Gritting my teeth, I rip the journal out from my satchel and toss it at his boots. Cole rubs gentle circles on my back, reminding me of how Marge did it back in Silkwood. Pushing off my knees, I walk back to the cliffside as the reality settles over me thicker than the fog in the chasm below.

Cole wraps his arms around my torso and reels me back away from the edge and into him. I fight against him, unable to take my eyes off the darkness and where she disappeared.

"Stop it! Marge! Marge!" My voice breaks as reality crushes me. "We have to get her, we have to—"

"I'm so sorry…" Cole's soft whisper brushes my ear.

I shake my head firmly, biting back tears. "She's down there! I can't leave her…"

Cole turns me toward him, his hands gentle on my shoulders until he gives me a quick tight squeeze. His eyes search mine, eyebrows raised in sympathy. "We can't, love. She's gone."

My chest caves in, and I blink back tears, my lip quivering. "No, she—"

"We need to move," Sethan commands in a low voice. "Even if

there is a bottom to that pit, we can't get to it without a dragon—and you might not want to see her, anyway."

"Father," Melaina scolds, her hand laced with Archie's, whose soft gaze settles on me.

But he's right.

Even if I find her down there, even if the sight doesn't ruin me, it would tempt me. I have to leave her there. Not because she deserves it but because the temptation of doing everything in my power to bring her back would overwhelm me.

"About time you rats showed up," Darian grumbles as he stands.

The throne room and grand dining hall beyond it is washed in sinister shadows, lit only by a dragonfire torch Bristol's holding on to. The stench of rotting flesh washes over me, the dragon carcasses hanging like grim chandeliers haunting my vision.

Bristol, Nolan, and Gavin rise from sitting on the floors with Gavin holding Darian's chains. A'nala, Nadja, and Daeja all bow their heads, confirming Sethan must have shared the news with A'nala.

Marge is dead.

She's gone.

"I'm so sorry," Daeja whispers, and walks up to me, nudging her snout into my chest and warming my still damp clothes.

Though nothing compares to the numbness seeping throughout my chest. Mindlessly, I brush a hand up her snout, my fingers bumping over each of her thick scales.

Marge is dead.

She's *gone.*

"Darian, for once will you shut the fuck up," Cole barks.

I slide away from Daeja, squeezing Cole's arm to brush back the hostility rolling off him in waves. He's just as upset as I am.

"What happened?" Gavin mumbles quietly, assessing each of us with silent precision before his face falls as he realizes who is missing.

Darian looks like he might explode until our eyes connect. Something shifts within him, his irritation melting away as his furrowed eyebrows relax. He blinks and scans our group, his head whipping left and right. Looking for her.

He thunders closer to me. "Where is Marge?"

Cole takes a protective step in front of me, his hand brushing me back behind him.

"Where is she!" Darian snarls, ignoring Cole and stepping to the side to look at me.

None of us have to answer Darian. It dawns on everyone all at once, each dragon and person's head sagging.

But Darian lights like a fire, his head shaking furiously as his breath hitches. "No."

My eyes say it all.

"No!" He attempts to shove Cole out of the way, and Gavin tugs his chains back. "You were supposed to protect her!"

"Back the fuck off!" Cole palms Darian's chest, sending him back a few steps.

But I can't bother with either of them.

Marge is dead.

She's gone.

When Darian and Cole get in a shoving match, Sethan and Archie slide in to break them up. After tossing me a cautious glance, Sethan decides we're far too exhausted to leave the castle, and we'll rest here in the throne room until daybreak. Some of our squad members complain of the stench, and I back away from them until my calves hit one of the throne chairs. I slide down to sit in front of it, my knees bent against my chest. Daeja curls up next to me, pressing herself into me silently.

We take turns watching as the others sleep until the sun rises, but I'm unable to close my eyes. I sit with my arms wrapped around my legs, my eyes fixed on the staircase winding down into darkness. Waiting to hear that tapping sound of her staff on the steps and her wheezing breath. Like all of this was just some fluke. I'm tempted to lean down into the stairwell and scream all the obscenities I can think of, just to get her to scold me. I wrestle with that hopeful part, trying to pin it down and kill it.

Because she's not coming back. Marge is dead.

She's gone.

A dam of numbness builds inside of my chest, walling off my heart and weighing down my body. Despite the suffocating exhaustion tearing at my every movement, I stare at the staircase until the sun peeks through the windows lining the grand dining hall, and Archie rests a hand on my shoulder.

"Kat…" he whispers, then shakes me gently when I don't move. "Hey…we have to get going."

Mechanically, I nod my head, still lost on that top step. Eventually, the rest of the group stands, stretching their bones after lying on the cold marble floors.

Daeja nuzzles my cheek. ***"A'nala says we must leave."***

"She's…she's still down there, somewhere."

"I know you loved her…" she whispers. ***"Just as she loved you."***

Loved. Now it's become past tense. And it was never a word I had even spoken to her. Somehow, I thought we'd always have the time. And yet…now it's too late.

Too late to tell her. Too late to ask her if she knew.

Daeja burrows her snout beneath my bent knees, then nudges me up. ***"I am with you. And I love you. Come with me."***

Melaina steps in, offering her hand to help me up, and I shake my head, not able to handle her pitiful gaze. I stand on my own and brush my hair back out of my face, my eyes not wandering any higher than anyone's knees. Because if one more godsdamned person looks me in the eye with that sad, mournful expression, it's going to crack the dam I'm trying so hard to put up.

Now's not the time to cry. Not the time to mourn.

We have to keep moving.

Slamming the wall down between me and my pain, I set the Blood Ring back into the groove on the throne and raise the room to the ground level once more. My heart slams painfully in my chest, knowing I'm closing the door to her.

We all leave the grand dining room and make our way throughout the castle grounds and courtyard. The birds chirp and water gurgles, the air heating in the sun's rays. It all feels too light for the storm brewing inside of me. All the conversations between our group are muffled, and I focus on putting one foot in front of the other. As we join the rest of the group waiting on the opposite side of the bridge from the castle, everyone's eyes fall on me. Cole brushes my arm affectionately, stealing my attention for a moment.

"I'm fine," I say in a small voice.

He waits for me to mount Daeja and buckle in, then performs his ritual of checking every strap and restraint before patting Daeja's side and tossing her a quick look.

She blinks at him before her voice rumbles in my head, *"Ready?"*

I nod, and even though she can't possibly see it from this angle, she stalks forward and launches into the air.

FORTY-EIGHT

Katerina Blackwind

Later that evening, Cole escorts me to the room designated for me in Everden. He lights the wall sconces, chasing away the darkness as I shrug off my satchel and toss it onto the bottle-covered desk, missing it by an inch.

Cole takes a step forward. "Here—"

"No, no, I got it," I mutter as I walk over to the desk and kneel.

Did the Vitalans seriously think I'm going to drink away my feelings? At least seven bottles of liquid are lined up on the desk, all different shapes and sizes. Bet Darian will have a field day with this one once Gavin returns with him from Everden's bathhouse.

"Kat?" Cole asks gently, watching me from a distance, in case I might explode. Or implode. "We should talk about what happened last night."

My pulse begins to pick up its pace, and a frenzy buzzes beneath my skin. I can't quite pinpoint the sensation, but I know I have to keep moving before it catches up to me.

With one hand I hold open the bag and with the other I take the items that spilled and toss them back inside, one by one.

All the items I've kept on me this entire time: a dagger, a flask, my father's journal, a chunk of bread wrapped in paper, the metal bracelet Melaina gifted me, the empty dragon's breath vial necklace, and…I freeze. Gloves.

Her gloves.

Cole takes a few steps toward me and pauses, the floor creaking under his boots. "…Kat?"

With a trembling hand, I slip my fingers under the leather gloves as if they'll turn to ash in front of me, before cradling them to my aching chest. If I wore them, perhaps I could have held on to her longer. Perhaps she…perhaps she wouldn't have…

My lip begins to quiver, and my throat gets so unbearably tight it's hard to swallow. Hard to *breathe*. Tears edge along my vision, just waiting for the split second I break. I clamp my hand down tightly on the gloves as I stand, trying to shut out the torrent of emotions that rise and threaten to overtake me. But then the wave crashes, and I'm ripped under.

With a guttural scream, I throw the gloves at the ground before backhanding all the liquor bottles off the desk.

Arms wrap tightly around me, preventing me from causing further damage, and I'm pulled back from the desk as I cry and kick. I wriggle against Cole until he spins me around to face him, his calloused hands cradling my face as he scans my expression, his thumb brushing my cheek. "I am so, *so* sorry."

He tugs me into a tight embrace. Squeezing like if he holds me tight enough, he might stop me from falling apart. A sob wracks my body, and I shake uncontrollably at the depth of sorrow and grief roaring over me. Like a hurricane flooding every valley of my mind, and all that's left to do is drown.

He says nothing.

He just stands there, holding me tight, his hand rubbing my back in delicate slow strokes, allowing me to feel it all. And Gods, does it give me the slightest breath of air. To not feel so alone. To not force myself to feel okay. I heave with each sob, and just when I think we're as close as we can be, he pulls me in more. Something about it breaks me further, and my legs begin to fail. I sink to the ground, and he follows me, still cradling me until we're kneeling. I lean into him, burying my face against his shoulder, my tears spilling onto his shirt.

"I'm here," he whispers. "I'm right here with you. And I'm not leaving."

He turns and softly kisses the side of my head. He sways us back and forth slowly, rocking us as I fight for breath between my wails.

I stir when a knock sounds at my door. I'm lying on Cole's chest, and the fingers pulling long strokes down my hair stop. Slowly, he edges out underneath me. When the bed lifts from when he gets off, I peek open my swollen eyes to see Cole strolling across the room. Another knock sounds as he reaches for the door, then opens it.

"She's…she's grieving right now," Cole whispers, his head poking out between the door and doorframe, blocking my line of vision. "Can't you give her some time?"

"We don't have time," Sethan snaps back in a tight whisper. "If we take any longer, we risk losing even more people. What then?"

"She's still a person. She still has feelings," Cole bites. "Let her grieve."

"Let me in to talk to her," Sethan commands.

Cole straightens and braces his arm against the side of the door. "No."

His shoulder jerks back, as if pushed.

Cole's voice dips to a dangerous warning, "I have a 'you get to threaten me once without retaliation' policy. After that, it's on you what happens next. You'll leave her alone until she is ready. Is that clear?"

Cole shuts the door without waiting for a response, and I squeeze my eyes back shut, feigning sleep. The bed dips under Cole's weight as he sits down. When he whispers, I strain to hear it. "I am so sorry we couldn't save her, my love…"

He brushes a hand gently through my hair, and his soft lips graze my forehead, lingering for one long moment before his touch disappears.

The next day, I wake alone in the bed and Cole returns with breakfast.

He sits on the edge of the mattress, lifting his tray toward me and setting it on my lap. "I brought you something to eat. Or…I could get you tea?" He shoves up to his feet, anxious to find something to alleviate my distress. "Maybe even—"

"No," I whisper. My throat is still raw, burning as I swallow. My gaze settles on the display of food in front of me, so carefully picked out. I begin to slide the tray off my legs. "Thank you, though. I'm not quite hungry."

"Alright. We take it at your pace, okay?" he murmurs, dropping to his knees beside the bed, staring up at me through his dark lashes. "I do have something for you, though. Will you come take a walk with me?"

I nod, my chest heavy with emptiness. He has me slide to the edge, where he works socks onto my feet. He puts my boots on and laces them up my shins.

"Where's Darian?" I croak, glancing over at the wall with the hooks.

"Gavin and Nolan kept him overnight, per my orders," he says, eyes still fixed on my boots. He licks his thumb and wipes a spot of mud off the tip of my left shoe.

Was that because he didn't like the thought of me alone with Darian? Or because he didn't trust Darian after the outburst he had in the throne room yesterday?

Cole leads me out of Everden, taking the sideroads to avoid all the bustling main streets. I keep my gaze down on the ground, my gloveless hands in my pockets. Because I still can't quite bring myself to wear her gloves.

Cole's footsteps pause once we reach the forest, the distant Serahaven mountains hiding Vitalis stretching above the pine trees. Daeja stalks toward me and bumps her nose into my stomach until I rest a hand on her. Her sympathies roll off her like an unspoken promise.

When she pulls back from leaning into me, she lowers herself to the ground.

Cole turns to me, resting a hand on my shoulder as he offers me a small hint of a smile. "Go. Remember who you are."

"But Sethan—"

Cole shakes his head. "Don't worry about him or the rest. I'll handle it. You take the time you need. Just…be careful, okay?"

He knits his fingers together into a foothold, dipping his head with silent encouragement before boosting me up over Daeja into the saddle. He checks each strap and buckle as he always does, and I notice the straps seem longer than usual. He pats Daeja and leaves without another word.

As I grab the belt to loop it around myself, still hooked into the saddle where I left it last, my heart skips a beat. A small sprig of purple alliums is tied with a string to one of the belt's holes. And there, engraved into the leather so subtly only the wearer would notice it, is my name.

Katerina Blackwind.

I glance over my shoulder back into the direction where Cole left, but he's gone. My heart quakes in my chest. I haven't seen my full name written in so long—my last memory is the time my brother fought to teach me.

He knew just what I needed.

Knew me almost better than I knew myself at times.

"To the skies?" Daeja asks quietly.

"And the stars," I whisper back.

She flaps her wings and lifts into the air.

FORTY-NINE

MEANT FOR MEMORIES

By the time Daeja and I land back near Everden, my eyes are stinging and dry from the wind and tears. My hands are chapped—it was the first time I'd flown without wearing Marge's gloves.

The sun dips below the treetops, the sky melting into a haze of orange and purple.

"I'm still here," Daeja whispers, leaning her head against mine after I dismount. Those three precious words are a reminder she's gifted me since I had to leave her outside the military outpost back in Arterias.

For the first time since Marge's death, my lips lift into a soft smile. *"I know."*

"Now go get something to eat." She nudges me toward Everden. *"Your growling stomach is going to scare half the town if you don't take care of it soon."*

An echo of a giggle rumbles in my chest, and I rub the end of her nose affectionately. *"Thank you."*

Pressing a kiss to the bony ridge, I walk toward Everden and pause mid-step to look back at her over my shoulder. *"Hey, Daeja?"*

She perks up, her tail swishing back and forth behind her as she tilts her head. ***"Yes?"***

"I love you."

"And I love you," she purrs.

When I make it back to my room, Cole is sitting at my desk, and he jolts to his feet when I slide through the door.

"Hey…" He relaxes slightly when he realizes it's me.

"Hey." I grin, leaning back against the closed door. "Thank you…for that."

Cole nods, not wanting to take his eyes off me, but forcing his attention back to the desk. "Sethan's been…adamant, that whenever you're awake, you read this." He grabs a letter and holds it out for me.

I raise an eyebrow and clear the space between us, taking it from him and flipping it over. The letter is still sealed, the fresh wax stamped with the A symbol for the Dragon Lands. "What do you mean when I'm awake…?"

"I may not have told him you were gone with Daeja all day. Just said you were sleeping." He shrugs. "Not that it's his business anyway. You're a grown woman who doesn't need to bow to anyone's demands."

My heart skips a beat. The Cole I knew years prior would never have risked his integrity. But then again, the Cole before me is so different from the boy and man I had grown to know and fall in love with. This man before me is sharpened into somebody else entirely, even beyond the chiseled muscles, rough beard, and long auburn hair sweeping past his jawline.

"If he had found out you were lying…" I whisper.

"Then what?"

"Then…"

"Exactly. I'm not afraid of Sethan." He crosses his arms over his chest, regarding me with a confident head tilt and grin.

"You should be. A'nala would torch you on the spot."

"I could outrun her."

I chuckle. "You're not fast enough to outrun a dragon."

"Says who?"

I snort. "Says the person who outran you one time."

A rumbling laugh bumps his words, shaking his arms and chest. "You mean like the time you split your pants?"

My mouth drops open, and I playfully smack him with the letter, the warmth of embarrassment and fondness washing over me at the memory. "I did not!"

We both erupt into laughter, watching each other through squinted eyes.

He has to contain his chuckling just to say, "I don't think I had ever seen you run so fast. Not even the time when you almost got sprayed by that skunk."

As I quiet down, a smile still warms my cheeks, a new light cracking through the grief in my chest. "I definitely thought you hadn't noticed my pants."

"Oh, I *definitely* noticed," he laughs with a nod.

We stand a few feet away from each other smiling, until our faces relax as the memory becomes just that—a memory. And a reminder of a simpler, more joyful time.

He clears his throat, and I break our eye contact to look to the right.

"Well…I'll let you get settled in for the night. Unless you need anything else?" he asks.

I almost ask him to stay with me tonight. To hold me. But knowing it's not fair, I shake my head, tucking a strand of my hair behind my ear. "No, I should be all set."

He dips his head then takes a few steps for the door, and I slide toward him, stopping his advance. I wrap my arms around him, kissing his cheek before closing my eyes as I lean my head into his chest and whisper, "Thank you."

He flinches before he wraps his arms around me, holding me in a tight embrace and resting his chin on the top of my head. "Always."

When we break out of our hug, his cheeks and eyes are warm. He squeezes my hand lovingly. And walks out my door.

I've read the letter Cole gave me from Sethan multiple times over. But it's pointless. Ten read throughs later, and I know nothing more than I did on the first. The strange language stares back at me, taunting me for not being able to decipher it.

Gavin knocks on the door later that night with Darian in tow, coming to collect Darian's rucksack after being commanded by Sethan to take Darian to his office. While I've been able to build my trust with Sethan, I hesitate over him being alone with Darian. And given Sethan's growing desperation to save this realm, I wouldn't put it past him to try the same tactic again to glean information.

"Bring him in here. He's staying with me," I whisper to Gavin and open the door farther.

Gavin eyes me hesitantly but hands me Darian's shackles all the same. After I pull Darian inside and close the door, he's already eyeing the bottles on the desk. I managed to break two of the seven bottles yesterday. Bless Cole for cleaning it up sometime after I'd fallen asleep.

Darian tips his chin toward the liquor. "I see you've finally decided to hold up your end of the bargain?"

"Knock yourself out," I mutter before turning my back to him.

He clears his throat, and I turn slowly, finding him lifting his shackles and shaking the chain. Sighing, I remove the key from my brassiere and unlock his shackles without looking him in the eye.

"Did she still have that fire in her eyes?" he asks softly.

I jolt my attention up to him, meeting his gaze. "What?"

"Marge…" He clears his throat, before swallowing. "Did she suffer? Was it quick?"

My heart flinches inside my chest. Marge said she had known Darian since he was a boy, just as Sethan had. But her soft spot for him was apparent through her half-hearted scolding toward him and her discreet defense of him when he wasn't in the room. I figured he would have heard by now what exactly happened and how she died.

I shake my head and return my attention to removing his second manacle. "She wasn't even scared. She saved us—me—without hesitation."

The second shackle clicks as I release it, and I take the restraints and gently toss them to the floor. "We were running from the Stone Gods. I tried dragging her with me across the bridge. But we weren't fast enough. So, she sliced through the bridge and—"

Emotion chokes my throat as roughly as any hand, and I stare down at the shackles on the floor as I slide the key back into my brassiere. His chains are reminiscent of those back near the bridge. The same ones Marge used to save me. I bite my lip to quell my trembling chin, and a hand brushes the side of my arm.

When I look up at Darian, tears blur the edges of my vision. His expression is deadly serious, and he nods, slowly. The silence between us is filled with a heavy understanding.

She died for me.

But I can't stare into his eyes for too long, so I look away and swipe a stray tear off my cheek. He drops his hand from my arm.

"Why did you tell Gavin to leave me here with you?" he whispers, diverting the conversation.

"What kind of question is that?"

"Why? Is it hard for you to answer it?"

That gains him a teary-eyed glare. But with each slow pounding of my heart, bits of my composure crumble like a wall. "Because Marge would have wanted me to."

"That's not it. I'm going to ask you again. Why did you want me to stay?"

I fight against the next swell. But even as I clench my teeth, I can't brace against it. Instead, it slams against my chest and spills out the cracks of my heart. "Because I don't want to be alone, okay? Is that what you want to hear?" I manage to get out through a tight throat, but each word slips into a deeper sadness. And as another tear rips free from my eyes, hot and wet against my skin, it splits open the dam I've built up over the last several hours. I take a half-step back from him and begin to cry.

He grabs me by my arms and walks me back to the bed until I sit on the edge.

Resting my elbows on my knees, I hide my face in my hands. And I can't stop now. I'm a sniffling, babbling mess. "I'm so fucking sick of having to say goodbye to people I love. My family. My friends. I feel like…nothing ever works out for me. As soon as I'm close enough to someone, they die. So, I don't want to be alone. Not tonight. Because sitting with myself, thinking of all the people who have died because I couldn't save them—because it was my fault—will destroy me."

I slip my hands from my face and find Darian on one knee in front of me, his hand resting on the side of my thigh.

He shakes his head and whispers, "I'm not the one for this."

"I know you're not. But can you just pretend? Even if it's only for one night?" My voice cracks into desperation. Borderline mania. "Please. Please, Darian. Don't leave me alone. Even if you have to be a dick. Even if you have to piss me off to make me feel something other than this emptiness. This loneliness. Please just spare me from being alone with myself."

He sucks in a breath and holds my gaze for a long moment. Then he gets up and walks away, and I sink back onto my hands. But it's not long until I feel a tap on my shoulder. I look up to see Darian biting the cork off a bottle of liquor, spitting it out to the side, then he offers it to me.

"Forever was never meant for people," he whispers. "It was meant for memories."

I drag my gaze off him and take the bottle. A quick sniff of it and the hollow pit in my stomach coils. Shaking my head, I hand it back to him. Without exchanging another word, I change into my nightwear and slide into bed. My back is to Darian, but I hear him drag the chair out from the desk and take quiet swish after swish of liquor until I fall asleep.

I dream of a knock at the door, and when I go to open it, ready for a late night training session with Marge, nobody's there. Every time I wake from it, tears wet my cheeks. I close my eyes. As soon as I slip back into sleep, I relive the dream. Over and over again.

The next morning, I wake to find Darian's face resting on the pillow wall between us, his eyes closed and breathing steady. Quietly, I lean up out of bed and glimpse two bottles of liquor on the desk, completely empty. Glancing back down to Darian, one hand is fisted in one of the pillows, with his other arm slipped underneath the one I had been lying on.

I slide out of bed, careful to not disturb him, and begin to braid my hair back out of my face. Once I've finished, I change into my leathers and cloak. I stare long and hard at Marge's gloves on the desk.

"And if you only listen to one thing I ask of you…" her voice echoes around me in a distant memory from when she gave them to me in Midkeep. *"Keep these on at all times."*

As a single tear races down my cheek, I wipe it away and grab them. Finger by finger, I tug them onto my hand.

While I step into my boots and begin to lace them, a knock sounds at the door. Whipping toward Darian, his eyes flash open, and he shoots to his feet. I clear the space between us and lock him back into the shackles and lead him to the chained wall.

"Just a minute!" I call.

I race back to the door and open it to find Bristol, who reports Sethan is demanding my immediate presence. Gavin and Nolan are a few steps behind him, no doubt here to escort Darian off while I chat with Sethan. Gavin and Nolan take Darian with them as Bristol leads me out into the streets and toward the northern part, where Sethan's temporary residence is.

As I slide my hands into my pockets, a letter of some sort brushes my fingertips. With Bristol a few steps ahead of me and unable to fight against my own curiosity, I tug the paper partially out of my pocket, only to find it's blank.

Tossing one more cautious glance at Bristol and the towns-people passing us by, I pull the letter completely out of my pocket. It's folded into a quarter of its size, with both sides blank. A small, dark stain blooms on one corner, smelling an awful lot like whiskey.

With a thundering heart, I unfold the paper to find a stunning depiction of an allium. Each brushstroke of vivid purple petals is precise; elegant shapes any masterful painter would struggle to emulate. And there's only one person I gave paints to.

I half-crumple, half-fold it and shove it back into my pocket with the heavy feeling like everyone we pass is staring at me. Heat creeps to my cheeks, and I breathe it out before I can linger on it.

Bristol tosses me a glance over his shoulder, far too many steps away. "Is everything alright?"

Swallowing, I nod and begin walking again. I push the gesture to the back of my thoughts and instead attempt to focus on the next task at hand. Bristol drops me off at Sethan's building, leaving me alone with him.

"You're two days late," Sethan grumbles, unwilling to mask his lack of sympathy.

I lift my chin. "I showed up. What do you want?"

He motions for me to take a seat at his desk, and I slide into the chair.

Resting my fingertips on the wooden chair's arm, I ask, "Did you assume I'd be able to translate that letter you sent me?"

"No. But I figured it might spark your curiosity enough you'd come to me."

I snort and lean back, crossing my arms over my chest. "Well. You have me. What is it?"

"I've shown the elders here in Everden this journal, but they're suggesting we head down to Nightfort, as there's another elder there who might be able to decipher it." He opens Queen Elara's black journal, spins it, and slides it across the desk toward me.

Even though the journal is facing in my direction, I wouldn't be able to tell the difference between it being upside down or right-side up.

He taps his index finger on the page. "But the ones I spoke to here were able to translate this. They interpreted it as saying something about a *celestial event*."

"So…that doesn't give us much."

"It gives us a timeframe. The prophecy says the realm will be restored by air and *night*. The darkest night of the year is during the—"

"—winter solstice," I finish on a breath.

"In other words, a celestial event."

My breath picks up in pace. "Okay…that still gives us a year. That's next winter—"

"What did you see when you touched Queen Elara's body, Katerina?"

I swallow. I hadn't quite thought about it, and instead was processing Marge's death. And perhaps I should have—perhaps I should have put my feelings aside and prioritized figuring out what Queen Elara's memories meant. With a sigh, I recount all her memories as I experienced them, and Sethan's eyebrows pinch as he leans back in his chair and listens, occasionally nodding and rubbing a hand down his short, gray-stricken beard.

"I…I think Queen Elara was pregnant. I think that's why her dress was shredded—not because she had been mutilated. But because someone tried to save her baby," I whisper quietly, my eyes falling to the journal filled with entries beyond my own comprehension. "And if they did, they would have had to save that baby with Vue's dragonblood."

"Creating a hybrid," Sethan confirms. "Part human, part dragon."

I glance up at him. "You…already suspected?"

"Yes, I had a theory. And I believe you're right. I think Cyrus was the son of Queen Elara. In the Gods' language, Cyrus's name translates to 'sun.'"

"But how would he be a hybrid instead of a Spoiled?"

Sethan laces his fingers together and rests his mouth against it, his eyes distant. Finally, he says quietly, "Because they used a sun dragon's blood. Think about how overpowering the blood of such a rare dragon would be in a newborn. It would taint their fresh human blood and likely bind to it. And if it subdued his human blood, he could have essentially been more dragon than man."

The theory slaps me in the face with a force that stings my cheeks. I shake my head, because if I'm Cyrus' granddaughter, and he was Queen Elara's son…

"I can't be related to Darian," I blurt, trembling like a leaf.

"No, no. Darian isn't related to you."

My voice comes out shaky, "And how would you know that? How can he possibly be the heir to the Arterian kingdom if he isn't?"

"Because Darian isn't Jurrock's son, but King Aaric doesn't know that. And nobody *can* know that."

"So then how do you know that for certain?"

He crosses his arms over his chest. "Because Jurrock told me as much."

Then who in the hells is Darian? And what other secrets is the crown hiding? I lower my head into my hands, rubbing my temples like it'll clear all my racing thoughts and questions.

Why does King Aaric need a celestial event? For what ungodsly reason would he need to harness all that power? Something like that could obliterate everything, perhaps to the extent he wouldn't even need the Blood Ring…would he?

Yet, in the dying moment of Queen Elara's memories, King Aaric's last words echo in my ears like a haunting phantom. *"Wait, I still need him!"*

I drop my hands from my face, and as the clouds begin to lift with each slowing thought, I'm dragged back to my father's journal entry on the sun dragon.

He could control the position of the sun, channel solar power into beams of blasting light, manipulate dragonfire, and it was even rumored he could resurrect the dead.

King Aaric needed Vue alive because Vue had the potential ability to resurrect the dead. And if Vue was born of the magic from the Gods themselves?

I straighten to look at Sethan. "…I think I know what the King is up to."

"Go on?" Sethan tilts his head to the side.

"I think he's trying to resurrect his wife and daughter. That's why he needs both rings."

FIFTY

Between death and silence

Sethan orders us to stay in Everden until we've received a letter back from Nightfort confirming the translator for Queen Elara's journal is still in the city. Sethan's convinced there's more we need to know, and even though the darkest night isn't for another three seasons, the looming deadline is enough to stir a swarm of anxiety underneath my skin.

Despite the heaviness still clouding my heart from Marge's sacrifice, I know what I must do. After dinner, when everyone's turned in for the night, and Darian seems to be fast asleep, I slip out to the forest.

I stand in the darkness, staring at the tips of the mountain range in the distance as tears slip down my cheeks. Thick flakes of snow fall from the sky, collecting until the earth is dusted in white.

Marge should be here.

As I wipe my face with my hand, the bracelet Melaina gave me all those weeks ago shifts on my wrist, and I pinch the metal and spin it around until the moonlight catches on the engraved words.

You can go through it, or grow through it.

Removing my black leather gloves, I take a deep breath and lower to the ground. Marge's last words whisper to me in a silent wind.

You have never let me down, Katerina Blackwind.

I brush my fingers across the cold, wet earth and am immediately entangled in the power thrumming below. It's right there… tempting me. I close my eyes and press both palms flat to the earth. And slip into The White.

"Marge?" I call out, swiveling in every direction and finding nothing. I try my damndest to not let my hope skyrocket, but I recall her conversation about there being a fifty-fifty shot of seeing someone in The White.

It just has to be wanted from both sides.

"Marge?" I call out again, sensing a pulse of warmth from one direction. I follow it, walking blindly into an endless sea of white and not knowing how far I've gone. Or if I've even gone anywhere at all.

I cup my hands on either side of my mouth and let out, "Marge?"

But the silence is deafening.

My hope seeps out of me, like blood from a wound, as I whisper, "Why don't you want to see me?"

The same words she told me all those nights ago in the forest, echo inside of my head.

Magic like this is old, ancient, and dark. Many of the spirits are well aware of the temptation to revive an at-peace spirit. Especially when it's someone you love. So rather than showing themselves, they avoid contact entirely.

I bite my lip, nodding as the realization washes over me. She won't show herself to me. Not when she knows how tempted I'll be to possibly bring her back. I swallow the tension building in my throat but hang on to that small kernel of peace.

She knows I love her.

When I slip back out of The White and return to my senses, I snap open my eyes. Even if I was so desperate to speak to her one last time and didn't get that chance, I can already anticipate what she'd want me to do next.

I press my fingers down through the thin layer of snow to the earth while that hum rises around me, my hair billowing in a nonexistent breeze.

*Come to me…*I call out to it. *Yield to me…*

My vision blurs, and I lift my hand an inch off the ground, pulling small wisps of blue flames. The fog-like tendrils of blue waver, threatening to slip back into the ground. Gritting my teeth, I throw out my other hand to trap it, then raise both my arms to pull the flames higher.

Come to me…
I will not be shaken…
You will yield to me…

The flames shriek like a wild animal pinned in a cage. I lift them, pulling them until I'm standing, and they're shoulder high. I sweep my hands left, dragging them with me, then slide my grip back to the right, breaking their hold on the ground. We become a dance— swaying back and forth as I gain more and more control, like reeling in a rope, until they completely surrender to me.

It's the most I've ever been able to pull.

With a strangled scream, I slam them back into the ground, my breath shaking my shoulders. A new surge of emotions crashes over me, and I laugh as tears line my eyes. It's a victory she would have been proud of.

Throwing back my head to stare up at the sky, snowflakes land on my skin. Just as I begin to close my eyes, I swear one of the stars in the night sky above me winks.

By the time I return to my room, the moon is at its highest peak. Enough snow has collected on the streets that my footsteps leave a trail. Silently, I slide into my room and take off my snow-dusted boots while trying to contain my chattering teeth.

Darian lifts his head to glance at me over his shoulder from his side of the bed, his brown hair a chaotic mess. He looks me up and down, not a lick of amusement in his face. "What were you doing?"

"Nothing that concerns you," I whisper, and unclasp my cloak at my throat.

Surprisingly, he has not a single thing to say back. I welcome the silence, and as I hang my cloak up and run my hands down the material, I brush a bump near the pocket.

The painting of the allium.

My heart skips a beat, a warmth rising to my cheeks as I retract my hand and stare at the cloak. Slowly, I remove the rest of my clothing and change into my nightwear before slipping into bed next to Darian. His back is turned to me, and I pull the sheets over my chest.

"That painting you made for me…" I whisper, staring up at the dark ceiling as if the shadows will consume me before I embarrass myself. "Thank you."

Silence.

Painful, long silence.

To the point where I'm convinced he's either somehow already sleeping or ignoring me.

And then, "You're welcome."

The next morning, Gavin takes Darian to the Everden bath-house, and I dress and head toward the main dining hall. As I approach the massive building with a drawbridge for an entrance, I catch a familiar dirty-blond man walking my way.

Archie pushes past me, eyes on the street with moisture collecting at their corners.

I spin and try to grab for his shoulder pack. "Hey—"

He dodges me wordlessly and pulls his pack on tighter as he continues.

I glance back at the direction he came from, and Melaina stands holding her arms at the elbows, head down. As I stride toward her, her head whips up, eyes narrowed with pain, before she turns and begins to walk away.

"Stop," I command.

Reluctantly, she does. But she still won't face me.

"What's wrong with Archie?"

She shakes her head again, frozen at the spot but not wanting to look back at me. "It's none of your business."

I grab her shoulder and spin her toward me, her brown eyes regarding me with hesitant bitterness.

"It is my business when he looks like that. He's my best friend. What happened?"

She bites her lip as if it'll seal her mouth from answering me. With a sigh, she replies, "I told him we don't work."

"What do you mean you don't work?"

"I mean, we don't belong together. It was just a silly crush, a simple distraction—"

"How can you say that?" I drop my hand from her shoulder, shaking my head. "He loves you—"

"It's complicated."

"It is if you make it that way," I bite. "What is it really, Melaina? I know you care for him. I see it in the way you look at him—"

"It doesn't matter!" she snaps. "We can't. I'll break him. And it's better that I do it now, than if I do it later."

"Will you break him, or will he break *you*?" I challenge.

"We live in a world where we are ravaged by war. Either of us can die at any second." Her voice trembles. "And I don't want to be the one on the receiving end of losing him. It's easier this way."

My jaw relaxes in realization. "This…this isn't you. This is Sethan, isn't it?"

"Just leave it alone, Kat," she warns, tearing her gaze away from me.

I grab her hand in mine, daring her to look at me. "Your life is not Sethan's. It is your own. He may be your father, and he may be the commander of the Vitalans, but he does not rule your heart. And if you let Archie go, you're breaking him anyway. You don't get both—you have to choose. Your heart or his."

"Then…I choose neither," she whispers.

With a grunt, I turn away from her and break into a run, chasing after Archie. Scanning every building, every road and alley, my worry intensifying. I catch a glimpse of his blond locks heading south and follow him through the swarm of pedestrians. I lose him for a moment in a thick crowd bottlenecked near a side street. I push through until I'm off into the forest.

Archie's distant figure disappears into the treeline.

"Archie!" I pick up my speed. "Wait! Please!"

Trees flash by me in blurs of green and brown, the cold air sharp in my lungs. Finally, I catch up to him, breathless.

He whirls, eyes round in shock as he grips the bag on his shoulder. "What are you doing here? Why are you following me?"

I lean forward, bracing my hands on my knees as I fight to catch my breath, panting out each word, "Don't…Don't go."

"I'm going home, Kat." His voice trembles. "I have nothing left—"

"You have me!" I straighten and slap a hand to my chest. "I know it hurts. I know you're in pain. But you can't leave—you can't go. I need you here. With me."

He scoffs. "You've never needed me. You've never needed anyone."

I grab his shoulder, digging my fingers into his jacket in the event I can actually stop him if he decides to run. And if he does decide to, I'll fight him. I'll throw him down, wrestle him to the ground, and pin him until I can talk sense into him. I need him with me.

My words come out in an impossibly long string I'm hoping will pull him back to me. "I have always needed you. I wouldn't have survived the first time we were attacked back at the outpost. Just as I needed you to be the one who discovered Daeja back in Arterias. You were the one who suggested I use a regular blade rather than a dragonblade to get us through the door in Vitalis. You've guarded all my secrets. Whether you realize it or not, you have saved me more times than I can count—emotionally and physically. You're my best friend, and I love you. I don't know how this is going to end or what's going to happen, but all I do know is that I want to do it with you by my side."

He shakes his head, trying to turn out of my grasp.

I blurt, "Do you know why you're my best friend? It's because of who you are. You're naturally joyful. It comes so easy to you. And for some, it may be aggravating because it's so difficult for them to feel what comes so easy to you. But you know what?" I grab his hand in mine, then drop my voice to a cracked whisper, "Even in the darkest of these nights, even when I feel low, scared, and incapable. When I'm around you, I find myself optimistic. Even joyful, sometimes. Because I have you. Because you're such a light in my life, when all else feels dark."

His lip quivers, his voice growing strained, "You don't…you don't mean that."

I smile with a firm nod. "I do. I mean it, every day. And I will work harder to remind you of it."

We burst into an embrace, hugging the other as tight as if we held every piece of each other together.

I whisper into his sandy-blonde hair, "Remember what you told me back in Arterias? We both might suck, but at least we suck together. And we both might hurt—but at least we hurt together. This doesn't work if you're gone."

His fingers grip my back, painfully sweet. I bury my head in the crook of his neck, squeezing my eyes shut.

A loud snap of wood rips us both out of each other's arms. A group of dark shadows creep toward us, a glimmer of metal catching the dappled sunlight between the pine trees.

"Run," Archie whispers and shoves me away.

FIFTY-ONE

God relics

I don't have time to question why we're running, but even if I did, the masked faces and drawn weapons I glimpse are enough to catapult me. We break into a sprint, the frosty ground crunching beneath our boots, the group of heavy footsteps not far behind us. We aren't going to be able to outrun them. And I don't have any weapons.

"I need help!" I call out to Daeja.

"Don't you always—" she snickers, then recognizes the fear in my voice. **"Where are you?"**

"South of Everden with Archie! Someone's after us!"

Archie wraps his hand around my forearm, then drags me to the right unexpectedly. We lurch forward as the ground beneath us dips down into a steep hillside. We aren't quick enough to stop ourselves from falling.

Archie loses his grip on my arm as the both of us tumble down the slope, each bump slamming into my chest, back, and legs. I wrap my arms around my head to protect myself until I finally slow to a stop.

When I open my eyes, my back flat on the ground, I stare up at the spinning kaleidoscope of treetops and gray muddled sky.

I drag my head to the left to find Archie slumped forward face-first on the ground, his eyes closed. Approaching footsteps steal my attention up past the hillside.

"Archie!" I whisper, tugging at his shoulder. "Get up! We have to move!"

His eyes drag open, a bruise already blooming at the corner of his eye. "What…"

"Up!" I groan as I pull myself up off the ground and slide my arm underneath his chest.

"Come out!" a man calls in the distance. "There are twelve of us and two of you. You're severely outmatched. If you come willingly, no one will be hurt. We promise." The jovial tone chills my blood.

I don't trust it for a second. They have to be the rebels. Though, I still can't see anyone up on the edge of the hillside. There's only a matter of time.

I whip back to Archie, and he's sluggish to move his hands under his chest.

"I…I can't feel my foot," he groans, trying to force himself up, then winces and grips his left leg.

Fuck.

I help flip him onto his back and then clasp hands with his and yank him up. He's careful not to set his left leg on the ground. But as I turn to look up at the ridge, I see masked figures moving through the trees. Edging closer to overlook the lower part of the forest where we are.

Pulling Archie's arm over my shoulder to brace his weight against me, I race us toward a thicker grouping of trees crowded with a leafy underbrush. As we trample through the bushes, we both grunt as thorny branches scrape at our legs.

"You're testing our patience!" one rebel calls.

"I'm going to devour them," Daeja growls. ***"Stay hidden. I'll catch them by surprise from behind."***

"Don't get too close! They might have dragonblade!"

"Dragonblade will never be enough to stop me."

"Now's not the time for arrogance!" I tear Archie to the ground with me behind the cover of a tree. His breath puffs out of him when he lands. Hard.

"Shhh, shhh," I warn, dragging him to lay with his back against the tree.

He grits his teeth, digging his fingers into his leg like it might dull the pain. When I go to assess his foot, he bats me away. "No. Don't. If I see it, it'll only make the pain worse."

I peek around the tree trunk, scanning the ridge and forest above. But I find no movement. "I think they moved on."

I've spoken too soon. A group of masked people sweep past a cluster of trees, now on the same level as us. Their weapons glimmer in the sunlight. Full-face, black metal masks only expose their eyes.

I shift back behind the trunk, sitting next to Archie and trying to slow my beating heart.

Archie's eyes widen when he sees my face. "Wha—"

I slam a finger against his lips. The only hint of someone approaching is the eerie feeling of pressure on my skin. Pulling off my gloves finger by finger, I tuck them into my belt and press my hands down to the ground. As I draw magic up through the soil, a breeze picks up my hair and carries it across my face. That liquid heat burning up my arms.

"She's here! Quick!" someone shouts. "She's pulling!"

Archie withdraws two daggers from his side and jerks up to his knees. Facing the tree trunk, he slips out from behind the cover to fling one dagger out at the incoming rebels. A scream punctuates his success. It's a damn good thing I'm with one of the most skilled dagger throwing soldiers.

Gritting my teeth, I pull blue wisps out from the dirt beneath my hands and stagger to my feet. Barely maintaining my grip on the magic, my knees tremble. Sweating, I form the ghostly blue wisps into a ball, as Marge had prompted me to all those nights ago. Spinning it in slow circles until it forms into something familiar.

Dragonfire.

Archie whips behind the cover of the tree trunk, and a split-second later, an axe shaves off a chunk of bark before it sinks into the ground ten feet past us.

"When…I…throw this at them…" I say, panting as I glance at Archie. "I…want you…to run…for Daeja…"

He white-knuckles the dagger in his right hand, while he grabs another strapped to his side with his left. "Not a chance, Kat."

As if on cue, Daeja's roar echoes through the trees, followed by a scream. Archie pops out from the tree again and flings both daggers, one after the other. And now, I can hear the drum of their footsteps through the underbrush.

I slide out from the opposite side of the tree, taking the ball of dragonfire, now the width of my shoulders, and just as I'm about to hurl it at them, something strikes me on the side of my head.

Everything snaps to black.

Slowly my senses begin to creep back in. My breath echoes, pain lacing my skull.

"You didn't kill her, did you?" a feminine voice hisses, followed by something round and pointed prodding my ribs.

"No, my liege," a gruff voice responds. "Just knocked her out. As you requested."

"Good. We'll need answers before we kill her," that icy, smooth feminine voice responds. "And where is her dragon?"

"We pinned it with nets and dragonblade hooks. It won't be getting out unless we let it."

"Do not kill it until I'm done with her. Is that understood?"

"Yes, my liege."

The cold firmness pressed to my right cheek and underneath my chest tells me I'm lying face down. I fight to keep my eyes closed and face still, despite my skipping pulse. When I reach out for my bond with Daeja, it's like a door is closed between us. Slowly, I shift my ring finger and sense I'm still wearing the Blood Ring.

They can't be Arterians in the Dragon Lands, considering they know I'm wearing the ring, and they're still willing to kill me. Which means they have to be Vitalan rebels.

A tight fist grips my shoulder and flips me onto my back. I let my head roll lazily, keeping my eyes closed. Fingers scrape my chest as someone grabs the front of my shirt and lifts me a few inches off the ground. A tight, hot flash of pain rips in my cheek as someone slaps me. I can't fight against the natural hiss that slips out of my mouth, nor my eyes flinging open.

A woman is crouched over me. Her pale hand fisted in my shirt. She puffs her short cropped black hair out of her face, her calculating blue eyes piercing me. A sinister grin splits her thin lips as our eyes connect. I glance to my left, looking for Archie. He's face down on the wooden floor, knocked out. Another slap across my face spins my attention back to the woman.

"Eyes here," she commands. "I'm going to ask you some questions. If you fail to answer me in a timely manner, your little boyfriend over here dies first. Second strike, and I'll kill your dragon. Do you understand?"

Biting into my tongue, I fight against the rage boiling up through my chest and screaming to rip out of my mouth. Thinking better of it, I nod, holding her gaze without a lick of fear. She smiles. And it takes everything in me to not smack it off her face.

"First question. Which ring do you bear?"

Tapping the wooden floor with my fingertips to channel my anger into some other movement, I search for the magic underneath us. And find nothing. We must be far away from a ley line.

I focus on my peripheral vision while locked into her eyes. We're in a dimly-lit room, with daylight spilling through a dusted window on my left. Which means I've either been out long enough it's been a full day or it's been very brief.

Farther back in the room behind the woman are several guards with their attention trained on us through their masks. The rest of the space looks to be a makeshift gathering room with chairs, a table, a desk with a stack of books on the surface, and a wardrobe.

"Do not have me ask you a second time," the woman warns.

"The Blood Ring."

"Good. Where is the Bone Ring?"

I can't help but laugh. And she tightens her grip on my shirt and shakes me until I quiet.

"King Aaric has it," I reply.

"Who?"

I blink at such a simple question. How would she not know who King Aaric is? I respond again, in case she didn't hear me clearly, "King Aaric…"

"And where is he?"

"I'd imagine in his castle back in Arterias. But I've never seen him, nor have I ever been to the capital, so I can't be certain."

"Daeja…can you hear me?" I call out into the chasm of my mind.

Silence.

The woman pulls out a small, round golden object from her side. And for the first time since I've been awake, she tears her gaze away from me. Flicking open the object's lid, I get a glimpse of what looks like a compass. Details etched into the back of it whisper of something foreign. Something ancient, and ethereal. Whatever she sees in the compass, she snaps it closed and slides it back into her pocket with a grin. Then she retrieves a dagger and points it at my chin. Releasing her hold on my shirt, she backs off, holding me hostage with her dagger all the while. "Get up."

Sliding up off my back and rising to my feet, I hold her stare. Trying not to worry myself with Archie slumped on the ground. The slow rise and fall of his back is the only thing keeping me calm right now.

"What do you know of the god relics?" the woman asks as she taps her blade underneath my chin. She's only a few inches taller than I am.

"I don't know what you're talking about."

"Are you sure about that?" She tips her head to the side, and two guards slink away from the shadows toward Archie.

"I swear, I don't know what you're talking about—"

Archie groans and stirs when two masked people lift him off the floorboards. His eyes are half-lidded as he blinks through the haze until his attention settles on me. Those brown eyes flash wide-open, and he tries to slip out of the masked soldiers' grip.

I shake my head at him to warn him, before looking back at the woman. "Please don't hurt him. I'm trying to cooperate, but I don't know what the hells you want from me."

"I'm losing my patience here. Tell me what I want to know, and we'll let you go."

Liar. I clench my fist to still my fidgety hands. Desperate to pull magic to demolish her and all her henchmen.

She continues, "Where can I find the Book of Magic?"

Book of Magic… I've heard that once before. Back when Cole and I stole the *Breaking Magical Binds* journal from Sethan. But that was just it—a quick mention.

"I. Don't. Know." I punctuate each word, pleading she won't hurt Archie.

"I've had enough. Kill him," she orders over her shoulder.

I drop down to a crouch. Shifting my momentum through my

leg, I clip her at the ankles. The two soldiers wrestle Archie as he slams a knee between the legs of one masked person, then headbutts the other. While it's not enough to knock either of them unconscious, it's enough to loosen their grip on him. He slides out from their grasp. And as the woman drops back on her ass, I lunge. Throwing my weight entirely on her and snatching her throat in my hands. With my hands on her, I feel a light pulse of magic. My eyes light up, and I dig down into the source and begin to pull it.

She gasps, her eyes widening. "Don't you dare!"

Digging her fingers into my bare forearms, she throws her weight to the left, toppling me off her. We scramble for the upper hand, and I glimpse Archie being detained.

A roar vibrates outside the room. The door bursts open behind her, bits of wood spraying out from the violent contact like an explosion of small arrows. The door shrieks as it's torn clear off the hinges. Light spills in from the outside, stretching a long, dark shadow across the dusty floor. Cole's silhouette is stark against the light background, but his honey eyes flash, his broad chest heaving up and down. Violence beams from his features, his lips pulled back in a scowl as he rakes his gaze across the room. The entire set of soldiers stiffen. A few of them inch backward.

Cole's sword, clutched tightly in his veined hand, is stained in crimson dripping generously from the blade. "Where is she!" he roars, two cups on the desk rattling with his thunderous demand.

Everyone freezes. And as mine and Cole's eyes connect, the rest of the soldiers in the room swarm toward him.

The room explodes into chaos.

The woman springs back on me, wrestling me with my back down to the ground. I grapple for the upper hand, and she strikes me across the face again before pinning me. Her legs bracket my waist and hands imprison my wrists. Bridging my hips and swinging my arms down toward my ankles, I dismantle her balance and throw her up over me. Before she can recover, I trap her right arm in mine, wrap my leg around her right thigh, and throw her over. Slamming her onto the ground, I rear up and throw all my anger down through a punch.

My knuckles split as they connect with her face.

When her head smacks back against the wooden floor, I glance up at Archie and at the masked soldier tearing Archie's arms back behind him, exposing his chest. While the other one rears back his sword. Ready for a clean, killing blow.

Glass explodes from the window, showering Archie and the two soldiers with slivers of it. Daeja snarls and snaps forward, seizing the man with the sword and plucking him out of the room. I shove off the woman and race toward Archie as the soldier holding him hostage backs up against the wall.

"If you don't leave now, you're next!" I bark.

The soldier's eyes meet mine. Wide with paralyzing fear, framed in black metal. But he doesn't have long to consider it because Daeja's head pokes back in. Blood drips from her maw and trickles down her throat. She lets out a high-pitched screech before stretching her head across the room. Archie elbows the soldier and ducks with Daeja snapping forward a second later, snatching the soldier by the shoulder. She drags him out slowly, only to terrify the rest of the soldiers in the room as he screams. I race toward Archie and help him off the ground, turning to who lies in wait.

The black-haired woman is gone.

A soldier swings their blade at Cole. And Cole jerks back with breakneck speed, the blade nearly grazing his nose. Each movement is fueled by his wild rage, with each strike and swing something of a dance. Wrath so palpable it rolls off him in waves filling the entire room. Bodies lie deadly still around him.

Cole hurls himself at the remaining soldiers until they drop to the floor, eyes wide with lifelessness and splattering more pools of blood across the walls. One soldier is left, and they back up until they bump into the wall. They hold out a blade in front of them, practically begging for the space between them and Cole. Cole's expression is unreadable from this angle, but his red hair swings as he lurches forward and seizes the blade in his hand and squeezes, his own blood dripping down his forearm.

The masked soldier gasps. They release their grip on the sword and raise their hands. A male voice shutters, "I-I surrender! Please!"

Cole throws the man's sword to the side and devours the space between them. Grabbing the man's throat, he says in a lethal voice, "You forfeited that right once you took her from me."

And then he snaps his neck. Tossing the limp body to the side, he turns to face Archie and me. The fury alight in his gaze makes me shiver.

"They're gathering a group and weapons! Quick! Come out the window!" Daeja's deep-throated growl warns.

I snag Archie's hand and pull him to the busted window, trusting Cole will follow. "We need to go! Now, this way!"

Daeja reaches through the window again, and I guide a limping Archie to her first. She plucks him by the collar and pulls him off his feet, then out the window. I spot Marge's gloves on the desk and grab them, tucking them into my waistband.

Cole grabs the side of my face and turns me to look at him. "Are you hurt?"

"No. You?"

He shakes his head as Daeja reappears and grabs my shirt to lift me out of the room. When she sets me to my feet outside, the sky is growing a darker shade of orange.

"We should have seen where they put my daggers." Archie pats his sheaths like they might have forgotten one.

"No time."

Daeja places Cole next to us. The two of them are both caked in blood and grime. But before I can ask how they both got here, Daeja's head snaps up to something in the distance. A black-masked mob turns the corner, their weapons raised and ready for blood. When I look to

Cole, he takes out two daggers from his belt and wordlessly offers them and his sword to me and Archie.

Shaking my head, I motion to Archie. "He's the best with daggers. But even two won't help." I swing my attention to Archie. "Get on Daeja and get out of here."

"I'm not leaving either of you!"

"If your foot is broken, you won't be able to run!"

"I don't give a damn if I can't run!" Archie snaps.

"Daeja, I need you to get Archie out of here. Cole and I can fend them off until you get Archie a safe distance away."

"Don't you dare! I can tell you're talking to her!" Archie screams at me and shoves at Daeja who stalks toward him.

"As long as you aren't telling me to stay away," Daeja responds, then scoops Archie up in her front claws and lifts into the air. ***"But only far enough for A'nala to pick him up. They're on their way."***

"Great. Thank you." I allow myself a quick breath of relief.

"Kat," Cole mumbles in warning.

The mob splits. A group of at least twenty circle around us, all dressed in black with their weapons drawn, staring intently at the two of us.

"Surrender," the black-haired woman calls at the lead, slipping out from the throng.

"Fuck you," Cole growls, pulling me behind his back. He hands me his sword and clenches the two daggers in either hand. Understanding, I turn to press my back to his, staring out at the other side of the group surrounding us.

Two of us. One with a sword and one with two daggers. Back-to-back. Braced against a group of twenty armed men and women perched to slay us. Or capture us…though, given the sheer amount of carnage left in Cole's wake, the chance of being hostages don't look likely. That, and I'm sure the woman won't entertain asking me any more questions.

Either way, the odds aren't in our favor.

I search for the magic beneath our feet. Tunneling down into the earth and praying it can assist us. But I'm far too drained to pull such a massive amount of magic it'll take to defend us. Especially given the fact I'm already exhausted from pulling straight from the source before I passed out. And the ley lines still feel too far away. The throbbing in my skull pounds louder from when I was knocked out.

The mob lurches forward with a disjointed cry, and I shift Cole's sword into my left hand and raise it. Here's the moment I can prove myself. Cole's sword in my hand, void of magic and rings and dragons. What happens to me after this comes down to what I'm capable of.

And I'm not going down without a fight.

Everything explodes into a crackle of metal and screams, sweat running down my forehead and coating my palms as I swing again and again. I cling to the sword's hilt for dear life, damn near praying it won't slip from my grip. The contact breaks between mine and Cole's backs, and I shake away my worry, trusting he'll manage fine without me.

I manage to disarm one man, and the next I slice above their knees. But it's no use, there's no way I can bring down ten soldiers on my own. And perhaps I'll never be able to. They fall on me like shadows after the sun sets, evasive and deadly. As Darian's taught me, I find that deeply rooted anger within me and use it slowly to feed each stab and block. Even if it's only enough to keep me alive for the short term.

Daeja's roar trembles the ground beneath our feet, and seconds later her massive black shadow falls across the valley and a blast of flames scorches a line in front of me, catching two soldiers on fire and backing the rest of the group away. Daeja passes overhead and flips into a tight, spiral-like turn, redirecting herself back to us. She flares open her black, jagged jaws and belts another formidable jet of flame behind me. As I turn to follow her, I find myself and Cole in the center of a circle of flame.

Cole's eyes meet mine, the flames dancing in the reflections when I notice blood dripping from a cut in his forehead, slipping down his skin near his eyelid. I scan the rest of his body, before he nods as if noting my silent evaluation, his breath still shallow in his chest. Then he assesses me. I nod back.

After he sheathes his daggers, he grabs me by my waist and lifts me into the air. Daeja's flapping wings flick the flames out in separate directions as she hovers a foot above my grasp. Cole thrusts me up higher, and I snag one of the stirrups and heave myself up and over. As soon as I sling my leg over her back, I reach down for Cole and snatch his hand before trying to pull him up with all my strength.

Daeja roars out another blast of fire at the rebels attempting to brave the flames, and they scatter like ants. *"Hurry up!"*

Cole grips my wrist, but he's far too heavy for my own strength. *"I can't pull him up!"*

Daeja grumbles, turns her head and bumps him up with her nose.

With a breathy grunt, Cole pulls himself up over the saddle in front of me. I wrap my arms around his waist, and he grabs hold of the saddle horns.

"Go!" I call out loud.

Daeja snakes up into the air, and I squeeze my thighs around the saddle as Cole and I lurch back and forth.

"Holy shit," he grunts, fighting to keep himself up and pressing himself down into the horns to keep himself on Daeja.

Quickly, I wrap the waist belt around him and clip him in before holding onto his waist. The wind whips around us, and the burning camp disappears, fading into a distant cloud of black.

"Fuck, fuck, fuck," Cole whispers quietly, and the only reason I'm able to hear it is how the wind carries it.

I slide my hand to his on the horns and squeeze for a moment before I let go. We pass the other dragon riders with A'nala at the head. *"A'nala says one of the other dragon riders picked up Archie and should be back at Everden now. The rest of them are going to make sure no rebels are left."*

"*Do they need backup?*" I twist to look over my shoulder as they fly into the distant smoke.

"If I dare question A'nala's capabilities, I may very well not live to see tomorrow."

"*Fair point.*"

"And Sethan's already pissed anyway."

"*Of course he is. When is he not?*"

It's a short flight back to Everden, luckily. And as we land, I unclip Cole, and he jumps off immediately, bracing his hands on his knees as he fights to regain his breath.

I slide off Daeja and lean down to rub a hand on his back. "Nauseous?"

He nods, unable to get a word out of his gritted teeth.

A small smile pulls at my lips in nostalgia, unable to stop myself from asking, "First time?"

FIFTY-TWO

NOT YOUR TURN

"Were you out of your mind?" Sethan roars, slamming a fist down on the table. "What were you thinking?"

Everyone in the Everden community hall stops and swings their wide-eyed gazes to us.

I pluck the wine glass served to us for dinner and take a sip as I lean back in my chair. "I don't owe you any explanations."

As far as he knows, Archie went out to stop *me* from leaving. And that was when we ran into rebels and were captured. He doesn't need to know Melaina and Archie's situation or that Archie left because of it. It will only make Sethan think Archie is weak. And love isn't weak.

I set my glass of wine back down before crossing my arms over my chest. "The fact of the matter is none of us died. So, I think your scolding is pointless. You can give us the verbal lashings when we fail."

"That's what you don't understand. You're bound to fail if you risk so much. It was foolish of you to run away. And for what?"

"She wasn't the one who ran." Archie stands up from a few seats down, his weight still shifted to his non-sprained ankle.

I throw him a glare, hoping if I stare hard enough, he'll sit back down and be quiet. But he holds mine and Sethan's gaze as if he's dealing with two toddlers instead.

"I was," Archie admits.

Melaina on the complete opposite side of the table lowers her head, twirling her fork as if she may melt into another universe.

"And why is that?" Sethan challenges, though with the way he tilts his chin up, I have a feeling he already knows.

"Because I was hurt…" Archie tosses a glance toward Melaina, his confidence breaking each second she doesn't return his gaze, until his attention finally settles completely on her. "Melaina, please. Please, just look at me."

She blinks, sucking her lips in before finally dragging her gaze off her plate to him. Water lines her brown eyes.

He leans slightly forward to her. "I love you. I am *in* love with you. And if you don't feel the same anymore, just tell me."

"She doesn't," Sethan growls.

Archie slams a fist down on the table and swipes a knife from his setting, flicking it in his expert fingers and pointing it directly at Sethan. "Stop talking. Not your turn."

I flinch at the seriousness in his voice, but pride bubbles within my chest. A small grin pulls at my lips at the sheer shock slapped across Sethan's features.

Archie pins his attention back on Melaina as he whispers, "I can handle it. Just tell me you don't love me, and I'll leave you alone. I will let you go."

Melaina shakes her head, her chest rising and falling as she glances between Sethan and Archie before she shoves up from her chair. "I can't," she says with a cracking voice and bolts toward the exit.

Sethan pushes up from his chair, and Archie stabs the knife down into the table, staring Sethan down before warning, "No. You stay here. This does not concern you."

And then he follows Melaina out.

When silence settles over our group, Sethan obeying Archie's command, I turn back to face Sethan. "What do you know about god relics? The woman who captured us mentioned them, and she wanted to know where the Book of Magic is. Did you take any survivors for questioning?"

Sethan's brown eyes narrow at me. But he answers, "No, there were no survivors. Your dragonfire destroyed them all. As for god relics…" He looks down at his wine glass and mindlessly runs his middle finger around the lip. "Never heard of them. And the Book of Magic has been long lost. For more years than I can count."

FIFTY-THREE

LIKE I HATE YOU

"You're pissed off," Darian points out.

I pause from taking my braid out, then shake my fingers to loosen the strands. I'm not sure if I should be mad at Melaina for not sticking up for herself or mad at Sethan for thinking he had a say in her love life. Not to mention, Archie is an incredible man. And I don't just think that because he's my best friend but because it's true. He deserves all the happiness the world has to offer him, and if that source of joy is Melaina, and she feels the same, there shouldn't be a reason to keep them apart.

Yep, definitely pissed at Sethan.

Especially considering all the past transgressions I have with Sethan. Torturing Darian. Admitting to witnessing him being beaten by his father and not doing anything about it. Constantly cutting Archie down, despite him being an asset to our group, just because he felt like he didn't deserve his daughter because he thinks he's *weak.* Questioning many of my decisions because he thinks I'm *weak,'* too.

"Great observational skills you have there," I finally mutter a response to Darian, flipping my hair to my back and unlacing my boot.

"Take it out on me," Darian whispers silkily.

I look up at him through the wall of my hair sliding into my face, then toss my boot to the side before removing the other one. "In what way?"

He smirks. "In whatever way you want."

I blink and straighten, anger still pumping through my veins as thick as my own blood. It should make sense to continue our training… right? If we only have until the darkest night to take down the King, I'll need to be the sharpest tool I can forge. And channeling all my negative emotions into something productive feels freeing.

He follows my exact train of thought. "You go off and do your own training every night, even without Margie. But I'm still here. And…" He slides his gaze over to the bottles on the desk with a sly grin. "I still love liquor. So, here's what we'll do. We'll still uphold our fragile little agreement of exchanging liquor for lessons. You win, and I win."

I chew on my lip, mulling over the tempting offer and glancing over at the bottles. Had it not been for him teaching me how to channel my anger and use my left hand to wield, who knows if I would have been able to defend my side against the rebels. I know for a fact, even if I don't want to admit it, Darian's training is working.

With a sigh, I stalk across to the bottles and grab one, flipping off the lid and taking a swig before turning to him. He rises expectantly from sitting on the stone floor, his chains rattling with the motion.

What he's saying is right. Even if I won't say it. And even if I feel like I can't move on, the world won't stop spinning for me.

I need to keep training.

I stride over to him, unlock his shackles, and then hand him the bottle of liquor. As I walk to the farthest wall to grab my sword, he takes a few drinks and groans in pleasure. I reach for my sword's hilt, and hesitate. Darian won't kill me, and fighting him without a weapon wasn't doing me any favors in terms of learning. Glancing at him, I snatch my daggers instead and return to him, handing him one.

"Interesting," he purrs, running a fingertip up the sharp edge. "You know, daggers are personal. Intimate, even."

I take a few steps back from him, readying my stance and waiting for him to drop the conversation.

He pricks the tip of his finger on the blade and flicks his thumb across the small bead of blood, smearing it. He looks up at me and whispers, "So you don't feel bad when you make the first cut."

I fight against the smile creeping up my cheeks at his brazen confidence in me. "Are you going to keep talking out of your ass? Or will you actually teach me something?"

And Gods, does that bring the most brilliant smile to his coy lips.

We dance in a series of jabs, sidesteps, and swipes, each growing closer and closer to slicing the other and eliminating the space between us step by step.

"I noticed…" he grunts as he jerks back out of my wild swipe. "You've been wielding with your left—" He ducks. "Fuck, you might be better with the dagger than you are with a sword—"

I slam my dagger into his and our blades lock. Sliding my weight forward, I creep us back toward the wall, digging deep into that anger sitting beneath the surface.

I grunt, raising an eyebrow. "You were saying?"

He flashes me a quick smile, something like pride in his expression. "But…not…quite…good enough," he grits out, then forces our blades far to the right, breaking my balance.

"You're breathing a little heavy there, Darian," I snicker and jerk back to my stance, ready to block his advances.

"Make no mistake, I've handled two women at a time. One is no challenge."

I snort and slash out at him. "Why does that not surprise me."

"I must say though…" He catches my blade again, leaning his head down daringly to whisper, "I used to think that was my greatest fantasy. And then I met you."

I bite down a shiver, his words driving straight down to my core, heating my cheeks instantly. I grunt, shoving my dagger away and ducking in time to dodge his swing.

Sexual prowess drips from every one of his movements and snide remarks. Gods, and it fucking pisses me off. Part of me is pissed at him because of the feelings he stirs in me. And the other part? The other part is pissed at myself. I'm so conflicted about how I feel. How completely and utterly out of control I am. I'm caught on his confident strides, how his messy brown hair is swept in ways that should be disheveled—but make me yearn to be the reason it looks that way. With my fingers tangled in his hair. Dragging my lips and teeth over his throat to keep him from saying some ridiculously stupid flirtation. He shouldn't be as good looking as he is. And what's even more infuriating?

He knows it.

Just as well as I do.

He's back on me quick, his blade meeting mine, and we lock together once more. He steps closer to me, as if he doesn't give a damn that I could stab him—whether on purpose or not.

"Nothing could compare to when I…" he leans forward and inhales the air near my ear, dangerously close. "Smelled you."

He drags a tongue up my neck, and the grip on my dagger trembles in my hand. "Tasted you."

He flings the dagger out of my grasp effortlessly, and the weapon skitters pathetically across the floor. He tosses his own, never breaking eye contact, his green eyes heated with desire.

He grabs me under the chin, brushing his thumb across my lower lip. "Touched you."

Then he leans in, slowly, eyes fluttering nearly closed. His lips so near and yet too far from mine. "Kissed…you," he breathes.

Subconsciously, I tip my head back to brush my nose to his, wetting my lips in anticipation.

His lips tease mine as he says an inch away, "Tell me, do you think about me, as much as I think about you?" He drops his hand from my face and, instead, grazes the back of his finger down my side to my hip.

"No. I don't."

"I don't believe you," he hisses against my ear and edges closer. His hand cups my hip and pauses, his fingers tightening on me. "Tell me to stop," he whispers, his voice hot against my neck.

And yet, I don't want to utter the words. I don't want to make myself vulnerable by admitting how bad I want him. That I do think of him. Often. And that part of me is eager to touch and taste him again. Despite the danger of it.

I remember to breathe before I can black out. "I…"

I *can't*. Can't tell him to stop. His hands are on me. The perfect distraction.

His voice is tight with strain, pained and desperate. "Fuck… show me some mercy, you ruthless woman. Tell me to stop. Rid me of this endless torture of wanting you but not having you. Tell me not to touch you. Tell me you don't feel good with me. Tell me you don't want—"

Me.

The words are choked in his mouth, refusing to leave his lips. He knows it's all a lie, as much as I do.

He takes his hands off my hips, stepping back with his head low, not daring to look me in the eyes. "I…" he breathes heavily. Muttering like it's more of a conversation with himself, "I'm out of my fucking mind for—"

You.

The word hang between us.

He turns away from me, and I lurch forward, breaking through my own self-restraint and snatching him before he can leave me.

"I can't tell you to stop. Because I," I pull open his shirt, hungry for his skin, then push up to my toes to graze his lips with mine, saying between each slow kiss, "Don't. Want. To."

He groans into my mouth, capturing the side of my face in

his hands and leaning into me with a controlled step. His thigh wasn't enough to satisfy my craving for him. Neither was his mouth or fingers. And while I've already had him twice—I can't help myself. I want more. Need more.

Need *all* of him. I need him to come undone, and I need to be the one to do it. To have the sheer power of stripping away all that conceit and crassness. Unraveling him down to the simple desire of his flesh.

He's supposed to be a distraction from Cole. But it's become more than that. I find myself fantasizing about the way he touches me. Kisses me. Fucks me.

We shuffle step by step back to the desk, our mouths moving and never parting, our hands exploring in a frenzy. We're a tangle of heat and desire, obliterated by the all-consuming *want*. Never breaking our kiss, he uses one hand to sweep off all the things on the desk behind me. Everything falls to the ground with a thud, a flutter, and something shattering. But I don't care. All I care about at this moment is him.

And how badly I want him.

He grabs the back of my thighs and rips me off my feet, then plops me down onto the desk before untucking my shirt from my pants. I pull the blouse off and throw it to the floor. He takes the key out from between my breast and brassiere and tosses it on the desk. And I remove my brassiere. Grinning, he slowly teases kisses closer and closer until he—

Gods, those sinful lips.

—flicks his wicked tongue across my hardened nipple. He generously sucks it into his mouth as he fondles my other breast. Moaning, I stretch to try and stroke him, but he's out of reach. Sucking and nibbling my nipple eagerly until he switches to the other one.

His hand slithers down beneath my pants, between my legs. Those dastardly fingers slide up and down my entrance, testing my arousal. Teasing with slow strokes.

He takes his lips off my nipple to look up at me. "My…so wet…"

He slips a finger inside of me, the palm of his hand cupping me as he burrows it as far as he can. I curl my body up, grabbing hold of his shoulder as I quiver.

He moves his attention from my breasts to my ear, whispering as he fingers me, "Was it the thought of me fucking two other women? Does that excite you?"

"No," I moan, my eyes fluttering shut as he adds in a second finger and begins to massage the heel of his hand into my clit.

"Good. Because when I have you, I want you all to myself. I won't share you. And I don't want to divide my attention, unless it's across every part of your body." He sucks my earlobe into his mouth and nibbles. Then shakes his hand against me, playing into my sensitive clit until my legs wobble around him.

He works me on his hand, his mouth on my neck until I cry coming around his fingers. After he removes his hand, he pulls my pants off. Less than a minute later, and we've removed every article of clothing separating the two of us. I bask in his attentive touch, his lingering kisses, and his sweet tongue trailing up and down my unbearably hot skin. Then he crouches down, positioning his head between my thighs and grabbing hold of my legs to place them on his shoulders.

Shifting back onto my elbows, I lift my needy hips to him, and Gods, that fucking smile of his when I do. Mercifully, he doesn't make me ask like he normally does and places that delicious set of lips onto my clit.

Moaning, I slide my fingers into his silky brown hair, tugging at the strands as he teases me. He buries his face deeper into the crook between my legs like a starved man, devouring every inch of me with a frenzy and determined hunger to push me over the edge.

Every whimper and broken sigh of mine fuels each flick of his tongue, and just when I think it can't feel better, he proves me wrong, switching tempos and pressure. Testing each of my limits to find out what makes me cry. The knot in my stomach builds to a hopelessly tight tangle, begging to be released. As I tip-toe closer to that euphoric cliff, I clamp a hand over my mouth to silence the oncoming scream I feel building.

His eyes meet mine, and he removes my hand from my mouth, his voice rumbling between my legs, "If you want me to fuck you with my cock tonight—" he pushes his fingers back into me with an agonizing slowness that makes me want to ride his fingers myself, "—you won't quiet yourself as you come. I want to hear your cries for me."

I writhe as he lowers his head back down and flicks slow, hard licks across my clit and combines it with the curling of his fingers inside me. Once he has that pressure ricocheting inside of me again and my legs trembling around his head, he picks up his speed. He moves his fingers and swirls his tongue in a heated, precise rhythm until I'm arching my back off the desk and letting my head fall back against the wood as I squeeze my eyes shut. Before I know it, he unleashes the knot of pressure in my core, and I cry out as I succumb to my pleasure.

He switches places, driving his tongue inside of me as his thumb rubs against my clit to draw out the full extent of my orgasm. I greedily grind into his face as he laps up every drop I give him.

"That's my girl," he mumbles into my cunt.

Once he's driven me past the point of aftershocks, he stands, ushering in a cold breeze between my thighs that prickles my skin. I heat even more at the vision of him naked between my legs—his nose, mouth, and chin glossy with my arousal. My gaze follows the curves and angles of his body. How wide his shoulders are, dipping down to his firm pecs and chiseled abs. Down to his cock, hard for me. His hands are resting on my knees, eyes dark with an untamed desire to ruin me— but also restraint, as he waits for me to grant him permission to do so.

I nod with parted lips and a heavy chest, tilting my knees open wider for him.

He smiles.

He pulls me up off the desk to flip me around and face the

wall. Placing a hand on my shoulder, he bends me over the desk until I'm ass up and legs-wide for him. He takes his cock and slaps it against my pussy a few times for me to hear just how wet I am. I swallow a squeal as he pushes himself inside of me. It steals every breath of mine as he buries himself inch by inch, and I adjust to the fullness. He leans down over me, his arms braced on either side of my head, and he leans his forehead into the back of mine.

"Fuck," he moans, sliding himself in until he's fully seated. "Do you know how much I think of your tight little pussy? How much I fantasize about fucking you into the morning, hard enough you can't sit down without thinking of me?"

"Then stop talking…and do it," I challenge breathlessly.

He pulls out just enough to smack his hips hard into me, jolting me forward and shaking the desk underneath us, all while stealing my breath. Brushing the hair on my neck off to one side gently, he bites into my skin possessively and begins to pound me.

I moan, my eyes fluttering closed as I arch my back into him instinctively. Relishing the feeling of him filling me, our bodies sliding together in molten friction. The desk squeaks underneath us as he thrusts, followed by the wet, smacking sound as he rams into me over and over.

"Harder," I whimper, wanting to see just how much more he can give me. To show him I can take it. "Fuck me like you hate me."

I can feel his fucking *smile.* He obliges, grabbing my arms and pinning them behind my back with one hand. With the other hand, he grabs the front of my shoulder and fucking *pummels* me. Fucking me so hard my legs quake, and every plunge of his has me seeing stars. Each snap of his hips sparks a mix of ache and heat between my legs. My eyes roll back as I stare back up at the ceiling as he takes what he wants from me, and yet, gives me exactly what I need.

With each thrust, he forces out, "Is. That. To. Your. Liking?"

"Yes," I half-cry, half-moan. "Gods, yes."

As a testament to how hard he's rutting me, one of the desk's legs snaps, and we slide to the right. With an irritated grunt, he pulls out of me, picks me up, and carries me to the bed. After he lays me face down, he grabs something off the ground and crawls over the bed toward me.

Desperate and hungry to have him back inside of me, I arch my back again. He's on his knees, his eyes dark and a devilish grin on his lips when he lifts what's dangling in his hand.

The shackles.

"You want me to fuck you like I hate you?" he whispers, sweat glistening on his muscled body. He leans over me and clamps one of the metal bands over my wrist, his eyes narrowed and lustful. "Or me to fuck you like *you* hate me?"

I offer him my other wrist and nearly plead, "Both."

He loops the three-foot chain connecting the shackles around one of the posts at the headboard. Then attaches the second shackle to my wrist with parted lips, his chest rising and falling with anticipation. As soon as I look at the restraints on my wrists, an achy feeling fills my gut at the split-second thought that this all could have been a trick to trap me. He could easily leave me here, chained naked to the bed, and he could escape through the door if he so wanted to.

But instead, he pulls my hips up until I'm on my knees, ready for him. I wrap my fingers around the chain to give me leverage, pulling it tight. My lips part as he begins to push himself back inside of me.

Once his hips are flush with my ass, he withdraws and explodes into a frenzy. My knuckles turn white as I grip onto the chains, and that spark of lust ignites within me all over again. We slip and slide, our naked bodies slamming into each other like if we try hard enough, we might become one.

I cry his name as he fucks me hard, lost to his control and borderline delirious with the fullness of him. He sets off moan after moan in me, rewarding me by brushing just the right spot and moving at just the right tempo. His fingers dig into my hips assertively, with a pressure sure to leave bruises in the morning. And all I can do is lay here and take it. Something about the utter loss of control consumes every thought I have, until the only thing I can think is I don't want it to stop. And Gods above, those breathy moans of his gives me the chills. How it flirts with a soft, jerky whimper with each thrust, beyond pleased with how tight my pussy wraps around his cock.

His hands leave my hips, and he lowers himself over me, brushing my hair off my upper back and dragging his tongue up my spine to my neck, until he finds himself at the one spot that always has me quivering.

He pauses his thrusts as his hot breath warms my neck. Planting a soft kiss behind my ear. "You can scream about how much you hate me," he whispers huskily. "But we both know how much you love me fucking you."

Then he slides his mouth down to the crook between my neck and shoulder and bites with a delicious sting before his hands are back framing my waist. Crashing his hips against me in short, hard spurts that drive each breath out of my lips. My eyes fall closed, body quivering with each thrust.

He unleashes his bite on the spot between my neck and shoulder. Then purrs, "Shaking for me?"

Clearly noticing my trembling legs threatening to give out beneath me, he grabs a pillow, tugs my hips up a little higher, and shoves it underneath me for leverage. Once I've relaxed onto it, he's back at it. I can't do anything but moan as he pins me under his weight and mercilessly fucks me. I drown in the all-encompassing ecstasy of him filling me. Of that deliciously rough friction. When deep, throaty grunts slip from his lips, I splinter into a thousand pieces, crying his name and every obscenity I can think of.

"So pretty when you're coming for me," he growls near my ear. "All night. You're going to make a mess on my cock until the sun rises. I don't want you to stop."

His hands grip my ass hard, nearly pinching the skin as he holds me wide open for him. I find myself bouncing my hips back against him, hungry for every inch of his cock. One of his hands slips down between my legs and rubs circles against my clit until I cry 'yes' as I climax again.

He groans, drunk on each of my orgasms he elicits and pushing me closer to the next one like it's a race. Flattening himself against me, his chest presses to my back. One of his hands slips around my shoulder to collar the front of my throat. Holding me back to him as he bounces us on the mattress. My vision turns to stars, and I can't help but cry in the euphoria.

"Oh, fuck," he growls near my temple. "Keep crying like that and you're going to make me–"

"Come," I moan the invitation, leaning my head back into him.

His grip on my throat tightens, with his other hand clenching over my hip. Each of his movements become quick and erratic as he roars, holding me as he spills himself inside of me. His thrusts slow to a stop. He pulls out of me and gives me a playful smack on the ass.

I finally look at him over my shoulders, snickering through pants, "What happened to until tomorrow morning?"

He snorts, his lips pulling up at one side in a crooked grin as he dips two fingers into me, wetting his fingers with the mixture of his cum and mine. "Who said I was done with you? I only wanted to look at how well you take all of my cum."

He replaces his fingers with his cock and lowers himself over me. His lips brush my ear as he whispers, "I don't want you to walk tomorrow without thinking of me."

For the rest of the night, we go round after round. I've never had so much sex. Eventually, after my wrists ache from the shackles, he removes them.

And somewhere in between rounds, exhaustion claims us.

I wake to a shuffling sound and open my eyes to Darian's back. He's off the bed, his shirt already back on as he slides into his pants. Blinking the sleep out of my eyes, I shift up onto an elbow, watching him clothe himself in the moonlight before he reaches for his shackles to put them back on.

"What are you doing?" I ask plainly.

He flinches, then tosses over shoulder, "Going back to where I belong. In the dirt…on the ground."

"Since when?" *He's never refused to share the bed with me?*

He pauses, thinking. Then works at fastening the belt at his waist with jerky movements. "If you knew any better, you'd know not to trust me."

"Why? It's not like you're not going to kill me—"

"As far as you know."

"You would have already, if you intended to. If you wanted to."

"You know nothing about my intentions," he quips and takes a few steps over to the opposite wall. "You should be scared of me. I'm fucked up in the head. Do you not realize how stupid you are to test me?"

I recoil at the insult, gritting my teeth against it and biting back, "Because you think I should be scared that you killed your own father?"

He flinches as if I slapped him before pointing a daggered glare at me over his shoulder. "Excuse me?"

"Why?" I press on. "If you're going to insult me by calling me stupid for not being scared of you, then at least give me a reason why."

He scoffs, ignoring the question. "I can't believe you're insinuating such a thing."

Still naked, I pull the sheets off the bed and wrap them around me as I get to my feet. Dawn can only be an hour or two away, based on the sky outside the windows. "Sethan told me."

"Sethan's a fucking liar," Darian seethes, his nostrils flaring as I stalk toward him.

"Is it…because he hit you?" I ask gently, brushing his arm. That wicked rage burning in his eyes when I smacked him in the face all those weeks ago when he was training me wasn't because he was embarrassed I caught him with such an assault.

No, it was something far more sinister. I had a theory it unlocked some painful memory in him. Reminded him of some dark, traumatic past. And now the longer I sit with it, the more I can't ignore it. I can't look past and forget it.

He jerks away from my contact, not looking me in the eye. "No."

"Because you felt like he might kill you first?"

"No," he growls in my face.

"Then why?" I whisper, trying to just *understand* him. Back in Arterias, Marge had spoken of how similar Darian and I are, that we both lost our mothers. That hurt things bite. And he didn't have anyone. No friends…not really any family, aside from Celeste, who he just pushed away.

"Because I'm a ruthless piece of shit. That's why." He turns his back to me.

"I…I don't believe that," I murmur, hesitantly reaching out again and pausing.

"Then I've failed to show you who I really am."

My fingertips graze his back, my skin tracing hidden ridges and bumps. It dawns on me…*scars.* I can't even hide my gasp. Perhaps that's why he never could have sex with me face to face, and why he always spun me away from him. Because he's hiding.

He swivels to me, ripping his shirt off and flinging it to the ground. "Is this what you want? Is this what you want to see?" he thunders. "Here, take a gander."

My heart cracks when he turns away from me again. The barrier of his shirt between my fingers wasn't enough to prepare me for what's before me. Faint, jagged scars rip down his shoulder blades, his spine, and all the way down his dimpled lower back. I might have gotten a glimpse of his back once or twice before, but I always brushed it off. Assuming it was from the night back in Midkeep where I found him in a dungeon getting beaten by Corvin and Sethan. I never stopped to give it much thought.

Oh, Gods. How could someone do that? And to their own *child?* My eyes grow blurry at the sides, a thickness collecting in my throat, and I rest my fingers against my chest.

He glances at me from over his shoulder. "Now have you had enough?"

Something crosses in his face when he recognizes the pain in my expression, before he rips the shirt off the floor. "Don't pity me. I deserved every lash. And if I had the chance to kill my father again, I would. Every day, for the rest of my miserable fucking life."

"Stop," I murmur, taking a step toward him.

His eyes flash, and he pauses, watching me with hesitancy.

I take a few more steps, closing the distance between us and gently tracing my fingers up his forearm, his bicep. My voice is softer than a breath. "If you don't want my pity, you won't have it. But don't lie to me. Why did you kill him, Darian?"

His chest rises and falls heavily, his eyes searching mine as if fishing for something I'm not even aware of. He bites his lip, shaking his head firmly. "Because I wanted to."

"I don't believe you…"

"Because it felt *good.*"

He's trying far too hard to push me away. He doesn't want me to see him—he doesn't want to admit the pain he's holding. But I have to try. Secrets are painful, heavy things. Lonely. And he has no one.

"Try. Again," I prompt gently.

"The fuck you want me to say, Katerina!" His pulse races in

his throat. "Because he didn't just hurt me? Because he also hurt my mother? And I couldn't stand him putting his hands on her? Is that it?"

My breath catches in my throat as the impenetrable wall between us explodes.

He leans closer to stare me in the face. "Shall I go on? The day I killed him is the day I found him over my mother, his hands wrapped around her throat and choking the life out of her. I fucking flung myself at him, knocking him off her, and even with his hands gone, she was still unresponsive. I fucking killed him. Right then and there. Strangled every breath from his pathetic fucking lungs because he didn't deserve another. Because I couldn't stop myself. Because I was…" His eyes cloud, reliving the memory for the first and millionth time since the incident, his bare chest rising and falling even more dramatically.

"You were scared," I whisper with a small nod.

When he breaks our eye contact to stare at the floor, avoiding me and saying nothing, I brush my hand against his stubbled cheek.

I grip his chin, turning his face to look at me. "I understand. I've been scared before, too."

Fuck. The way he's looking at me. The green of his eyes is agonizingly beautiful and haunting. His jaw clenches, a softness to his gaze as he shakes his head. And then he grabs me.

And *kisses* me.

For the first time, I realize what this means to him. Where I buried myself in this mindless, explosive sex to escape from the reality of my future, he does it to escape the haunting of his past. Because his pain is so deep, it lingers with each breath. I suddenly understand him, seeing him in a new light. Every flirtatious innuendo. Every venomous threat.

He's calloused. Hardened by someone who broke him over and over.

How much has changed between that small boy painted in his room back at Windmere and the man in front of me now?

I hold him, running my fingers through his long hair, chasing away all the thoughts and memories haunting him. Our lips melt into kiss after kiss, until a few soft, intimate moments later, he pushes at my shoulders to create space between us.

"I can't do this," he mutters, avoiding my eye contact.

I grab his hand before he can move away. "Wait—"

"I can't." He pulls his hand from mine, then he takes his spot on the floor across the room, locking his wrists back into the manacles himself.

FIFTY-FOUR

MEANT TO BE YOURS

The next day at breakfast, I shift uncomfortably in my seat. A delicious soreness aches between my legs. Every time I push Darian out of my mind, I move and it sparks a distant reminder. I have to bite my cheek to not blush. Later, Sethan commands us all to gather near the eastern outskirts of Everden in the forest for sparring. We haven't had much time to practice since traveling to and from Vitalis. While we wait for the letter from Nightfort to confirm the elder's presence who can potentially translate the journal, we might as well be productive.

The smell of pine sap calms my nervous system as we all gather in a clearing set in the forest. I find Archie immediately and pull him to my side as we wait for some of the matches to end. Tossing sly glances at Archie, I look for every hint of emotion in his features. Pain, sadness, joy...*something* to tell me what happened after dinner the other night with Melaina. But his face is stone-cold, his attention set on the two soldiers in the middle of the circle sparring.

As soon as the match concludes, I elbow him with a smile. At breakfast, he told me the Everden healer gave him some dragon's breath to heal his ankle. "You up for it?"

He half-grins. "Always up for kicking your ass."

With a laugh, I pinch his elbow, and we both stride toward the center and draw our blades. I toss my sword into my left hand as Archie's eyebrows quirk up.

"Oh…getting really cocky now, are you?" He chuckles. "Going to take it easy on me by using your left hand?"

"Don't be so sure," I whisper with a grin.

We burst into a series of strikes, swipes, blocks, and advances. I replay all the moves Darian taught me over the last few lessons, and within minutes, I disarm Archie.

Sweat sticks his sandy blond hair to his forehead, and he bends over to rest his palms on his knees as he looks up at me, panting. "I'm sorry, where did that come from?"

As I open my mouth to answer him, Sethan thunders from the sidelines, "I suppose you've outgrown your sparring partner, so it only makes sense to move to a more skilled one." He motions to his daughter. "Melaina, if you'll please."

I sweep an angry glare at Sethan. Archie pats my shoulder to soothe my irritation, shaking his head before he retrieves his sword and returns to the sidelines.

Melaina stalks toward the center, and we both hook each other with an intense glare. Her metal bracelet feels extra heavy around my wrist now. I haven't had a chance to speak to her since we returned. Based on her and Archie's expressions, nothing has been resolved yet. Or if it has, it's not in the direction I'd prefer. Without words, we burst into swipes and swings. Except this time, I've become familiar with her movements, and I have Darian's training at my advantage. This time, she is equally matched—if not more.

"You can do better than that," she coos, striking again.

I block her advance with a grunt. "Funny, you were the one to teach me that one."

"I didn't teach you everything." She smirks and swings out at my legs.

Her sword knicks the front of my boot, slicing open the leather. I glare and rear back to kick my opposite heel out toward her knee before she dodges, and I use the opportunity to swipe my blade toward her chest.

She smiles, barely blocking my attack in time, and her eyes soften slightly. "Better. Good."

We move swipe for swipe as we rotate around the ring, until she swings down toward my shins, and I catch her blade with mine and redirect her up. She sweeps her blade off mine in a half-circle, opening herself up but moving so quickly that she aims her downward swing right toward my ribs with her eyes glittering with triumph. It's too bad she doesn't know I've been training with Darian.

Sometimes, you just have to get creative.

I drop like a stone to the floor, my weight shifting immediately into the balls of my feet as I catch myself in a crouch, and then I fling myself at her lower legs, driving her off balance. Her breath whooshes out of her as her back slams into the cold, frosty earth. Before she can regain her breath, I scramble over top of her, pinning her arms underneath my knees and holding the long edge of my blade to her brown throat.

Applause explodes around us like thunder, and I linger, staring her down.

"Well done," Sethan calls.

I lift off her and extend my hand. Despite her pinched eyebrows, she grabs me and allows me to help her up. She dusts off her pants and her back, rolling her shoulders to test how sore she is. Drunk on two wins in a row, I scan the onlookers as I hold my sword, ready for someone who will give me a challenge. Each face I turn to, everyone is staring, and yet no one steps up.

Heavy footsteps sound behind me, and the gazes of the

Arterians and Vitalan soldiers I'm facing widen. I turn, facing my approaching opponent.

Cole.

My mouth falls open. *He's offering to fight me?* When all this time he's refused to put me in any sort of danger or pain?

He nods, so slightly I barely catch it, then raises his sword as he stops a few steps away.

Shit. I'd always wanted Cole to take me seriously and treat me as if I were any other person in his squad. But now that I stand in front of him, facing down his broad shoulders as they roll back in preparation, his proud chest steady with unhurried breaths, and his jaw set with his warm eyes trained on me…

I'd seen him back in Blackfell with his first kill. And the entire group of soldiers he slaughtered when I was captured only yesterday. He's brutal. And no matter what hand I use, there isn't a single chance I have against his sheer power. But the recognition of his respect for me settles between us.

I swallow my apprehension and call upon that deep-rooted anger like Darian taught me. The anger he created by not telling me of his engagement to Celeste. The downfall of what we once were.

I dig into it as if I were sinking my fingers into the soil and drawing it up from the depths of my soul. I rush forward, swinging my blade out toward his knees, and he blocks me. We flow into swings and spins. It doesn't take me long to recognize his hesitancy. While he strikes me, it lacks the speed and strength of what I know he's capable of.

Channeling that anger, I grit my teeth and feed that rage into my attacks. Without caging my strength, I lunge forward and drag my sword straight toward his throat. My blade slams into his as he blocks, a vibration ringing up through my arm.

He holds my blade in place with his. Not a single bead of sweat collects on his brow, as if we're doing something as simple as slow dancing. My muscles strain against his brute strength pressed into the blade, my arms trembling until my legs do as I fight to hold him at bay, and yet…

He's still.

Holding.

Back.

He can easily knock me on my ass. Right here. Right now. In front of everyone.

"Do it," I grit out between my clenched teeth, pinning him with a glare.

He shakes his head slightly, jaw tense.

"You're still…holding…back," I growl, shoving every last bit of my weight and power into him. "I am not some fragile…little—"

He explodes with a grunt, releasing his power and knocking me backward. I fall in slow-motion, the trees and sky a blur as I plummet. I squeeze my eyes shut and tense, waiting for the impact. My ass hits the ground first, followed quickly by my back, my shoulders, my—

Something catches my head before it can slam into the ground, cushioning my fall. Opening my eyes, I find myself staring back into Cole's golden ones.

Eyebrows furrowed, his mouth parts in a small whisper, "Are you…?"

I nod, pushing myself up off the ground. He slips his hand off the back of my head and offers me a hand, pulling me up to my feet. One by one, the onlookers explode in a clap, cheering just as loud as when I defeated Melaina. I turn, meeting each of their gazes as a small smile spreads my lips.

I glance over my shoulder and mutter, "You—"

He's already gone.

I slip off to the forest after dinner and sit near the river's edge, staring at the water as I absentmindedly brush a hand up and down Daeja's massive snout until she dozes off next to me. Marge's gloves are piled on my thigh. I find comfort in Daeja's scales, still warm from the fading winter sun, my fingers gliding over each ridge. Every exhalation she breathes nearly flattens the crisp, frosty grass.

"I've been looking for you," a thick voice calls. Cole shifts in, taking a seat beside me.

"You were the one who left earlier?"

Daeja lifts her head to glance at Cole before she settles back down, tucking her wings into her side even tighter.

He glances at me sideways, warily. "Are you alright?"

I nod and roll my shoulders back, my eyes still glued to the rushing water as an ache ripples through my muscles when I move. "All you did was knock me on my ass. It's not like you hurt me."

"That's not what I meant."

His unexpected answer finally tears my gaze away from the water.

He clears his throat when our eyes connect and shifts his gaze down to a patch of grass he fiddles with. "I umm…look. I know you've lost a lot of people you care about. And it feels like it's constantly one thing after another. And…I just wanted to make sure you're okay."

"I suppose I'm as okay as one can be," I mutter. Glancing down at Daeja underneath my hand, with her eyes closed and breathing easy, a soft smile creeps up my cheeks. When I glimpse the Blood Ring on my finger—Cole's mother's ring—my smile fades again.

He must be looking at me now because he asks, "What? What is it?"

"I feel wrong wearing it, you know?" I admit in a whisper.

"Why?"

"Because…" I clear my throat, struggling to form my thoughts into words. The truth of it is because his mother's ring had always been a promise of our relationship. Of our love. Our future. It feels unfair to wear it now—for him and for me. It makes me feel wrong for wearing it during my nights with Darian. When all I really want— if I'm honest with myself— is the one thing I can't have. Him.

I continue, "Because it's your mother's. And I feel like you should be the one who has it—"

He rests his hand on mine, his voice gentle. "Stop. It was always meant to be yours, whether you loved me or not. Whether it was prophesied about you or someone else. I don't want you to feel guilt over it. The day I met you, I couldn't imagine it on anyone else."

I bite the inside of my cheek, my gaze shifting to his strong hand resting overtop of mine. Shaking my head with a laugh that is anything but comical, I mutter, "Gods…I would have never thought we'd end up here…"

"Yeah…" He glances down at our hands. "There are many things of mine that belong to you. That are inherently yours…"

A tension builds in my throat and chest. He doesn't have to spell it out for me.

He whispers so simply. So honestly. "I am…*so* sorry, Katerina Blackwind. I'm sorry for who I was. I'm sorry I hurt you. I don't deserve your forgiveness—I know that. But I will try my damndest to make it up to you someday."

Then he gives my hand the tiniest squeeze before rising to his feet to leave. After he takes a few steps, and the warmth of his hand fades from mine, I turn to watch him walk away.

"Cole…?"

He pauses mid-step and glances over his broad shoulder at me, his expression unreadable.

"I do forgive you." The words tremble on my lips, tears sting at my eyes.

He smiles sadly and dips his head. "I know, love."

Then he continues his walk back to Everden.

FIFTY-FIVE

BEYOND THE HEIGHT

We received the go-ahead from Sethan's contacts in Nightfort, and we're making the trek south. Daeja and I join Sethan and the rest of the dragon riders in the sky. Away from formation, Daeja glides in and out of clouds, each puff whipping me in the face with a bitter moisture.

I wave each assault away, coughing as I tighten my other gloved hand around the saddle horn. *"Too high, too high!"*

She dips her nose down and dives into the massive gray cloud, my stomach dropping down into my toes, and my eyes watering as the wind rakes its sharp claws up across my face. My knees lock around Daeja as I silently thank all the Gods for these blessed straps and hooks. Otherwise, my ass would have been half a mile higher from such a massive drop.

"Trying…to make…me…piss myself?" I ground out through each breath.

Without responding, Daeja releases her wings, snapping them open and jolting me forward, the saddle horns slamming into my chest hard enough that it knocks the wind out of me.

"Too quick, sorry about that."

She's still learning, and there's not a single bone in my body that can be angry with her. Plus, it's not like I'm an expert at maintaining my balance and weight, either. Dragon riding is definitely a skill I need to hone. Forcing myself to straighten, I glance down at the ground hundreds of feet below us, my stomach churning at the thought of how long of a fall it would be.

"Get out of your head," Daeja warns, sensing my queasiness.

I swallow, attempting to force down my nausea. *"Hard to get out, when you're already in here."*

"Isn't it a nice view at least? Just take a look. Look beyond the height."

I focus on the colors first: the splash of various evergreen shades from the pine trees, the dusted grays frosting earth, and a snaking blue river cutting through the land. The jagged edges of the forest versus the smooth liquidity of the river. How the water ebbs and flows, as easy as if it were…

Wait.

I scan the rest of the valley and the peaks spanning out around us. The gargantuan Serahaven mountain range, framing the distant Vitalis castle with waterfalls spilling down into pools, spurs a flicker of a thought. The river whips and flows throughout the land, connecting at different branches and clustering in distant areas to form lakes.

Flows as easily as if it were blood. And as if the rivers were *veins.*

I turn in the saddle, staring out beyond Daeja's tail to the south. The river twists through the forest, and out beyond what I can see. Memories of the Arterian map flash through my head in rapid succession, luring me into a trance. *"Daeja, tell A'nala and Sethan we're taking a quick detour. I need to see something. Head south along the river."*

"In case you were wondering, A'nala is just as ornery as Sethan is."

"Good thing you match them in sass," I giggle and pat her neck.

"If I recall correctly, you still owe me more examples of how much better I am than you."

"I think your ego is already large enough to last you to next winter, don't you think?"

Her rumble of a laugh vibrates underneath my legs, and she dips her head and neck until we're perpendicular with the ground. She tucks her wings into her side, plummeting us down like an arrow whizzing through the air. The wind screams in my ears and rips tears from my eyes. I fight against my own body to keep myself from losing my balance and sliding face first over the saddle.

She twists into a corkscrew, spinning the ground below us into a whirl of green and gray and blue until it's as undecipherable as my breath. My heart and blood freeze. *"Daeja…too…much…"*

Suddenly, yet not sudden enough, she whips left into a wide turn and nearly gives me whiplash as I grip the horns and tighten my thighs to keep myself upright. I laugh through the fear shaking my arms and legs, a rush of adrenaline washing over every buzz of my racing thoughts. She straightens out, and the two of us fly farther south, following the river until Dragon's Back Ridge rises in the distance.

But I don't have to get much farther to piece it together.

Because I know part of the reason why King Aaric moved south to Arterias and didn't stay at the castle in Vitalis. Why I couldn't pull from the ley lines when Archie and I were captured by rebels southeast of Everden. And I never stopped to consider if Aaric would ever venture outside of Arterias to take control of the entire realm.

Marge, all those weeks ago, explained ley lines were like underground rivers. And all this time, I should have sensed the humming but had grown accustomed to it. When I found serenity at the river back in Padmoor, it wasn't because of some unknown reason.

The rivers *are* the ley lines.

Arterias would have the most power, as all the rivers lead south. But many of them in Arterias dried up long ago. He's been draining them.

Then why not move north of Dragon's Back Ridge to claim the rest? Unless of course…it's only a matter of time.

FIFTY-SIX

DON'T GO GETTING SENTIMENTAL

Daeja and I backtrack to Nightfort, sticking to the eastern part of the river and working our way toward the city. The massive stretch of dense forest thins out to plains. The river snakes through a gorge with plummeting, rocky cliffs at either side. Daeja extends her wings out to her side as she glides gracefully over the water. The cliff sides curve to the east the farther north we get, and Daeja cuts up over the ridge. The roofs of Nightfort are stark black against the yellow plains, with clusters of boulders littering the landscape below.

Daeja lands near the outskirts where we find A'nala, Sethan, and the others. Sethan's addressing the group about keeping a close eye out for anyone following us as we walk through the city. The dragons will stay back so we can keep a low profile. The idea is to get in and out without much notice. Only here for what we need and nothing more.

An ancient translator, who might be able to decipher Queen Elara's journal.

A'nala swings her golden glare at me and Daeja in a silent

reprimand before turning her attention back to Sethan as he retrieves his scabbard from her saddle and slings it over his shoulder. I unhook myself from the saddle belt and slide off Daeja, then unpack my own weapons and arm myself. We all gather and head into Nightfort together, following Sethan's lead through the streets until he stops and knocks at a stone building.

A small metal peephole slides open on the door, before shutting again. After a few moments, Sethan knocks again.

"She's not here anymore," someone calls on the other side of the door.

"I don't believe you." Sethan pounds harder on it.

The peephole slides open again, and this time a set of brown eyes narrow in on us. "You better leave before you're noticed."

"Shall I have you sent to Millton for non-compliance?" Sethan growls into the doorframe.

A series of what sounds like metal twisting fills the silence, and a second later, the door parts open.

A bald man, short and stocky, appears on the other side of the door. "Get in here, then. Before half the town knows you're here!"

Sethan turns back and motions for me, Melaina, and Cole, who's holding Darian's chains. Then, he gestures to the rest to stand guard outside. I narrow my gaze at him for the exclusion of Archie, but Archie takes it in stride, leading part of the group back through the streets to watch from afar.

Our group of five slides into the dark building. Blankets drape over the windows, and a small candle with barely any wax left burns against a far table. A musty smell smacks me over the face, and I turn to exchange a look with Melaina as the man closes the door, sealing us in shadows.

"You'll get me killed, too, if they know you're here!" the man grumbles, then kicks a stool away from the door leading up to the peephole.

Sethan cuts straight to it. "We need your help. Your council confirmed Elder Honora—"

"Our council is *corrupt,*" the man warns as he grips the hilt of a shortsword at his side. His gaze bounces from person to person until it settles on me.

Sethan slides in front of me, blocking his view. "We need to know where Elder Honora is. Tell us, and we will simply be on our way."

"She…she's dead."

Sethan draws his sword from his side and lunges forward, racing the man back to the wall and pressing a blade to his throat. "Tell me the truth!"

The man's voice is a panicked, shrill mess. "I…uhh…she's…"

"Now!" Sethan thunders.

"Sh-she snuck off to Bayrock! They knew you'd come for her—"

"Who is *they?*" Melaina interjects.

As if on cue, a knock sounds at the door, and we all slide our attention to it. Sethan takes a step back from the man and motions him to answer it, following him to the door with his blade still pointed inches from the man's neck. Melaina and I, along with Cole leading Darian by the chains, all slink over to the farthest wall out of sight of the door if it were to open.

The man grabs the stool, slides it under the peephole, and peers out. "Can I help you?"

"Yes. We need to come inside," someone answers.

Melaina shifts to grab her sword, ready to unsheathe it, and I do the same as I exchange a look with Cole. He transfers Darian's chains into his non-dominant hand, then readies himself for a quick draw.

Sethan presses the tip of his blade into the man's back, and he winces. Whoever is on the other side beats against the door, and the man slides the cover over the peephole and jumps off the stool, despite Sethan's hissing.

One more thud, and the door springs open, sending the stool flying into a table.

Sethan backs up, putting himself between the group of men on the other side and us as he widens his stance.

"Daeja…we might be in trouble."

"A'nala's already on it. The other part of the group has been attacked in the streets, and we're closing in for backup."

"Shit. We've been ambushed. I don't know if these are Close Circle members who have crossed the border or Vitalan rebels. Arterians won't kill you…but Vitalan rebels will. If they are, stay back!"

"Pfft, I'm not staying back! Either way, beat those bastards, and I'll meet you in the outskirts of town."

"Be careful!"

"Don't go getting sentimental on me."

Melaina, Cole, and I all withdraw our swords in a harmonious chorus of metal as a group of men spill through the doorway, beheading the short, screaming man.

Bastards, indeed.

Cole looks at me and tosses me Darian's chains. I catch them with my breath stuttering as Cole dashes to stand side-by-side with Sethan and take on three men. More of them bleed into the room, and Cole and Sethan explode into a frenzy of blocks and side steps. Even as Melaina joins the fray, one thing is for certain.

We're easily outmatched here.

Darian meets my gaze, his face deadly serious. "Remember what I told you? Anything is a weapon if you're creative enough."

I swivel to the candle burning in the corner and nod. Praying I can trust him, I drop the chains and race across the room. Ripping my gloves off and tucking them into my side, I raise my hands to the candle and pull it toward me like I'm tearing a sheet off a bed.

The flame sputters off the wick and gathers into a ball as a hum of energy flows around me, through me. I funnel the distant ley line magic into it. Within seconds, I pull it inches from my chest, now a ball the width of my shoulders. My fingers tremble as I fight to contain it, then I turn back to the group.

"Duck!" I scream and throw the flame toward the fight.

Melaina and Cole drop immediately, and Melaina rips her father down just in time for it to barrel over him and blast into the wall of soldiers, knocking them onto their backs and exploding into screams of men on fire.

Darian tosses me a small grin, and I race over to grab his chains and pull him toward the door. Cole helps Melaina stand, and Sethan stumbles to his feet, the tips of his white hair colored black.

"You'll pay for that one later," he grumbles, brushing a hand over his head.

"Not my fault you can't duck fast enough," I toss back with a chuckle.

The soldiers all lie on the ground, some of them twitching. I splay my hands over the fire and tamp it down to the floor until it disappears completely.

"Let's go!" I whisper, then pull Darian along with me as I tiptoe around the charred bodies, scanning their armor for hints of what side they were on but not slowing to find one.

We all exit the building into an eerily empty town, then race down the street we came from. I slide my gloves back on, just in case. One block over, a chaotic symphony of metal roars out from the distance. Several townspeople dash past us, screaming and disappearing behind the corner of a building. We cut down dusty alleyways, until we get to the last street leading out to the plains.

It's a mesh of humans and dragons, with flashes of metal in the sunlight and smoke billowing up into the air, filling my nostrils with the unmistakable scent of burnt flesh. The numbers aren't in our favor. But it's a damn good thing we have dragons.

"Get to your dragon!" Sethan commands, then looks at Melaina. "And you! Stay behind the lines."

"I will not cower in fear!" she roars.

He lurches over her. "You will as long as I am your father!"

I take a step forward, ready to speak on her behalf, when she fires back, "And you *still* will not dictate my decisions! Father, or not!"

She races into the throng, disappearing into the chaos. Cole shifts a look at me with a small smile, then launches into the battle without another word. Sethan cuts to the northwest where A'nala's red figure rears back and snaps at a soldier advancing at her with a spear.

"Let me help you!" Darian begs from beside me and holds his fists up, the metal of his chains clinking with the movement.

My eyes meet his. My heart thunders in my chest, my breath quickening as I look down at his shackles.

"Trust me!" he shouts over the roar of the battle.

I fumble the key out of my brassiere and shakily shove it into one of the locks, twisting until one of his shackles springs free. A set of thunderous footsteps approaches us, and my attention is dragged up to three soldiers racing toward us, eyes narrowed with menacing determination and their swords raised. I rip a dagger out from a sheath at my side and shove it into Darian's hands. No time to unshackle his other wrist.

I glance back at our opponents and draw my sword. Without taking my eyes off the soldiers, I tell Darian, "Once I get to Daeja, I can give you my sword instead!"

The closest of the three closes in. I barely have enough time to block his attack, the force of his blow making my steps falter, and I fumble backward.

"Kat!" Archie calls, and he bursts across the group from my right. His flash of sandy blonde hair whips as he stabs his sword into the soldier's side, and the man collapses to the ground with a scream. It affords me enough time to dart my gaze to where Darian—

Isn't.

I spot him running away. Toward the south and away from the battle.

"You *fucking* asshole!" I scream, loud enough it burns in my throat like I swallowed fire. Anger bubbles my blood, threatening to combust me, but I don't have time to think about it because the other two men close in. Archie and I fight side by side, matched in skill but losing our energy.

"Above you!" Daeja roars overhead a split-second before outstretched, black-as-death talons swoop down and claim the faces of the two soldiers fighting Archie and me. She drags them up off the ground as she lifts into the air, taking a few flaps before tossing them thirty feet from the ground into the battle.

"She's badass." Archie watches her with awe. "When am I going to get a dragon?"

"No time!" I grunt and elbow him, pointing at two more soldiers racing toward us.

They descend upon us quickly, not giving us much of a break from the last group. Archie steps away from me to take the man on the right, and I slide to the left to ready myself for the woman running toward me.

Daeja swoops down and nabs the woman's hair in her mouth and rips her from the ground. The woman screeches as Daeja flings her off into one of Nightfort's buildings behind us, the body colliding with the stone walls in a sickening crack.

The man fighting Archie gasps and books it down an alley, with Archie chasing after him. Daeja circles around and descends until she lands into a run in front of me, her head dipped down and eyes burning as another set of soldiers charge for me. With a panted breath, I raise my sword, readying myself once more.

Thirty feet.

Twenty feet.

Ten.

I roar as I swing my sword up into the closest man's chest, funneling all my anger from Darian's betrayal behind my swing and surprising even myself when my blow slams into his ribs and knocks the man sideways. I pull my sword back just in time to block a new attack from a woman, and I spin our connected blades until I direct hers away from me.

Another soldier creeps behind the woman to attack me from the side, but Daeja springs forward and swats them twenty feet to the side. Striking like a snake, she lunges forward and seizes my female attacker in her daggered jaws, clamping down on her body until it splits with a crunch and explosion of blood before she tosses the limp body aside.

"Thank you—" I pause as a group of men and women charge for Daeja, their swords and spears raised.

"Go!" I grunt and smack her hind leg.

"I'm not leaving you."

There's no time to argue. I race to her side as she lowers herself to the ground, and I grab hold of one stirrup and swing myself up onto her back. As I settle into the saddle, she begins to gallop forward, and I cling to the horns while squeezing my legs around her to keep me upright. The saddle belt dangles to my right, slamming against her side with each stride, and too far below for me to try and fish it up now.

Daeja roars, and pain spiders throughout my nervous system. I spin to Daeja's rear and find a man holding on to one half of a sword, the other half embedded into her thick, muscular tail.

"Swing him toward me!" I cry. *"I'll make him fucking pay!"*

She slows her pace and turns inward to whip her tail toward me. The man's eyes widen in fear as he realizes how fucked he is the closer he swings toward me, and yet he still can't seem to pry his fingers off the blade. But before he can talk some sense into himself, I push up through the stirrups and rise off the saddle to slash through his forearms.

He screams and falls to his demise as I face back forward in my seat, Daeja launching up into the sky. I press myself down into the saddle until she levels out.

"That fucker. Are you okay?"

"Yes…it hurts—"

"Get us down and I can take it out."

"I'll be okay."

"It's hurting you, and I can feel it. Get your ass down now!"

She growls but dips low, the wind ripping my eyes open and keeping me from blinking until she lands with a force that whips me forward then back.

Spinning in the saddle, I crawl to my feet and run down her spine toward her rear. *"Raise your tail!"*

She lifts it, creating a nearly horizontal path to the blade gleaming at the end of her tail. As I race down her tail, I skid and almost slide off as it thins. I drop down and crawl forward until I get to the blade. *"This is going to hurt—"*

She roars as I rip it clean out of her tail, drawing a string of her blood almost dark enough to be black. I toss the sword to the side.

"Hop off!" she commands with an urgency that spikes my heart rate.

I jump and roll sideways on the ground to avoid her heavy, clawed feet as she whirls her body toward me. Her tail swings out away from me and sideswipes into three soldiers racing toward us, knocking them over like they're made of straw. She continues her circle to face them head on with a mighty roar that trembles the ground beneath me.

I jump to my feet as her head plunges down again and again, each time pulling up with more splattered blood and flesh. Lunging for the stirrups, I pull myself into the saddle to find a horde of soldiers racing toward us.

"Fly, Daeja! Get off the ground, more are coming!"

She whips away from the incoming group and gallops until she pulls us up into the air again. As I toss a glance behind my back to make sure none have snuck onto her tail, my body rolls with each wingbeat. She careens down back toward the battle, and I brace my weight as we've always practiced. Though, it's the first time without wearing a belt. This high up and without it, my breath quickens for an entirely different reason as I scan the battle below. Fear creeps up my throat as I search the sea of bodies for all the people on our side.

The citizens of Nightfort must have come to our aid, considering how many people now fight back.

A glimmer of red near the northwestern edge catches my attention, and my hope picks up a breath in my chest when I recognize A'nala with Sethan, the other dragon riders at their side. A'nala roars and blasts a shot of fire at a swarm of soldiers with blades glowing in a ghastly blue.

Fuck. That's not good.

"We have to get back down there! We can't let them defend themselves on their own! They have dragonblades!"

"A'nala says we have to stay back!"

"I don't give a fuck what A'nala says! She and Sethan do not command us!"

"When this is over, you'll be the one to get their heat, then." She dips back down.

"Good. Tell them it was all my idea." I tighten my hands on the horns and lean into her.

We land close to forty feet away from them to give us enough time to assess a plan.

I scan the field beyond Sethan, A'nala, and the other dragon riders. The battle surges like the tides as men and women attack and recede, with figures dropping dead left and right. Melaina fights back-to-back with a Nightfort commoner. And Gavin is gesturing to another unfamiliar person to take up a weapon from a dead body. To the northeastern side of the battle near Nightfort, I glimpse Archie backing up and drawing a dagger from his side until he bumps into a wall, cornered by a soldier.

No…

The color drains from my face, and I break into a sprint toward him, each beat of my heart matching the drumming of my hurried steps. Everyone is distracted by their own battles, and even from this distance I can see Archie's panic.

Where the fuck is his sword?

Even if he can manage just fine with a dagger, he doesn't notice a second soldier stalking forward from the side, ready for the kill.

The first soldier is only a distraction.

FIFTY-SEVEN

Too late

"Archie!" I scream, pumping my arms harder and hurdling over the downed soldiers littering the ground. "Archie!"

Hands snatch me from behind, and Daeja roars, ***I'm trapped!***

An unfamiliar voice calls behind me, "This is her. Have they secured her dragon?"

"Yes, sir."

"Good, both of them must remain unharmed."

I wiggle against them, trying to free myself while never taking my eyes off Archie. *"They won't hurt you, Daeja…but I have to get to Archie!"*

I can hear her snapping jaws somewhere behind me. She'll manage on her own.

In the distance, the first soldier strikes Archie, and he deflects the blade—barely—with his small dagger. The second soldier prowls toward them as Archie fights for his life against the first one. He still hasn't noticed the second man.

I rip my left arm out from my assailant and fling it forward with curved fingers, channeling the ley line magic below the earth and pushing it until it erupts from the ground into the first soldier attacking Archie. It slams the man against the wall.

My kidnapper slaps my arm down, and I lose my grip on the magic. The man I've pinned against the wall slumps to the ground, knocked unconscious. The second man tackles Archie from behind. Out of the corner of my eye, a flash of red appears before I'm knocked sideways to the ground. When I land face-to-face with a dead soldier, I clamber up to find Cole scrapping with my attacker.

When Cole affords me a glance as he grapples with the man, he mouths, *"Go!"*

Belly down, I crawl through the bodies for a moment until I can spring up to my hands and knees. I look up as Archie is pinned down by the second soldier. The man pulls a fist back and smashes it down straight into Archie's face.

"No!" I cry.

Someone snatches me by the ankle, dragging me backward through the dirt as I watch the man rear back and begin to wallop Archie as he writhes on the ground. I reach out a hand to him, like I'll be able to stop it in the devastating distance between us.

Everything slows while my memories with Archie flash in my mind. Him throwing the dagger to save me back in Arterias. Us staring up at the stars and pointing out a constellation that looks like a soup ladle. Him taking it easy on me in sparring. Him finding Daeja and protecting me against her before he even knew she wouldn't hurt me. Letting me rest my head on his shoulder to sleep.

Every laugh.

Every smile.

My *best* friend.

I flip onto my back to face my attacker and fucking kick the man square in the face. Giving me enough time to scramble away and turn my attention back to Archie. All the pain surges around me like a power source, filling to the brim.

"Archie!" I lift my hand again with a cry, tears blurring my vision as if I reach hard enough for him, I can save him. I begin to pull the magic again—

The soldier rebounds and falls on top of me, pinning my arms behind my back and shoving my face down into the dirt. I lose my grip on the magic. All I can see is Archie getting hit, again and again. Tears slip from my eyes as I'm forced to watch, fighting to free myself.

A figure flashes across the scene and tackles the soldier off Archie to the ground. The figure rears up. Brown hair swept into a mess.

Darian.

He plunges a dagger straight into the man's throat, pausing for a slow moment, before slicing it across his neck and ending the soldier's jerky movements.

The person pinning me rips me up off the ground by my hair, their other hand on my wrists. When I see Archie roll off his back onto his hands and knees, relief breaks through my chest. He's *alive.*

The person holding me hostage grunts, then gurgles. Something slumps behind me, and I turn to see a man collapse to the ground with blood pooling out of a wound in his chest.

Melaina looks at me and nods, then springs back into battle. When I glance back at Daeja, she's shaking nets off her back, fifteen soldiers lying limp around her.

"I have an idea," I pant.

"Don't you always?" she purrs, flicking her gaze to me across the battlefield.

"Light it up. I'll draw the flames to protect our group."

"Good thinking." She rears back onto her hind legs and blasts a shot of fire near me.

Sucking in a quick breath, I power my stance and grip the flames with clawed fingers. I work to move them around the battlefield, like drawing lines in sand. Eventually, I've blocked off our group, protecting them from any attackers.

The clamor of the battle fades into an eerie stillness, broken by crackling embers, until we all stand amongst the carnage, flicking our gazes back and forth between those still standing.

"Bristol…take the others and fly overhead…See if you can pick off any stragglers," Sethan commands breathily, his hands braced on his knees.

Bristol dips his head and mounts Nadja with the other riders as they push off the ground and climb into the sky. I slide the flames down back to the ley lines, sweat soaking my brow.

I make eye contact with Cole. Even from this distance, the amber of his eyes glows with rage, blood smattering the side of his face and clumping bits of his flame-red hair. He nods slowly to let me know he's okay, blinking the anger out of his eyes like a cat might do when the sun comes out after a dark night.

"Father!" Melaina screeches behind us.

Everyone turns as she catches Sethan, folding forward onto his knees. Melaina struggles against his strong frame to lower him to the ground, and when she does, all of us swarm in around her.

I sweep the soldiers in front aside to get a clear look. "Let me see him!" I drop onto my knees beside Melaina as she cradles her father's head in her hands, her eyes round with fear.

"What's-what's happening?" Melaina pants, her voice pitching higher with panic. Her shaky hands gently pat up and down his torso, his sides. "I don't understand. He isn't injured. What is happening?"

Sethan's eyes stare up at the sky, his fingers pulling at the top of his gorget. His lips bloom to a tinge of purple.

"Kat!" Melaina screams. "Please!"

I scan his body with my eyes and hands, not finding any critical wounds or blood. Frantically, I unfasten the gorget encasing his throat. "Poison? Maybe? I can try to—"

My heart stops as Sethan slides his brown eyes to mine.

I look over at A'nala as she collapses onto her side to the ground. Her head bounces off the earth lifelessly, and her yellow eyes are blown wide in a glassy stare. A shining blue blade protrudes from the elegant curve of her throat.

I scream to anyone who'll listen, "Someone! Quick! Take that dragonblade out of her throat!"

Several rush over to her and pull the sword out. The blade is soaked in blood, glittering in the sunlight with a beauty belying the horror. Her blood spills out onto the ground in ruby pools, shining with magic and poison. Poisoned by her own kind. Twisted by the sinfulness of man.

I jump to my feet, determined to pull any poison from A'nala's bloodstream—

Sethan catches me by the wrist, his fingers locked around me with a waning strength. He takes a strangled breath.

When I look back down at him, he chokes out with his eyes half-closed, "It's…too late."

Melaina's cry breaks something in me, and she curls her shoulders inward as if she can protect her father from his own looming fate. Archie comes up behind her, resting a cautious hand on her shoulder.

Sethan's grip on my wrist intensifies. "Success is…a decision."

He lets go of me and rests his hand on Melaina's forearm as his head begins to lull back, fighting with every staggered breath and drag of his eyelids to stay conscious.

"I may have never been the best father to you. But…I never wanted to leave you, Melbell," his voice is mangled by blood, spilling out of his mouth in gurgling streams. "I want you to be happy. I… love…"

You.

His hand slips off Melaina's arm, and the gurgling in his mouth ceases. His head falls back as the life in his eyes fades.

Melaina screams.

FIFTY-EIGHT

AND THE STARS

After those Nightfort civilians who've fought on our side have helped us settle into the city with fresh baths, clothes, food, and any wound care, we head to the northernmost point of Nightfort after sunset. Melaina lingers at the edge of a stone pit, staring absently at A'nala and Sethan's bodies in the center. A blanket covers Sethan's body, and A'nala is wrapped around him, her nose touching the tip of his head and tail curled around him in an everlasting sign of oneness.

Even in death, their bond is evident.

The torch in Melaina's grasp flickers as she stands at the pit's edge for a few still moments, tears slipping down her cheeks at a furious speed. Dipping her head, she tosses the torch out onto her father's body.

This was what they wanted.

The old, ancient way of burials.

One by one, Daeja and the other dragons blow soft breaths of fire onto them, intensifying the flame until it drowns out the silhouettes of A'nala and Sethan.

The group of us circling around the pit watch the flames grow higher and higher until it reaches up for the heavens.

"To the skies…" I murmur, my head tilted back as I watch the smoke waft into the air.

"And the stars," Daeja finishes sadly.

Archie leans his head into my shoulder, then wordlessly offers me a flask. I flick my gaze up to him and shake my head. Melaina stands to our left, her arms wrapped tightly around her chest as she stares up at the flames. Her eyes glisten, and her hair whips in the gentle breeze.

I squeeze Archie's arm. "Go to her."

He looks up at me, his eyes wide and sad. "I can't."

"She *needs* you," I whisper, patting his cheek.

He bites his lip, then nods as if he was internally struggling with the decision and only needed one small push. But I don't have long to watch the situation unfold because Darian slinks off between the flames, away from the group and into the darkness.

He's avoided all eye contact with me since the battle. I haven't even proposed to put his shackles back on. I'm not sure why—maybe because, for the first time, it seems like he's finally come to terms with being on the right side of this war.

He saved Archie. He came back for *him.*

And yet…something doesn't feel right.

I dip my head in respect to Sethan and A'nala and leave behind the warmth and light of the fire to slip into the brisk cold air of the winter night. *Maybe he's injured and didn't want to admit it. He can't possibly be…upset? That he killed someone?*

As I stride farther away from the bonfire, he's nowhere to be found, and I'm starting to wonder if he actually ran away this time. Until I catch a glimpse of someone sitting on the edge of the cliffside overlooking the river and distant Serahaven mountain range hiding Vitalis. Throwing a glance over my shoulder, debating if I should go back to the fire and leave him alone, I decide against it and walk toward him. The wind picks up and ruffles my hair, the cold air kissing my skin and sending a shiver down my spine. I pull my cloak tight across my frame, my body tensing as I stop a few steps away from him.

He has his legs dangling over the side of the cliff, which drops hundreds of feet to the ground below. The sliver of moon hanging in the sky is barely enough for me to see his outline against the explosion of stars and brilliant darkness in front of us.

Darian tilts his head back to guzzle down the liquid in his flask. He pauses, but he doesn't turn to look at me. "What do you want?"

My mouth parts, but nothing comes out. I'm not quite sure how to answer him. When I try again, I shake my head and settle down next to him. I sit a foot away from him and only dare an inch of my heels over the cliff's edge. But he still won't look my way, his eyes fixed on the distant star-streaked sky.

"Are you…okay?" I ask cautiously, glancing sidelong at him. It feels as if I were trying to pet a snake, waiting for him to lash out.

A breathy sigh escapes his lips. "Seriously?" He finally turns to look at me, his eyes narrowed and that icy characteristic back in his tone.

"Seriously…" I breathe.

When he doesn't respond, I creep my hand on the ground slowly toward him. His gaze darts to my hand, and then he offers me his flask by placing it at the tips of my fingers. I awkwardly take it, unsure if he misunderstood my intentions. To save myself the embarrassment, I lift it to my lips and take a few sips. The fiery liquid burns and slides down my throat, warming my insides. The moment feels too tense for me to ask him where he got it.

"I knew him," he says at last.

"Sethan? I know—"

"No. The guy who almost killed Archie. I knew him." His voice is tinged in regret.

It's the first time I've ever heard him call Archie by his name. Here I was thinking he had no capacity to feel remorse or regret. It makes me feel like an asshole. "I'm sorry, Darian."

He snorts at my, admittedly, lackluster apology, and takes another gulp from his flask.

"Do you…" my voice drops to a whisper, "want to talk about it?"

He whips his head to me, holding my gaze captive in his.

Before I can regret it, I swallow and press on. "Why did you come back?"

"Because I heard you."

"You heard me call you a fucking asshole? No different than most days."

"No…" He rips his gaze from mine, back to losing himself in the distant sky. "No. I heard you scream for Archie. Watched you crawl for him. And I…I just knew I couldn't let it happen to you. Not again. Not after Marge."

My breath catches in my throat. The painting of the allium I found in my jacket pocket flashes behind my eyes. And the simmering realization bubbles to the surface, even when I threaten to smother it.

He *cares.*

Even if I don't want to recognize it. Even if he doesn't want to admit it.

I take the key from my brassiere, grab his forearm, and unlock the last manacle still on his wrist, releasing him. He watches me, a silent breath sucked into his lungs when I finally free him and drop his arm. His thumb strokes the inside of his wrist, scarred with all the weeks of wear and fighting.

Clearing his throat, he tips the flask back to his lips again, his muscled neck working the liquid down his throat. When he stops, his eyes are a little softer. A little duller, as they stare out at something I can't see. The tension collected in his jaw from earlier dissipates. "I've…killed plenty of people. More than I care to admit to. And yet…I haven't felt like this since my mother died. Killing someone I knew…"

He takes another hearty swig from the flask.

My heart flutters as I remember Marge telling me all those months ago how his mother died, too. He was…

…he *is* just like me.

I know that feeling all too well. The heaviness and emptiness, all at once. A reality where I cling to every ounce and breath of a memory, and who she was. And yet, no matter how hard I longed for her or how much I wished I could see or feel her just one more time—it somehow could never be enough. Until the day I die, we'll be separated by this invisible rift. The only thing to bring me the smallest morsel of peace is knowing she might be out there with my father and brother. And perhaps, wherever they are, they're looking back at me. Watching. Proud of me.

"I understand," I breathe gently, careful not to spook him if I'm any louder.

He shifts his gaze back to me, and before I can think better of it, I rest my hand on the back of his. The tension in him flares as he flinches at my touch, his chest inflating as his breath stutters. He looks down at my hand perched on his. But to my surprise he doesn't shift away from me. We're both frozen, staring at where we touch. Neither of us daring to break contact first.

Unable to take my hand off his, I whisper, "My mother died, too. I wouldn't wish the death of a parent on my worst enemy. You live your whole life knowing nothing else but them, and then they're gone. And you're supposed to figure out how to live in a world without them and….and it's not fair. It's not easy. Even when they're gone, you see them everywhere. In the set of your jaw or the color of your own eyes…"

"Yeah," he mutters, so softly I almost second-guess it. But his eyes snap up to me, watching me with an intensity that makes me swallow. Staring at me as if he knows it all too well, and my words aren't only unnecessary, but they're *useless*. And yet he appreciates it all the same.

He shifts his gaze back up to the stars, his hand rigidly still under mine. "She used to tell us the stars were lights of a far off city in the heavens where people went when they passed away...and then she died." His throat bobs as he fights through the tension in his voice.

My thumb skitters across the back of his hand, slow and gentle. I don't know why I feel so desperate to make him feel better. Maybe it's because it's such a stark contrast against the Darian I know...I feel like he's a stranger. And I'm just trying to do the right thing for someone who has done all the wrong ones.

He continues, "After my mother was gone, my little sister would stay up for hours looking for movement in the night sky. She'd sometimes fall asleep on the balcony, just waiting. And then one night, she told me about this beautiful streak of light that flared across the sky. That it was our mother, telling her *I love you.*"

He stops and shakes his head profusely, his gaze falling down to the bottom of the cliff as his breath snorts out of his nose. "It's a bunch of bullshit, though. I've never seen one. I think she was so young she was making it up to make me feel better."

I remove my hand from his, and instead, grab his chin in my fingers to turn him to look at me. "Love is not bullshi—"

The words die on my lips. Out across the sky in our peripheral vision a vibrant flash catches our attention. We turn and watch an incandescent trail of light streak across the star-studded sky. My breath is stuck in my chest as the shooting star fades into the black of the night.

Darian stumbles back onto his forearms, his boots kicking at the cliff's edge as he fights to find his feet, showering rocks down into the valley below.

I reach out for him. "Darian—"

"I-I've got to go," he croaks, avoiding my gaze as he stands.

"Wait!"

"Leave me the fuck alone," he growls and quickly walks back toward Nightfort.

I watch him for a moment. Unsure if I should press on or leave him be. My gaze lowers to the ground, where my hand was resting on his. He had been in such a hurry, he left his flask. I snatch it off the ground along with his shackles and head back toward Nightfort.

Anxiety weighs in my stomach like a bag of stones with each step. Now that I released him from his binds, where is he even going to go? My room?

I burst through the door of Cyrus' old residence room and find Darian gathering his knapsack before he slings it over his shoulder.

He turns his head slightly but not completely looking at me. "Don't close that door—"

I close the door, my shoulders falling back against the wood.

"Can you fucking listen for once in your godsdamned life?" He swivels, his eyes meeting mine with an intensity that makes me pause.

I flinch, frozen at the spot and unsure how to respond. But I try anyway and hold out his flask. "Look, you left this—"

"You think I give a flip-flying *shit* about alcohol?" He seems to grow larger as he thunders toward me and snatches the flask out of my hand.

I toss his shackles off to the ground, irritation flaring inside me at the contrast of this callousness in comparison to our vulnerable moment just minutes before. "What is your problem?"

It's the wrong thing to say.

He throws the flask at the wall, the glass shattering inside the leather container. I shrink, inching backward and finding myself bracing against the wall. My left hand instinctively dips down to my sword.

He swivels to face me. I don't think I've ever seen him so angry. His brows are drawn down and tight, chest heaving with each breath as he tries—and struggles—to maintain any semblance of self-composure.

"You! You are my fucking problem!" He prowls forward and stops only inches from me. When he dips his head to stare me in the eyes, his hair falls into his face, strands partially hiding his glare.

His hands seem to move with a mind of their own, accentuating every word with a flick of his wrist and clench of his fingers. "You are so godsdamned infuriating and incredibly fucking foolish. It's a heavens-sent miracle you haven't died yet, as it should have happened ten times over at this point. You put so many people in danger, all because you think it's the morally right choice. You fuck up *everything*!"

My fear spikes at the volume of his voice, but my anger simmers beneath the surface. Even if I don't want to accept it, his brutal truth hits home.

He sweeps the hair out of his eyes and pins it at his templates, tightly, until he slides his hands down his face, his expression still fuming. "And I hate *everything* about you—"

"Good, I hate you, too!" I throw back, my eyes narrowing. "You are a massive fucking asshole!"

"Shut up! I'm not done! I hate the way you can't seem to keep your fucking opinions to yourself. I hate that you can't seem to recognize when you're in danger, and when you do, you still charge in head *fucking* first! I hate the way you have all this determination despite not wanting to take the help you need from other people. And I can't fucking *stand,*" he screams, "the way your lip pokes out when you're mad."

The anger in his eyes swirls into an entirely different emotion, his voice softening, "Or…or the way it quivers when you're sad…"

The only thing filling the silence is his heavy breathing. And the pounding of my heart. The realization settles over me. He hates the way I make him *feel*.

He slams two fingers against his heart, so hard that my own chest hurts, and his voice cracks. "And yet, I can't fucking hate you. No matter how…*fucking*…hard…I try. You'll destroy my life, and everything I've worked for, and…for some godsforsaken reason…I would let you—"

I swallow up the last bit of space between us and crush myself against him, pressing my lips to his. We turn into a tangle of greedy hands and melting mouths.

I just want him to touch me.

Have his lips on mine.

Every second he isn't touching me is unbearable.

His hands grip the back of my skull hard enough to make my scalp scream. His own desire is feverish as he claims my mouth, holding me to him like he's scared to let me go.

My hands frantically pull at his shirt, untying the top of it with a messy, frenzied speed in case he changes his mind. He gasps surprise into my mouth, and jerkily begins to rip his jacket off, shrugging the material off his shoulders as his lips are locked onto mine. We break apart as I unlace my own top, and rather impatiently, he brushes my hands aside. Quickly, he removes the article of clothing at three times the speed I would have been able to. He tosses my shirt off carelessly, followed by all the other articles of clothing separating us. Once we are both naked, I push back into him with a kiss until we fall onto the bed.

I land on top of him, my hair swinging forward and curtaining the both of us in this experience far different from what it has been before. He might have wanted me all the times before, but now? Now he *needs* me. He tucks my hair behind my ear, and I can see it in his eyes. How he holds my gaze. And kisses me.

Gone is his usual bravado and arrogance. His expression is deadly serious, like this means something to him. Like this isn't just some silly fantasy way to pass the time or form of manipulation.

I kiss him with everything he's supposed to hate about me. Fueled by every desire to shove those things he hates in his face. Giving him every reminder of why we wouldn't work. Why this is just sex.

I bite his bottom lip and tug at it, hoping to convey what this is supposed to mean for both of us. This is just sex. It doesn't need to be more.

He groans, then holds the back of my head in one hand and braces his other hand against my lower back before he rolls himself on top of me. But as he hovers over me, his muscled arms on either side of my head and his brown locks sweeping down toward me over those soft green eyes…

Face to face.

It shouldn't be this tempting, but…the way he looks at me stirs something within my chest. It makes me completely forget what I just tried to convince him we were doing here.

He pushes up away from me to kneel, then grabs behind my bent knee. Pulling it across my body to roll me onto my hands and knees. Our silent agreement. Just. Sex.

I catch his forearm, removing his grasp from my leg and sliding my hip back open. "Not tonight," I whisper. "I want you to see me."

A wave of shock and hesitation washes over his features, and before he can argue with me, I pull him into another kiss. Every muscle in him relaxes, bit by bit, as if he's surrendering himself to me. I swipe his lips open with my tongue, and we turn into a slow spiral of heat. Without breaking our kiss, I reach down between us and grab his hardened cock and pull him to me. Arching my hips up in a silent plea, he obliges, dipping low to sink himself inside of me. I wrap my legs around his waist, locking my ankles.

Rather than fucking me with unmatched vigor and carnal need, he breaks our kiss and rolls his hips into me. Slowly. Burrowing each inch deeper inside of me with every staggered breath we share. He moans as he fills me to the brim, until our bodies are completely flush with one another.

He hangs his head before pulling out slowly and gliding into me again. I snake my fingers into his hair as he adopts a steady motion. He must feel my legs trembling around his waist because he flicks his attention to me and shifts up to grab my ankles. Gently, he directs me to bend my knees to my chest. He arches over me again and is back to rolling himself inside of me.

And oh, Gods, does it do something to me. At a depth and angle I've never experienced, I come undone around him. My cries drip from my lips as stars cloud my vision, and wave after wave of ecstasy rolls over me.

His face tenses, his jaw nearly wired shut as he squeezes his eyes closed. As if he's close to his own climax. I slide my legs out from between our chests to bracket his hips once more, locking my ankles again at his lower back. He groans at the new position, his head hanging low and avoiding my eye contact.

"Hey…" I breathe, my heart racing, the words fumbling out before I can stop myself as I grab his face in my hands. "I want to see you, too…"

He flicks his eyes up to me, locking into my stare. Pinning me with his eye contact, where it feels wrong to move. Wrong to even *breathe*. Not that I wanted to.

I nod, understanding just how close he is. "It's okay," I whisper.

His forehead bumps mine as he gently rests his head against me, his hips still rocking slowly. His mouth parts into something fragile. Every angled, angry line of tension etched into his face from the hardened years melts as his eyes blink slowly. And yet, he doesn't look away.

He doesn't look away.

He looks at *me*.

All at once, I see him. Everything he's tried to hide, every corridor of horrific secrets and monstrous flaws. A chasm of pain masked by violence and sarcasm and sex. Every distant flicker of happiness, every shimmer of hope and longing, all swept into one abyss of green. The green of new beginnings. Of the forest. Of the trees I once called home, and of the one place that made me feel safe.

Yet, here he is.

And I can't move away.

I can't *look* away.

He doesn't rush. He doesn't pummel me straight into the mattress hard enough for my eyes to flutter closed. To be sore the next morning. He rocks into me gently, with each push and withdrawal deliberate and intimate.

All the times before, we chased the highs. Climbing each step with fury and haste, minds centered only on the pleasure that shocked our entire nervous system. But this is something different.

Instead, we settle into something deep and slow. Quiet. Controlled and gentle. Something I can't quite comprehend. We focus on sharing breaths, touching like if we let go, it will break something within us. I'm lost. But not lost in myself and fleshly pleasure.

I'm lost in *him.*

I touch his face, my fingertips skimming his stubbled cheek, as if we own every second in the world at this moment. As if there's nothing else in the kingdom but him and I.

The times before felt like flying. But this? This feels the opposite.

It feels like falling.

I stretch forward, brushing my lips against his. We kiss, slow and easy. I hold onto him, settling into the intimacy.

When he finally breaks away from my lips, his dark lashes flutter, and his breath rasps out, "Katerina."

My name, without taunt, sends a chill up my spine. I speak onto his lips, "Come undone for me. Show me who you really are, for tonight I am yours."

He laces his fingers into mine and holds onto me with a need that breathes security. His forehead tilts down to rest against mine, his eyes fluttering. Those carved muscles tense, and he slides his hips flush against mine, unraveling before me. Something between a soft moan and whimper slips off his beautiful lips. He can't help squeezing his eyes shut.

We hang there in the silence for a long moment, filled only with our pounding hearts and heavy breaths. When he opens his eyes again, he kisses me. Slowly, easily. I loop my arms around his neck, locking him to me.

For the rest of the night, we take our time. Each climax he unleashes in me is unhurried, gentle, and purposeful. Until I finally pull him into me, holding his head to my heart racing for him in my naked chest. His weight is comfortably heavy on me as I rake my fingers through his hair, until both of us fall fast asleep.

FIFTY-NINE

GOOD.

Darian is gone when I wake in the morning, but next to the bed is a cluster of pennyroyal flowers. *Odd, considering he mentioned he was barren.* I pluck one of the petals off, examining it with distant uncertainty, before I drop it.

The realization of our intimate moment last night hits me over the head, as if someone struck me with a rock. I can't get his eyes out of my head. That deep, forest green. A swarm of warmth, with the depth of all the things buried in his past. Yet, he brought it to the surface in a single, vulnerable moment. The same moment I felt myself slipping into, replaying it over and over in my mind.

It was supposed to just be…sex.

I start hyperventilating, raking my fingers through my hair with trembling hands and attempting to calm myself. Pulling in long breaths through my nose, I can't seem to calm my racing heart. *Fuck.*

He looked…at me.

I shake my head, my eyes shifting back down to the ground. This all feels too scary. Too hard. Now I feel an even heavier responsibility, holding on to something more fragile. More tender.

Oh, Gods. *Why* did he look at me like that?

A knock sounds at my door, and I rush to pull clothes onto my body. "One moment!"

As soon as I slip a shirt over myself, slide into pants, and pull on my gloves, I flatten my hair and open the door to find Archie. His brilliant smile would usually lighten the anxiety in my chest. But this time, it's not enough.

His joy fades as he recognizes the truth of my state before looking me up and down. "What's wrong?"

I shake my head and lean against the doorframe, attempting to look more casual than I feel. Bruises discolor his face, his lip still swollen from yesterday. "Are you alright? Have you seen any healers yet?"

"Pfft, I don't need healers. There are soldiers and citizens who suffered far greater injuries. I look worse than I am. Except…" he flicks his tongue between a new gap in his teeth at the back of his mouth, "that asshole knocked out one of my teeth."

He pauses. Then tilts his head sideways to glance into the room behind me and flicks his brown eyes back to me. "You sure you're alright? You seem…off?"

I promised him no more secrets. Even if it's an awkward conversation to have, I say, "Darian and I…last night…we kind of had…I don't know." I sigh. "A moment?"

His eyebrows shoot up his forehead. "Oh…really? Umm…that's…great?"

I scratch the back of my head. "Yeah, I don't really know."

An awkward silence settles between us. He breaks it up by saying, "Well, if you ever want to talk about it. I'm here!"

We both smile until we blow out laughs at how awkward the tension is between us.

He continues, "Anyway, I came to tell you Melaina is calling an urgent meeting. Someone ratted us out to King Aaric, telling him we'd be in Nightfort before the battle. And it couldn't have been anyone in the council because they wouldn't have been able to make it happen so quickly. The only people who knew we were coming to Nightfort before the council are the ones traveling in our group."

"*What?*"

"We have a traitor in our midst."

Oh, Gods, if it's Darian… my heart thunders in my chest as we all gather in Nightfort's community hall. *How could I have trusted him? How could I have been so stupid? He told me so many times I shouldn't trust him—*

"Yesterday's battle was an unnecessary slaughter. Had the citizens of Nightfort not come to our aid, I firmly believe more of us wouldn't be standing here today," Melaina calls out, her voice still hoarse with grief. She's standing on a small platform near the grand hearth at the northernmost part of the room, looking out across our group of Arterians and Vitalans.

"Had King Aaric's Close Circle members not been tipped off, many of our friends, our family—" Her voice cracks, and she clears her throat, before continuing in a steadfast tone, "Would still be here today."

With her chin lifted, she exchanges a glance with the Nightfort guards posted beside her. They all shift toward us, with more of them coming up behind our group. Trapping us.

"Detain them all for questioning," she announces as several soldiers snatch those on the outside perimeter of our group. "And search their rooms."

Archie lifts his hands in surrender as one nabs him by the back of the neck. Cole willingly offers his wrists as three of them approach him. Darian smirks and lifts his manacled hands to remind one soldier there's no extra step needed. The rest of the crowd shifts, and a soldier rests a hand on my back to guide me out of the throng and up the steps to where Melaina is.

"Is this necessary?" I hiss. "You're making me an exception?"

She swings her attention to me. "You don't need to be detained nor questioned. There'd be no reason for you to betray us."

I glance over my shoulder at the rest of our group, now mostly shackled and gripped by one or more guards. But what about Archie? Cole? Gavin or Nolan? The ones who've been with us since the beginning? "And the dragon riders? They made a pact to Sethan, too. Why arrest them?"

"It'll make for a fair trial if we question everyone," Melaina responds. Not bothering to look me in the eye. With one gesture, the guards begin to shuffle everyone shackled back out of the building.

As soon as they all leave, I look at her. "Even Archie? You know for a fact he wouldn't betray anyone."

"Do I?" She finally looks at me.

"You're upset. Your father died, and I understand—"

"What do you mean you *understand*?" she spits. "You never even met your father, right? So how can you possibly talk to me like you understand?"

"This isn't you, Melaina. This is grief. And while I may have never met my father, I still grieve for him all the same. I didn't have the tender moments and memories you had. I had hopes. Wishes. The 'what ifs.' Someone once told me forever isn't for people—it's for memories. And you have that. You have to hold on to them."

"Get out."

"Melaina, what if this is a mistake? You already knew the King had undercover soldiers in the Dragon Lands. For all we know, they could have been following us!"

"I said get out!"

A guard grabs me by the forearm, and I rip out of his grasp as

I spit back, "What happens when you question everyone and get no answers, hmm? Are you even questioning the council?"

"I owe you no answers."

"You do when you hold my friends as prisoners!"

Her expression darkens. "If they won't willingly give me the answers I need, then I suppose I'll have to force them, won't I?"

My face falls as I realize what she's implying. "You will not become like your father. If you torture *any* of them—"

"What? Tell me what you'll do, Kat? You became blinded as soon as you started fucking the Arterian prince! If anything, you've betrayed us by proxy!"

Rage swarms my chest like angry bees, begging me to release them. As I storm up the steps toward her, two guards capture my arms and tug me back.

"Go ahead," she continues. "Lie to me. Tell me you only fucked him once."

But as I hold her gaze, my limbs trembling and breath heavy in my chest...I can't. I can't lie to her, even if I'm pissed. And maybe there's a small truth to what she says. Even if it hurts to swallow.

"That's what I thought. If it's him—if he's the traitor—I'm going to kill him. Slowly. And you can be the first one to watch," she seethes. "Now, if I have to tell you to get out one more time, I'll throw you in the dungeons with the rest of them just to show you I can."

"Then do it. Who's to say you have any authority over me? Any authority to make these calls?"

Gods, does fury twist her features into something sharp. "I am Sethan's next of kin. And since he was killed by the actions of a traitor, that means I call on how to avenge him."

I fight against the two guards until I lose my balance and they tug me backward away from Melaina. I call to her, "You touch any of them, and it'll be the last thing you do!"

She snorts as they drag me out of the door and close it.

As I get to my feet, I turn my attention to the two guards and offer them my wrists. "Take me to the dungeons."

When they hesitate, I realize they're weighing my word against Melaina's. Which means they know who I am. I lean into their knowledge of me as the prophesied one, and they comply. I convince them to shackle me, and they lead me to Nightfort's dungeons. On the way there, they fill me in on Melaina's plans of questioning everyone overnight, with the hopes of cracking a traitor by daybreak.

I call out to Daeja, *"Don't freak out…but—"*

"What have you gotten yourself into now?" Her voice is low. Sad. It breaks my heart that she's hurt by A'nala's passing.

"I'm going down to the Nightfort dungeons. Melaina has everyone detained for questioning. She thinks someone in our group has betrayed us. But don't worry about me, Melaina and the soldiers won't hurt me. They can't."

"That's not to say someone from Nightfort won't try to kill you to end the King."

"Fair point. I'll call you in for backup if I need you."

"I'll stand guard. The other fire dragons aren't happy the riders are being detained, either. I'll gather them and wait for your command, if you need us."

"What's one silly little underground dungeon against seven dragons?"

"Exactly."

"And Daeja? I'm sorry about A'nala."

"Me, too."

When we enter the dungeons, the air is cold and wet, with water dripping from somewhere in the shadows. The stone prisons are lit by torch lights at the end of the long path. Lining it are at least twenty cells bared in iron. Every one of them full with Vitalans and Arterians. The guards lead me past each one, and I watch as head after head snaps up, eyes wide as they realize I've come to join them.

I stop at the cell with Archie, Cole, and Darian, the soldiers a half-step ahead pausing as they realize which cell I'd like to be put in. They turn and unlock the creaky door, swing it open, and usher me in. When they lock it, they look at me. I nod. Then they disappear down the corridor, a door slamming shut before a key locks it.

"What are you doing here?" Cole whispers.

"She came for us!" Archie grins when I turn to face them.

Darian is sitting in the corner, calmly, like he's done this one too many times. Our eyes connect for a split second before he looks down. I scan the cell and find Gavin and Nolan in the darkest corner.

Taking a seat next to Archie, I relay the information about Melaina's intent to question everyone, with the possibility of torture. Archie waves me off, claiming Melaina would never. But I remind him of who her father was. Archie never witnessed how much he beat Darian when we first arrived, and I have a hard time trying not to glance Darian's way.

"She won't," Archie whispers. "I know her. I love her *because* I know her."

"You've known her for two seasons," Nolan grumbles. "We've known her for years. So yes, I wouldn't hold your breath on the thought she won't."

Gavin elbows him to quiet, then murmurs to me, "Did she send you down here, too? Why would she think you'd betray us?"

Heat prickles in my skin because there are three people in this cell who know the answer. Archie, me, and Darian. And that isn't even the beginning of the secrets. They still don't know Cole and I aren't siblings.

"No. She didn't," I answer softly. Even though, based on my transgressions, maybe she should have.

"Then why did you come?" Darian rumbles, flicking his gaze up to me momentarily, before Cole answers.

"Because she didn't want us to be here alone."

The rest of the evening I toy with the idea of pulling the fire from one of the torchlights. Though, seeing as everything here is iron and stone, I'm not sure what I'd do with it. The minutes tick by more and more painfully. We all sit in silence. Waiting.

I manage to fall asleep on Archie's shoulder, and wake when someone opens a door. We all edge up off the cold, damp floors as guards come in and unlock the cells. Shouting to form a line. When I glance back at our group, I'm met with confused looks.

Either Melaina's changed her mind. Or…she already found something.

We're all led out of the dungeons by the sounds of swinging chains and wet boots. Escorted back to the community hall where Melaina is standing at the pedestal platform, the upper half of her body rising above the heads of the prisoners.

"Have you heard any news?" I ask Daeja.

"No. But we're right outside the community hall. Say the word, and we'll burst in."

As we get closer, my heart drops when I see her father's sword in her hand. Unsheathed. Her face is stone cold. She flicks a look at me, then down at my shackled hands, before she looks away.

She calls out across our stilling crowd, "It is standard to send traitors to the prison in Millton to await a trial. But given I'm kin of the recent Vitalan leader, I am given the privilege to decide."

But what if she's wrong? My breath quickens, and I search for any hint of magic, as if I'll be able to wield it and turn back time in the event of a mistake. I scan the room for all the familiar faces.

What if it is someone I know? What if…Gods, what if it *is* Darian?

Melaina lifts her sword and points it directly at someone in the center of the group. "In the name of my father, Sethan Silverstone, all of dragonkind, and the Gods above, I hereby sentence you to death."

Everyone steps away from the center, leaving Nolan glaring back at her. He growls, "You have no proof."

"We found your correspondence with the King's Close Circle hidden within your bag. Come and kneel with any last scrap of honor you might have," Melaina bites back.

Shock rolls over us all in waves, stilling our feet to the ground. A guard shoves Nolan forward, and he headbutts them before more guards swarm in and drag him up to the pedestal at Melaina's feet.

Nolan spits at Melaina's boots. "I am not the traitor here!" He pushes up onto his arms and turns, scanning the crowd. "You all are! You all turned your backs on Arterias and our King! On our homes and our people!"

I shut my eyes and bow my head, unable to witness another death as Melaina rears back her sword.

"You are responsible for my father's death!" she roars.

"Fuck your—" Nolan's voice is cut off by the deathly sound of metal through flesh.

I flinch when his body slumps to the ground.

When I walk back to my room and swing the door open, Darian is collecting his things at the farthest wall. He picks his manacles up off the floor and regards them before tossing them back to the floor with a precise callousness.

"Come to say goodbye?" He swings his gaze to me, his

expression set in cool casualty. As if nothing changed between us two nights ago.

"Goodbye? What are you talking about?"

"Melaina's granted me my own separate quarters, after proving my loyalty by saving Archie. That and…since Archie has made up with her, there's a spare room."

"*What?*" I'm glad Archie and Melaina have reconnected…but to give Darian his own room? To essentially let him walk free, after she was just giving me shit about him yesterday?

"Don't look so disappointed," Darian mutters and tosses his rucksack over his shoulder.

"Why did you look at me, then?" I blurt in a half-hearted demand.

"What do you mean, kitten? Do you prefer I look away when you walk into the same room as me?"

"*Stop* calling me that."

He snorts. "Why?"

"Because…" I swallow. Remembering my name on his lips two nights ago. How soft and tender it sounded, unlike anything I'd ever heard. It ruptured something in me—something I'm failing miserably at trying to stuff down. "Because I don't like it."

He smirks and walks toward the door. "Have you ever considered it's *exactly* why I call you that?"

Doubt sneaks into the back of my mind. Perhaps I'm wrong. Perhaps our last night together was only a figment of my imagination—an over-exaggeration of what really happened. It was always just sex with us…

I seriously need to stop before I get ahead of myself. Before I do something even more stupid than sleeping with him. Before I fall. And not just into his sheets.

But *fall.*

"Oh…one last thing before we bid our farewells." He pulls a dagger out of his rucksack—*my* dagger—and places it in my hand. He wraps my fingers around the hilt and lifts my hand to position the tip of the blade right above his heart.

He whispers with a tone that aggravates me more than it does settle me, "I still need you alive, so next time you're in an unforgiving scenario, this is the best angle. Three inches deep is all you need."

I rip my hand away and out of his grasp, never taking my eyes off him as I chuck the dagger a few feet away from us. "Why are you acting like nothing happened between us?"

"Because nothing did happen. And it won't happen again," he responds coolly, patting my shoulder before taking a step toward the door.

"That's bullshit, and you know it!" I snatch his bicep as he attempts to move past me.

He has the decency of not plowing through my grip and continuing on his way, his brows lowering down over his eyes as he locks into a rigid stance.

I tilt my head, searching his eyes for the man I saw that night. "Please...let me in."

"There's nothing I have to let you into."

"I don't believe you!"

He flicks his head to me. "There is *nothing*, Katerina—"

"You're lying!" My voice comes out angrier than I intend. Him using my full name is proof enough. "I saw it. I saw you—"

"You saw nothing." He pulls out of my grasp and continues his way to the door.

"That's why you're acting this way?" I laugh shakily at his back. "Because you're scared?"

"I am not scared!" He whips around to face me, his eyes burning in fury. "I am *not* scared, kitten. You seem to think I'm someone who needs to be saved, someone hiding some better version of himself from you. But there is none." He slams a fist into his chest. "This is me!"

I slap his fist away from his chest. "I refuse to believe that!"

He looms over me, his voice slipping into a whisper as he

grinds the words through clenched teeth, "And why? Because I'm not good enough for you?"

"That's not—"

"Because you can't *possibly* stomach the fact you're wrong about me?"

"No—"

"Because you have this *sick* perversion of helping people?" he roars. "I don't fucking want your help!"

I glare at him, not flinching underneath his hateful attitude as I warn, "You're being an asshole—"

"Good!" he grits out. "It's better for the both of us if you remember that. I'm not some cuddly man head-over-heels in love with you, dying for your hand in marriage, and begging at your fucking feet to simply look my way. I don't want to be with you. I don't fucking *want* you. Do you understand? So, before you start fantasizing about all of that and who you think I am, let me set you straight. I have used you. For just about everything. From fucking you back in Arterias to try and get the Blood Ring. From getting out of that dungeon back in Midkeep. To avoiding being beaten by Sethan and his henchmen and drinking myself silly with those bottles of liquor at night. You're nothing but a tool to me. You're a shoddy fuck, and since I didn't have better options, I settled for what's between your legs so I might have a meager ounce of pleasure every once in a while—"

I fucking slap him.

As soon as my hand connects with his stubbled cheek, my skin heats almost unbearably, triggered by the mix of anger, hurt, and shock. As soon as I realize what I've done, I take a step back, blinking the tears at bay as my entire body trembles with the anger it struggles to contain.

He drags his face back to me. His eyes round with shock before being drowned out by anger. We stare at each other, the godsawful silence filled with our heavy, exaggerated breaths.

He leans forward and spits at my feet. "Good."

And then he's out the door. When he slams it shut, the walls around me quiver from the sheer force.

SIXTY

After being given directions by Gavin, I knock on the door where Melaina is staying. When it swings open, I smile at the man on the other side.

"Hey…" Archie clears his throat and rubs the back of his neck. The bruises still mottle his face, and he grins through his swollen lip.

Melaina strolls up behind him and when she sees me, she glances at Archie. "Do you mind if we have a few moments alone?"

"Absolutely," he answers as he dips his head and slips past me, squeezing my shoulder before walking down the cobblestone street and disappearing behind a row of shops.

"He's a good man…" Melaina whispers, her attention still fixed on the distant spot where he disappeared, with a bittersweet smile on her lips.

"He is." I swing my gaze to her. "And you had him imprisoned just last night."

She jerks her head back to the room. "Can you come in?"

Working through my consideration by grinding my teeth, I finally nod and sweep into the room.

Once she closes the door, she releases a heavy breath, her hand still on the handle. "I'm…really, really sorry, Kat."

As I open my mouth to fire off all my anger, she flicks her brown doe eyes to me. And Gods, are they so much different than they were yesterday. Tears line them, her lip quivering. "I was…out of hand. I didn't know how to cope. How to handle it all again. And I lashed out…and…I said some *awful* fucking things to you."

My anger dies down a bit, each of her sincere words washing it back. "You were right though, about there being a traitor. I just didn't want to believe it."

"It doesn't even matter if I was right or not. How I treated you, how I treated everyone, was terrible. Despicable. It's been haunting me. And I thought finding the traitor and killing them would make me feel better. But if anything…"

"It made you feel worse," I finish in a whisper.

She bites her lip to still it, tears racing down her cheeks as she drops to her knees before me. "Please, forgive me. I know it means nothing, but I never intended to torture anyone. I used it as a threat. I was keen on finding the person who hurt me, but instead I hurt you. I hurt Archie. I hurt everyone."

She covers her face with her hands as she cries. Each passing second breaking me down further and further until it shakes off my fury. The time I discovered Daeja's egg is an example of how familiar I am with being emotionally overwhelmed. With reacting in the wrong way. Lucky for me, I got a dragon out of it. And while my father might have died once…she experienced Sethan dying *twice*.

I drop down and rub her arms. "Shhh. Grief can bring out the…less than ideal sides of a person. Someone once told me, 'hurt things bite.'"

"Marge," she sniffles in her hands. "Yes. She used to say that all the time."

Her name alone is like a punch to the gut. But I smile wistfully. "Yes. Marge…"

Melaina lifts her wet face out of her hands. "But you handle it all so well. How? How can you possibly maintain such grace with all that's happened to you?"

I can't help but laugh at such an absurd statement. "Me? Handling it well? While I'm flattered you think so…it's far from the truth. If anything, I've come to learn loss and grief aren't a linear path. It's cyclical. It doesn't disappear over time, you just learn how to move with it. Each loss is like carrying an unsheathed dagger, and eventually you learn how to stride without cutting yourself back open. You just have to be mindful. To take it slow, until you can run. But it will always stay with you."

I twist the metal bracelet she gave me off my wrist and hold it out to her.

A silent truce.

Her eyes flick back and forth between the bracelet and me. It's the same exact gesture her best friend—Celeste—did when she thought her father died the first time.

I can only imagine how hard her brain is trying to trick her into believing it isn't real, since he hadn't died the first time. Even now, the reality of losing Marge is a painful stab. There are still times I catch myself subconsciously looking to ask her a question. Or share with her a finding. Expecting a whack anytime I use profanity. And yet, I have to remind myself she's *gone*.

What awful, hellish things the human mind can do under grief's nasty veil.

Melaïna's lip begins to quiver as she grabs the bracelet and looks at it.

"I'm so sorry, Melaina," I whisper genuinely.

The walls of her self-assurance crumble, and I pull her to me in an embrace. She dips her head into my shoulder, crying quietly as I rub her back. After a few moments, she leans back as she wipes tears from her eyes.

"Thank you," she whispers. "And I'm sorry for what I said about Darian—"

"Don't. You're right. Which is why I'm not going to be…" I tilt my head to the side to imply it, "him. Again."

I stand and help her up off the floor. "Though, I'm glad to see you and Archie are back on the same page."

She smiles sadly. "He's just as gracious with his forgiveness as you are."

"I'd argue, even more."

We both giggle, the lightness of it cutting through the sadness.

She takes her hands out of mine to wipe the wetness away on her cheeks. "The Vitalan council sent notice they want us all to report to Millton for discussions on who should take my father's spot. They want us there in two days' time."

"But…shouldn't we head to Bayrock and see if we can find the elder Honora to translate the Queen's journal? What happens if she moves again before we can locate her there?"

"I know. I have the same concern. We still don't know what it's going to take to kill the King, nor a plan to execute it."

"What do you think we should do?"

Her head rears back. "You're asking me?"

"Yes, why wouldn't I?"

"Because…" Her shoulders relax. "You're supposed to be the chosen one. You're supposed to lead the Vitalans, so you should be the one to make the decision. And after what I did last night—"

"I'm sure there are many people who'd love to argue that. Preferably with swords. But…I forgive you, Melaina. Don't let your grief override your heart and kindness. I want to know what you think."

"Thank you…" She clears her throat before continuing, "Millton is a two-day trek from here, and Bayrock is at least a week away. I think we can split up our forces. If we have the dragon riders take the journal to Bayrock, they could get there in less than half the time. The rest of us can travel to Millton, and after the council meeting, we can meet them back here in Nightfort."

"I think that sounds like a solid plan. Though, do you feel like you can trust all the dragon riders on a mission of their own?"

"If my father trusted them and forged a blood pact with them, I will trust them, too."

That's right. With Sethan dead… I glance down to my palm where I sliced the skin to make a blood pact with him. The scar has lightened to a shade that makes it almost invisible. The only way I can see it is if I angle my palm enough the light catches it just right.

"There's one more thing." She retrieves a paper on her desk and holds it out to me.

I take it and scan it, only to find it's filled with the same five lines, repeated over and over in a foreign language. "What is it?"

"Before he died, my father said this was written multiple times throughout the journal. And the few words he did know were *'air and night.'* He seemed to think it was important, so I wrote it down on a separate paper, just in case."

I brush a thumb over the corner of the page as if it'll reveal what the incomprehensible words really mean. "I think it's the prophecy."

"What's odd, though…" She leans over to me, then underlines the top sentence with her finger. "Is he said this wasn't translating the same as the prophecy we all have known since we were children. Some of the words look similar but are different."

I blow out a breath. "Well, I really hope the dragon riders can find Elder Honora quickly."

"Me, too."

Positioned three buildings down from mine are Cole's temporary quarters. Wanting to check in on him, I take the two steps up to the door and stretch a fist forward to knock. The door is already parted open a few inches.

"Cole…?" I call out gently, and when he doesn't answer, I edge the door open with my fingertips and peek inside. Hoping seeing him will settle my heart. Because maybe distracting myself with Darian all this time was foolish. Perhaps I should have closed myself off. Or accepted that since Cole is still technically engaged, I should just be alone.

Cole stares blankly at the wall adjacent to me, his eyes blank and distant. Even when I tap against the inside of the door to announce my arrival, he's frozen.

"Cole?" I close the door behind me gently.

He clenches a paper in his right hand, his arm trembling slightly. I tip-toe over to him and toss glances at the wall he's fixated on, finding nothing but a standard pattern of worn rocks. Resting a hand on his shoulder, I tilt my head to the side to try and catch his eye. His skin is pale, with his stare round and flickering back and forth as if he's reading something on the wall.

"Hey, tell me what's wrong?" I whisper, squeezing his broad shoulder.

"Read it," he mutters, then offers me the letter.

I take it slowly, watching his face all the while for some sort of hint. He dips his head and then walks over to the window, leaning up against the wall next to it on his forearm as he stares outside.

The letter has a broken red seal on the back. But rather than the ancient symbol of Arterias with a dragon perched on top of the A, it's plain.

King Aaric.

"Why do you have a letter from King Aaric? How did he even get a letter here—" My voice dies off when I open the letter, and my eyes scan the first line.

Cole Ashbourne,

Report to Arterias at once. I will be holding your sisters as ransom until you appear, and if you do not show in three weeks' time, I will kill them one by one. Starting with the youngest.

I gasp, glancing over to Cole who hangs his head in anguish, his eyes squeezed shut as he shakes his head. I scan the rest of the page.

Bring the ring, and come alone. Try anything, and I'll kill them without hesitation and destroy all of Padmoor in your name.
— King Aaric

I clench my gloved hand tighter around the paper, and as I open my mouth to vocalize my disbelief about its authenticity, I whisper, "Where did you get this?"

"It was slipped under my door this morning."

Just when we thought we removed any spies in Nightfort. What if we were wrong about Nolan being the only traitor? What if he isn't the only one on this side of the border working for the King?

I toss the letter onto his desk. "It has to be a trap."

He shakes his head, pounding a fist into the wall. "Fuck…I mean, maybe? But I'm not willing to risk their lives by calling a bluff."

Arabella. The King will kill her first. How could he threaten such a thing, when he lost his own daughter who was only a few years younger than her?

Seeing Cole's expression, him struggling with splitting pain crushes me with guilt. I tear my glove off my left hand and touch the ring. "He doesn't know you're not the one wearing the Blood Ring…" I murmur, sliding it up and down my finger. It snags on my knuckle as if refusing to leave. I've been pulling too much magic, tipping dangerously close to being sealed. Forever. "We have to review this with the rest of the group. Have a meeting and see what can be done—"

"There is nothing that can be done, Kat." He turns to me, tears lining his eyes. "I have to go."

The tension from my ring slips, and the metal band slides up off my finger. But I can't take my eyes off Cole. "No! He's luring you, and there has to be some way around it—"

"I don't care. He can dangle them in front of me, and I will come running. Every. Single. Time." He pushes off the wall, grabs his cloak, and secures it around himself before slinging an already packed rucksack over his shoulder. He glances at the Blood Ring, now off my finger. "Put that back on."

I slip the ring back onto my finger with a swiftness that may convince him to stay. "Then give yourself a chance to think this through for a second."

"Unless you can somehow kill him before he kills them, there is no way around it." He gently shoulders past me for the door.

I whip, snatching the back of his shirt so he'll listen to me. "You can't. He will *kill* you, Cole!"

He still won't turn to face me, his voice soft with resolve as he slips out of my grasp. "Then so be it."

"How do you expect him to release your sisters? He won't just let them go without the ring. Do you truly think he's capable of negotiations?"

"I have to try." He pushes open the door and exits.

I race after him, pulling my glove back over my hand. We descend the front steps into the street. "I know you're scared, but you can't make such a rash decision. We have to think this through, together!"

He continues on, his head low and pace steady. With a grunt, I jog past him and turn to face him head on. But he won't stop, and I walk backward as I fight to get him to look me in the eyes.

"Look at me," I whisper.

He still won't. His eyes are on the cobblestone street, his hand white-knuckling the strap of his rucksack.

"I said look at me!" I roar.

He stops in his tracks, his body flinching like I've hit him.

I grab the front of his shoulder and take one step closer to look up at him. "You can't go."

He finally looks up at me, his amber eyes soft. "And why is that?"

It's a simple question. One that should be easy to answer. And the look in his eyes is so legible it makes my knees tremble.

"Why? Because I still—" I choke, my heart racing like a rabbit for its life in my chest until pain wraps around it like a snake constricting it from breathing.

Love you. I still love you, even if it hurts. Even if at times it feels wrong, and I try to ignore it. Or distract myself from it. Even if it aches to admit it to myself—I love you, Cole, and I don't want you to go.

But I can't say the words. They won't slip past my heart.

"...because I still *need* you," I finish, in a voice so quiet the rest of the pattering footsteps around us nearly drown it out.

His confidence wavers with the softening of his eyes, the slow sag of his shoulders. But then he squeezes his eyes shut, closing me off, and shakes his head. "I'm sorry."

"No. No, you're not." I prod his chest with two fingers. "You're scared, and you're rushing into this. You're not in this alone—"

He presses a soft kiss to my forehead and slips past me again.

I seize his rucksack and yank him back, my voice cracking. "Don't you fucking dare. Don't you take one more step."

He freezes, and I swallow against the constriction in my throat. Against the tears rising to the corners of my eyes. There's no way the King will let him survive if he returns without the ring. And I know there's no logic in sending him with it, even if there was any chance I could convince him to take it. "Please don't make me beg you. Please...I just barely forgave you. Don't give me another reason to hate you."

His head dips. "Maybe it's better if you do."

"Look me in the eyes and fucking say that." My voice wobbles, and a tear slides down my cheek.

He turns his head, and I shift in front of him again. But he proves me right—he still can't look me in the eyes.

I bite down against my drowning terror and desperation. "If you love me as much as you say you do…give me this chance. Out of the two of us, you've always been the one to lead with logic. At least let us see what the others think. Maybe they can help us come up with a better plan than the two of us can on our own."

He doesn't respond, but he doesn't move.

"You told me your word means nothing if it's not for me… right?" My lips tremble. "In Arterias, you promised me we'd stay together. And in Mossmead, you said you were always here for me. What changed?"

"Nothing *ever* changes about me when it comes to you," he whispers and looks up at me with eyes that tear into my soul. With a deep breath, he nods. "We'll take it to others and let them weigh in."

SIXTY-ONE

WHEN THE DEAD REST

A nervous rush of chatter washes over our group in the Nightfort community hall. We discuss the original plan to send the dragon riders to find the ancient translator for Queen Elara's journal in Bayrock and the rest of us to Millton to speak with the Vitalan council members on the future of the Dragon Lands' leadership.

As I actively try to avoid looking at the spot where Nolan was executed, my gaze slips to Darian who looks at everyone but me. We switch gears to the King's letter Cole received.

"Will the council members in Millton allow us to venture back into Arterias with Cole?" Gavin asks quietly. "Maybe we can just kill the King while we're down there?"

"We can't kill the King without risking Kat," Melaina says.

I tug the ring up and down my finger in the event it decides mid-conversation to bind to me. But it slides past my knuckle with a little force. "The ring isn't sealed to me yet. So, I can take it off if we get within a kill shot."

"As if us Vitalans haven't tried all this scheming already? What makes you think this time would be any different?" Bristol challenges.

"We have her." Archie points at me with a beaming smile, radiant with pride. "She'll kick his ass and take his throne."

I shake my head and hold my hands up. "No, I'm not interested in ruling. But Bristol is right, we don't know what the King is capable of." I swing my attention to Melaina. "Do you think we could request the council to arm us with soldiers to storm the castle? Perhaps we can take him by surprise and numbers?"

"No, I don't think they'll allow a plan so last-minute like this. They've spent decades strategizing, so they must know something we don't," she answers.

"Then what do you propose?" Cole's arms are crossed over his chest.

"We bring this discussion to the council in Millton, as we originally planned," Melaina answers.

Cole unfolds his arms and leans up against the table with a twitch in his bearded jaw. "That'll cost us at least half a week traveling there and back. And then if I travel south to Arterias afterward? We don't have that much time."

"Daeja and I could fly you there," I offer.

Everyone swings their attention to me, Cole included.

"If…you fly on dragonback, it should only take us a week at most to get there from Millton. We could consult with the council and still make it to Arterias in the deadline," I whisper, my attention pinned directly on Cole, willing him to consider it.

"You're going to fly through Arterias? Are you insane?" Bristol murmurs from a few seats down to my left. "The council likely won't allow it."

I meet his gaze, then sweep it across everyone else. "Even so, we still have to try and ask for their help. But ultimately, it isn't their decision. It's mine."

Archie nods, leaning back in his chair with a sure smile as he absentmindedly twirls a table knife in his fingers.

Bristol continues gently, "If you move against the council's orders, and you are not the appointed leader of the Vitalans, you risk yourself being executed."

"They wouldn't kill her. The prophecy states she's the chosen one," Melaina chimes in.

Bristol lifts his hands. "Look. I don't know what they'd do. I'm just stating the normal protocol."

I stand up from my chair. "Prepare yourselves for the journey and get a good night's rest. At daybreak, we'll all make haste to Millton. Dragon riders, you'll take Queen Elara's journal to Bayrock and see if you can locate Elder Honora to translate it. If the seven of you can locate her and get the translation in the first two days, send your fastest rider to Millton."

Later that night, I wake up in a cold sweat, my skin tight with goosebumps and a heavy pressure weighing down my chest. I scan the dark room to find it empty, then brush my sweat-dampened hair back off my face. And if it weren't for the tight cord of tension running between Daeja and me, I would have guessed it's from my recurring nightmares.

"Daeja? Are you alright?" I ask as I lean up off my back.

"What? Yes…fine. Just…bad dream."

"Do you want to talk about it?"

"No."

Her response is like someone threw cold water on me. *"What's wrong? I can sense something isn't right."*

"Just go back to sleep."

I throw my sheets off my legs. *"That's it. I'm coming to see you—"*

"Do not," she warns.

This isn't like her. Not like her at all. I freeze, staring at the moonlit wall across my bed. I want to respect her space, if she needs it for herself. Feeling for our bond, I caress it, trying to understand what it is that's troubling her. Perhaps she just doesn't want to give the feeling words. *"You're...nervous about travelling tomorrow?"*

She snorts. **"Never."**

"Is it...is it A'nala? I know how much she meant to you..."

Silence stills the sounds between us.

"Ever since my mother died in the fire back in Padmoor, I've had nightmares, too. About everyone who has died since. The ones I wasn't able to save. It's okay if you don't feel up to talking about it. I just wanted you to know I'm here for you. Always. I'm still here."

"Thank you...now go back to sleep. We have a long day tomorrow."

As I lie down, I have trouble falling asleep. But I flood our bond with as much love and warmth as I can muster. Hoping it's enough to comfort her from afar. Until she'll let me in.

The next morning, I meet our group near the northeastern outskirts of Nightfort and shield my face from the blinding sun climbing up over the horizon. Melaina gathers the horse-drawn wagons, and we bid farewell to the dragon riders. The sight of the incomplete formation sparks pain in my chest. The dragons fly in a V formation with no one at the head.

"Ready?" Melaina calls behind me.

I stride over to Daeja and heave myself up and into the saddle. As I lean down to retrieve the belt pre-hooked into the saddle, I instinctively glance down at my left for Cole.

Where he…isn't.

I look up to the horse-drawn wagons, searching all the faces for his when my heart drops into my stomach. For the first time, I realize how accustomed I've grown to our silent ritual before traveling.

"Where's Cole?" I shout out, my heart skipping beats into a full gallop.

But he's not here. Not with any of them. I check the groups three times just to make sure, scanning faster and faster. Melaina searches, and when her eyes meet mine, I already know.

I rip off the buckles and hooks when I see a small sliver of paper tucked underneath the front of the saddle and Daeja's neck. As I pull it out, a soft breeze carries strands of my hair across my face, and I frantically tuck it behind my ears as I unfold the letter.

Kat,
If this is the last time you ever hear from me, know this:
I love you.
Even when my heart stops beating, it'll still always call your name.
I trust in you, just as much as I hope you someday trust in me.
Cole

I crumble the note in my hand, a frustrated grunt ripping in my throat as I slide off Daeja. *"It wasn't a bad dream last night, was it?"* It must have been her guilt. I whisper, holding up the letter as I face her, *"How could you let him go?"*

She blinks, slowly. ***"My first priority is always you."***

"And you didn't think this would destroy me?" My voice wavers. *"You lied to me!"*

"He asked me not to tell you."

"And since when do you listen to him?"

She ducks her head, avoiding my eye contact as her tail whips back and forth behind her.

I grab her chin to pull her attention back to me. *"Listen to me, please! This is wrong, he shouldn't have left."*

"What's done is done."

"How can you say that?" I nearly cry down our intimate bond.

She lifts her chin. **"Because I did not bond him. I bonded you."**

"Then you know how I feel. Remember? You told me that back in Arterias. I shouldn't have to say it. You know what he means to me! You know I lov—"

"Is everything alright?" Melaina calls behind me and rests a careful hand on my shoulder.

"Cole's gone," I murmur, numbness creeping throughout my chest as I'm still locked into Daeja's white, slitted eyes.

"I thought I noticed a horse was missing but..." Melaina glances to the distance where the other dragon riders had disappeared. "What do you want to do? It's your call."

Breaking eye contact with Daeja, I look to Melaina. "You all move ahead. Daeja and I have to search for him. If we don't find him by tonight, we'll circle back and meet you at Everden."

Daeja and I fly south in silence. A cold, bitter wind whips my hair back from my face, my cheeks numb and chapped. Even with Marge's gloves protecting my hands from the cold, it still pierces through to my bones.

"I'm sorry..." Daeja whispers. **"I only wanted to do what's best for you."**

I reach forward and pat her neck. *"I'm sorry, too."*

"I couldn't stop him. I tried. He wouldn't listen to me."

"He didn't listen to me, either..."

We fly hours south until Dragon's Back Ridge rises from the cloudy gray distance, my eyes scanning the ground and forests for that blasted red hair, my heart sinking deeper and deeper the more time stretches on.

There's no sign of him. Not even hoofprints of the horse he stole treading through the frost-tipped grasses.

When I see a glimmer of several wild fire dragons gliding off to the left of us near the mountains of Eldire, I tell Daeja with a defeated sigh, *"Let's return."*

"Are you sure?"

No, I'm not sure. But one thing's for certain. *"Even if we find him, we won't be able to convince him to come back with us. He's made his decision. The best thing we can do is try to convince the council and our group to come with us so we have the numbers to take the King down before he gets there. And given the fact you and I are prophesied to save this realm, if they listen to anyone, they'll listen to us."*

As soon as we land at the northeastern outskirts of Nightfort after the sun has dipped beyond the horizon, I unhook myself and drop to the ground. If we leave in a few hours, we'll be able to catch up to the rest of the group heading to Millton, and it'll give Daeja a bit of time to rest.

"Who said I needed rest?" she retorts, then settles to the ground anyway, tucking her front legs underneath her chest and folding her wings.

Despite the exhaustion weighing on me after having flown for an entire day, I immediately press my palms to the ground and close my eyes. The rush of energy sizzles beneath my hands, lying in wait for me.

I'm praying to all the Gods above someone will meet me on the other side. Someone who can guide me to what I need to do to fulfill the prophecy and take down the King before he gets ahold of Cole.

"What are you doing?" Daeja asks with a pointed stare.

"I have to try and get answers. Something." I lower my head and pull until the pain floods my body and unravels me into a senseless, blank white. The cold fades from my body, along with the stinging pain from channeling the ley lines until I feel nothing. The White hangs around me like a fog, and I scan every direction.

My heart stops in my chest as a shadow emerges from the mist, transforming into the outline of a human.

SIXTY-TWO

THE LIGHT IN A TRUTH

As if in slow-motion, a man appears. His pale skin is flecked with freckles across the bridge of his nose and dirty blonde hair swept back neatly. When he smiles, my chest caves in. Because…

Because it looks just like mine.

"Hello, Katerina. It's so nice to finally meet you."

"Father?" I cry.

I race to him and am suddenly stopped by an invisible barrier. Though the sensation of feeling and touch is gone here, I'm encompassed by warmth, safety, and an overwhelming torrent of love.

He steps through whatever invisible wall was between us and brushes a hand down my head as he stares at me. "Gods, look at you. You are absolutely beautiful. You look just like your mother."

I laugh, a smile cracking my lips as tears stream down my face. "I thought…I thought you shouldn't touch me?"

"Do you know why your mother named you Katerina?"

I shake my head.

"Because it means pure. I know you'll do what is right." He

swipes a tear off of my cheek with a thumb. "You have come so far. And we are all so proud of you, my love."

The word proud makes me flinch, and I bite down on my lip. I didn't realize how much I needed to hear it. And the fact it's coming from him of all people.

I glance around him, desperate to see the rest of my family. To see Marge or even Sethan. To see all the other people I failed to save: the little girl, her family, Corvin.

"Just me…walk with me." He offers his elbow.

I wrap my arm around his, and we stroll in one direction, off into the expanse of white. The motion seems silly, to walk aimlessly into nothing. But I enjoy his company and will take anything to stay in this moment with him.

I glance up at him. "I finished reading your journal. I still have it with me."

He flashes me a smile. "You do? I'm glad to hear it. It's something of a family heirloom. It was originally my father's, but he died before he could write in it and before I could meet him. So, when my mother gave it to me, it was always such a sentimental item for me. It gives my heart much joy to know you still have it."

I mirror his smile, thankful for the times I second-guessed destroying it, and even more grateful Cole had hidden it for me. "You never wrote after settling into the Northern Forest in Padmoor. What happened? How did you meet my mother?"

"Well…your mother was a skilled archer for the King, as you might have known. And after a few days hiding out in the Northern Forest, she caught me red-handed with Daeja's egg. Miraculously though, her arrow only grazed my face." He taps his left cheek with an index finger, pointing at a faint scar. "I'd like to think it was just a warning shot. Your mother never missed. When our eyes connected, it was as if something instantly changed in her. She captured me and took me as a prisoner. Except…she never reported me. Never turned me in. She read through my journal after she took me, and it transformed her perspective. She began to question the King and the kingdom she served. Even during her time in Arterias as an archer for the King, she was commanded to perform many questionable things. Things that broke her morals and haunted her."

"That's…that's why she lost her sanity, isn't it?" I ask quietly, sadness shrouding over me at the thought. It feels worse than if it was just a natural decay in her mind. But knowing now that it might have been caused by the King? Caused by events she witnessed? If I have nightmares of the ones I failed to save, what kind of horrors did my mother experience?

My father answers, "No. Or…maybe. But the real catalyst for her downfall was dragonblood."

I gasp, meeting his gaze. "She was a Spoiled? Why?"

"When your mother and I fell in love, we wedded. I had always intended to return to the Dragon Lands, and while it took some convincing, your mother and I decided we would make the trip. But, Gods blessed, she got pregnant with your brother. We were elated but knew it was far too risky to travel north while she was with child. So, we decided to wait until he was a few years old and the three of us could go. Shortly after your brother was born, she got sick. Knocking-on-death's-doorstep sick. I was out of my mind and desperate. I couldn't live in a world without her, and I couldn't let your brother live without his mother. So, I broke a cardinal sin. I cashed in almost all our coin for dragonblood to save her."

His head drops as he scans the blank white ground beneath us, before continuing, "While the dragonblood saved your mother's life, it was the final nail in the coffin for us returning to the Dragon Lands. As soon as the rebels found out she was a Spoiled, they'd either execute or imprison her. We found out, as she got better, she was pregnant. With you. We weren't sure if she had been pregnant while she was sick or while she consumed the dragonblood. With dragonblood…Gods." He shakes his head, then looks up. "It's a brutal thing. It has incredible healing properties, but it's highly addictive. At the dosage it took to bring her back to health, it gave her severe withdrawals. Your mother struggled with managing her cravings. Shortly after you were born, she rapidly declined. It got to a point where I had no other choice. I had to get her more. Willard came to see her and advised she take micro doses in order to maintain her health and sanity."

I stop in my tracks. "Willard?"

"Yes, Willard. The problem with it though…it was too late. While the dragonblood saved her life, it meant she would have to spend the rest of that life taking it. And no matter what, it would erase parts of her with each dose. Her memory, her sanity, her skills. Your mother fought so damn hard to not take it. But it wasn't a fight either of us could win…"

I stare at the white beneath my feet. Not even my shadow shows here. A soft mist ripples over my boots, and when I look up at him, tears line my eyes. "How?"

He tilts his head at me, his brown eyes hooking into mine.

"How…did you die?" I whisper.

He shakes his head.

"I must know. Please," I plead.

He sighs heavily, dragging his gaze away from mine and staring back off into The White. "The Padmoor council caught me with the dragonblood. I couldn't turn Willard in, not when he had helped us so much. And I knew I was already caught—I knew I was dead. If I kept Willard a secret, he could continue to help her."

"So, Willard…knew who I was? All along?" My head spins with the realization.

"All along." My father smiles sadly. "He's known you all your life."

All the years he spent trying to help me get my mother medicine. How he was always so willing to trade for the fish I caught. The day I brought him Daeja's egg…perhaps he didn't turn me in. He wouldn't have had a change of heart after years of looking after me and my family, would he?

"Is he…is he still alive?" I ask with a small voice.

"Yes. He still dwells within your realm."

I lose a shaky breath.

Half of my father's face fades a few shades lighter, and he darts a hand to cover it before tossing a glance behind him. When he turns back to me, his uncovered eye is round. "We don't have much time left."

"Left…?" I nearly forgot where I am. I scan the surroundings. *Where…where are we again?* It all feels peaceful. Lovely. The only thing I have missing is my mother, brother, Marge…

My father claps his hands over my shoulders, turning me to face him. He shakes his head, more of his features beginning to fade into the white mist behind him. "Listen to me. I love you. Marge trained you well. But you're still missing something. You've got it all wrong, but it's not on you. If you want to know more, you'll need to go back to my…"

The weight of his hands on my shoulders eases until it disappears completely. His entire body recedes from existence. The last thing I make out is the outline of his silhouette, until it's gone, too.

"Back to your what?" I call out.

But it's silent. Deafeningly so. I spin, turning all directions, if there are any, searching for him and an answer. "Back to your what?" I scream.

Panic races in my blood, and pain splits in my face. My eyes flash open. Everything that was white turns black in a blink. Cold seeps into my skin, my bones. I suck in a breath and bits of dirt stick in my mouth. I recoil, my head swimming as I come to my senses, using my hands to touch around me. Chilly, wet grass brushes my fingers. Small rocks bump against my palms. I slide my hands underneath my chest and push up.

I'm back in the forest.

I scan around me as if my father's voice will emerge from the trees, prompting me what to do next. "Back to your what?" I whisper, staring up at the stars. But the more I settle into this reality, the more my mind clears.

Journal. It has to be the journal.

I swivel to face Daeja, who's already watching me. The tip of her tail flicks back and forth as I drag my feet toward her.

"What did you see? Did you get the answers you needed?"

"I met my father for the first time. And…" I rub the back of my head, against the dull ache collecting in my skull. *"I'm not sure yet if I got much of an answer. But…"*

As I walk behind her, I run a hand along her neck. All the way down to the leather saddle clinging to her back. When I pull my father's journal out from our travel bag, I squint through the darkness. But it's no use—the starlight isn't enough to read in.

I'll have to wait until morning.

I slide the journal back into the bag. *"Are you up for a night ride?"*

"You look tired enough to slide out of the saddle and not care if you fall."

I smile, partly delirious. *"Is that a no? Guess it's a damn good thing we've practiced the art of falling and catching."*

"Your lack of fear would startle me if it didn't excite me as much as it does," she grumbles and rolls up to her feet. **"But I also know you won't take no for an answer. And I owe you."** She noses me up into the seat.

Pushing through the bone-weary exhaustion after a full-day's flight and dipping into The White, I strap myself in. At least if I can't read until the sun rises, we can fly and get back to Melaina and the rest of the group. My attention once again settles to my left where I'd usually find Cole double-checking all the belts and buckles. The lack of his presence hits me with another wave of fear and pain.

"We'll get him back. I promise," Daeja whispers.

We fly for a few more hours under a sea of stars and expanse of moonlit forests. Even the frigid temperatures aren't enough to keep me awake and alert. I find myself sagging forward and snapping up again.

"You need to rest."

"I'll rest when I'm dead," I rumble, the stars ahead of us in the distant sky blurring as my eyes threaten to seal shut.

"I don't think I like that attitude. And if you push yourself too hard, you just might."

"Once we get there…" I whisper back, and my body starts to lean as my eyes close.

Daeja growls beneath me. ***"You're going to be permanently bent to the side like that when you wake in the morning."***

"Mmhpmm," I grumble, too tired to care.

My body shakes, and when I open my eyes again, we're back on the ground. Daeja's snorts blow hot air against my abdomen as she begins to nibble on the belts strapping me to the saddle.

"What are you doing?"

"Get off. Or I'll chew through all these straps and you'll have to ride me without a belt for the rest of your life."

Palming her snout away from me, I grumble as I undo my belt and slide down off her back. She grabs the back of my jacket and drags me until my spine hits her solid, warm muscled ribs. She shifts one of her wings over me to cut out the bitter night chill.

"Rest," she demands. ***"This time I'm not asking."***

SIXTY-THREE

AN APPETITE

Daeja and I catch up to the rest of the group outside of the dreary, gray-washed city of Millton. I've reread my father's journal entries multiple times during the daylight, unable to pinpoint exactly what he was telling me. When we meet up with the group in the outskirts of Millton, Melaina looks to be anything but positive as she heads in our direction.

"You didn't find him…did you?" she mutters.

I shake my head, hugging my arms closer to my chest as a cutting wind picks up and blasts me nearly sideways before it disappears.

Melaina sighs and stops a few steps away. "We haven't had much luck, either. The council refuses any meetings with us about the King's letter. They're saying they need time to deliberate without our outside interference."

"We don't have a few days."

"I know. Which is why I informed them of the deadline the King gave and stressed we need soldiers. And we need them now."

"And that didn't change their minds?"

She breaks our eye contact, already preparing me for what I suspect. "No. They're still deliberating. But they offered us to stay while they decide. The vote must be unanimous. Some of them already side with us, but others need a bit of convincing. Many don't feel the need to risk the lives of so many soldiers for someone as…I'm sorry, I swear these are their words not mine…dispensable as Cole."

I clench my teeth. "How long is it supposed to take until we get a decision? By the time they finish their *'deliberating'* we might not have any time left in the King's three-week deadline."

She sighs and asks sincerely, "What do you propose, then?"

"No news from the dragon riders, I presume?"

She shakes her head.

I scan the skies like it'll tell me something I'm not thinking of. The bright sunlight causes me to squint. I dip my head and run a hand through my hair as I squeeze my eyes shut. "Gods-fucking-damnit…I don't know…"

"Hey…" She jolts forward and grabs my forearm. "Listen, it's okay if you don't know what to do. But maybe you sleep on it."

"That's just a waste of time," I growl, pulling out of her grasp.

She holds up her hands to me. "I'd argue a strategic plan from a well-rested mind is better than a last-minute, reactionary one. One night. That's all I'm asking. I can work with Archie on some ideas while you rest. Even if you only take tonight to rest on it, you will still have enough time to fly back if you have to."

"She's got a point. And your eye bags are looking real bad," Daeja chirps from behind me.

I throw her a quick glare before deciding against jokingly chucking my father's journal at her.

"What?" Daeja chuckles. **"You're not your best when you're exhausted. And you've hardly slept over the last few days of travel. Plus, you've pulled and gone to The White."**

"Fine…" I grumble, dragging my attention back to Melaina. "One night."

"Kill her!" a haggard old woman screams, pointing her crooked finger at me from the sidewalk.

"End this now, coward!" another middle-aged man calls from the other side of the street as Melaina walks me and Daeja through Millton.

More shouts of protest and disgust rise from around us, melting into a chorus of anger the farther we get into Millton. Something hits me on the side of the jaw before it splatters to the ground.

A…fucking *tomato?*

I turn to the direction from which it came and this time a handful of rocks the size of coins hits me square in the chest. Daeja swivels, her wings flaring out to the side that envelopes the entire width of the street, and roars with a fury that sends crowds scattering like frantic ants.

Melaina removes her cloak and wraps it over me, then pulls the hood up over my head and tucks me down in between her and Daeja.

"Keep your head down!" she whispers. "Some of these people will kill you to end the King!"

"But I'm wearing my gloves—"

"I know! But word is getting out of what you look like, and it's hard to miss the massive black dragon." She ushers me quicker to the northern part of town. "And now that my father is gone, with no one yet appointed to rule the Dragon Lands? Things will only get worse…"

Worse. I don't like the sound of that.

The next morning, after a night of tossing and turning, I wake to a knock from Melaina. When I open the door, I recognize the defeat on her face. While the council of the Dragon Lands still won't meet with us, they've granted us private, guarded use of the community hall. They feed us breakfast, and while the others eat around me, I can't find my appetite. I pull out my father's journal and the one page Melaina shared with me from Queen Elara's journal.

"Aren't you going to eat, Kat?" Archie asks from across the table, his eyebrows pinched in worry.

I shake my head. My mind is the only thing hungry. Staring at the pages, I examine each letter. *What did my father mean? What's in his journal and the page excerpt from Queen Elara's isn't new information… what am I not reading that he needs me to know?*

I set the excerpt from Queen Elara's down next to my father's journal and stare at the language I do know. The prophecy.

The one son, chosen to lead them all.
Wasn't a son but a maid.
Until binds of death did that grave deed bade.
In death, blood is shed. But from blood there is life.
Restored by air and night to end all strife.

"I don't have much of an appetite either…" Archie mumbles, pushing his food around on his plate with a fork.

"Since when?" Melaina asks, then takes a bite of an apple.

"What do you mean since when?"

Melaina laughs. "You've always had a good appetite."

Archie gasps, insincere with his pained tone, "Is that supposed to be insulting?"

"No. It's just you've always had a wide range of foods you enjoy."

"Oh, yeah? Like what?"

"Remember the time you ate all those mussels?" Melaina prompts.

"Did you find it endearing?" Archie smirks, leaning back in his chair as he throws one arm over the back of hers.

She looses a bell-of-a-laugh that rips me out of my concentration. I grit my teeth, straining to block them out as I refocus back on the letters in front of me. "Can you guys keep it down? I'm trying to focus…"

In true Archie exuberance, he continues, "Ha! It *was* the mussels that got you to look my way, wasn't it?"

"Archie!" I hiss a reminder to lower his voice.

He flexes his arm, his scarred bicep bumping up under his shirt. "But you meant these muscles, didn't you?" he waggles an eyebrow at Melaina.

I freeze.

It couldn't be…right? I look back down at the page, staring at the letters. Melaina's words echo throughout my mind from a few days ago.

"What's odd, though…is he said this wasn't translating the same as the prophecy we all have known since we were children. Some of the words look similar but are different."

"Give me a pen!" I shout and everyone turns to me in confusion. But I can't take my eyes off the words, for the fear of losing my train of thought. "A pen! Hurry!"

Gavin races off and returns with a pen, Melaina and Archie watch me in confusion.

"The translation is wrong…" I explain as I search the page. I cross out words and replace them with other similar sounding ones.

The one ~~son~~ sun, chosen to lead them all.
Wasn't a ~~son~~ sun but ~~maid~~ made.
Until binds of death did that grave deed bade.
In death, blood is shed. But from blood there is life.

Restored by ~~air~~ heir and ~~night~~ knight to end all strife.

Archie whispers, "What does it mean?"

Unable to drag my attention up from the page, I shake my head. My thoughts buzz as all the pieces come together. Cyrus had a son. And considering Cyrus was born of sun dragonblood…it would have made his child a hybrid as well. Granted, that child would likely have a more diluted bloodline. But still magical all the same. Ancient whispers flutter around me.

Fire incarnate. Flame in flesh. Blood of power.

Brushing my fingers across my father's journal, his voice echoes in my mind, *"It's something of a family heirloom. It was originally my father's, but he died before he could write in it, and before I could meet him."*

I stop. *Wait…*

I tap my finger against the page as I wrestle my way through each tangled cord of thought. And despite the hushed whispers around me stilling to a silence, my mind roars.

If my father never met his father because he died…why would my father have written a letter to Cyrus labeled as *'sire?'* Unless he meant it as a title of respect. But then that would mean I'm not related to Cyrus. And if I'm not…how could we have possibly made it through the invisible barrier at Vitalis? Or unlocked the door into the royal tomb?

I glance down at the Blood Ring on my finger. Could it have been magically strong enough to negate the need for Cyrus's bloodline to enter?

The entire room whirls into a blur of color, becoming a wash of varying shades of red. All those nights back in Arterias where I dreamt of fire and blood resurface like a current screaming for my attention.

Until I pinpoint exactly where I've seen those shades of red—vibrant like any roaring fire, and rich like fresh blood.

Everything is drowned out by flashes of my memory played back in slow motion.

The wall of fire I saw back in Blackfell. The figure behind it a shadow, until a man emerged from the other side. His glowing amber eyes with slitted pupils burning with otherworldly wrath as the reflection of flames danced in his eyes. Concealed raw power rolling off him in waves. How inexplicably drawn I feel to him. His tousle of flame-red hair.

"He's not even my father," his voice echoes in the deepest roots of my mind.

Just as I begin to accept the truth that's been in front of me all along—I'm overwhelmed.

Using my blood to pass through the Vitalis barrier and the tomb only worked because it wasn't *just* my blood.

How my nightmares always disappeared when he was near.

How his eyes almost glowed amber, and the way they reflected flames so clearly.

How he roared in battle like he was more beast than he was man. That pulsing, drowning rage.

"Find Cole, and take her back to the Dragon Lands," my mother's voice calls in my memory.

The chants creep in around me, prickling my skin. Like the archaic collection of whispers recognize that I finally understand. After all this time.

Fire incarnate. Flame in flesh. Blood of power.

Fire incarnate. Flame in flesh. Blood of power.

Fire incarnate. Flame in flesh. Blood of power.

"What?" Melaina snaps me back to reality, her eyes searching every inch of my body as if it'll give her a clue. "What is it?"

Finally, I look up at her. "I was never the chosen one…"

I swallow.

"It's Cole."

SIXTY-FOUR

Even if you were gone

I roll the hilt of my dagger across my bare palm. Back and forth, as the rain hisses on the ground around me. My clothes are soaked to the bone. As I fixate on the way the raindrops splatter against the blade, all I can think of is that the Gods sent me this sign, I'm taking the right path.

Cole's voice repeats in my head over the pouring rain. *"It was the closest I could feel to you…even if you were gone."*

My heart cracks, allowing each wave of emotion to spill into my chest, drowning out each breath.

I'd reflect on every last breath I shared with you. Every smile, every laugh, every kiss, and every touch.

The memories, the years, and every bit of Cole flashes through my mind in an endless torrent, threatening to sweep me down and out of sight. My eyes flick up to Daeja, and she blinks slowly at me in full understanding.

"Are you sure?" I ask, voice wavering.

"If you think it is the right thing to do." She presses her forehead to mine, her eyes closing. ***"I will follow you into the dark and***

into the next life. And though we might not have had a lot of time together in this one, we will have it in the next. It is only destiny."

Squeezing my eyes shut, I lean my head into hers as I wrap my hand tighter around the dagger's hilt, with my other hand scratching underneath her chin. Her throaty purr rumbles through the air like deadly thunder, and tears spring to my eyes. She shouldn't be involved, and no matter how hard I try to convince her I can try and break our bond, she never wavers with that headstrong stubbornness of hers.

"Where you go, I go," she murmurs again, reminding me. Like it's anything but a question.

I pull my head off hers and meet her white, cat-like eyes. Raindrops snake through the crested ridges of her black scales into rivers gushing off her muzzle. She blinks.

Slow. Easy. As if her trust in me is as simple as breathing.

Shakily, I raise the dagger and press the end directly above my heart. Three inches, Darian said. That's all I'd need. Each thundering beat, the thought grows louder and louder until it develops lungs of its own and fucking *screams.*

Do it.

Do.

It.

This is the easiest way. The quickest way. It would be such a simple sacrifice. I'd save Cole before he even got halfway to the castle. And knowing what I now know, that he's truly the one the prophecy is about, it feels selfish to not sacrifice for the greater good of the realm. Two lives to take out one. To save hundreds of thousands. The math is simple.

But the equation is not.

The shaking in my hand rackets up into a violent quake, and I wrap my right hand around my other hand to try and steady it. More tears slip free as I stare down at that beautiful, black ring around my middle finger on my right hand. The very physical piece of Daeja's bond.

I've fought so hard to keep her alive, and yet, I'm the one who will end her.

All because she loves me.

Squeezing my eyes shut and gritting my teeth, I force the dagger down through my jacket, my shirt, my—

An overpowering resistance blocks me from sinking the blade further, like I've hit an invisible wall. And that invisible wall pushes my hands farther away from my chest.

"Don't you *fucking* dare!" a growl rips out from behind me a split-second later.

I flash open my eyes and find two scarred hands wrapped around the blade between my hands and my heart. Forcing the dagger away from my chest, blood seeps through their fingers as they slowly pull it away.

"Let it go!" the voice roars in my ear.

I fling my head back and connect with a hard mass, and the hands slip from my blade with a pained grunt before strong arms wrap around me, pinning my arms down to my sides. I fight against it, and Daeja rears back with a roar. I fight to free myself before I'm spun around to face my attacker.

Darian's narrowed green eyes meet mine, his face hard with unkempt anger as he digs his fingers into my shoulders.

He slaps my hands down and attempts to keep the dagger from rising higher than my hip, then grapples for it. "Stop it! Let it go. I said, let. *Go!*"

He pries the weapon from my hand and chucks it off into the river. A sob works its way up my chest until I cry. As I sink to my knees, eyes fixed on the water, he snaps forward and catches me.

The two of us kneel on the ground, his bloody hands grabbing my face as he roars, "Look at me, look at me!" He fights desperately to pull my face up, before his voice softens. "You can't. You can't do that—"

"Why? Why not?" I whisper, tears still blurring my vision. "It would be the easiest way—"

"You don't give up that easily! We don't do easy!" He holds my face in his hands, and his gaze collides with mine.

"You shouldn't be here…" I whisper, my voice trembling like I'll crack and melt into his arms.

"I know, I know. But I didn't mean what I said—" His breath comes out in quick, heavy rises and falls. "I—…I fucked up. And I…I hurt you. I'm…"

Everything slows around us.

He searches my eyes and brushes a thumb underneath my cheekbone. His voice trembles like it'll collapse. "I'm…*I'm sorry.*"

The words pierce me, sinking deeper than any blade straight to my heart. I've never heard him speak those two simple words. Never even hinted at it, after all the awful things he's done. He's never one to be sorry, but here and now…he means it.

I can see it in his eyes.

He shakes his head, the rain plastering his brown hair to the angles of his face and dripping off his thick lashes. His anger melts into an array of other chasmic emotions I can't quite place. All at once, he pulls me into his chest, pinning my face right above his heart and holding me. His heartbeat pounds underneath my ear, one hand wrapped around the base of my skull and the other rubbing my back. He holds me in the silence.

Silent tear after tear slips down my cheeks until I focus on the rise and fall of his chest, his gentle strokes down the back of my head.

"I'm sorry," he whispers again into my ear. "You were right, okay? I lashed out at you. I was scared."

As my emotional overwhelm slows, he pulls my head back to look at me for a moment before darting a glare at Daeja behind us. "How could you let her even get to such a thought, you stupid flying lizard?"

"Tell him I'll bite his head off and toss him downstream if he wants to call me that one more time," she growls back.

An echo of a chuckle rumbles in my chest. All this time he

called me kitten to taunt me. Flying lizard is just another one of his nicknames.

He directs his attention to me. "There's another way, okay? We'll save him. I'll take you to Arterias."

"How? The King will never let me within a league of the castle."

He drops his hands from my face, his shoulders relaxing as he breaks our eye contact.

"What?" I murmur. "What is it?"

"You're not going to like it."

"You've never been one to hold back saying what I won't like. Let's not start now."

He drags his gaze up to meet mine, snorting like it's a dastardly notion he already knows the answer to. "You'll have to accompany me as my consort."

I flinch, drawing back from him. "What—"

He nods, slowly. His throat bobbing. "You'll have to come with me…as my wife."

A long growl rolls off Daeja's lips, but he doesn't break his eye contact with me.

"He can't be serious. If you accept, you'll have to lick my talons before I let you ride me again."

I hold out a hand behind me like it'll silence her displeasure and rise to my feet. A heat creeps to my cheeks and flutters in my chest. I'm waiting for the arrogant, mocking laugh that doesn't come. As I stand with him kneeling before me, his eyes search mine. Waiting for an answer.

My voice is as shaky as I feel. "Y-your wife? You…you want me to…marry you?"

There's that pompous grin. "You say that like it's such a bad idea."

I blink through the confusion and the absurdity of such a notion. I'm dumbstruck. He *actually* means it.

Rising up, he looks down at me from his full height. "It doesn't have to be real. King Aaric just has to think it is. That's how we're going to get you into the castle."

AFTERWORD

Thank you so much for spending time in my world! I hope you love this story as much as I did! Feel free to tag me in any reviews/posts that are 4 or 5 stars. My DMs are always open, if you have any questions or simply want to share if you enjoyed it! I personally respond to each one. :)

OBAB is also on Amazon, Barnes & Noble, Goodreads, Storygraph, and Romance.io. I sincerely appreciate reviews, as it helps push this book for others to see.

On occasion, I also have page overlays, art packs, and signed copies available in my shop. I do all of my own artwork, including my covers.
Please make sure to visit my website at **courtneywhims.com** and sign up for my newsletter to get updates surrounding the release of book three, other book series I'm writing, giveaways, beta and ARC signups, as well as bonus chapters!

You can also follow me on Instagram or TikTok. My handle is **@courtneywhims**

Thank you for reading and I hope you loved it!
- Courtney

COURTNEY WHIMS

Courtney Whims is a self-published independent author. *Of Flames and Fallacies* is her debut novel, and the first in the Arterian series. Courtney has hand-drawn and designed all of the artwork you see in this book; from the cover, chapter headers, interior design, and map. She lives in Los Angeles, California with her husband, toddler, black lab (who inspired Daeja), and cat.

For updates on book two, news, bonus content, and events, sign up for her newsletter here: **courtneywhims.com**

ACKNOWLEDGMENTS

This book would have taken a long time to write had it not been for my husband. Everything has a cost, and I'm so thankful for my husband's support. Trying to find time to write is challenging with a two-year-old, full-time job, a broken foot, all the holidays, birthdays, anniversaries, etc. I've squeezed 60-80 hour weeks between writing this book and my full-time job. And let's be honest, it meant more time away from my family. So, the first person I want to thank is Adam. Thank you for pulling extra hours and giving me the time and space to write. Thank you for being an inspiration, for the late-night brainstorming sessions, acting out scenes to make sure it logistically makes sense, being the first person to show up to signings, hand-cutting over 1,000 art prints, and bragging to everyone who will listen that your wife wrote a book. My number one fan, always. ♥

Thank you to my family and friends who've been sharing my book with their circles!

Brooke–my very first alpha reader. And who somehow saw a gem in the rubble of a second draft enough to want to beta read, ARC read, and be on the street team. I appreciate you!

A thank you to my beta readers, who also helped shape this! Several scenes I added in because of their commentary. Thank you Rita, Shaelin, Kaitlin, Brooke, Sarah, Jess, Georgia, Kyra, Becca, Mikaela, and Emilie!

Noah Sky–so thankful for your guidance and brainstorming sessions! And a lot of your commentary makes me LOL.

Katy, thank you for being my PA and helping me manage the chaos!

Sometimes I get a little carried away with all my ideas…thank you for being my sounding board and bringing me back down to earth. ;) You've been incredible in helping relieve stress by managing all the things so I can focus on writing and drawing!

My street team, who always make me giggle and warm my heart with how supportive you are. Some of y'all have been around since day one. Thank you for rallying behind me, even in the moments when I'm quiet.

Thank you to Brit at the Author Experience for polishing this baby up, even when I delivered a book with almost 30,000 more words than we anticipated.
To my author friends who have become a support system I'll always be thankful for. I'm so grateful to look at you while we are all in the trenches. Cortney L. Winn, Rachel Schneider, M.A. Frick, and Gretchen Powell Fox. And A.N. Caudle who has become my author bestie and I talk to daily–someday I hope to eat brownie mix with you IRL haha.

Rebecca Yarros, you'll probably never read this. But if you do, I would never have written this series without being inspired by yours.

To any reader who decided to take a chance and spend time with me, my world, and these characters. From the bottom of my heart–thank you. It warms my heart to know you read my work and loved it.

Lastly, thank you to God–I am nothing without you.

www.ingramcontent.com/pod-product-compliance
Lightning Source LLC
Chambersburg PA
CBHW030326010826
48973CB00004B/887